ALWAYS ENOUGH

Sally,

Thank you for your kindness
in providing a special class
for our grandchildren . . . .
It sure was a great success.
Hope you enjoy the novel. No
matter how far you read, the
ending can not guessed !!!

Warm Regards,

Linda

L. K. Craft-Hisayasu

ALWAYS ENOUGH

A Novel

L. K. Craft

iUniverse, Inc.
New York Lincoln Shanghai

ALWAYS ENOUGH

iUniverse books may be ordered through booksellers or by contacting:

iUniverse
2021 Pine Lake Road, Suite 100
Lincoln, NE 68512
www.iuniverse.com
1-800-Authors (1-800-288-4677)

ISBN-13: 978-0-595-39551-4 (pbk)
ISBN-13: 978-0-595-83949-0 (ebk)
ISBN-10: 0-595-39551-1 (pbk)
ISBN-10: 0-595-83949-5 (ebk)

Printed in the United States of America

In 1983, I met a kind, gentle, humble man. I couldn't possibly know that everything in my life would change because of him. It is with much gratitude that I thank my husband, Gordon Hisayasu, for his amazing love and support.

Contents

CHAPTER 1

Poor Ol' Sue

I am standing in front of the mirror, crying. My vision blurred by tears, I force myself to look at my reflection. Everything appears normal, except for the chopped-off hairstyle my mother has given me. I can't see anything to suggest that I am disadvantaged or abnormal. Opening the drawer of my bedside table, I take out a report card and look at my grades. I have all A's with one B in gym class. Apparently, I am smart and capable of learning. I sink onto my bed and bury my face in the pillow, hearing the echo of Mom's voice and those infamous words. This time she has said them to Mrs. Emerson: "Well, poor ol' Sue will appreciate the book." Only fifteen minutes have passed since I listened in on their conversation as they drank tea and chatted in the kitchen. It was like so many other times when I heard my mother refer to me as "poor ol' Sue." Why? What is there about me that warrants this negative framing of my name?

Regaining my composure, I tiptoe back downstairs and am shocked to see that Mrs. Emerson and Mom are still talking. They had said good-bye earlier, which sent me sprinting upstairs so they wouldn't catch me eavesdropping. Looking down at my feet, I silently move to the edge of the carpet at the doorway. Years of eavesdropping have worn the spot where I always stand. Now, at thirteen, I am angry that I have no better understanding of why Mom refers to me as "poor ol' Sue."

"Well, Beth, it's so hard trying to fit everything into a day's schedule. I keep telling James that someday I'll have more time to give poor ol' Sue. But for now I can barely stay afloat with everything I do in the community."

"I'm sure Sue learns a lot about cooking and cleaning from just observing. You've always been such a wonderful homemaker and mother."

Sure enough, they are still talking about the virtues of my mother. Again my stomach churns as Mom says poor ol' Sue. Things haven't changed. It has been over a month since I heard her refer to me as poor ol' Sue. I'd hoped that she had stopped. Those words crush me, weighing me down like the heavy knapsack I lug to school. Why does she pity me? Why isn't she proud of me? Why does she insist on calling me this? It's like a subtle warning, preparing others for the fact that there is something wrong with me. It hurts because I believe my mother is credible, so what she's saying must be true.

Those horrible words have given me a perspective about myself. If I am not normal, I need to be careful when I'm with others. I've become such a good actor that no one suspects something is wrong with me.

My tears welling up inside, I tiptoe to the front door.

"Hey, Mom. I'm going to the park. I'll be back in an hour."

"Okay, sweetie. Be careful—and stay on this side of the brook."

"Okay. Bye, Mrs. Emerson. See you later, Mom."

I walk down the sidewalk, ready to get beyond this moment. The sky is filled with billowing clouds, with the sun peeking through them. Mrs. May's lilacs smell like heaven as my shoes brush the fallen petals on the sidewalk. Two classmates, Shelley and Clara, are walking toward me. Although we aren't close friends, we always speak to each other. As Shelley looks up and sees me, she whispers to Clara. My stomach begins to churn, my eyes become tearful. I feel they're talking about me. Poor ol' Sue is plagued with insecurities, I tell myself. Obviously, Clara and Shelley know there's something wrong with me.

"Hi Shelley! Hi Clara! How are you?"

"Okay. Sorry Sue, can't stop to talk. We have to get home. Bye."

I enter the park. It is majestic and inviting, with huge willow trees swaying and lush velvet grasses beckoning me to lie down. Going to my favorite spot beside the brook, I collapse on the ground, again in tears. Everywhere I go I feel conspicuous. My mind races as I think about how hard I work in school to prove to others that I am intelligent. All this uneasiness has forced me to keep people at a distance. Finally, I wipe my face with a sleeve and make myself a promise: I will not allow Mom's words to affect me like this again.

I sit up. I want the wind to dry my tear-stained face and clear my red eyes. I look across the brook. I love sitting here and daydreaming about the other side. It is so alluring, with its vast wooded terrain. All my life my mother has forbidden me to go to the other side, which piques my interest all the more. She tells me that it isn't a safe place because people hide there, drinking and smoking. All at once I realize that time has slipped away from me. I jump up and head out of the park. Just as I reach the sidewalk, my father pulls up at the curb.

"Hi, hon. Why don't you hop on in and ride a block with your papa?"

"Sure," I say, opening the passenger door of the old Ford station wagon and sliding onto the vinyl seat cover. Dad is listening to big band music on the radio. He tousles my hair and winks at me, and I smile back at him.

"Did you have a hard day?" I ask, trying to sound grown up.

"No, just really busy. After dinner I have to go to Wayne's house to build booths for the festival. Bet you've got plenty of homework to keep you busy tonight."

"Yes. I have a lot to read, and I have to study for a test. Well, we're here. Thanks for the ride."

I love my dad because he talks normal to me, and he tells me the truth. He's no secret or mystery to me—just a sweet man who loves me and never hides from me. My mother, on the other hand, is distant and doesn't share much.

I rush into the house. Mrs. Emerson has gone, and Mom is busy fixing dinner.

"Hey Mom, can I help you with dinner? Maybe I can set the table or make the salad. I promise to be careful and not make a mess."

"Not now, Sue. Go do something with your brothers or father. Dinner won't be ready for another hour or so."

I feel disadvantaged because my mom doesn't teach me the things most mothers teach their daughters. She is always pushing me out of the kitchen and laundry room. Her refusal to teach me how to do household things makes me believe she thinks I'm not smart enough.

Dad has changed his clothes and is working in the yard with my brothers. Being the only girl in the family is nice to some degree. Dad treats me like a princess. I have two brothers. Grey is a year older, and Mark is a year younger than I. Dad keeps both of them quite busy with work around the house. He always says that my brothers need to develop a strong work ethic. Yet no one seems to push me toward work.

"Hey guys, what can I do to help?"

"Hon, go make some lemonade and bring some glasses out with it."

"Sure, be back in a bit."

I know this will upset Mom's apple cart. She does not like me making anything in her kitchen. My mom looks up from stirring a pot of homemade noodles when she hears me open the refrigerator.

"Sue, what are you doing?"

"Dad and Grey and Mark are all sweating out there. Dad told me to make some lemonade and bring it out to them."

"Go back outside and tell your father I will make it and bring it out in a minute."

"But Dad asked me to do it."

"Sue, just go out there and do what you are told. I don't want you in here making a mess. Tell your father I'll bring it out."

I knew this was exactly what she would say. Anything my father directs me to do will be taken over by Mom. My little life is so predictable.

I go upstairs and begin my homework. Time flies by, and I soon hear my mother hollering to come to dinner. As we are eating Mom's delicious noodles with chicken, my father asks, "Elizabeth, how was your day?"

"Hectic as always. I went to the church and wrestled with those wild roses in the back. Then I had to go to a membership committee meeting at the auxiliary. By the time I got home, Beth Emerson stopped by to talk about the church bake sale. By the way, she reminded me that I've been heading that annual bake sale since 1964, and now, five years later, I'm chairman of that committee again this year. Anyway, I feel just exhausted today." Mom looks too tired to eat.

"Well, you're surely busy. You need to slow down and let others pick up the slack, Elizabeth. I know that's hard for you to do. But really, hon, I don't like seeing you so frazzled."

Yep, here we go again, I tell myself. At the end of every day, Dad asks Mom how her day went. Mom always gets a lot of sympathy for her exhaustion, as everyone knows how hard she works. Today, like every day, I feel her exhaustion is my fault because I can't hold up my end. Maybe Mom created the image of poor ol' Sue so others will sympathize with her more. Sympathy is what she wants, and sympathy is what she gets. Tons of it. No one feels sorrier for her than I.

"Sue," says my father, "I have the day off tomorrow, and the only thing I have to do is help your mother move some things in the basement. I want you to go with me to Sandy Whittingham's. I have something very important to show you. This will be the perfect opportunity to do that. We'll leave when you get home from school. About 3:30, okay?"

"Sure, but I don't understand what you want to show me. What is it?"

"You need to go with me. Afterwards we can talk more about it."

"Okay. It sounds strange to me, but whatever you want, Dad."

After school the next day, my father is waiting to take me with him. As we reach Sandy Whittingham's office, he looks excited.

"Honey, you're about to see one of the fastest typists around."

"Hello, Sandy. I brought my girl, Sue, with me. I think it will be good for her to watch you type this letter I need."

"Well, sure. Nice to meet you, Sue. Come on in here, and I'll get this letter typed for your father. Your family has used my in-home secretarial services for years."

Standing beside her desk, I watch as she quickly presses the keys on the typewriter. She is so fast that it's mesmerizing. I look up at Dad, who is impressed with her speed. "If only you could get half as good as Sandy, you could support yourself when you grow up," he says to me. "I think typing would be a great career for you. Sandy makes a lot of money doing this. You could become an executive secretary if you learn to type well."

In one way I am inspired. My father thinks I can do something. Yet on the other hand, this goal is too limiting. I'm saddened that the best career Dad thinks I could have is as a typist. But at least Dad is not like Mom. He believes I can do things.

On the drive home he cannot stop talking about Sandy Whittingham's typing speed. I'd hoped my parents would believe that I could be a doctor or teacher. My grades are great. Surely that's evidence that I can become more than just a typist.

"Wouldn't you like to learn to type that fast, Sue? Are you going to take typing in school?"

"Yes, I'll be taking typing, and it looks like fun. But Dad, don't you think I could become more than just a typist? I think I can," I say, feeling sad about all this.

"Well, hon, women's opportunities aren't equal to men's. I think you need to be realistic about what you can do to support yourself. Typing can certainly be a great opportunity for you."

That night I lie in bed thinking about my life. I feel so worthless and limited. Dad's excitement about my future as a potential typist is so disappointing.

The next morning I awake with a new outlook on life. I've signed up to take 4-H cooking classes. There I can gain my own education about cooking. I look forward to finding out the name of my instructor and where we will be meeting.

As the final bell sounds for the day, I run to my locker and then out the door to the fairgrounds to find out about my cooking class. Out of breath, I rush up to the bulletin board. I nearly faint when I see the instructor's name: Elizabeth Martin. My mother! My mother has signed up to teach, and they've put me in her class.

Last year I signed up for sewing class. My mother got involved and demanded that I be assigned to her best friend's class. Thanks to Mom's influence, my sewing teacher basically made my entire project for me, believing I was incapable of doing it. I got a blue ribbon, and Mom told me how proud she was of me. Later, I overheard her talking to my grandma. "Daisy was kind and made poor ol' Sue's skirt. I am so happy she got a blue ribbon, and I know it made Sue feel great."

That was so disappointing and left me so sad. I imagine my cooking class experience will be the same, if not worse.

At dinner that evening I know I have to say something about it. First I let Dad talk to Mom about her day. Then, when the conversation falls off, I take a deep breath. "Mother, I found out today that you signed up to teach cooking. I was upset that I had to be in your class, since you won't even let me help in the kitchen. Why did you do that to me?"

"That's no way to talk to your mother," says Dad. "My lord, girl, why are you so insensitive to her? She is the hardest worker I know. You should be appreciative that she cares so much about you that she signed up to teach a class. She did that on top of all of her commitments. I won't have you being disrespectful. Now apologize."

"I'm sorry, Mom. I don't mean to be ungrateful. But I don't..."

"No buts, Sue...just a straight, sincere apology."

Dad's voice trembles a bit, and his face is flushed. He is upset and shaking. I have never seen him this way, not with me. With my brothers it's different—they're used to Dad being stern with them. But he has rarely even raised his voice to me, ever. I can't stand to disappoint him, even if it means that my mother will have her way again.

My hand shakes as I take a drink of water and stare down at the tablecloth, ashamed. Dad taps his fingers on the table impatiently, glaring at me, and Mother just keeps eating her dinner, resting her fork primly on the edge of her plate after each bite. My brothers have stopped filling their faces and are staring at me, no doubt wondering how I will react to this rare scolding by our father. "I'm sorry. I really am," I say weakly. "May I be excused?"

"Yes, you may be excused," Father says.

That night it is hard to focus on my homework. I feel myself fuming about it over and over again. My thoughts are all over the place. I am upset that Dad always takes her side on everything. He only looks at the best in her. How can he ever see what she is doing to me if he can't be objective?

While walking to school the next morning I think about how I crave to make friends, yet my fears of being inadequate always restrict my attempts. I want to be popular with my classmates, but instead I hide alone in the park. My brother Mark is the heartthrob of all the girls. I can see him walking ahead of me, swamped with girls trying to talk to him. He is so good-looking, and loaded with sports talent.

As I come up to them, Stacy calls out, "Sue, your brother is so nice. You are so lucky!"

"Mark's the lucky one, 'cause I always defend his butt with Mom. By the way, Mark, where were you last night at the dinner table? You let me go down hard with Dad," I say, still upset that no one stood up for me.

"Don't mind her. She had a bad night," Mark says, looking disturbed at my comment and then turning away to talk more privately with his friends.

Mark and I are close, but with Grey…it's different. He is a very confusing individual. Grey is the smartest kid in school and seems to live in a world of his own. When not doing his chores or working with Dad, Grey lives in books.

Approaching school, I see Grey sitting on the ground reading. His curiosity keeps him busy doing experiments and reading tons of books. Yet there is a sad side to him. No matter how well he performs academically, my parents take his success for granted and ignore him. His accomplishments, for the most part, go unrecognized. The lack of attention and celebration by our parents is what connects us. We know our parents are capable, because we've watched them celebrate Mark's victories over and over.

"Hey Grey, look up. Mom said to remind you to take all those books you stuffed in your locker back to the library."

"Mom worries too much. Stop being a nag. I won't forget."

With ten minutes until the first bell, I sit on the lawn and look around at everything and everyone. There is nothing exciting going on in my life. I have nothing to look forward to in the days to come. Saddened by the exchange that occurred last night with my father, I feel tears welling up inside me. It is hard to get away from my thoughts. At last the bell sounds, and I am on my way to class.

CHAPTER 2

Struggling with Adolescence

As summer draws to an end, I am apprehensive about going into eighth grade. I am at the top of my class, but feel uneasy about being in the same building with high school students. I am facing a more sophisticated environment. I fear my inadequacies will be obvious to others, even though I have no idea what they are. I can no longer be theatrical. If I am to explore my potential, I have to be courageous enough to show up as myself, not some theatrical production of my making.

This is a period in my life where everything is going to count. I don't underestimate the importance of fashion, hairstyle, and accessories. Makeup is extremely important, symbolizing my move toward womanhood. I've known the day would come when makeup would be an issue in my home.

Tomorrow is the first day of the school year. I've been practicing putting on the makeup I bought with my summer earnings, and as I enter the living room, my mother immediately notices. With much anger, she screeches, "Sue, you are not going to school looking like that! You look like a girl looking for trouble!"

"What do you mean by 'trouble'?" I ask.

"Painted girls are going to school to be noticed by boys," she says, with intensity and outrage.

My immediate thought is rather rewarding: obviously I'm looking good enough to get noticed, all right! But she is relentless in telling me what she thinks.

"You are going to school to learn, not to get in trouble. I won't have you looking this way! Now get up to your room, wash your face, and throw that stuff away!"

Dad chimes in with his semi-supportive help that falls like a double-edged sword. "Elizabeth, leave her alone. Let her use makeup. If the barn needs painting, then paint it!"

Although I think he is standing up for me, this, too, feels like a put-down. Pained and upset, I go to my room. After crying awhile I feel that I have no other choice but to become deceptive and defiant. I am not about to succumb to Mom's directives regarding makeup. I already feel totally inadequate going into eighth grade. Earlier in the day, Mom chopped my hair off because she believes heavy girls should only have short hair. That was her final butchering, I promise myself. In addition, she has bought a new school wardrobe for me that is outrageously hideous.

Mother never feels that I can choose appropriate clothing. She believes that I have no taste for style and color. I heard her say to my aunt one day, "Well, I took poor ol' Sue school shopping. It is so sad because she wants things that are so unbecoming for someone of her size. I had to draw the line and pick everything out for her."

I am sick of her disregard for my feelings. When I was younger I trusted her taste, even though I hated what she picked out for me. Mother always buys the most hideous plaid clothing for me. It makes me feel like I am competing to be the biggest, ugliest sight walking down a street. Every school picture has me in bright plaid. Last year a photographer commented on it, saying "Oh my lord, girl. How can I capture you under all that bright plaid hoopla?"

What is Mom's need to keep me in plaid? The clothes she buys support her inaccurate representation of me: poor ol' Sue. Well, enough is enough. I'm tired of being a walking billboard of her creation. No more! I've purchased black slacks and a black blouse—a couple of basic pieces to tone down the raging plaid. I am so happy with my new clothes. They cover up my usual chaotic look that seems to scream out, "Poor ol' Sue has arrived."

The next morning I awake all excited about school. Being an eighth grader is like being a little person in some big league. I dress in my black slacks and blouse. I don't feel conspicuous. Instead, I feel elegant and secure in my new look. I prepare myself emotionally for Mother's comments as I move through the house. I know the makeup and the outfit will bring a reaction from her. I anticipate that she will rapidly spew criticism in a demanding tone, and I'd better be prepared to hear it. As I enter the kitchen, she looks up at me.

"Sue," she says, "you are no longer my child with that stuff on your face and body."

Before I can stop myself, I respond with biting sarcasm, "I know. I'm not your creation anymore. I am myself. Get to know me."

"I hope you know how hideous you look," she exclaims.

After this the conversation changes and she doesn't continue to challenge my use of makeup. I eat quickly, and my brothers and I leave for school. They take off in a different direction as I turn toward Patty's house.

Patty is my closest friend. She comes from a rather wild family. Her father has been in trouble for car accidents while driving under the influence of alcohol. Her mother is also known to drink. Both my parents are outspoken about them. However they do like Patty. They allow me short visits to her home but no overnight stays. Somehow we have worked out our friendship with my parents' blessings. Patty has adult brothers that drink and party all the time. The contrast between our worlds is huge. Patty adores my parents. To her they are the perfect couple. I, on the other hand, find the honesty and straightforwardness in her home quite refreshing.

Patty has spoken many times about my mother being the greatest mom in the world. Mom always goes out of her way for Patty, cooking little dessert surprises for her. She is very affectionate toward her, always hugging and putting her arms around her. All of that seems really strange, as I can't ever remember that level of attention being given to me. Mom constantly reminds Patty that she is like a second daughter. Mom is calculating and theatrical around others. She plays her roles well, and my friends are captivated by her.

I am fascinated by Patty's relationship with her parents. They are very authentic and affectionate toward me and make me feel at home. Mrs. Williams's alcoholism is obvious a lot of the time, in spite of her attempts to appear sober. She is warm, kind, and always answers my questions truthfully. Patty's parents seem accepting and never judgmental of others. Despite their alcoholism I find this family fascinating because they use feeling words. They ask about each other's thoughts and ideas and give honest accounts of their own experiences. They are so different from my parents, who tell me how to think, how to feel, and how to act. My parents talk *at* me and Patty's parents talk *with* me. My parents always talk from the perspective of telling me how to *do* life. In Patty's home they simply *live* life. I love it there. No one needs to be anything more than what he or she is. They have a genuine acceptance for differences in people. But most of all, they know how to celebrate life.

Patty is excited. "Hello, Sue. Isn't it a great day to start another year of school?" she says.

"Yes," I reply. "But I'm a bit uneasy about being around high school students. I guess I'm intimidated."

"You are so smart and mature, Sue. You'll fit right in, trust me," she says.

On the way to school, we see Carrie crossing the street to meet us. Carrie and I became close friends last year after I realized that no one acknowledged her at school. No one ever spoke to her. She ate by herself and never entered a classroom with anyone. She is an average-looking girl but quite withdrawn. Carrie is so intelligent, and that impresses me a lot. I had gotten to know her when we became study partners in science class last year. She told me about her life, about how she was given up for adoption at birth. When she was three years old, her adoptive parents were killed in a car accident. After that she was placed into the foster care system. She had been shifted around from home to home and learned to never get too comfortable. She had been so guarded when we first talked; every answer was one word…"okay"…"yes"…"fine." All her words were compliant, detached. Slowly she started to smile, and then laughter and friendship followed. By the end of the class year, Carrie and I were friends. She had been to my home on a few occasions, and Mom treated her as someone special.

"It's good being back in school," says Carrie. "It's so hard to live in the foster home. I hardly have any time for myself, taking care of all the people. I've really missed both of you."

"Well, I worked with Mom and Dad on a lot of church projects this summer. My only excitement was when we three met at the park," I said.

"I've had a good summer except for mom's drinking," Patty says. "She's really started drinking so much more. Please don't say anything. My father became so concerned that he stopped drinking to care for her. All of us are trying to persuade her to go for treatment. Well, I don't want to talk about it. I'm just glad to get out of the house…even if it is for school." Patty lets out a sigh.

We spend the rest of the day getting situated in our classes, renewing our friendships, and sharing stories about our summers. We are more mature and excited to be moving up a grade.

I will no longer spend my days living life as I have been directed by my parents. I will exercise my independence and seize my opportunity to finally become a real, live teenager. My excitement comes with struggles and challenges, but my dreams are greater than my fears. My hopes are stronger than my negative thoughts and doubts. I know my strong faith will see me through.

For the most part, I am emotionally independent and no longer in need of parental approval. Although I have longed for closeness, communication, and support, I have received a very different type of parenting.

My friends don't know the truth about my relationship with my mother. They are lost in her kindness and involvement with them. I believe her love toward others is theatrical because I cannot accept that she can love so genuinely and yet not love me. I am not about to open up to my friends and share my thoughts, beliefs, and truths about Mom. Nor would I want to diminish or reshape their impressions of her. I have to admit there is a payoff for me as well. Vicariously, I can live through my friends and enjoy a different mother than the person who is my mother when others are not around. It also pleases me to see my mother's joy. They are all so important to each other, and I am happy for all of them.

CHAPTER 3

First Date and Soaring

I don't think much about dating—until I turn sixteen. My active imagination leaves me pondering what it would feel like to have the attention of a special guy. In my world, it seems like an impossible thing to have happen.

I test new things, such as new hairstyles and a new wardrobe. My hair has grown out, and I've survived what I consider to be the final haircut by Mother. As I walk into gym class, I feel my usual uneasiness—as if this were the most anxious moment of my day. I am fortunate that my gym teacher has taken an interest in me. Now, sitting in Mrs. McCall's office, she talks with me about my health. "You know, Sue, you are a brilliant and beautiful girl," she says. "Get rid of the fence that protects you so the world can see your beauty."

"Huh?"

"Your weight's not bad, but you could lose the excess. And I can't begin to tell you how it can change you."

I take a deep breath, knowing I have to tell her my truth.

"You see, Ms. McCall, my mother says I have big bones and come from a family of big-boned people. It's hereditary."

"Sue, that is not true," she replies, continuing to take measurements of my body. "Look here. I've diagramed your body structure. You don't have big bones and you can get rid of the few extra pounds. The choice is yours."

This is so exciting. And yet I feel anger toward my mother for that deep-rooted message she planted, telling me that I have big bones. But now I have hope. It's as if someone has found a cure for my problem. I'm apprehensive, but the feeling is minor compared to my excitement. Now I can improve poor ol' Sue. I am not offended at all that Mrs. McCall cared enough to talk with me about this.

"Here are some articles to read and a healthy eating plan. It is imperative that you eat right and exercise daily," she explains.

On the way home I wonder if I should share this information with my family. A healthy family would be supportive, but in my family, sharing is an act of self-sabotage. My mother has her theory that I am big-boned due to heredity; if I contradict her she will only dim my hopes. I decide to go it alone, to modify my eating and begin exercising, and see if change occurs. This approach feels so right, and I am so ready for it! I won't make any verbal proclamations to anyone—just a silent personal challenge with dedication and the hope of producing evidence of great success.

I have learned to enjoy my secrets. Exercising and changing my eating habits will be a private experience. I've heard that everyone needs a support system to provide encouragement. But my history with Mom has taught me that sharing anything too special means submitting it to ridicule. I know my plan is important enough that I must keep it private. I'll be my own cheerleader.

My head is in the clouds, and I barely hear a voice calling to me as I walk down the sidewalk.

"Hey, Sue, wait up! I want to talk with you."

I turn around to see Gary Waltham running toward me. We've been classmates throughout the years, but I don't know him personally. We've never spoken, other than a quick hello as a gesture of courtesy.

"Oh, wow. You're a fast walker. I'm out of breath. Could we sit here on this bench?"

"Sure."

"I was looking for you earlier. I wondered if you'd like to go to the dance on Friday."

Wow! What an unanticipated question. He is looking for a response. I am so shocked and unprepared.

"I'd like that very much," I reply, "but I do have to ask my parents. Can I let you know tomorrow?"

"Sure. I understand. You're so fortunate to have parents who care and want to be involved. Thanks, Sue. Don't study too hard. I'll talk to you tomorrow."

My mind races all the rest of the way home. Gary thinks I'm going home to my warm and perfect parents. He probably thinks I'll talk with them about our date. In all truth, Mom will think there's something wrong with the guy because he asked me out. She'll be in shock that poor ol' Sue got noticed. I dread sharing this moment with her. It isn't right that I have to offer it up to be analyzed and destroyed. This moment should be on the highlight film of my life; after all, it's my first date.

I'm excited in anticipation of dancing with him close, having his arms around me, and feeling like a normal girl. I feel chosen, special, and elated beyond all my dreams. I do not want to surrender or share my excitement with my mother just to have her make light of its importance.

I could ask Mom if I could go to the dance on Friday but not mention that I have a date. I could have Gary to pick me up at Patty's house if I went there after school and Patty's mom did my hair. After the dance, I could let him walk me home. Maybe Mom wouldn't see our good-bye at the door. And if she did, she'd think he was a guy I met at the dance. Surely it would be worth the deception.

Then I think about how it might be if I simply told them the truth. I have no idea what my parents would be like if he came to the door to get me. My family has this huge need to embellish their own importance. I start thinking about it in vivid detail, imagining high drama: Dad shaking Gary's hand and having him sit; Dad asking about his plans and career objectives. Dad would have some ethical questions to ask as well. And, knowing my family, anything less than astronaut or president of the United States would be rather weak goals to set. I am laughing, thinking about all of this. I imagine Mother commenting, "It's so nice of you to take poor ol' Sue to the dance." She would let Gary know that I've never before been out with a guy, apologizing that I might be a bit awkward. My thinking turns into the painful realization of what will surely happen in the future. I choose to stop thinking about it.

I decide that before the school year ends I will grant myself growth-producing wiggle room from my deeply rooted family ethics. After all, I'm now a teenager. The most important feature of my plan is that I have freedom to anticipate, to think, and to celebrate this period in my life. In the past, Mom made all my realities appear abnormal, but I won't let that happen from now on. I will silently celebrate my first date and my first dance alone.

At dinner I eat a modified meal, which Mom notices. "Why are you eating so little these days, Sue?"

"I just feel better and have more energy when I'm not bogged down with heavy food," I reply.

"Well, be careful," she cautions me. "You could get sick, eating so little."

Such conversations about my eating habits subside as the week wears on. Finally, Friday arrives. It feels like it has taken forever to get here.

"Mom, I'm going to Patty's after school, and we'll be going to the dance. I'll be home after the dance and before curfew."

"Are you looking forward to your first dance?"

"I'm looking forward to it; won't know how I'll feel about it 'til I go."

"Grey will be there because he helped organize it."

"Well, it's just another school activity. I need to get going—see you tonight."

At school Gary and I confirm everything. The rest of the school day seems to drag by. Finally 3:30 arrives. Patty is waiting at the lockers, talking to James.

"Hi, Sue. I hear you're going out with Gary," James says. "He's a nice guy. Shy, a little hard to get to know, but nice. I hope you two have fun."

I don't say much. I don't want anyone to know the excitement inside me. In truth I am way beyond excitement. I'm beyond any feeling I've ever experienced. I feel as if I must be on the edge of nirvana. It is the first time anyone has singled me out as someone special. I do not want to forget this feeling.

We rush around at Patty's house as her mom does our hair. "Oh Sue," Patty says, "I like James a lot. How do you feel about going out with Gary?"

"I don't know him very well. His parents are very quiet people and not too well known. I think he's shy. I know he's an only child, not into sports, and reads a lot. Gosh, it will be interesting getting to know him. I think he's just a simple guy. I like that."

"Come on Sue, what do *you* think of him, really?"

Now embarrassed, I know I have to show my excitement.

"I am so excited, Patty. He's the first guy who's noticed me. That makes him pretty special. I guess I'm full of hope…but guarded, in case things don't work out."

My hair turns out great, and I am pleased with the nice sweater and slacks outfit that I've chosen. My makeup seems to highlight my facial features. Patty's brother walks through the living room and notices me. "Sue, you look terrific tonight. If that guy doesn't show, don't forget I'm upstairs." He's like a brother to me and is being very kind and complimentary.

The doorbell rings a couple of minutes early, and there is Gary, smiling.

"Gary, this is Patty's mother, Mrs. Williams, and of course you know Patty."

"Nice to meet you. Gosh, Sue, you look great! We'd better get going." As we're walking down the street, Gary takes my hand. It feels so wonderful and intimate, his fingers interlacing with mine. I am overwhelmed with the softness and warmth of his hand. These are my first experiences with this kind of feeling. I notice a beautiful, starry sky, highlighted by the sparkling interplay of fireflies glistening in their flutter and dance. Crickets singing, a full, romantic moon illuminating the night—I imagine that heaven must be like this. Everything seems so perfect.

"Sue, let's walk to the park on Lamont Street. It'll take a little longer to get to the school, but I want us to get comfortable with each other. Is that all right with you?"

"Oh, yes. This is great. I've always felt like daytime is humanity's time, while the nighttime is for other species. While humans sleep, God mists the forest with fog, illuminates the skies with stars, and puts the moon up there for the other species to enjoy—like these fireflies." Walking beside the brook, Gary lays his jacket on the grass, and we sit down.

"It certainly is beautiful," Gary says, "I love to be out at night—much more than during the day. I guess it's because we use more of our other senses. In daytime, we're so distracted by visual clutter. Just smell the night air and listen to the sounds. I think life is beautiful when it's contrasted against darkness."

Silence permeates the next few minutes, but the silent exchanges between us are ever so vivid. I feel the soft movement of his fingers as he expressively holds my hand. It is as if the gentle caresses are speaking for him.

"Sue, may I ask you a personal question?"

"Sure, I think." My half-smile leaves a hint of reservation to fall back on.

"I've noticed you for years. You don't seem to be shy, yet you distance yourself from others. That's interesting, because most people who stay to themselves do it because they're shy, like me. You speak with ease and intellect in class, and you stand up for your ideas without any hesitation. Yet at the end of the day, you're out the school door and very much to yourself. I assume that is by choice. I admire your communication skills, but I'm baffled as to why you stay to yourself…I'm sorry. This is none of my business."

Smiling at his awareness, I am pleased to know that someone in this world has been observing me.

"Good observations, Gary. I'm not shy. I have no reservations about expressing myself. But I have reservations about whom I share myself with. Some of my thoughts and ideas seem too important to share. Too many times, I've shared something with my family, and they've torn my ideas apart without regard for the importance I place on them. All those times became very painful and left me empty. I decided early on that I would only choose to share myself very rarely. Gee—I'm sorry. This is more than you wanted to know. Tell me about you. Why are you so shy?"

I am happy that we are talking about ourselves.

"Thanks for being so honest. I've been shy all my life. My family is shy. My mom is wonderful, and we talk a lot about things, but she doesn't have friends and is socially dependent on me. Dad really keeps to himself and works a lot. Both are smart and talented, but no one knows it but me. Mom writes music; she's awesome on the piano. Dad's a closeted inventor. He's built many things in our home. All our furniture is designed and built by him. They're both amazing. I wonder how many concertos die inside a hidden musician like my mom. Or how many designs and inventions die with their creator, all because of shyness. I wish I weren't so shy," Gary said.

"I know you are shy, I've always sensed that," I say. "But I am so happy you asked me out in spite of it."

"Well, Sue, it was the hardest thing I've done recently. I promised myself that I wouldn't be like my parents. Remember the assignment last week in Mrs. Biskow's class, where we had to write an amendment to the Constitution and then present it?"

"Yes I remember."

"And we got only one grade reflecting both parts? Well, on my paper, Mrs. Biskow wrote that it was very well done, but she gave me a C-minus. I figured out that if half the grade was on the writing and half on the oral presentation, I must have received an F on the presentation to end with a C-minus. I was angry and decided I was going to conquer shyness. I've wanted to get to know you but never had the courage. I decided that asking you to this dance was my first step."

"Thanks so much for asking me. I was so shocked that I hardly knew how to respond. I guess we both had some awkwardness, but I am so glad you asked."

I feel so close to him as we walk the rest of the way to the school. It is as if our new relationship is now a comfortable one. I feel like we have been friends for a long time. As we enter the decorated gym, my brother Grey comes over.

"Where have you been?" he demands. "Mom told me to watch out for you."

"I took my time getting here. Relax, Grey. I'm here now." My eyes are locked onto his eyes, trying to express my feelings silently: *back off, brother.*

"Oh, okay. Glad you're here. See you later."

They start playing the song "Vincent" by Don McLean. Gary holds his hand out to me. As we dance I hear Gary softly singing every word. He knows the song verbatim. It is amazing to be in his arms. It feels so intimate. When the dance is over, I can still hear him singing the words.

"Would you like to go for a walk, rather than stay here?" Gary asks.

"Yes, that's perfect," I respond.

We walk down the park side of the brook. Gary picks my favorite spot, and we sit. I wonder how he knew that. The night has become a bit brisk. We can see our breath as we talk. It is like seeing our words form works of art.

"I feel so good right now," Gary says, "because you have honored me by sharing yourself. I have loved every moment of being with you. You're very easy to be with. I am sure I appear awkward."

"Oh no, not at all," I reply. "You've shared a lot as well. I loved hearing you sing 'Starry, Starry Night.' Is that a special song to you?"

"Yes. It's a wonderful song, yet a sad song too. It makes me feel so much. I studied van Gogh's life. His art shows us his mind and the world as he saw it," Gary explains.

"Which of his paintings is your favorite?" I ask.

"All of his works are important. His paintings tell us his painful life story. People say a lot of things about his art. They say van Gogh painted for only eleven years. Back then his works seemed too intense, almost repulsively different. Many thought of him as an emotional, obsessively driven eccentric. I think it's recorded that he only sold one painting during his lifetime."

I realize that Gary has become lost in what he's saying.

"His critics thought he was anything but normal. But Sue, if he spent his life trying to be what others thought he should be, none of us would be viewing his thought-provoking art today. van Gogh's life pushes me to take advantage of my own talents and abilities. 'Starry Night' was painted from memory, with van Gogh writing about it something like, 'he thought he saw the sun, the moon, and eleven stars bowing to him."

"It is so special how you have taken to van Gogh's paintings and have come to appreciate him," I say. "You have given such value to his life."

"Sue, I think the sun, moon, and millions of stars are bowing to us tonight," Gary says. "I could talk to you forever because you really listen."

We both are filled with the warmth of a new, special relationship, and the night chill is hardly noticeable. Gary's fingers rub slowly against mine. I can tell there is something very important he wants to share, and finally he finds the courage.

"I have something I need to tell you. I've been attracted to you for years. You are so smart and so independent, and I like it that you are not so wrapped up in socializing. You appear confident, and that's so attractive to me. I wanted to find a relationship where both people could celebrate, and I didn't want one out of neediness," Gary explains.

I am really surprised and pleased that Gary views me as independent.

"Thanks for the compliment," I reply. "It means a lot. Unfortunately, it's getting late, and I'd better get home."

We slowly walk to my house. The night fog is setting in. I want to remember everything about this night. I want to remember the glances, the touches, and the wonderful exchanges that we've had. I am glad I didn't tell my parents that I was going to the dance with Gary. Now I won't have to offer up any details that could possibly be shaped into a "poor ol' Sue" moment. Tonight is so special that holding my memories safely inside is perfect.

As we arrive at the door, I feel anxious in the most positive way.

"Sue, I had the best time, may I give you a goodnight kiss?"

"Oh yes, I'd like that very much."

Slowly and very gently our lips touch. The intimacy of this moment is spectacular—a magnificent crescendo leading to something great. Our lips part. My eyes are still closed as I whisper to him, "I want to remember this always. Good night."

CHAPTER 4

Coping with Loss

Our family had always been very active in church. As a teenager, I had attended church camp every summer. I love church because they use words that I desperately want to hear. They talk about a God who unconditionally loves me. Then, there is a perfect place called Heaven, and through my profession of faith I will be transformed and never die. It takes faith to believe everything they tell me. Generally, I need evidence before I believe in anything. But faith I have, and it is the foundation that holds me together during the worst moments in life.

Many teens from our church go to summer camp. This is my last year, as I am going to college in the fall. I'm excited that Patty and Carrie are also going to camp and that we'll be staying in the same cabin. I enjoy being away. At camp I am just another person and not an extension of my family. There I will not be poor ol' Sue in anyone's eyes.

I look forward to having time to think about my faith. I have many feelings about organized religion. Often, people declare their church to be the right one; then, under the auspices of their religion and in the name of their God, they declare war on the religions of others. I am confused by religions because they proclaim to love, yet exhibit hate. How can someone say that everyone is a brother and then declare war on that brother? It is sad to think that all of this is in the name of God. I love the atmosphere of camp; it allows me time to think about such issues.

Our camp is for teens of various church affiliations. It's a time for friendships, fellowship, and celebrating our faith. As I pack, my mind races. The drive to Meadow Lake Campgrounds will take six hours. I grab my new journal and start to write. I've been recording special moments in my life since I was thirteen.

> *Today is full of great excitement. As I leave my family, I realize that I leave behind the enormous pressure of their competitive way of living. I leave behind a place where I am taught to do life and go excitedly to a place where I will choose simply to live life.*
>
> *I am leaving behind a place where big goals and hard work are required. Now I can breathe and celebrate the simpler things in life, like nature and friends.*

I close my journal and tuck it in my suitcase. Soon we're on our way. As Carrie gets into the car, she looks as if she's been crying.

"Are you okay, Carrie?" I ask. "Is something wrong?"

"I almost didn't get to come," she tells me. "Bella decided that she didn't have enough money for my expenses. I have fifteen dollars that I saved from my lunch money, but that's not enough for camp."

I can tell that Carrie is embarrassed as she continues to open up.

"When Ms. Reese came into the house, and I told her I couldn't go, she immediately said to get my bags and not to worry. I feel really strange going when I know I don't have the money. I'm so tired of being dependent on others."

"I'm so glad you came," I say. "I'd have missed you a lot. I have enough money for both of us, and I hope you'll allow me to share. Gosh—think of it as payment for having tutored me in algebra."

After a while, Carrie starts to relax and smile again.

Patty, Carrie, and I sign in and are assigned cabin 131. We have arrived first. Three more girls will join us. We pick the side of the cabin where the sun comes up and shines in the window. The cabins are very small. After we get settled in, we make a sign reading *Welcome New Roommates* and hang it over the other three beds. Then we head for the camp's hangout place, called "The Shack."

One of the few buildings on the grounds, The Shack is a store with a soda fountain, café, ice cream stand, and gift shop. The camp's lake, tennis courts, softball field, and pavilions serve as outdoor meeting places. There's plenty of hiking terrain, too. Meadow Lake, mostly surrounded by fir trees, is beautiful, with a lovely shore and a sandy beach. In the middle of the lake is an island filled with trees. It's large enough to explore—a magical place to enjoy nature and solitude.

While at The Shack, we choose our classes. I sign up for writing and art. I love writing and often record my thoughts in sonnets and haiku. Writing lets me purge what I hold inside; it lets me express and defend my ideas. I've taken writing classes each year, and my camp writings are something I take home as a reminder of the summer.

We spend the rest of the day scouting the campgrounds and attending orientation sessions. When we return to the cabin, we meet our three new summer roommates.

"I'm Jacquee," says one, "And this is Charlene. We're from Detroit. Thanks for the welcome sign. You guys are in for the time of your lives. We're here to let go and have some fun!" Both are African Americans who describe themselves as "wild children from the 'burbs." We laugh and welcome them.

The third roommate, Denise, seems shy. "Gosh," she says, "I'm sorry to say that my father is camp chancellor. I assure you that I'm not a snitch. I just want freedom from my family. This year I refused to stay in the chancellor quarters. I made my parents promise they won't interfere and will keep a distance."

"I can easily identify with your need to be away from family," I tell her.

We all become better acquainted over dinner. Afterwards, we decide to attend the night bonfire on the beach. By the end of the evening it is as if we have known each other forever. Patty leads the nighttime devotions, and each of us shares a little about her life.

The next morning, we hear the ringing of the camp bell. We dress quickly and hurry to the daybreak service. The minister greets all of us and introduces the chancellor and his wife. Denise slinks down in her seat, as if she doesn't want to be seen. Chancellor McLean welcomes everyone. At the end of his short statement, he looks out among the campers.

"By the way," he says, "there is one girl out there—and she knows who I am talking about; we love you and hope you are having a good time."

As he steps away from the podium, the five of us look at Denise. She is red in the face.

After the service we have breakfast and rush to our first class. My writing class is held in one of the eight pavilions. The instructor is John Reed, a fiction writer who has written three novels.

"Today," he says, "we are going to breathe in the aesthetics of an object and then express it in a short essay. Each of you will be challenged to experience an intimate relationship with an inanimate object. I know this may sound silly, but each of you must create a personal attachment so that you may access your emotional side."

Mr. Reed gives a brief lecture about emotionally connecting ourselves to what we write. He passes around a box of sealed envelopes, and each of us takes one. He explains that each envelope holds an inanimate object, and we are to write about the object in a short essay of approximately 150 words. We have thirty minutes to write.

Laughing, we rip open our envelopes. One camper has a rock, another a blade of grass, another a nail, another a small vial labeled "raindrop" and containing a drop of water. Inside my envelope is a rubber band.

This is perfect for me. First I study it carefully, pulling at it, expanding it, and playing with it. My mind runs wild with deep appreciation for my object. I quickly write down the simple truths about my rubber band. Thirty minutes doesn't seem long enough, but when the time is up, Mr. Reed stops the class from writing.

"Okay, let's get started. Who'd like to go first?"

A camper introducing himself as Barry reads his essay about his rock. It is funny—using levity, yet expressing value in the rock. Then Sandy reads her essay about the raindrop, using similes and metaphors to create the feeling that the raindrop sustains life.

Many unique writings are shared, and finally my turn comes:

> *Rubber Band, you are so wonderful. You bind together my things that would otherwise blow helplessly in the wind. You are flexible and capable of shaping yourself to fit my needs. When I stretch you, you generally snap back, as often I expect too much from you. You are giving of yourself, over and over, to be useful for different purposes. When I try to mold and shape you, you fit my needs but eventually return to be yourself. You withstand greater pressures than most things bigger than yourself. You give and give and are always ready to give again. You have a limit, and if I become unreasonable in my demands of you, you snap back. Never forget that I remain reasonable and appreciate you always. But most of all, thanks for holding my love letters together and never telling my secrets.*

The instructor is smiling as I speak. "Great, Sue," he says. "You've written a personal appreciation to the object. You humanized it, so to speak, removing the inanimate aspect. Good. This kind of thinking is what all of you will need in future writings. Just breathe in, feel, and appreciate the beauty of what you are writing about. Try to connect with your subject personally. I hope this exercise has helped everyone. In the next days as you're relaxing, take time to breathe in your surroundings and feel the importance of all that surrounds you. Being a good wordsmith is insignificant if you're unable to experience what you are writing about. See you tomorrow."

I am surprised at how the weeks fly by. I spend most of my time in class, but every free moment is spent writing. Meadow Lake is beautiful, and every day here is like waking up someplace really special. Now, sitting under my favorite tree, I decide it's time for me to mentally leave Meadow Lake and write home. I couldn't wait to get away from home, yet I find myself thinking about my family a lot. I know Mom has been busy with her community projects. My father would have little time to sit under a big tree and feel the sweeping gentle breeze as I do at this moment. He's never taken time to ponder the questions of life, let alone think about anything so silly as a rubber band. He's probably keeping pace with his to-do lists that grow bigger each day. I wonder how Mark and Grey are. Probably spending the summer working too hard.

What's all this about? It's the same old pervasive reality. Even Meadow Lake can't erase the ever-present feeling of guilt that I carry inside. This type of thinking is always able to bring me down if I am having too much fun. And now is a perfect moment for the guilt to unleash itself. After all, I've found a refuge from my everyday life. I am celebrating new skills and enjoying everything about the people around me. More important, I'm enjoying being myself. But just when I get to the edge of what feels like Nirvana, my internal saboteur, guilt, pulls me back to reality, leaving me feeling like poor ol' Sue. It's a rushing emotional pain that brings me down. I was born into a world of great disorder, into a family I did not choose, and into circumstances that I don't understand. Even though I felt helpless as a child, I've always developed ways of pretending. I envision dreams, develop goals, and map strategies that will certainly lead me away from home. Now, my head on the grass, I am sobbing from the conflict of missing my family and yet am glad to be so far away from them. Emptying myself of sadness, and wiping away the tears, I sit up and write a postcard to them:

∾

Dear Mom, Dad, Mark, and Grey,

I miss all of you! I love camp but feel guilty that I am not home somehow being part of your daily lives. I have two more weeks until I come home. My greatest challenge is allowing myself to be away. Take care of yourselves and just know I love each of you.

Love, Sue

I read my brief note again. I realize that I have shared nothing regarding how wonderful it is to be at camp—an omission clearly due to my guilt. After all, I am so happy being away. But then, I realize that my being deliriously happy at camp is not very important to them. Their only desire is to receive a postcard or note simply letting them know that I am okay.

Carrying the postcard to The Shack, I hope to find mail waiting for me. As I walk in, I see Patty holding a large box.

"Sue—it's for all of us from your mom." Patty pushes it toward me.

"Gosh. Mom is being our hero. I know she probably sent us some awesome goodies."

I love the fact that everyone is excited as I rip open the box. Inside is a sealed letter addressed to me, along with packages of cookies, fudge, and raisin bread.

"Dig in, everyone," I tell the others. "Patty, could you take the box to the cabin for me? I want to take my letter and go to the island."

"Sure. But the box may be weightless the next time you see it! Gosh, this is great!"

I'm happy to hear from my family, yet I also dread it. I know the letter will be filled with information rather than feelings. I decide to not open it until I'm on the island. I'm afraid its contents will somehow leave me shipwrecked on the shore once I've read it.

I walk along the edge of the water until I reach a little cove that I remember from previous years. There I open my bag and spread my little beach blanket. Sitting down, I take a deep breath and open the envelope:

ॐ

Hello Sue,

We have missed you. Your absence is so obvious to each of us. Mark was talking about how silent it is at the table. He said he missed your questions and dialogue. I saw Patty's mom in the store and she said that Patty had written a huge letter sharing her busy schedule. She was laughing when she mentioned that the two of you tied in a watermelon seed spitting contest. I do hope you were polite and not making a spectacle of yourself. Your dad is very busy helping with the Chamber's fall festival. I finished canning the garden goods. Well, I had better get going. Don't eat too much of the chocolate. I put that in there for Patty, as she could use a few pounds. Here is some extra cash from Dad, who was concerned that you did not have enough. Please write and let us know you are okay.

Love, Mom

It is just as I expected. I am happy to hear from Mom, but sadly, the letter does not contain anything personal. That's our relationship. I wish she could reach inside herself and tell me how she's feeling—what she's thinking rather than what she's doing. The last line says it all: please write and let us know you are okay. My heart longs for her to say, "Please tell us about camp because we don't want to miss out on anything." But Mom is theatrical, detached from her emotional side. She performs life perfectly, especially in the eyes of those who deeply admire her productions.

I am okay after reading the letter; it could have been worse. I had anticipated that I would be left feeling guilty and that everything would be padded in humor for poor ol' Sue. Letters have been exchanged both ways, and poor ol' Sue has filled her family obligations. Now I can put my family aside for a while and return to being that fun-loving camper, Sue.

As camp quickly moves into the final two weeks, I am sitting on a cloud—feeling emotionally refreshed and independently strong. Along with growing closer to my friends from home, I've also found a new friend in Denise.

Throughout the weeks the four of us have shared a lot about our lives. Denise has been very kind in supporting us when we've shared painful stories from our pasts. Her own life hasn't been easy. Her family has moved five times. Denise struggles to find peace in the eyes of the public. She says that being a preacher's kid is difficult; the phone rings daily regarding people in need. Some are sick and in need of visitation and prayer. Others are struggling with various family issues. She lives with death being a daily reality in her home; her father provides family comfort and performs funeral services often. Denise is a great testimony to her rich faith and trust in God.

She and I spend a lot of time alone. She is the first person to whom I have fully opened up about my family. Denise and I come from two very different families, yet we struggle with some of the same realities. While visiting the island, Denise asks about my issues.

"I haven't heard you share much about your family, Sue. Patty and Carrie talk a lot about their life and challenges. But you seem reserved. Why is that?"

"That's a fair question," I reply, "especially since you've shared so openly about your family life and difficulties. You and I have some of the same issues. My parents are totally wrapped up in the community—even to the point of taking my brothers and me for granted. My mother appears theatrical to me. She is very giving to everyone. Maybe I frame it as theatrical because I can't deal with the fact that she gives so little to me. She does a lot of great things for others. I don't know if I can solidify my feelings into specific issues. From the earliest time I can remember until now, I can't remember my mother really enjoying being with me. She's never been authentically affectionate toward me."

"What do you mean by 'authentically'?"

"Mother is very loving in how she speaks about me to others, and somewhat loving toward me when others are around. But she's never told me that she loves me. She has always dismissed me when we are alone. She frames me by calling me poor ol' Sue, which leaves me to believe there's something wrong with me. When I was a child she decided everything about me, without listening to anything I would say. I was a little heavy, and she'd say it was just my bone size and discourage me from dieting."

"But Sue, you are perfect. You look great!"

"I learned later, in junior high, that I could lose weight. Now I know how to eat right and exercise."

Reflecting on these matters, I feel emotion choking me. But I continue to open up. "I can't share important things with Mom. She's shown over and over that she doesn't value my thoughts, ideas, and desires. She takes care of me very well, but there's something missing. I've watched her with my friends, and she is affectionate, kind, and always shows concern for them. My friends adore her. In many ways she's their second mother. I'm happy for them and I love seeing her with them. But when no one is around, our relationship has always been strained. I've been very pained over it."

I start to cry, fearing to go any further, and decide to not say anything more.

"Sue," Denise says, "I am so sorry you've had such pain, and I am lost as to what to say."

"It feels good just saying it, getting it out. It would be different if I believed Mom was limited in her ability to have a close relationship. But seeing how close, open, and intimate she can be with others clearly leads me to believe she doesn't want a close relationship with me. That tears me apart."

Denise puts an arm around me. I wipe away my tears and feel myself calming down. "Thank you," I tell her, "for letting me share some of my feelings, whether they're legitimate or not. You're the first person I've shared this with. Patty and Carrie don't know that I struggle inside with issues about my mom. Mom's so loving with them, and she supplements some of the deficits in their lives. Patty has a neat mom, but she drinks heavily and Patty worries about her. Patty talks a lot with my mother. The progression of Mrs. Williams's alcoholism has slowly eroded her relationship with Patty. My mother is so important to Patty now. Then there is Carrie, who was raised in foster care. Carrie has been up for adoption all her life, and although couples "tried her out," as Carrie calls it, no one adopted her. My family is important to her, especially Mom. My mom gives so much to them, so I refuse to confuse them by sharing my feelings."

It helps to talk openly with Denise. She is not part of my home community, so I can just unfold.

Time flies by, and in the final days I spend a lot of time with Denise when I'm not in class. On our last Friday together, Patty, Carrie, Denise, and I decide to go on a picnic. We stop by The Shack and pick up sandwiches, cookies, chips, and sodas. As we are going out the door, Sam calls out for us to get our mail. There's a letter for Patty from her brother. She quickly tucks it in her pocket.

We find a great place to spread our blankets and begin sharing our plans for after graduation. No one is more excited than Carrie. She will finally be on her own. "I'm so looking forward to college," she tells us. "I hope I'll get some financial assistance. But best of all, I'll be able to be myself for the first time. Growing up in foster homes, I've always had to live everyone else's agenda."

Denise looks moved by Carrie's words. Patty and I listen silently.

"What do you mean, Carrie?" asks Denise.

"Well—I am to stay with Bella until I graduate, and then I'm out of the foster care system. Bella took me in so that I could help her with the elderly people who live with her. She really didn't want me to come to camp this year. Life in the foster care system has so many unknowns. I've had to learn to accept today and never think about tomorrow because I have no control over it."

"Is the thought of being on your own also scary?"

"I'm looking forward to being on my own, Denise. It would be different if I were in a permanent family where I could be myself, disagree from time to time, or debate things without worry of being sent away. But I always feel I must be compliant and gracious and never upset the apple cart. I stay as long as they want me. I've spent my life trying to stay desirable at all costs. But inside, I choke on my emotions. I have no idea what stability feels like. I've never thought of anything so far away as next summer and have always focused on one day at a time. While here at camp I've been thinking about Bella. She was shocked when Mrs. Reese said that I was going to camp, even if Mrs. Reese had to pay. Bella looked disappointed. In the past, disappointed foster parents have sent me packing."

I am astonished by the truth of Carrie's words. I've known Carrie for some time but have never asked about her life in foster care. Why, I wonder? I thought I couldn't do anything about the situation. But now, observing the exchange between Carrie and Denise, I realize that I could have done a great deal just by supporting her.

As we lie back in the sunshine, I have a revelation like no other: I've chosen not to ask about other people's lives out of fear that they would ask about mine. Afraid to show my naked soul, I always speak light-heartedly about life in general. Carrie's descriptions of foster care make me feel I hardly have any reason for real sadness. The contrast between her world and mine has stirred me deeply.

Patty remembers the letter from her brother. She takes it out of her pocket, opens it, and begins reading to herself. Suddenly, she starts to sob. "What's wrong, Patty?" I ask. Without answering she rolls over and buries her face in her blanket, continuing to sob. She is so upset she cannot talk. I gently place my hand on her back to assure her that she's not alone. Denise has her head bowed silently. Carrie comes and sits on the other side of Patty. Tears spill steadily down her flushed cheeks as she looks up and hands me the letter.

❧

Sweet Sis,

I miss you and can't wait to see you on Sunday. I hope you are enjoying camp and trying to get your mind off things here. You have been missed a lot by all of us. I can't wait to hear about your camp experience.

There are some developments regarding Mom. She has been getting sicker and sicker for the past few days. Dad took her to see the doctor yesterday and put her in the hospital. Mom has continued drinking a lot, and Dad is sure the sickness is from the alcohol. She will be going through a series of tests after they detoxify her. She has been having various problems, as you know. She continues to have pressure in the abdomen and is somewhat jaundiced, they say. It will take a few days for the tests and some specialists to see her. They should know more by Monday. You will be home by then. She's sleeping a lot right now and *really is not up to visits from any of us. Mom is in better hands now that she is in the hospital. Hopefully, they will find out what is wrong. Probably its her drinking.*

I know all of this causes you a lot of sadness, but I thought it might be a relief for you to know she is in the hospital rather than home, continuing to drink.

I have to run and want to drop this at the post office on my way to work. We love you. Tell Sue I said "Hi." Take care. Will see you Sunday.

Love, Dale

By the time I finish the letter, Patty seems to have calmed somewhat.

"I am so worried about Mom. Not a day has passed when I haven't felt bad about being here, rather than at home where I could help her. Oh Sue, she is so much worse now. That's why I haven't had you over. Most of the time she doesn't even know what she's saying; sometimes she calls me 'Vickie,' who was her best friend who died of cancer a few years ago. Mom has been having serious abdominal pain but has refused to go to the hospital. She isn't herself, and she gets so angry now. It's good that she is finally in the hospital. It's a relief, but I'm afraid of what the doctors might discover."

"Hey," I say. "I want to be there for you, and I know Mom and Dad will want to help too." Carrie gives Patty a big hug. To try to help her relax, we eat, talk about silly things, and then pack up and head back to our cabin.

Somehow the afternoon's sharing has changed our relationships. We are no longer merely a diversion or an escape for one another. Nor are we just there for the silly moments of fun and laughter we have shared. We have converged on a new pathway, becoming extensions of each other's lives. No longer will any of us feel alone. Nor will we cry silently, having no one there to care. The demons of aloneness will be driven away because we have each other. Our last year of camp has led us to a deeper level of intimacy. Each of us built walls to protect others from our truths, but we walled out the love and support that could have helped us through our painful times. Now the walls are slowly coming down. The gift we offer each other is a powerful message: we are not alone.

The next morning we return home to our lives. Our summer at camp will always be remembered.

🍁   🍁   🍁

The next weeks pass by slowly, with the sad realization that Mrs. Williams is not getting better. Even though summer seems like ages ago, camp has changed my life. I no longer feel sorry for myself and I start seeing my mother in a different light. I see how much she means to others and how she gives of herself. She is a remarkable individual. Now Mother is very busy helping Patty and her family.

Mrs. Williams's abdominal pain, weight loss, and jaundice turn out to be symptoms of pancreatic cancer, which has metastasized. In her final days, she stays at home, extremely sedated. Mother spends most of her time fixing meals and caring for the Williams family. She's there in a special way for Patty. I drop by daily to help Patty keep up with her class work. It is our senior year.

On an early winter Saturday, I decide to get Patty out of the house. Walking along Elm Street, with light snow flurries gently caressing on our faces, Patty begins talking about the horror of watching her mother die.

"How can life give us so much and then rip it from us?" she asks. "I am so lost in all the suffering Mom is going through that I can barely welcome another day in my own life. Oh, Sue—I don't like being like this, and I certainly don't want to inflict any of my pain on you. I'm not fit to be with anyone. Mom is slipping away, and I'm trying to prepare for that. I don't want her to keep suffering."

Patty is sobbing as we walk. Arriving at a café, we see a booth at the back and make our way to it. We order hot chocolate with our traditional ton of whipped cream. Wanting to express my desire to help, I attempt to open up.

"Please, Patty," I say. "I want you to talk with me about whatever you need to talk about. Thanks for not pushing me away, because I want to be here for you."

"You and your family have been such a help to us. Your mother has literally cooked most of the meals, and your father helped Dad get the car fixed so he could get meds and have transportation. Your mother had a wonderful talk with me the other night about grief. She had me tell her about the things that Mom and I did before she got sick. I was smiling and laughing as I shared the good times. Your mom pointed out that I still have those good times and they will always be alive in me as wonderful memories, unless I choose not to focus on them. She spoke of celebrating Mom's life. Reflecting on those wonderful years brought some momentary peace. I haven't been that calm since this all came crashing down on me." As I listen to Patty's words, I am overcome with appreciation for my mother.

As I walk home I think about the fact that no one lives forever. The only guarantee in life is death. That truth is always there. Eventually, every life on earth will simply become nothing. As I find courage to entertain these thoughts, I realize how really short our time on earth is. I need to spend less time worrying what others think of me and more time giving to others. After all, our mortality is the one thing we all share.

The next few days drag by, filled with weighty periods of watching Patty suffer with the ongoing reality that her mom is slowly slipping away. I continue to be overwhelmed by the dedicated and compassionate actions of my mother. I can't help but think how fortunate I am that she is still here. It's as if she is a great vision and I am left breathless by her beauty and strength. She is endless in her giving, and extremely sensitive in her outreach to Patty. I love her so, but still, it is as if I am on the outside looking in—an unknown admirer of hers from afar.

It is a Sunday and I'm getting ready for church when Mother comes into my room.

"Mr. Williams just called," she says. "Mrs. Williams has just passed away."

As I look into Mother's solemn face, I start to cry. She looks sad and distant.

"If you want, you can go over to Patty's with me. I'll be leaving in a few minutes."

"Okay, thanks," I reply. "I want to go, but I don't know what I can say or do. But I will go."

"Sue, this is all part of life. We all try to avoid dealing with this great pain. We can help them by just being there."

Mom hugs me in a reassuring way.

"I know," I say. "I'll be down in a few minutes."

Alone in my room, I'm sobbing. I am lost in a painful abyss, lost in the fact that my friend is torn apart. I hope I can help Patty by being there. I want her to know she is not alone in her deep sadness. Although no one can ever replace her mom, she is not without love, because I love her dearly. I quickly phone Carrie and Denise and share the sad news.

As we arrive at Patty's, the coroner is taking Mrs. Williams away. Patty is sitting on the couch, sobbing.

"I am so glad you came. I was there when she passed away. It seemed peaceful, but I worry that she feared death. The minister spent many hours with Mom, talking about life after death. He said she made peace with God."

Mom spends time with Patty's brothers. It is a somber environment, and the thick reality of death permeates every aspect of the home. Now an empty hole of darkness looms, as her presence is nowhere to be found. This home and the hearts of its people are now altered by the death of Mrs. Williams. Mom stays to help them with all the arrangements.

The day of the funeral service, I hear the doorbell ring as I'm getting dressed. Mom calls up to me that a friend has stopped by. I go down the stairs, and there stands Denise. I'm surprised to see her. She has driven four hours to come to the funeral.

"Oh Denise," I exclaim. "It is great to see you! But I am so sorry it's on such a somber occasion."

I hug Denise and introduce her to Mother. "Sue and Patty have shared a great deal about you," Mother says. "It's wonderful to finally meet you. I hope you plan on staying with us a while."

"That would be nice," Denise replies, "but I don't want to put anyone out. It's only a four-hour drive, and I could go back later today."

"Oh no, Denise," Mom says. "Please spend time with us. You are welcome to stay as long as you want."

"I need to call my parents and let them know I arrived safely. And if you don't mind, I'd love to stay the night. I have to get right back to school and can't stay longer."

We go up to my room to relax. We have a couple of hours before the funeral. I share in great detail the past few weeks and talk to her about Patty. Denise is used to comforting people at the time of death. I am glad she is here for Patty and her family. But deep inside, I cannot help but think that she is somehow here for me. Strangely, in her presence I feel so needy, but guilt for having such a feeling quickly represses my neediness. After all, this is not about me.

"How are you holding up during this difficult time, Sue?" Denise asks. "I know your deep love for Patty, and you spoke a lot about her mom at camp. Death is painful not just for the immediate family but for everyone connected in special ways to any of the family members."

Fearing that I will break down and wanting to concentrate on the funeral, I quickly insist that I am okay. Denise can see through me and says that we will talk later.

I ride to the church with Denise. It is a beautiful day, providing a glorious backdrop to such a painfully sad time. Entering the church, Denise and I see Patty at the head of her mother's open coffin. We immediately walk up to the front and hug Patty. Denise whispers words of condolence and comfort as I reverently gaze at Mrs. Williams. I've seen funerals in the movies, and heard all the old clichés about how peaceful the person looks, but I am overcome by the loss of Mrs. Williams. Her lifeless body is a stark reality that she is no longer here. She is dead, absolutely dead, and gone forever. She does not look as if she is sleeping; she looks plastic and lifeless. They have made her into someone who is not the Mrs. Williams I knew—a person full of life and laughter. I feel my emotions well up inside. I need to get away, to breathe. Not wanting to interrupt the soft talking of Denise and Patty, I turn away and walk quickly down the aisle.

The overwhelming image of Mrs. Williams being so dead fills my thoughts. Tears stream down my cheeks as I turn the corner of the church and move toward the backyard. Then, through my tearful gaze, I see my mother in the distance—in the rose garden behind the church. I am startled by her presence, confused as to why she is here. I quickly tuck myself behind a tree and do not disturb her. What irony, I tell myself. I am overcome by the stark reality of Mrs. Williams's dead, lifeless body, only to find my own mother so colorfully alive here in the flower garden. I know my mother loves this place, but it seems strange to me that she is here at this moment. Mom is looking attentively at each rose, smelling one after another, as if every single one were important to her. My heart is filled with the overwhelming contrast between having a mother who is alive and not having one. She looks up and, catching a glimpse of me, motions for me to come over to the garden.

"Sue, this reminds me of you when you were a child," she says. "I would always catch a glimpse of you out of the corner of my eye. What are you doing out here?"

"Oh, I left Denise talking with Patty. And I needed some air, so I thought I'd get a little before the service starts." It is not my nature to ask about Mother's actions, but for once I'm not going to let the moment go unquestioned.

"Mother," I ask, "why aren't you in the church? What are you doing here?"

"Well…when I find myself about to collapse from exhaustion or despair, I have a few special places that are helpful to me. This garden has always been my favorite place. I am somber and sad today. I really need to be here right now, experiencing these wonderful roses. I don't feel so fragile in the midst of such magnificent natural beauty."

I am stunned. I have never thought of my mother as fragile. She seems so different here in the rose garden. I am moved that she has shared with me how important this garden is to her. I am stunned that she is human and, like the rest of us, needs to be replenished.

CHAPTER 5

Welcoming the New Year

The coming New Year brings a great deal of excitement as I look forward to graduation. Getting ready for New Year's Eve, I am thinking about my growing relationship with Gary. We have a level of intimacy that allows us to speak openly about everything. We don't discuss the future; we focus on the moment. We have become each other's little refuge from life. Tonight we'll attend the school dance in celebration of New Year's Eve. At school dances now, we usually show up, have a couple of dances, and leave to be alone. Through the window I see light snow falling on the ground, already snow-covered. I fix a thermos of hot chocolate and pack Christmas cookies and a warm wrap. Mother has lifted my curfew. She knows the kids will party until breakfast.

Tonight feels so different. My life is changing, and my mind races as I quickly dress. How will I feel when Gary and I depart in different directions for college? I don't want to define our relationship, yet I don't want to lose Gary or the special bond that we have. I love the way we celebrate each other. I think about Gary's smiles, laughter, and intellect. I love his poetic nature, his love of art, and his richly detailed expressions when communicating. We have connected on so many levels. I'm excited by the thought of being with him, always like a mini-vacation away from reality. The times with him mean everything to me. They have turned my world around. Every time I come away, I am rejuvenated and have a better outlook on life.

Hearing a car door close, I glance out the window. Gary has a bounce to his walk.

"Sue," says Mom, "you look warm in that outfit. Guess you'd better get going before you have a meltdown. Gary, be careful driving. Too much celebration and bad weather makes it unsafe."

"I will be very careful, Mrs. Martin," Gary replies.

As we shuffle down the snow-covered sidewalk, Gary takes my hand and helps me with the slippery walk. With excitement in his voice, Gary says, "I am so happy to be with you this New Year's Eve. It makes sense that I want to spend the last day of one year and the first day of another with you."

"I know," I reply. "I feel the same way."

"I have some special plans after we visit the dance for a bit. My parents have gone to my Aunt Ida's for New Year's, and I stayed behind to work on my research paper. I asked my parents if I could have you over tonight, and they said I could."

"That's great, I want to be alone with you. I brought a thermos of hot chocolate and a blanket in case we decide to sit outside in the snow. But it will be best if we stay inside on a night like this."

I am excited about the thought of our being alone. I don't really care about the dance. We go in and visit with our friends. Then, having danced one dance, we quickly say our good-byes and leave. The snow is coming down hard as we slowly work our way through the streets to Gary's home. Gary lights the fire and I pour mugs of the hot chocolate. We spread my blanket in front of the fireplace.

"Sue, I think about you all the time. It's as if you are so important that my thoughts don't exist without you in them. What we have is very special."

Smiling, I felt a rush inside. I feel my breathing change and I am overwhelmed by Gary's words. I fear he wants to verbally define our relationship, so I'm feeling vulnerable. I have my own thoughts, ideas, and dreams about all of this. I love the mystique and feelings that our relationship generates, but I don't want to define them. I like the anticipation of what it all means, but I fear that to define it might strip it of its magical powers.

As we rest in front of the fireplace, Gary gently pulls me closer into his arms. This closeness feels natural, yet we've never before had such an opportunity. Having his arms secure and warm around me feels wonderful. It is the first time I've felt so much love. He looks into my eyes and I know he is lost to the moment.

"May I touch your face, Sue?"

"Yes."

Softly, he takes the back of his hand and very slowly and sensually moves it artistically along the left side of my face. It is as if I am his canvas; I feel transformed by his artistry and touch. I feel emotion welling up inside and moisture starting to flood my eyes.

"All the years of wondering if I would ever feel so special," I say. "Then, in a wonderfully magical touch of my face, I am overwhelmed."

I see emotion in Gary's eyes. He can barely speak. "You are so special to me, Sue."

Silence fills the room as the unbelievable truths of our relationship slowly unfold. A few minutes pass, and then I must share my thoughts.

"How does this wonderfulness get all used up in the beginning of a relationship," I ask, "and then later everyday worries and monotony take over, until couples just exist with each other? Seems like everyone is wrapped up in young love or new love, but you never see emphasis on growing love or sustaining love. In life everything new is exciting, like new objects, cars, toys, whatever. But in time, everything loses the specialness that once existed. Unfortunately, I see relationships deteriorate with time, and slowly people end up just existing together. You know what I mean, all the specialness is gone? I don't get it. With millions of facets to each of us, how can boredom set in? Is love that fickle, that shallow, that limited?"

"Please don't stop now, Sue. What you're saying is interesting."

"It comes down to: what is love? When you ask others about their love for a person, they always go back to the beginning and talk about when they met. I wonder what characteristic one needs to sustain fifty to sixty years of marriage? It can't be a person's appearance, since aging is a given. It can't just be sex; that changes with time, too. I want to be with someone who has a positive outlook on life and is not trapped in disbelief. I like people who are realistic, yet delight in dreaming. I want authentic laughter, which I believe comes from good self-esteem. I desire to be with someone who is a survivor of life, not a victim of its circumstances. I could go on and on. But love for me is not some magical moment of awareness. It's the growing respect and deep valuing that comes with time and commitment. I'm a romantic and I love the breathless anticipation that comes at the beginning of a relationship. But more than that, I am a realist, and I see love as a growing process that involves commitment and dedication. Gee, I have never shared these thoughts with anyone."

"Its amazing that you have thought this all out, Sue. I've thought a lot about love, but what is love? Is it a by-product of choices and development? I've never thought of it as magical—as something that presents itself without work.

Some people spend an entire lifetime in pursuit of love. A good example is Vincent van Gogh. I've looked at his short unacknowledged loveless life. I see where society never supported or valued him. I think about his funeral, how his brother surrounded his coffin with all his paintings. And that was easy to do since no one valued or liked them enough to buy them. I don't know if you've ever seen his painting called *Couple Walking and Crescent Moon*. Supposedly, it was painted when he was in the mental asylum at Saint-Remy. If you look at the faceless man in the painting, you see red hair and a red beard, and he's wearing a blue shirt. Vincent had red hair, a red beard, and was known for his blue shirts. Anyway, this is believed to be a self-portrait, and he gave himself a companion, which is something he wanted. I believe it was his dream, an idealized scenario he visualized. He longed to be loved in the midst of the fields and the radiance of the sun. That is my favorite painting because I relate to it. I have a desire for that one companion. I fear, like Vincent, that I may spend a lifetime longing for that one person. But I am convinced love is a creation that evolves from commitment and dedication of two people who value and respect each other. Vincent may have been like most, who expect love to be magical, and when it does not happen that way, they're left feeling love is not for them. I don't think that way. Love is something that is inside of all of us. I believe it is a choice, and we must seek it, create it, and nurture it. I think about the value of love, feeling love, living love. You are so right about it being so much more than the early, fresh, new beginnings. Love needs endurance and growth, and it evolves from deep respect and gratitude. Why does society place little emphasis on growing love, sustaining love, and enduring love, as you have said? Sue, I really love our relationship. I haven't tried to define it; rather I simply let it be whatever is. It has evolved into something special. I am not about to define it. I'm very much taken by it, but in an open way."

My face is beaming, and I am slightly embarrassed. Gary has given me the depth and understanding I need about who he is. He realizes we are a relationship in progress. Only time and staying open will bring forth whatever our relationship will become.

"You seemed so relaxed as you expressed yourself, Gary. I'm so glad that our relationship is one of depth and mutual respect. I really like what you said."

I am peaceful and relaxed with his arm around me. Nothing is defined, yet everything is confirmed. We have a wonderful relationship. We spend the rest of New Year's Eve celebrating and having fun.

❦   ❦   ❦

The following Saturday morning I am awakened by Mom. "Get up, Sue," she says. "Carrie is on the phone."

"Hi Carrie! Is everything okay?"

"Oh yes, fine here,' she says. "I was wondering if you'd have time to meet me in the park this morning? All of my chores are done, and I have some things I want to talk to you about."

"Sure. How about 10:00 AM?"

I am pleased that Carrie is reaching out first. Even Mother, who was concerned that Carrie has called, quickly asks if she is okay.

It is a beautiful day. It's exciting being a senior, with anticipation of all the hoopla that comes with it: the senior prom, senior trip and graduation. I think about it as I walk to the park. The sun is dancing in and out of the clouds, and a cool breeze starts to sweep in. Focused on the glorious beauty of the trees blowing in the wind, I think about the aesthetics of it all. Gary would be quick to point out that this is the art of God.

In the park, I see Carrie sitting on a bench waving her arms at me. "Thanks so much for coming, Sue," she calls out.

"Sure. I just love this weather."

"Well, I don't want to take your day away from you, but I need to ask you a question. Now that we're in our senior year, I need to make some decisions about my future. Next birthday I will be free from foster care. I'll become fully emancipated. It's crucial that I start planning my independence and life. The thought is so exciting, yet I have fears. It will be the first time that I have no one to depend on. Most people go to college and move toward being on their own. But they know that if they ever need some help or assistance their parents and family are there. I've always known that, once emancipated, I'm fully on my own, and alone."

"I want you to know that I will always be there to support or help you in any way I can," I reply. "Mom and Dad care about you. Even this morning, Mom was concerned when you called."

"Your mom is such a giving person. She has always been kind and caring toward me. What I'm trying to do now is decide on what college or colleges to consider. I'll seek loans and work while going to school."

I am pleased that Carrie feels comfortable sharing this with me. I am surprised by all the work she will have to do to succeed in college. My parents are paying for me to go to college, and I cannot imagine having to become totally independent without some resource available in case I desperately need it.

"You've really thought this through, Carrie," I say. "I know it must be exciting, and a bit scary, to come to this point in your life. But I want you to know that I'd love to be there for you as much as possible. I don't want you to ever feel alone."

All it once, I have an inspiration.

"Carrie, why don't you and I go to the same college and room together? I'd love to have you with me, so we can share the next chapter of our lives!"

Carrie is laughing and has tears in her eyes at the same time.

"Sue, that's exactly what I wanted to talk to you about."

Now we are both gushing and laughing and so excited. Still, Carrie has concerns, and she opens up to talk about them.

"I am so excited! There is nothing I'd love more than to be your roommate. But before we get too deep into this discussion," she says, "I'm wondering what schools you're considering. I know all colleges are expensive, and it's hard for me to get accepted at some of the more prestigious ones because of my lack of family background."

"I've applied at three colleges," I tell her. "Only one is the one I'm really hoping for, and I know it is open to all. I really want to go to Broctren Harbor College in Illinois. It is an interfaith college."

"Oh, I know all about Broctren Harbor. Yes, it's one that I've thought about. too. This is so exciting. I already have an application for Broctren Harbor. A year ago, Bella was taking care of an elderly lady, and her niece came from Broctren Harbor and spent the weekend with us. She was so nice, and she and I stayed up one night and talked about the college in detail. She said it has such a great family atmosphere, with the professors being more attentive. Sue, I've filled out the application, but held up submitting it until I could talk to you. I'm frightened to be released from the system, and yet it's what I've lived for throughout the years. I never realized I would be this overwhelmed. But then, I thought about keeping in contact with you, so I wouldn't feel so alone. Then I thought about us attending the same college, and I got excited and hopeful."

"I love it, Carrie," I exclaim. "I love it! The idea of college felt both scary and exciting before, but now the scary part is gone, knowing I'm not alone. This is exciting!"

The rest of the morning we exchange our thoughts about Broctren Harbor College. As I walk home, I think about how my life is coming together. I am no longer saddened at ending my high school years. I'm eager to start college and have Carrie with me in this new adventure. I am overcome with a profound sense of gratitude for my life. Coming upon the church, I decide to go in. I always feel the presence of God in church. Logically, I know it is just a building, but spiritually it represents the house of God. Reverence is something I often crave, especially when I am full of gratitude. Acknowledging that I could not have created the good things in my life, I can trust that surely something greater than myself is in control. I am not too religious, but I feel I am very spiritual.

I never go to church out of neediness, nor do I beg God for things. I'm confused by people who say that God has a plan for their lives and then beg God to do things differently instead of trusting in that plan. Faith is my key to my life. When Patty's Mom was in the last days of her life, people were telling me to go to church and pray for her recovery. Throughout her sickness, I never asked God to heal her. I definitely prayed, thanking God for her life. Asking God for favors feels like a lack of faith. I never think myself wise enough to tell God what to do, nor do I feel as if God needs me to share my insights. Yet, I respect those who believe differently than I. I don't know what is right or wrong when it comes to another person's relationship with God. I only know that my faith is the foundation of my relationship with God.

After breathing a prayer of gratitude, I leave the church. Outside, I see my mother in the rose garden behind the church. The winter vines are now bare. Quickly tucking myself behind a tree, I gaze upon her there. She appears lost in thought, with her hands folded behind her in a submissive and reverent way. I cannot remember her ever looking so open and so patient. My image of Mom includes a great deal of movement, with her arms always in front of her, busily doing things. Even in church she sits holding a hymnal, going through pages, or flipping through the Bible. I used to wonder if constant movement was her way of avoiding eye contact. She never really relaxes in a chair at home. Even at the dinner table she moves about, busily taking care of everyone.

Gazing upon her now, I am stunned that she is standing so attentively still. It appears that she is somehow captured by something. It feels wrong to be covertly watching her. I think about having seen her in the rose garden the day of Mrs. Williams's funeral. Mother is a mystery to me. I long to understand her but probably never will.

CHAPTER 6

The Awakening

A couple of months into the school year, Carrie and I receive our acceptance letters from Broctren Harbor College. We are both so excited. I try not to allow the anticipation of college to outweigh the importance of my senior year activities. Soon we will be going on a senior trip to Washington DC, and in April there's the senior prom. But the greatest excitement will come from graduating in early June.

Looking forward to so much has my head spinning, and I can't get to sleep. Sitting by the window, I open it to feel the cool night air. I like being momentarily chilled to the bone. It makes me feel so alive. The moon and stars fill the night with a beauty that always sets my mind to dreaming. Tonight the stars look like a massive tiara crowning the earth with glory.

My thoughts drift to Gary. I have seen people fall in love and close off the world. Neither of us could do that. As strongly as we feel about each other, we cannot limit ourselves to each other's worlds. I know couples who have limited their lives by marrying too early. They settle down in their childhood community and shadow the lives of their parents. There's nothing wrong with that, but Gary and I want to experience more of what is out there. I need to be away from my family. I want the opportunity to explore and make friends with people who have no preconceived notions about me. I don't want to live off the good graces of my parents, or be sought after because my brother is a heart-throb. Planning any part of my life with Gary would be like attaching another defining characteristic. Yet, he is a soft haven where I can find comfort. He paints a better world for me with his words and touch. I am always transformed and renewed after spending time with him. But now I need to find out more about myself.

I can't stop thinking about how much I care for him, how difficult it will be without him in my daily life. I think about his touch, his electrifying, ever-so-gentle caresses. We have experienced deep intellectual intimacy, yet up to now we have held our physical relationship in check. But he has awakened my sexuality with intense feelings. Now, closing my eyes as the gentle air of night caresses my face, I think about his soft kisses. Many times Gary has stirred me physically—leaving me panting on the edge of something unknown.

Folding my arms as the coolness seduces me, my mind wanders to an incident that happened the day after my first date with Gary. I was at the library during an electrical power failure. The outside light, coming through the windows was dimmed by dark clouds. It wasn't bright enough to read by, but it was sufficient to be able to move about. I moved nearer to a window, hoping the power would soon return. Turning back to look inside the library, I saw everything in varying shades of gray. I leaned back against the wall next to the window, my arms softly folded across my breasts, my head supported by the wall, and relaxed. I slowly gazed through the gray shadows. All at once, in astonishment, I caught a glimpse of Gary in the library. Just recalling this incident causes me to gasp, and my skin is covered with goose bumps! Seeing Gary across the room, I could barely breathe. Trying to move my body seemed impossible—as if energy was draining from my legs. Why was I acting this way? Why was I out of control?

I remember that my mind could not outthink my body's reactions. My body was producing uncontrollable sensations and intense feelings. Even though Gary hadn't noticed me, when I saw him I lost control of my thoughts, as strong physical feelings invaded my body. I felt myself gasp, trying to gain some control. I was shocked and had to move away from the window before he saw me. It was all so surreal, almost an out-of-body experience.

I rapidly stumbled through the library. All at once I felt an intense pain in my hip, when I hit the edge of a table. I saw a restroom door about fifteen feet away. How far that felt! Finally, I reached the door—opening it only to find a pitch black space. I was even more panicked, finding that my refuge was gone. Then, suddenly, I felt a tap on my back.

"Sue." I turned around and, with no control over my body, threw my arms around him. He hugged me and said, "Shhh. It's okay, Sue. You're trembling! It's okay. It's okay. Gets a little scary in the dark, doesn't it?"

Now in the cold of a beautiful night, I recall how he gently held me, softly stroking the back of my head. I remember the panic inside, and how I had struggled to regroup. I had explained to Gary that I ran into a table in the dark and that the momentary pain was so sharp that I headed for the restroom to see whether I'd bruised myself. Gary had asked if I needed medical attention and I had assured him I was fine.

Thinking about this incident is still electrifying. The loss of control—and those sensations! It was a catalyst, unleashing my first real feelings of sexuality. Tonight is no different. Recalling those moments, I feel sexual arousal sweeping slowly over and through me.

I leave the window and stretch across my bed, the memories of those uncontrolled feelings now seducing me. My breathing becomes choppy, sounding like a gasping crescendo. As my hand gently moves over my body, every pore, every hair, every fiber of my being acquiesces in celebration. My back arches in intensity.

It is Gary who awakened my sexual beginnings. I think about the power of that incident in the library and how I have relived it over and over—always letting it take me. Savoring sweet exhaustion, I realize that I have barely touched the edges of my sexuality. I feel myself wanting to let go of my controlling nature. I so want life to spill all over me. I have to admit I was out of control, this incident becoming one of my best moments in recollection. I loved the unpredictable mystery of sensations permeating my body—feelings more powerful than my ability to control them.

My problem in life is that I am too much of a thinker. I control much of my life by overthinking, being logical, planning for certain outcomes. But this physiological phenomenon of sensuality and sexuality is something beyond my understanding. That loss of control arouses my curiosity. Control is about limiting and shaping an experience. Loss of control is much more intriguing. It offers the unpredictable and unimaginable. Now, quite relaxed, I turn over and finally fall asleep.

CHAPTER 7

Homecoming

During the fall, as leaves crown the earth and everywhere I look is beautiful, excitement fills every inch of my existence. It seems like every minute is filled with something special. But among all my activities are the endless times of over-processing life. Every aspect and every encounter offers me something to think about. Pondering has always been my way of breathing in life and giving meaning to it. Yet I have become giddy and light-hearted, especially about school activities. In the past I had little time to enjoy them, always pushing hard to get good grades and prepare for my college entrance exams. At last I am accepted at college and am now enjoying my senior year.

My classmates and I are trying to figure out what our senior homecoming float should look like. My mind reflects on previous years, and I have a silly thought. "I know what we can do," I say. "Remember our sophomore year, when the title of our float was 'The Royal Ball,' and we made a football that ended up looking like a huge potato? Then last year our float was 'Rocket Off to Victory,' and our rocket ended up looking like a big carrot? Well, this year we can use our leftover potato and carrot and title our float 'Stew 'Em.'" Everyone laughs. Every year we have so much fun making our traditionally disastrous float, which always comes in last in the competition. But no group of people has more fun than we do.

My thoughts of homecoming are filled with fun and romance—all the fun of doing the float and then attending the dance with Gary.

After the float committee meeting, I rush though the corridor. It's a gorgeous fall day and I know that Gary will be waiting for me outside by the willow tree. Shading the sun from my eyes, I see him standing there.

"Hi Sue," he calls out. "Great day to walk through the park. How did your day go?"

"Well, I'm full of energy, so it's hard to stay focused. I'm starting to daydream through class."

"Gosh, that doesn't sound like you. You're always so attentive."

"I know. I'm giving myself permission to really have fun this year."

Walking into the park, Gary looks at a particular pine tree growing between a gorgeous maple and an oak. Looking rather insignificant, the pine is overpowered by the beauty of the other trees with their brilliant red and orange leaves.

"Look at that," exclaims Gary, pointing high into the pine tree.

"What are you talking about?" I ask. I can't see anything but browning pine needles and cones. Gary holds my arm and points my index finger toward an area in the tree.

"Up there, Sue. See that unique pinecone? Isn't it really beautiful?"

Looking more carefully now, I see a pinecone of an unusual shape. "Oh. Yes. It looks like a bell."

"I love to see anything that diverges from the ordinary," he says.

When we reach the middle of the park, Gary glances back at the pine tree and then asks, "How would you like to go to homecoming with me? After all, aren't I the only guy for you?"

"I would love to go to homecoming."

At dinner that evening, Dad asks about my day. "I'm having a great time now that it is my senior year," I reply.

Quickly, he cuts me off. "Forget the fun. Get serious. You'll need discipline and focus for college."

Mom takes it further. "You should be studying at least a couple of hours every evening, Sue. Either you're goofing off doing some school activities, or you're with Gary. I'm getting concerned about your carefree attitude. You need to be careful. I think you are slipping."

These comments hurt, and I become irritated. Didn't my answer to his original question mean anything when I said I am having a great time? He asked a question without caring to hear what I answered. I have been so diligent in my studies throughout high school. Every evening I've studied until I fell asleep. I've completed my college exams and have been accepted with a partial scholarship. Now, when I choose to finally relax a bit and enjoy my senior year, my parents chime in, predicting disaster and doom if I am not careful. I immediately excuse myself from the table. Any further comment by them will surely release the avalanche of anger rumbling inside me. What have I done to them, that they have so little faith in me? Why can't they pick up on my excitement and delight in my being happy? Why are they so wrapped up in their thoughts and concerns that they don't listen to me? Once again I realize they are not interested in me sharing my thoughts. They are so busy talking *at* me that they do not know how to talk *with* me. Sobbing on my bed, I turn my thoughts inside, and once again I'm alone with my sadness. My whole life had been like this: rushing to my room to think and rethink everything a thousand times over. Sadly, I know they thought nothing of it and aren't sensitive enough to realize I left the table nearly destroyed. No one will come to my door to comfort me. They continue to parent me on how to *do* life and miss out on my joy in *living* it. So many times as a child, when I would hand Mom something I'd made she would only see what I could have done differently, never appreciating what I had done. Incident after incident floods my mind.

No wonder people suffer from depression, I conclude. If a mind stores up a lifetime of painful incidents, how can a person ever overcome that dangerous stockpile of feelings? At a certain point, I always force myself to turn to my faith. If I truly believe God is there for me, and that I am not alone, then I must stop feeling sorry for myself. This always breaks me away from spiraling into further depression. My faith forces me to refocus, to turn away from destructive thinking. Many times I've questioned why God would let me slip so low. But I know the answer: my faith is always there to turn to. Only self-pity allows me to dive into all the pain. How much will I put myself through? I am an intense person and want the intensity of my feelings. I want the high highs, but they do not exist without the low lows. I didn't realize how wonderful I had been feeling until my happiness was shattered by my parents' words. They have too much power and influence over my feelings. My way out of this mental torture is to return to my faith.

I decide to take a walk to the park. It is dusky outside, the sun has already folded itself into the edges of the earth. Darkness invades the now sunless sky, dimming the colors of the leaves. I can still feel the dampness on my face from the tears that fell earlier. Slowly, the night breeze from heaven will dry it. I feel comforted. I start thinking how houses confine us to the human conditions inside. They wall us in. They are prisons keeping us away from God's vast universe. So many times I have lain on my bed, feeling as if the walls and ceiling were trapping me. Now, resting under the heavens, I feel uplifted. I am transformed by the sky. Within seconds, I am thinking about all of life's possibilities. So many times I have lain under the skies and found a profound sense of freedom—freedom to think, freedom to explore, freedom to be me.

Feeling more in control, I return home. As I start up the stairs, my father calls me into the living room.

"You cut dinner short," he begins, "and I thought maybe it was something I said."

"No, it wasn't about what you said," I reply. "It was because you didn't listen to my answer when you asked how my day went. Well, it is over now. I'm fine. I just want to go read my English chapter and get ready for bed."

"Oh, okay. Have a good night."

I am shaking my head as I climb the stairs. He still doesn't get it, but at least I can feel a little reassured; his stopping me on the stairs showed me he cares.

The following week, I spend at least two hours every night after school working on the float. I don't see Gary, Carrie, and Patty, who are not involved in the activity. On the Friday night before Saturday's homecoming, I attend a casual party just for classmates who helped with the float. We are sitting around a big open fire pit in the back yard of Jim Weld's home. Everyone is laughing at our float; as usual, it is sure to take last place in the competition.

Steve Manning has brought a box of liquor and mixers. I've heard stories about parties where there is drinking, but this is the first one I've attended. As wrong as I believe it to be, something about drinking arouses my curiosity. I tasted beer once at Patty's house. I like the thought of losing control, even though I have no idea how it will actually feel.

I had thought about alcohol many times when Patty's mother was alive. Mrs. Williams told me that she'd controlled her drinking for many years and expressed how much she enjoyed it when she was young. I knew that alcohol had taken a toll on her physically and was a major factor in her death. Yet I couldn't stop thinking about the many stories she shared regarding the fun she'd had while drinking. She said that a little alcohol took away her mundane cares and worries, making her mind seem more creative. She'd have a few drinks and stay up at night, designing gowns.

I've read stories about great artists who created their finest pieces of work under the influence of alcohol. Although it is hard to admit it, I am intrigued by the thought of drinking. My parents drink a few ounces of wine with their evening meal a couple of times a week. It isn't enough to alter them in any way, just an enhancement to the entrée of the night. Seeing my fellow classmates drinking and laughing, I decide that this is my opportunity.

I am three blocks away from home and not driving. My parents have given me special permission to come home late, because it is my senior year, and they will be in bed by 9:00. All I have to do is open their bedroom door and let them know I am home. They never ask to talk; they just acknowledge that they've heard me. My watch reads a few minutes after eight. If I drink a little now but stop by 9:00, I tell myself, I will be fine by the time I get home at 11:30.

"So, Sandy—what should I try?"

"Here's a screwdriver. The vodka won't smell conspicuous. If you want to feel it, drink it quickly."

"Gosh. It tastes like a bad version of a glass of orange juice."

"One more and you'll feel whatever you want to feel," Sandy says, handing me another. "This one is stronger. They've put double shots of vodka in it."

Eric Barnett, a neighbor who lives two doors down from me, comes over and sits beside me. We have known each other since kindergarten and were play partners when we were young. As he grew older, Eric ran around with a fast crowd and dated girls with reputations for being wild.

"Gosh Sue," says Eric, "I can't believe you're drinking. That's not like you."

Buzzed from my quick intake of alcohol, I reply, "Eric, it's my first time. I was just curious, and it feels really strange but rather nice."

"Your family would be upset at your drinking. Maybe you shouldn't drink any more."

"Well, I don't plan on informing them."

I'm laughing as Steve calls to me from across the pit.

"Sue! Do you want another drink?"

Eric waves his arms in the air. "No, she does not!"

I know I'm feeling the effects of the drink. All I can think about is going to the park and looking up at the sky. I know I have to clear my head a little more before I can go home. I do fine standing up, but I feel buzzed, which feels good. I walk a few steps and feel like I'm still functioning okay.

"Well, I'll see you all at homecoming tomorrow."

As I leave the back yard and move toward the sidewalk, Eric comes up behind me.

"Sue," he says, "let me walk you home, please?"

"I'm going to stop at the park. I want to look at the sky."

"Can I come along? I just want to keep you safe and make sure you get home tonight."

I am still buzzed, so walking takes effort. At the park I sit down at the edge of the brook, and Eric sits beside me. He had quite a few drinks at the party, and I can tell that he is buzzed, too.

"You know, Sue," he says, "I'm shocked that you drank tonight. You're always so straight."

"Well," I reply, "I was curious. I didn't drink because it's the party thing to do, I drank because of the mystique. I've always wanted to know what it felt like."

I am lying flat on the ground looking up. Eric sits looking down at me. "What else are you curious about, Sue?"

"Shhh," I say. "Listen to the crickets. Listen."

Eric stretches out on his side, still looking at me. "You've lost weight. You're so nicely shaped now. I remember the little girl who played with me was a chubby kid."

"Well, I didn't really diet. I just started taking better care of myself and the weight came off."

"I see you with Gary Waltham a lot. Is he your boyfriend?"

"We've been dating for about a year. Sometimes I think he's my boyfriend, and other times I think we're just great friends."

"Have you had sex with him yet?"

Feeling impaired, I am not at all shocked by his question.

"No."

"Why haven't you two been sexual?"

"Well, I feel sexual when I'm with him, but we're both pretty responsible. We're going away to different colleges, and our lives might go in different directions. I think we just don't want to take that step. It could complicate things."

I am experiencing the full impact of the alcohol, and my head feels light and carefree. Unguarded and blithe, I feel seduced by the sky, the night breeze, and the man looking down upon me, asking me about my sexuality. I have no fears or apprehensions and instead am stimulated by everything. I feel goose bumps; every hair dances with heightened sensation from the cool breeze. My thoughts are filled with sexual imagery. It is a new kind of freedom I never knew existed, the freedom of enjoying a moment when my conscious programming can't hold me captive. My mind no longer processes anything, and my body is tantalized by everything. I am so free from myself that I have no idea I am at the pinnacle of vulnerability.

Lying beside me, Eric is quiet now, though I can hear him breathing. I am slowly losing myself to this moment. What could possibly happen? I have no thoughts of anything or anyone else. I sit up and look at him.

"What are you thinking about?" I ask.

"Ummm, about you being here beside me and how I would like to kiss you and touch you."

His words excite me, and when he sits up and looks at me he sees that my silence is an invitation. Slowly, he begins kissing me. His kiss is soft but so electrifying. I feel the lustful longing in both of us. Losing ourselves in the freedom of our lost inhibitions, we lunge into a kissing embrace. As he kisses me intensely again and again, I feel my body responding to him. He kisses on my face softly, and then his lips brush my ear. He rubs his cheek along my neck and then gently kisses my cleavage. Heat from his breath penetrates through my clothing as he kisses my breasts. His hand softly cups my breast. I so want to feel his hand on the flesh of my breast, not through my clothing. Kissing me, he slowly unbuttons my blouse. He unhooks my bra, and when my breasts are freed he gently touches them. It's unbelievable. My body consents to every electrifying touch. My breathing is out of rhythm, driven by endless crescendos of sexual sensations. My body dances inside. I feel an incredible inward contraction and rushing moisture.

Kissing me, Eric moves across and over me. Suddenly, I feel his undeniable arousal. It is a stark awakening. At once I become panicked. Reality floods back into my thoughts: what have I gotten myself into? No longer lost and free in the moment, I realize I've been out of control and must regain my composure before I do something I'll regret. I pull away.

"Oh Eric," I say. "I'm so sorry, but I'm out of line here."

I quickly put on my bra and button my blouse.

"Sue, its okay," Eric protests. "We didn't do anything that you have to regret. Please calm down. It will be okay. Please, please—it will be okay."

Eric seems upset that I am upset. He wants me to be okay with it. I look at my watch; it is 10:45 PM.

"Sue, its okay. Please, let's just sit for a minute."

"No," I reply, "I want to go home. Please forgive me for using you while I was impaired. I can't explain my actions. I want you to know that I won't look on this as anything but a moment in which you and I experienced a little piece of life. I am okay."

Eric walks me to my door and tells me not to worry, that tonight is a private matter between us. He says that if I need to talk about it sometime, to please let him know. Looking at Eric in the porch light, I realize that in my panic I have not once thought about him. "And are you okay?" I ask.

"Yes, I'm fine," he answers. "Just a little sad because I think you might beat yourself up for what happened. I hope you really do let yourself look at it as just an experience in your life. You're not just anybody to me. I know I had some drinks, but I think that allowed me to finally express feelings I've had for you for years. Maybe our loss of control was wrong, but I know it was a reflection of my admiration and attraction to you. Good night."

"Eric, thanks."

I glance at the hall clock as I rush upstairs. It's a few minutes past eleven. I open the bedroom door.

"I'm home. Okay?"

"Get some sleep. 'Night."

I take a quick shower. My head spins from the alcohol still in my body. As the hot water runs over and down my body, I touch my left breast and recall Eric's hand on it. How gentle he was, and how pleasurable it felt. Now, with water flooding and rinsing every crevice of my body, I feel vitally alive. I quickly dry off, get into my pajamas, and crawl into bed.

Reason and logic return. For the first time, I understand what drinking alcohol feels like, and it is something both good and bad. I had thought that tipsiness could release pent-up creativity, that it could wall off worries and free a person from nagging, conscious programming. That, indeed, had happened to me. I was free from my head—from processing and over-thinking, and from worrying about what people might think of me. But I hadn't expected such freedom to unleash my sexuality. I do not believe in sexual freedom, but want sexuality to be part of a special relationship. I hadn't considered that impairment would unleash raw lust, opening me up in such a sexual way. Exhausted from the night and from the aftermath of drinking, I soon fall asleep.

The next morning I feel a bit weak, but with no real signs of a hangover. It is Saturday, homecoming day. Kickoff is at eleven. My dress for the homecoming dance hangs on the closet door. I hold it to my body and, now looking in the mirror, imagine it on me. It looks great.

Downstairs, I hear chatter. I go to the kitchen for a cup of coffee and a slice of toast.

"Hello," says my brother. "Is someone in there?"

"Oh. Sorry, Mark," I reply. "I was thinking about homecoming and all the things I need to do before I leave for the game. What were you asking me?"

"Mom was asking if you'd tried your dress on."

"Thanks, Mom, its fine."

I excuse myself and return to my room. I continue thinking about last night, how the alcohol enabled me to feel everything more intensely than I'd known was possible. Making my bed and fluffing the pillows, I gently hold one to my body, feeling its soft presence against me. The pillow tight in my arms, I slowly lie down, thinking about Eric pulling me against him breathless and the passion escalating. Last night could never have happened without my being impaired, but the effects of the alcohol had liberated me. Now the memories of my spontaneity and loss of control continue to stimulate me.

Suddenly, my logic kicks in again. I realize how dangerous my situation had been. I surrendered my good sense when I drank, I tell myself. It was a high-risk experience, and much could have gone wrong. I had been in control when I chose to get drunk; then alcohol took my control away. Now I understand the progressive effects of alcohol. The person takes a drink, then the drink takes the person. Getting up from the bed, I desperately want to move away from my now painfully rational thinking. I quickly get ready for the game.

I don't really get interested in the football game, but the halftime parade of floats is exciting. As always, our float comes in last. When I return home, Mom tells me that Gary has just called. I immediately return the call.

"Hi, Gary. What's up?"

"My Aunt Ida passed away this morning. They live up north, about five hours away. We're going to leave in a few minutes. I am so sorry I have to cancel my date with you."

"Gary, please. No apology needed. Is there anything I can do for you? How long will you be away? Can I inform the school or get your assignments?"

"Well, Dad said we'll stay with Uncle Bob until the funeral is over, so that will be four days. Yes, if you wouldn't mind, please inform my teachers, because it's Saturday and there's no one at school for me to talk with."

"No problem. I'll take care of it. My thoughts and prayers are with you and your family."

Hanging up the phone, I go back downstairs and explain the phone call to my mother.

"Are you going to the dance by yourself?" she asks. "Maybe you can ask Carrie or Patty to go, and make it a girls' night."

"No, I'm fine."

In my room, I look at the dress I've bought for the dance. I think about the hard work Mom put into tailoring it and how I've imagined I'd look special for Gary. Taking it off the door, I put the dress in a zippered bag and tuck it in the back of my closet. It occurs to me that anticipating and planning something special has its own importance and value. I remember the excitement I felt when I found the dress. I've imagined myself in it, and I've visualized Gary commenting on it. My memories of how I imagined this night are no less important.

Now, thinking about the evening, I decide to make it something special. Mark has a date for the homecoming dance and will be gone. Mom and Dad are going to a dinner at the home of one of Dad's clients. The fall days are getting shorter, and soon I will be trapped inside because of the cold. I decide to pack a little picnic basket for myself and take a book to the park.

I make myself a chicken sandwich, fill a small thermos with some warm cider, and wrap up a few of Mom's homemade cookies. I dress in warm layers so I can peel them off and then put them back on as the sun goes down. With my book, basket, and a small outdoor blanket, I am ready for the park.

"Mom, I am going to spend my evening at the park, reading and relaxing."

"I think it's silly for you not to go to the homecoming dance, Sue. We spent a lot of time and money on that dress, and I know how you looked forward to going."

"I still the love the dress, and I'll wear it at college for special occasions. But a homecoming dance would only be something special if I were going with Gary."

"Well, don't stay too late at the park. Remember, we're going to the St. Clairs' and won't be back until late."

The setting sun has a little ways to go before it buries itself in the earth. It is beautiful now. Walking into the park, I pass the pine tree that so mesmerized Gary, and I can still see the oddly-shaped cone in the tree. I think about Gary as I pass under it. He is so attentive and has an eye for nature. I wonder how anyone could be so captivated by the smallest details of earth. How did he become so sensitive to it all?

Spreading out the blanket, I continue to reflect. I gaze across the brook into the beautiful, thick woods, where falling leaves are gliding on the breeze. Some trees have bare limbs and will soon cradle snow. It's pleasurable to absorb all the beauty. Gary awakened that part of me. Often, he has poetically described the beauty of a panorama lying before us. His words are like strokes on a canvas, words that paint the beauty he sees and bring me into it. He has stirred my senses, fine-tuning them so that I can enjoy his visual intensity. Gary is more than just a person that I love. He is a special gift from God to me. He is nothing like me but rather is an extension of everything that I am not. Being with him,

I have become so much more. I wonder how I will ever get along at college without him.

Then my thoughts return to the night before. All day, I have pushed them aside, again and again. But now my body begins to move with nervousness and anticipation as I recall it all. I remember what it felt like to just be in the moment. All the pretense and strain of trying to act properly, to say the right words to others—all of that had disappeared when the alcohol freed me. I had stopped worrying or even thinking, just feeling for certain that life was great. I had wanted only to lie down and absorb the sky, to be fully in the moment, living life intensely every nanosecond. I had experienced an acute sensitivity to everything, for once without any filtering. My breasts heave as I take a deep breath, recalling those wonderful physical sensations.

Would I ever again experience such physical freedom, perhaps without alcohol? I try to imagine getting that comfortably uninhibited, as I lay back and remember how everything unfolded. My lips and body had reacted naturally, and my responses had been filled with intense pleasure and ecstasy. I feel guilty recalling it all. Ah yes—guilt always takes away or destroys our pleasures. I open my eyes to see the sun now dipping into the earth. It is getting too dark to read. Sipping the hot cider, I am startled by a voice behind me.

"Sue! I thought you were going to the dance with Gary?"

"Oh! Eric. You scared me. I *was* going to the dance, but Gary and his family had to leave town because of a death in the family."

"Oh. Sorry to hear that. Mind if I sit for a moment?"

"Yes, of course. Would you like a cookie? Mom baked them."

"Thanks. They look good."

My thoughts fly all over the place. Why am I acting so friendly? Most of all, why am I so shaken? Why do I feel so weird?

"Sue, I am glad to have a moment alone with you. I want to make sure you were okay about last night and everything."

"I am okay, Eric. That is…it was the first time I ever drank, and it really loosened me up…and I know what happened and everything. That is not like me, but I don't wish it away. Maybe it would have been better if it didn't happen…all I know is that I will be fine."

"Well, I am sorry if you have any regrets. I figured you'd have some. I just wanted to apologize."

He stands up and dusts crumbs from his coat. "You enjoy your evening, and thanks for the cookie."

He turns to walk away, and I know I have to stop him.

"Eric," I call out. "Please don't go. I need to talk to you."

He returns and sits down beside me on the blanket.

"There's a lot about last night that I just don't understand—mostly about myself. The overly conservative, highly guarded Sue disappeared once I started drinking. Being impaired freed parts of me that I didn't know existed. It allowed me to live in the moment without any filtering or barriers. I could never have known what I'd be like. But now I do. Last night showed me that alcohol can free me sexually and that physical sensations can dominate my actions—with no regard for whom I am sharing them with. I'm glad you turned out to be the one I unfolded on because you didn't push me beyond what I was driven to do. And I trust that you will respect my privacy...and keep those unleashed moments something just between us."

I take a deep breath and try to relax.

"Sue," Eric replies, "I haven't spoken a word to anyone. I did return to the party after taking you home, but no one pushed me to talk. I only said I'd walked you home safely. I'd be lying if I said I haven't thought about last night. I feel some guilt over it because you're someone I've admired all my life. I knew last night that you were experimenting. I feel guilty that I participated. Maybe I could have seen you home safely without all the physical stuff unfolding. But I had been drinking as well. I was taken aback by your actions, but I still think that you are a very special person."

"Thanks Eric, really. Thanks so much for talking with me. I don't really know you well, but for some reason I feel close to you and feel that I can trust you. I don't regret your being the person with whom I ended up last night because I know I was safe with you. I remember that I was the one who initiated the moments that swept us away. Sure, you expressed your desires, but you never forced them on me. Even though I was impaired, I still have vivid memories of it all. Some things about last night are so hauntingly special to me. I can't explain it, but these are not memories that are going to fade. They were life-altering moments."

"Sue, thanks."

"Gee, Eric, I'd better get going home. My parents don't like it when I stay in the park alone at night."

"I'm walking home, too. Care to walk together?"

"That would be great!"

We make our way to my house and say good-bye.

Feeling itchy from a few bug bites, I decide to take a long hot bath. I light a candle and relax with my head resting on the back of the tub, thinking about my talk with Eric. He had seemed so concerned about how I was feeling. Obviously, he has some feeling for me; that makes me feel good. Now I am more relaxed about what happened. I can breathe and think more about it as I lie submerged in this wonderful warm bath, the washcloth now softly kneading the soap against my body. On my breasts I feel the cooler air in contrast to the heat of the water.

And then the memories of that night flood back into me: his gasping, hot breath penetrating my clothing, awakening incredible sensations in my body, his flesh making its way to my flesh. Tilting my head back against the tub's edge and gasping a bit, I slightly open my eyes to a blurred, steamy vision that seems to beckon me. Closing my eyes, I slide back into the warm water. The washcloth glides gently down my stomach and dips in an electrifying move that sends my back arching.

Depleted, I feel my breathing pattern slowly return to normal. How could two days of my life feel like a lifetime? Better yet, how could a lifetime of being one way be changed by two days? Exhausted, I go to bed.

CHAPTER 8

Contrasting Thanksgivings

Thanksgiving means a traditional midday meal with my family and Thanksgiving dinner in the evening with Gary and his parents. The Waltham's Thanksgiving dinner has rarely included anyone other than the three of them. I feel honored that his mom has invited me.

Thanksgiving day is beautiful, with a cold nip in the air. When the doorbell rings, I rush down the stairs as Mom and Dad greet my grandparents. Grandma and Grandpa drop their bags and immediately hug everyone. I love the hugs. My grandparents are especially affectionate toward me. Dad has told me his parents were not that affectionate as he was growing up, but Grandma squeezes and squeezes me until I can hardly breathe.

"Come over and sit with me, sweetie. Tell ol' Grandma whatcha been up to."

Grandma still treats me as if I am five years old, but I love it.

"You all sit and enjoy yourselves," Mom says. "I'll bring you some refreshments."

"Grandma, it's my senior year. I have been accepted at Broctren Harbor College, and so has one of my best friends. I'm so excited. Also, In March I'm going on my senior trip to Washington DC."

"You excited child!" Grandma exclaims. "You're having the time of your life. Enjoy it, for everything good passes by way too fast."

Across the room, I hear Dad talking to Grandpa about his work. I always feel sorry for my father because work seems to be the only thing he shares with Grandpa. The talks all seem so technical, so cold—especially in contrast to the warmth I feel from my grandparents. It always seems that Dad is trying to get approval by proving himself to his father. How can he be so different with his parents than he is with others? My father is a humble man who is known for his relentless giving to the community; I never think of him in terms of his career. But on Thanksgiving, Christmas, and Easter, when his parents come to town, this independent man regresses back to the role of an eager-to-please son. My happiest family moments with my grandparents are those that seem most strained for my father. Once, I asked Dad about his childhood. He quickly said it was "good" and avoided further discussion. But every holiday, my ever-inquisitive mind returns to thinking about my father and his childhood. My father's relationship with his father is exactly the same as his relationship with my brothers. While Dad has always treated me as someone special—I am his little girl, whom he adores—his relationships with Mark and Grey are based on duty and accomplishments, and he is always pushing them, directing them, and challenging them to do better. Maybe parenting is all about reproducing replacements of yourself to continue after you're gone.

Dad has said he doesn't like us to be involved in anything that isn't a solid academic course, so he dissuades us from art, music, and sports, calling them hobbies that people indulge in to puff up their egos. So my brothers have been cheated out of the space they need to evolve into themselves. I've watched my younger brother sabotage things, like his love of basketball. He was the high school's star player—until one day he suddenly quit. Everyone but my parents tried to talk him out of it; my father had told him that because basketball was not something he could do for the rest of his life, he needed to study and prepare for college. But Mark had been the best basketball player in the history of our high school, playing varsity every year, even as a freshman, when he led the team to a national championship. Dad had attended the games without Mark's knowledge by slipping in after the first quarter and watching from behind the bleachers. Then he would slip out just before the game ended. I know Dad admired the way Mark played because I saw it on his face. When I had told Mark I had seen Dad there, I could tell it made him feel good. Dad would tell Mark that he heard he did well in the game and then quickly admonish him not to get so wrapped up in basketball that he forgot his studies. Now, seeing Dad and Grandpa together, I feel I am starting to understand how our parents mold and shape us.

Next to arrive is Mom's sister, Elaine, her husband, Frank, and my cousins. Amy is ten and Cindy, twelve. Pulling into the driveway behind them is Mom's other sister, Freda, who never married.

Aunt Elaine and her family live across town. She is about as close to Mom as anyone can be and she and Mom are active together in the community. They don't talk intimately; it isn't their nature. They interact by giving their time to the school, church, and community.

Aunt Freda, on the other hand, lives about thirty miles away in a small lumbering village. She is quiet, rather shy, and always seems rather lifeless. Both aunts know not to offer to help Mother with anything because they've been dismissed by her on many occasions.

"How are you doing Aunt Freda? I've missed you."

"I'm fine, Sue. Still working at the mill. Never any real changes in my life to share. I have a few books for you in my car."

Aunt Freda is an avid reader of fiction, and she saves her books for me. She will have to sneak them in because Dad doesn't like me my wasting my time reading what he's decided are mindless books. Aunt Freda motions for me to follow her, and we sneak out the front door and open her car trunk. As she is handing me a stack of books, I spot another, lying off to one side, whose title is *The Contraindications of a Hysterectomy*; its author is a doctor. She notices that I've seen the book and nervously comments before I can ask about it.

"Oh, a lady acquaintance at work just had a hysterectomy, so I got the book for her."

I know my aunt is so private that she would never buy anyone else such a book. I know this book is for her. What does it mean? Why does she have it? Her sudden and unlikely excuse prohibits me from asking more, but I feel upset. Families are supposed to share and be there for each other. But so far this Thanksgiving I have already witnessed my father acting unlike himself in the presence of his father, and now my aunt is possibly hiding something about her health. All of this is actually none of my business, but I love them and want to help.

It occurs to me that the silence of an older generation affects generations to come. Father had been shaped by his father and was encouraged to focus on his career and making money. Now Mark has abandoned his love of basketball partly because of my father's hidden feelings. Then there is Aunt Freda, who lives in a world none of us know, dealing with life and health issues alone, and we can't support or comfort her. Grey had slipped into a silent world long ago, one Mom never tried to tap into, just as she never became involved in her sister's world. I see behaviors that are handed down from one generation to the next. Finally, there is that damned word "respect," which limits me from crossing what seem like rigidly defined barriers.

Grey and Mark join our relatives in the living room, and I decide to peek in to see how Mom is doing. Looking through the alcove into the dining room, I see her setting the table with napkin holders. She looks heavenly, very much at peace. She doesn't look stressed at all; if anything, she is in her element. The table is beautifully laid with her best china, wonderful silver candlestick holders, and a centerpiece of fresh roses from the florist's. The roses are especially stunning, with their light pinkish-lavender color and sweet scent. On the table Mom has laid out many special salads, hot breads, vegetable casseroles, sweet yams, puddings, ham…and of course a fantastic, artistically stuffed turkey. It's a feast only she can create. I quickly step into the dining room and ask if I can do any last-minute thing to help.

"No, Sue. Please invite everyone to come to the table now."

Everyone is salivating at such a feast. As we all talk at once, each of us finds a chair. Seated at the head of the table, my father speaks.

"Let us thank God. Shall we bow our heads? Dear Lord, father of us all, we thank you for this day. We thank you for this family and all the love it represents. We thank you for this meal and for Elizabeth who has prepared it for us. Father, out of all of our thanks, we most of all thank you for your son, Jesus Christ. Please help us to be faithful in serving and honoring you. Please keep us safe and close to you, Lord. Amen."

Dad begins carving the turkey, and we pass dishes around and across the table. Mother is the only one not seated; she is in and out of the kitchen, bringing more things. I love eating with my family on these special holidays because for once everyone speaks with feeling about their love of Mom's cooking. This is a compliment for all of her labor.

While we dine, we laugh at the silliest of things. My cousin Amy loves telling stories about her mom. "My dog drools and puts her nose on everything, leaving big ol' nose prints. A while back in church, Mom had to go up front to lead the congregation in a song. As she stepped out of the pew, we saw a huge, damp dog nose print on the back of her mom's dress. Cindy and I were afraid we'd crack up laughing. We had to duck under the seat and cover our mouths."

We all laugh hard because Aunt Elaine is a fanatic about how she looks. Right now she looks annoyed.

"My dog wasn't allowed into the house for weeks after that," says Amy.

Grandpa starts picking on Grandma.

"Your grandma must be out partying all night, because I wake up all the time and she is gone."

"My lord, man," says Grandma, "you snore so bad that I have to move to the other side of the house."

I love these fun, lighthearted, silly stories and times of sharing. However, when Thanksgiving is over and everyone is gone, I know I'll be thinking about all the important things that no one talked about.

The meal continues for quite some time. Finally, everyone retires to the living room and leaves Mom to clean up.

"Mom, let me help you, please?"

"No, you go relax and rest up for your dinner with the Waltham family."

Time quickly passes, and before I know it, Gary is at my door to pick me up. As we enter his home, Mrs. Waltham hugs me, Mr. Waltham takes my coat, and we walk into the beautifully decorated living room. On the coffee table sits a lovely woven cornucopia basket filled with acorns, dried wild berries, small gourds, and brilliantly colored fall leaves, all artistically placed between two flickering candles. The room is exquisite, its lighting soft and welcoming. Soft classical music adds to the wonderful ambience of the room—an overwhelming feeling that I am with special people. It feels like a place of safety, love, and trust. Gazing at the cornucopia, I am captured by the beauty of each item it holds.

"This is so lovely, Mrs. Waltham," I say.

"It is a special part of our fall decorations," she replies, "because everything inside the cornucopia was picked up at different times by one of us this year."

Mr. Waltham adds, "May and I go for a walk through the woods every day. In the fall, when we see something beautiful, we pick it up for our Thanksgiving cornucopia. It represents our thankfulness for the beauty of the world. Each item has fallen to the earth to expire. So we pick it up, celebrating its beauty by bringing it home for Thanksgiving. Gary is the biggest admirer of nature, so many of these beautiful leaves and cones were his discoveries."

Gary leans forward and picks up a pinecone.

"Sue, do you remember this?"

It is the uniquely shaped pinecone we saw hanging on a tree when we were walking through the park weeks ago. "Yes, I remember. But you didn't pick it, did you?"

"I looked at it each day I went to the park. After about a week it was no longer on the tree. I pushed through the fallen leaves, and there it was on the ground. I wanted it for the cornucopia because it is beautiful, unique, and it reminds me of that day with you."

Mrs. Waltham is now passing out beautiful crystal flutes of sparkling cider.

"All the items in the cornucopia represent the memories of when they were found," she says. "I love walking in the woods with Walter. Many of the wild berries and leaves were found on those special walks."

Mr. Waltham holds his glass high. "I want to welcome Sue to our home," he says. "May she feel welcomed and know we are honored that she is celebrating Thanksgiving with us."

"Thank you for the invitation."

I do feel welcomed by both of Gary's parents. As his mother is getting up to go to the kitchen, I quickly ask if I may help her. She tells me everything is done and invites me to relax. A few minutes later we are called to sit at a beautiful candle-lit dinner table with more fall colors in the centerpiece. Mr. Waltham then says that according to family tradition, each person is to share a thought about Thanksgiving. He asks Gary to go first.

"I am thankful for much, especially my parents who are so loving. I am thankful for the beauty of the world, art, and music. I am also thankful for Sue. You have enriched my life so. Also, I feel so fortunate to have such peace. I am sure it comes from God."

Next, Mrs. Waltham shares her Thanksgiving thought. "I am thankful for the life that I am allowed while on this earth, and for a husband who loves me. I am thankful for Gary. A child is the greatest gift because we may both give love and receive it. More important, it is wonderful to see his life unfold from birth into adulthood. It generates the richest feelings of gratitude. Out of all that has filled my life so far, nothing has been a greater gift than Gary."

Mr. Waltham asks if I have anything I would to like to share.

"I am just thankful for the chance to share these moments of celebration with all of you," I tell them. "I love Thanksgiving time and the reminder of how much we have to be grateful for. I am thankful most of all for my faith, which always strengthens me to push ahead in life. Thank you for letting me be a part of your celebration today."

Then Mr. Waltham offers his statement of Thanksgiving. "There are no guarantees in life. And I agree with you, Sue. I too am thankful for my faith—thankful and overwhelmed by the life the Lord has given me. He gave me this wonderful lady, and I am thankful for my son. Gary, you are a miracle in so many ways. We tried to have a child and when we finally relaxed and accepted that it might not happen, May became pregnant with you. You are so loved.

"Now, shall we all bow our heads? Dear Lord, we thank you for all that you have given us. I will always live in gratitude. Bless our lives and be with us always. We give thanks for this meal and for this Thanksgiving day, Amen."

I love this warm casual setting—the simple yet heartfelt sharing of the Waltham family. They speak softly, without any pretense or showiness. My parents are theatrical, especially Mom, who works hard to get recognition. My home has such an air of competition. Everyone seems in need of attention. Gary's family is different. I am stunned by their sincerity and the absence of a need to impress or entertain. Rather, they simply talk with each other from the heart. I am sitting in an unbelievable environment filled with warmth, acceptance, and gratitude.

After dinner we move into the living room. Everyone relaxes while Mrs. Waltham plays the piano. Before playing, she says, "Thanksgiving is a time to relax in celebration. I offer these pieces of music to wash over you. Breathe in their blessings, for great music comes from God."

Gary has told me that his mother is a wonderful pianist, and she is. After about twenty minutes, Mrs. Waltham finishes and quietly sits beside her husband on the couch. Mr. Waltham gently reaches his hand to hers. As he softly touches her hand, she slowly gazes up, and he winks at her. They say no words to each other, yet this gesture says more than most couples communicate in a lifetime. They do not need to speak; what they have to say is beyond words. The music was beautiful, but the love they exude is beyond anything I have ever seen. I so want to tell Mrs. Waltham how beautiful the music was, but I also want to savor this hypnotic atmosphere—and, after all, I am sure she knows we appreciated it. She is not needy of praise. No one in this family is needy.

This family seems so different to me. They display love and respect just by the way they breathe and move about each other. My family, on the other hand, seems like a group of people bumping into each other, pushing—so busy doing things that they rarely breathe in and simply live. The Walthams express gratitude; they appreciate things like the cornucopia filled with treasures richer than gold, each leaf, pinecone, acorn, or berry representing an awesome celebration of the moment in life it was found. My family is too busy to see and appreciate the gifts of life that surround them. Surely they would have missed all these wonderful gifts from God.

Relaxing on the couch, Mr. Waltham softly speaks. "I want to share a couple of thoughts I've treasured throughout my life. One is a French proverb that says, 'Gratitude is the heart's memory.' So many people seem to forget what has already been given to them. Their lack of gratitude results in an inability to find peace. Every day we should reflect and breathe in gratitude. Lastly, before I get up and go for a nice walk, I want to share another treasured quote, this one Helen Keller's. She said, 'The best and most beautiful things in this world cannot be seen or even heard, but must be felt with the heart.' So many miss out on so much because they are insensitive to all that is around them."

After a couple of minutes of reflection, Mr. Waltham rises. "Sue," he says, "thank you for sharing Thanksgiving with us. Now May and I will take a stroll outside and leave you and Gary alone."

They hug us.

It is getting late and time for Gary to take me home. "Gary, I can't begin to tell you how much I have enjoyed your parents and my time with you. It was beyond special."

"Thank you for coming, Sue. It was great having you with us."

He gives me a good night kiss at my door. The kiss feels special, and I feel renewed, alive, full of gratitude for Gary. The impact of my evening with the Walthams will be lasting; I have been taken by it and will reflect on it over and over again.

CHAPTER 9

The Woods

Fall's cold wind and bare tree limbs leave the earth altered. At this time of year I feel like hibernating, relaxing, just getting some sleep. It is a Saturday morning, and I don't have anything planned. Mom is busy finishing projects that will be Christmas gifts. A wonderful knitter, she has been working all year on an afghan for my grandmother. I so admire her talent. When I was younger, I had asked Mom to show me how to knit, but she said it was too complicated for someone of my age. I never again approached her about teaching me.

Mark has a part-time job at Willard's department store, where he has worked for several Christmas seasons. Grey is still at college and in a couple of weeks will be coming home for the holidays. Dad is away at a conference. Everyone seems busy with some great and important purpose for the day. Lying in bed, enjoying the warmth of the blankets, I wonder: what shall I do today? Gary spends most Saturdays at a studio working with an artist. Patty is no longer available on the weekends since she started dating Hale. Carrie is babysitting, trying to save up money for college. Why, I wonder, am I not connected to something important?

I still need to decide what to give Gary for Christmas. Suddenly, I have an idea. I'll go for a walk and look for gifts of nature, as the Walthams do. Maybe something special will present itself. I dress in warm clothing; the temperature is now in the forties and fifties. Hustling downstairs, I pour hot coffee and fix myself toast. I remember seeing some beautiful naturally dried cattails and wild winter plants and wonder if I can come up with a winter arrangement of some sort. However, I don't want to limit myself to the ideas in my head; I must try to be open to whatever beauty awaits me.

Soon I am crossing through the park to the bank of the brook. Across the brook I see wild winter foliage amid the trees. To cross to the other side I could walk about three miles along the brook to where a street crosses over, but that is way too far. If I can find dead trees or large rocks, I can work my way to the other side as I've seen others do. Walking along the water's edge, I soon come to a fallen tree that reaches across the brook, but its trunk is not very thick. I will have to balance carefully. I think about how I kept falling off the balance beam in gym class, and also how I am bundled up so tight against the cold that the last thing I feel is agile. I'm contemplating how I will move when all at once I hear voices behind me. It is Eric, Darrell, and Sam.

"Hey Sue, what are you doing?" Darrell calls out.

"Sue, why are you balancing on the end of that tree?" hollers Eric. "You're going to fall in if you aren't careful."

I back off the tree trunk and step back to the bank.

"Wow! You guys scared the bejesus out of me," I reply. "I want to go over to the other side and see what kind of wild life is over there. I want to collect some of those dried cattails and look at the wild foliage."

"Well, I don't think you should try it alone," Eric replies. "That trunk isn't lodged or secured, and it's still able to move. Let me hold the trunk securely, and then you can slowly move across it. You shouldn't have tried this alone, Sue."

Turning to Darrell and Sam, Eric says, "Hold the tree trunk, you guys. I want to test this to make sure it's safe to walk on.

Sam and Darrell secure the tree with their feet and hands, as Eric balances on the trunk and slowly walks to the other side.

"The guys will hold it," Eric tells me, "so you can walk across. I'll reach out and help you from here."

He reaches out with a long stick to help me balance as I cross. I grab the end of the stick and with Sam and Darrell holding the tree steady, I slowly walk across.

"Yes!" I scream, reaching the other bank. Pleased with myself, I dance around in a rush of adrenalin at the thrill of this little risky moment.

Darrell calls out, "Now that you two are over there, how do you plan on getting back? Sam and I have to leave."

Thinking about returning oddly causes me to feel a bit panicked.

"Sue," says Eric, "how'd you like to hike down to the road? It's about three miles downstream, so it will take time. You can see everything this side of the woods has to offer."

"Sure, I'm up for it," I say.

At first I feel good about Eric being with me. After all, he helped me get to the other side. But slowly I become uneasy about being with him. After all, I came to find some natural treasures to make a Christmas gift for Gary. I haven't owned up to the fact that I am intensely intrigued by Eric. I still have thoughts about the night we were intimate. Why don't I feel embarrassment or guilt about it? In truth, I have been enjoying the memory over and over again, at first telling myself the impairment was what fascinated me. But now, here I am again, alone with him and with these feelings, and it occurs to me that just being with Eric has some affect on me, whether I'm impaired or not.

"What are you looking for, Sue? Eric is looking confused. "Everything looks so dead over here."

I don't want to try to explain because Eric would not understand why Gary would care about a pinecone or a leaf. Even though I admire that side of Gary so much, I decide not to tell Eric the truth about my hunt.

"Oh, I like to find things like dried flowers, or unique leaves. And I love these dried cattails," I explain, taking out a pocketknife to cut three of them.

"Let's sit and relax for a bit," says Eric. "We've been walking these woods for half an hour."

"I brought a thermos of hot coffee," I reply. "Care for some?"

"Sure. Too bad we don't have a little Snobs or some Baileys Irish Cream to add to that," Eric says, laughing.

"Do you drink a lot, Eric?"

"I drink a little every day, but I only get buzzed on weekends. I like the feeling it gives me. It kind of makes the world an okay place for me, and it helps me because I'm shy. Liquid courage, as they say."

"You don't appear shy to me," I reply. "Have you had a drink today?"

"Nah, but I did share a joint with Darrell and Sam earlier. Are you shocked?"

"No, I know you guys get high. What does it feel like to be high on a joint?"

"Well, it's a lot more intense than alcohol. It makes me feel lighthearted and giddy about life. It really brings on the laughter."

My mind races. I've never thought about smoking a cigarette, let alone marijuana. Yet I can't help wondering what it would be like. But this seems too dangerous to consider. As much as I'd like to feel altered, to feel intensely again, I won't allow my curiosity and desire to get the best of me this time. To regain composure, I start looking around at the plants. But by the time I look back, Eric has lit up a joint.

"Sue, do you want to take a puff, just to see what it's like?" he asks, holding the joint out toward me.

I am stunned with anger at his presumptuous gesture. What is he trying to do? Yet, at the same time, I feel another little thrill.

"Eric, why would you light up and assume that I would try it?" I ask, my voice angry.

"Hey," he responds. "I didn't plan this. You asked me if I'd had a drink today and I explained I'd smoked part of a joint. You showed interest by your questions. I just thought this was a perfect place, since we're hidden from everyone. I thought maybe you'd like to try a little hit. Damn, Sue. I'm sorry if I've offended you," he says, taking a puff on the joint.

My mind is reeling; I'm of two minds, actually. Although I feel angry at being thrust into this situation suddenly, I do so want to try it. Conveniently, I have the whole day free. But what is Eric trying to do? Was he setting me up for this when he offered to walk with me? Seething, I go back to pretending to look for plants.

"Okay," I say then, my tone still angry. "I do want to try it."

But when I reach out my hand out to take it, Eric pulls the joint out of reach.

"Sue, don't push yourself. I must have read something into what you said that wasn't there. I am sorry if I've hurt your feelings," he tells me with sincerity. "I didn't mean anything by it. I'm not trying to get you high."

"Well," I reply, "I am caught off guard by this. You're right. This isn't your fault. I did say I wanted to, but I'm frightened by how much I want to try it. But damn, my parents have filled me with such moral hyperboles. They don't even know how what they've done has backfired." Tears well up in my eyes.

"Sue, if you are confused and upset, please don't try it." He pats out the ember, wraps up what's left, and puts it back into his pocket. "Nobody who has internal conflicts about using alcohol or anything should have to feel pressure," he says.

With the opportunity taken away—wrapped up in Eric's pocket, out of sight—my desire to try it is even stronger. I get up and start walking, looking down at the now uninteresting plants. My silence has made Eric uneasy.

"Are you okay, Sue?" he asks.

Slowly I turn toward him and feel compelled to hug him. I put my arms around him and pull him close to me. "Thanks, Eric," I say. "I'm confused, yet intrigued, by the thought of trying that joint. But my fear is greater than my sense of intrigue today. Thank you for understanding."

"Okay. Now tell me again what kind of plants you are looking for."

We continue to walk, and nothing special presents itself. After about an hour, we decide to rest again. I still have some hot coffee and a bottle of water left. "Thanks so much for bringing me over to this side of the brook," I say, wanting Eric to know I appreciate his efforts.

"I've been drawn to you since that party," Eric replies, "and I don't want you to think it's because of what happened. It's more than that. I've thought about it a lot. I don't trust or care for most people. But you've always been the same person throughout the years. You're someone who doesn't act better than other people, yet to my mind you are the best."

"That is so nice of you to say, Eric. I have to admit you're someone I've never really turned away from since childhood. We grew apart, but the distance made you seem more of a mystery as the years went by. It's like you were experiencing things that I was scared of, yet I was curious about them as well," I say, trying to explain my feelings for him.

"I'd hate for you to have a bad experience because of something I hurried you into," he says, rather concerned.

"I'm a big girl," I reply. "I own my decisions and don't need to blame anyone."

"Can I ask you a personal question?" says Eric cautiously.

"Sure. I can open up to you," I say, adding, "I feel like maybe you are getting to know me better than anyone. Go ahead."

"Are you still a virgin? Have you ever gone all the way with anyone?"

I am floored by the bluntness of his question. Why would he ask that? "Wow!" I exclaim. "That *was* pretty direct. But I did open myself up to any questions."

"Oh please," Eric says. "You don't have to answer. It's none of my business. Sorry," he adds, as if he regrets having asked the question.

"I don't mind telling you, Eric. I just wonder why you'd want to know?"

Clearing his throat, Eric replies, "In life I haven't found many people I care about. I don't get interested in people. I wish I could, but for some reason, most people disappoint me. But you've fascinated the hell out of me all my life, Sue. And even though it's none of my business, I would like to know a lot more about you. After the other night, I wondered if you had ever been that intimate with anyone else. You had seemed so natural, until, in the middle of every-thing, your abrupt stop made me think maybe not."

I decide to put aside the question of why he wants to know because I feel safe telling him the truth. "I have never gone all the way," I admit. "To be hon-est, what happened that night was the most I have ever experienced. When I got home, I was still woozy. I took a shower and my thoughts went all over the place, wondering what it would have been like to go the distance. My body wanted so much more. Even now, I know that had I not gone home when I did, I'd have unfolded completely. I was so lost to the moment. My desires were still raging in the shower that night. I thought about how I rolled over on top of you. The memory of all that had happened excited me, but most of all it served as a warning." Nervous and tense, I breathe deep again and try to relax.

"Wow, that was honest," says Eric. "What made you decide to stop so sud-denly?"

"All I know is that I was feeling my own body as never before. I was feeling my neck when you kissed it, I was feeling my body reacting to your breath, and I was feeling my breasts as your hand touched them. It was all about my own sensations until I moved over you. When I realized you were so aroused, some-thing snapped. I was no longer lost in my body's sensations—I was abruptly reminded that you were there. I knew that if what was happening did not stop immediately I was on the verge of being part of something that included more than me," I explained.

"I understand."

"Eric, I didn't drink that night for sexual reasons. That was far from my mind. I drank out of curiosity. I wanted freedom from my over-thinking and self-imposed limitations. I wanted to experience the night, the stars, and sky. I had no idea my sexuality would come rushing forth. Now, of course, it makes sense. Anyway, the experience has made my body more sensitive to everything. I still remember every detail—the kisses and touches, everything. But my sud-den awareness of your body shocked me, maybe because I have never been intimate with a man. I haven't ever seen a man naked, so even though I'm not ignorant about body parts, I was shaken to the core when I brushed against you. I'll never forget how it felt: electrifying and shocking all at once. But instantly, reality set in." I take a deep breath and hope that my explanation has made sense.

Eric is leaning back against a tree stump, his hands behind his head, fingers intertwined, as he gazes into the sky. "I'm glad you shared with me how it went down for you," he says. "I've been concerned that somehow you were blaming me for letting it happen. I've been afraid that your regrets would cause you to push me away. I never considered how it might make you feel to be with a man who was aroused," he says, taking a deep breath. "But I sure was aroused," he adds, softly.

Our conversation halts for the moment. I am fully aware of Eric's presence. I am stirred by our discussion, but I fear that if we keep talking I might give in to the desires that still stir inside me. Slowly, not wanting to look straight at him, I try to catch a glimpse of Eric in my peripheral vision. He is relaxed, looking into the sky as if lost in thought.

"What are you thinking about?" I ask.

"About what you shared," he says. "It is so beautiful to hear you talk about your body coming alive, how you were experiencing it all. Guys could never admit to that level of sensitivity or self-awareness. It was neat hearing you share the details of the joy you had in feeling yourself unfold. That's all I was thinking about."

I don't know what to say, but I know that I shouldn't keep talking about this because inside it's exactly what interests me the most. There is no telling what further talking might lead to. I try to move away from the topic.

"Well, we've only made it half the way," I say. "There's the road where we can cross. We still have to walk the other side of the brook back to the park." I stand up and close my thermos.

"Yep," says Eric, dusting himself off. "Let's get going."

On the road, we stop at the center of the bridge crossing the brook. As I gaze down on the woods below, I promise myself I will remember it as the place where I spilled my truth about the importance of that night.

Eric reaches out and takes my hand in his. Looking at me he says, "Sue, thanks for opening up to me. Don't worry, your words are always safe with me."

After he lets go of my hand, we walk the rest of the way back, giggling about everything and talking about nothing significant.

No one is home when I arrive. The three cattails I've been carrying now have other memories attached to them. I can't give them to Gary. They represent a special time with Eric and have become important to me. I had seen them from my side of the brook, and the only way to reach them was to take a risk and find a way across.

I have to admit that after today I am even more fascinated by Eric. But why? Nothing about his personality captures me. He isn't passionate, nor does he share any mutual interests with me that I know of. What attracts me to this guy? Is it merely because he represents the risk-taking side of me? Now that he represents the wild edges of life, I am intrigued. Surely, my maturity and strong desire to make the "right" decisions in life will prohibit me from making an irrevocable mistake. Nevertheless, I feel fragmented.

Would my family's standards and conservative upbringing overpower my urges at any fleeting moment of irresponsibility and high risk? Is Eric only a catalyst for this new confusion? I have to be honest; I found myself slipping toward the edge. If I had gone over it, could I survive? Would I be okay?

❧   ❧   ❧

The phone rings and I rush to answer it. It's Gary.

"Hi, Sue. Would you like to go out for hamburgers and shakes at Roxie's? It would be nice to spend some time with you." He sounds so bubbly.

"Sure," I reply. "What time are you coming by?"

"How about 5:30—in about an hour?"

"That works for me. See you in a while."

I'm happy that Gary called and wants to see me. I need to get out and stop all of my crazy thinking.

At Roxie's, Gary says, "I thought maybe you'd be busy with Christmas shopping or decorating."

Feeling a lump in my throat, I reply, "No, I've had a quiet day."

"So, what did you do on your quiet day?" Gary asks.

Caught off guard and not wanting to talk about it, I take a deep breath.

"I went to the park and just hung out with nature."

"Mom said she was crossing the old bridge over the brook and thought she saw you on the wooded side, talking to someone."

Suddenly I know I have to be more specific, and the words come rushing out. "Yeah, that was me," I tell him. "I wanted to cross over the creek to collect a few cattails. They're so beautiful now that they've dried out. Darrell, Sam, and Eric came by just as I was trying to shimmy across a dead tree trunk bridging the brook. They hollered and stopped me because it wasn't secure. After Darrell and Sam held the trunk securely, Eric went across to make sure it was safe to walk on. Then I went across. Eventually we had to come out at the old bridge. Eric's an old friend I used to play with as a child. He lives two doors down the street." I finally take a breath.

"Sounds like fun. My parents and I have hiked through that woods many times. They love it in the spring, when all the wildflowers start popping up everywhere. I love to hunt for the sponge head mushrooms; they're so delicious!"

Our food arrives, and I change the subject. "How excited are you about going on the senior trip?" I ask.

"Sue, you know I'm very excited to go away with you."

"Are you saying you wouldn't go on the trip if we weren't dating?" I ask.

"No, I'm not saying that at all. I love the museums and wouldn't miss this opportunity. But I am more excited because I'll get to experience everything with you.

"I've always wanted to know something about you," he continues. "What are the special things about you that you like best? I mean, I was wondering how you look at yourself, and what makes you feel good. You know what I mean?"

"Wow," I reply. "I've never really thought in those terms. What do I like about myself? I could probably spit out a list of things I'd like to change. Still, I don't have such low self-esteem that I can't answer you, though. Hmmm."

The answer is there all the time: the thing I like most about myself is the one thing I worry about. "Well," I continue, "I like the fact that I have great curiosity. That I want to taste all life has to offer. I want to go beyond my world and experience life to its fullest. I like that sense of restlessness inside of me because it makes the world an exciting place for me to explore." My answer is intentionally quite general so that Gary can't see through to what I am really thinking about today.

"That's a great quality," he says. "Now look at it from another side. What does it say about you?"

Now I feel trapped in the discussion. It is great that Gary wants to know me better, but I do not want to analyze this with him. Lord knows I think too much, and I have pondered the heck out of this issue already. But I take a deep breath and try to answer him.

"Well, restless could mean I lack peace. But I don't know if that is true of me. I do have gratitude for all that God has given me, and I feel fortunate," I say.

"I know you have gratitude, Sue. That's something I really admire in you. But I don't know if you have peace," Gary explains, "and maybe that's where your restlessness comes from."

"That's a good insight," I say. "I have thought about my restlessness a lot." I pause to allow this line of questioning to die out. "How is your hamburger? I love those huge chunks of dill pickle that they put on them." We eat without speaking for a couple of minutes.

"Have you finished all your Christmas shopping?" I ask, hoping to get Gary talking about something besides my inner life.

"I don't really go all out with gift buying," he replies. "I try to figure out something meaningful to give. Generally, that has little to do with department stores. How about you, Sue?"

"I have most of mine done. Just a couple of special people to do something for and then I can relax," I say.

"See," he says, "you used the word relax. Gee, how can I get my gal to relax? Let me see…hmmm. Maybe I could get her to go lie in the park with me and watch the night sky. Would you like to do that, since it is already dark outside?" he asks.

"That sounds great," I say, with a big smile. "I left Mom a note telling her I was with you and would be in before my curfew. I was hoping we could spend the evening together."

We drive to the park and Gary produces a couple of blankets and a picnic basket with hot chocolate and Christmas cookies. He has obviously planned for our evening. The night is breezy. Fall is almost gone, with the beginning of winter bringing its cold.

"Tonight might be one of the last times we can lie under the skies for awhile," Gary says.

"Yes. Snow will soon blanket the earth," I reply.

"Come closer to me, Sue" he says, pulling me into the cradle of his left arm.

My head now resting on his chest and shoulder, Gary pulls a thick blanket over us to keep warm. The clouds move quickly, and we can easily see the stars that dazzle the sky. It is wonderful to admire such a beautiful sight with Gary. He is a great absorber of beauty and has no need to chat. He's captured, as always, by the rich beauty of the sky. Softly, he marvels, "Wow, amazing!"

After about twenty minutes, Gary turns to me. Now we are both lying on our sides looking through the darkness at each other. "I love feeling your body next to mine under this blanket creating and sharing heat with me," he says, and softly kisses me.

Touching his face with my hand, I say, "You are fun to watch under the skies because you are so lost to the beauty. How am I ever going to get along at college without you to appreciate the beauty of the world? You've taught me how to absorb the beauty of nature. You always wrap the world up like a special package for me to open."

"Sue, Sue. Shhh. You are way down the road, feeling sad. Don't go there. That's down the road. Please just stay here. Be in this moment with me."

What he's saying is so true. Here I am, lying beside this extraordinary man in extraordinary conditions, and yet I can't experience it the way I want to. Why hasn't this moment captured me physically? I am lying here thinking about college and how I will miss him. With our bodies sharing their warmth and the gorgeous skies gleaming down upon us, why don't I feel swept away?

Gary's hand moves under the blanket and reaches behind me to rest on my back. He pulls me in closer, until no room remains between us. My head is tucked into his shoulder, and I can hear his breathing. "Shhh," he says. "Let's just lie here and absorb each other."

I hear crickets and the rustling woods on the other side of the creek. I am so aware of all the noises around us, but why am I not lost in the feeling of having his body against mine?

"Mmmm, you are like heaven," he softly whispers in my ear. "Sue you are something beautiful for me to experience."

Gary slowly moves his face into the curve of my neck. I feel his gentle kiss on my throat. Why doesn't my skin crawl with passionate sensations? Gary seems soft, gentle, and lost in the moment. He whispers, "May I lay my head against your heart? I want to hear it beat."

"Mmm-hmm."

He slowly unbuttons my coat under the blanket. I reach down and unbutton my sweater, inviting him to my flesh. In the dark night he slides his face down to the top of my breast. His breath warms my flesh. It is nice that we have this special closeness, but why isn't my body reacting? Slowly, I take his hand and place it on my right breast, over my bra. I feel his index finger softly moving over the end.

Softly whispering, he asks, "Are you okay?"

"Yes I am," I say, trying not only to grant permission but I encourage him to continue. I need to know if I will have any sexual feelings with Gary. But before long, Gary slowly moves away and buttons my sweater. He breathes excitedly and pulls me into his arms, taking one long deep breath. Then he shares what he is thinking.

"I love how I feel right now," he says. "I want to remember this."

"What are you feeling?" I ask. "Please tell me."

"I feel breathless. I feel desirous and wanting. I feel caught up in a possibility. I don't want these feelings to be displaced by hurrying to complete the experience. Let me try to explain it better. I think people have lost some of the greatest parts of life by circumventing feelings of desire. Instead, they race to complete themselves. You know I am a person who likes to savor every moment of an experience. Tonight is wonderful—better than all the dreams about you I have been having. I love just to anticipate seeing you and then to be with you, although, of course, I do think about us exploring each other more intimately. In fact, I've feasted on those thoughts for at least a year now. I remember the first time I touched your face. The anticipation of that moment had been long-lived, and then when I did it, the memory was vivid and over-powering. Tonight was even better, and pulling you to me under the blanket was unbelievable. I can't tell you right now everything I felt because I don't want to frame it or define it. I want it to spill all over me again and again with wonderment." He takes a deep breath and continues to unfold.

"There are many types of painters in this world. Some paint with speed, filling their canvas with a rushing neediness to see the completion of the painting. I'm different; I paint with passion. First of all, I spend a lot of time anticipating what I am about to paint. Then, when I start painting, I only do a little at a time, savoring each stroke and slowly reliving the moment as I paint. It always takes me a long time to complete anything, but that's because I take joy not only in its completion but in the creative journey along the way."

I am blown away by what he is saying because I am nothing like that. I always have to complete everything—my curiosity demands the outcome. A moment in itself is never enough; it is just a stepping stone to wanting more. That is the difference between us. Gary has instant peace because whatever he has is always enough.

Turning toward me, lying on his side, Gary says, "You are so quiet, Sue. That isn't like you. I wonder what's going on in that head of yours. Are you okay?" he asks, brushing the hair from my face.

"You are wonderful, Gary," I reply. "I am taken back by your word, 'savor.' That's why every moment is enough for you. You take satisfaction in what no one else does because you see value in every experience."

"Why would anyone want to fast-forward any moment with you, Sue? I was lost in our body heat and how our breathing patterns synchronized. My hands experienced more of you, and my body is left aching and wanting—such an exhilarating feeling!" he exclaims. Gary could hardly get the words out, he is so lost to them.

"I love hearing you talk about what this night has meant to you," I say. "You are so amazing, Gary. I feel so special, being the girl with whom you experienced tonight." I hope he hasn't noticed that I haven't expressed any intimate feelings myself. It is true that I am captured by him, but it isn't in a physical way. I admire his ability to experience life, and I so want to be like him—a person who enjoys each moment.

We both know it's getting late.

"I'd better get home, or Mom will worry," I say. "I wish this night didn't have to end. I really enjoy being with you."

Gary pulls me to him. "I have such strong feelings for you, Sue Martin," he says, and he kisses me.

"Well, Gary Waltham, you make me feel special. Thanks for this wonderful evening."

We pack up and he takes me home. We share a kiss at the door, and I wave as he drives away.

I head upstairs, my thoughts racing. Putting on my pajamas, I jump into bed and turn off the lights, still wondering: Why wasn't I physically responding to Gary? I go over everything piece by piece. I love eating with him, I love looking at him across the table. I love how he looks. He's attractive, very good-looking and tall, and I especially love his long arms. I also know I am captivated by Gary's intellect and also his sensitivity to the world. So why, I think desperately, can't I find any feelings, thoughts, or memories suggesting that I want Gary physically? Maybe I am misinterpreting what is going on. I hate the question I am about to entertain: Is he like a brother? I think and think. No, no way. I love being kissed by him. I love how his physical feelings escalated tonight. Yes, I see him as a man who wants me and loves me.

Suddenly, I snap inside. Is this about him, or is this about me? Thinking back to the time I was impaired, it begins to make sense. I admire Gary's softness, slowness, and his ability to savor each moment—certainly, all of that will serve him well when he needs to express such things on canvas. But no way will that work for me. I realize that I need Gary to be out of control.

I want to know that he wants that too. There must be some drive in him stronger than his preference for stopping and savoring the moment. While he finds beauty in creating a moment, I find beauty in being lost to it. I do not want his nobility. I do not need him to seek permission to touch me. The mere fact that I chose to lie down with him was affirmation of my desire.

Then I understand why I need Gary to lose his self-control: It would give me permission to let go with him. I don't want a sexual experience that is crafted and created like a fine piece of art. No, I want to be lost to the moment, breathlessly accelerated by a passion that can't be stopped. I want Gary's feelings about me to be unmanageable, with his lustful urges wreaking havoc with his inner peace.

Hot tears edge the outsides of my eyes. Why must we be so different? Do our differences mean we aren't right for each other? Why, oh why, am I this way? I know I am an intense person, someone who craves intensity in everything. I've had lustful feelings about sex for a long time, and my desire to lose control is strong. I want the freedom of the moment to take me somewhere beyond myself.

To Gary, intimacy is like art—a beautiful concept, a masterpiece that he envisions as a creation by two people. But the love I know has no such power. In my family, love means responsibility, duty, unspoken loyalty, and—most of all—unspoken emotions. Love is something you are somehow supposed to know exists. Had I been raised like Gary, I am sure we would be much more alike. In his home, the beauty of each person and the beauty of the world are celebrated daily. Everything about Gary's home is visibly shaped by love and reverence—an attractive way of living and loving, but not my way.

Sobbing, I wonder why I have to be so different. True, opposites attract and can offer new ways to look at life. But could our sexuality, something so rooted inside each of us, ever be reshaped or fine-tuned? I am not judging Gary's beautiful understanding of intimacy, but it would require me to be someone I cannot imagine.

Crying now, I am truly hurting, and I let myself cry until I feel wasted and spent. Trying to breathe normally at last, I foresee what may very well happen. We will enjoy the rest of our senior year together, but we have both agreed to go different ways when we depart for college, to let go of each other and focus on education and new opportunities. We haven't been clear about what all this means, but we know that the future of our relationship may be determined by those changes. When I am away at college, I will have the opportunity to let Gary go. I know that I have much love for Gary, and perhaps these next few months will bring us closer somehow. I can't possibly know how life will pan out. All I know is that right now I am not ready to make any decisions about anything.

CHAPTER 10

A Teasing Snowman

This year's Christmas is different because Grandpa and Grandma are unable to come. Christmas day is simple and very nice. It snows all day, leaving us with three feet of snow. The next morning, from my bedroom window I see Dad, Grey, and Mark shoveling the driveway. The house is warm and Mom is downstairs cleaning and cooking. I am waiting for a moment to get her alone. I pour a cup of cocoa for myself and sit down. This is a special moment for me; I want to express my appreciation for her Christmas gift to me.

"Mom," I begin, "I love the afghan you made me for college. It was a perfect Christmas gift. How did you find the time to make one for Grandma and one for me?"

"Well," she replies, "you watched me make your Grandmother's here in the evening. But I made one for you when you weren't around."

"How did you know I'd love the color?" It is a beautiful pairing of teal and cream—nothing like the bright, gaudy colors she dressed me in as a child—and her excellent, tasteful choice had really surprised me.

"You kept an old outfit in your closet, and once when I asked you why you said its shade of teal was perfect. From that day on I started hunting for that color in yarn. I found it in Chicago last year when your father and I went to that conference." I am overwhelmed by the effort and by her cleverness in not letting me catch her crocheting it—details that make the gift even more special.

"I can't begin to tell you how much I love it," I say. "It will look wonderful on my bed at college. Thank you so much!" A part of me wants to rush over and hug her, but that is not how we relate to each other. I know my spoken appreciation is enough, and I need to give her space.

I still have to deliver Gary's Christmas gift. He and his family had visited relatives in Boston the week before, and we plan to spend time together after he returns. His parents will stay in Boston through the New Year.

I bundle up and go outside to enjoy the snow and to see if I can help Dad and my brothers. They've moved down the street and are now cleaning out Mrs. Adams's driveway. As I am walking toward them, a snowball hits me in the head. I look around, wondering where it came from, and at first I don't see anyone. Then I spot a cloud of breath coming from behind a big oak tree in Eric's front yard.

"You can come out now, Eric," I call out. "I can see your breath."

"Gosh, I didn't mean to hit you so hard," he calls back. "Are you okay?"

"Sure! I'm well prepared to go to battle with you in the snow," I say, throwing a snowball back at him.

"Hey, damn! I mean darn," he says, trying to clean up his language. "Did the Martin family have a nice Christmas?"

"Sure," I reply. "How about you?"

"Well, Aunt Sarah, Mom's sister, has been with us for the holidays, which is nice," he says, adding a mischievous wink. I wonder what the wink is about.

"Glad you had a nice Christmas. See you," I say, and continue on down the sidewalk. Reaching my father and brothers, I ask if they need some help or something warm to drink. Dad says they're about done and don't need anything.

On the way back, I see Eric standing at his gate. I can tell he has something on his mind.

"It's a great day, Sue," he says. "Want to go to the park and see who can make the best snowman?"

"Sure," I reply. "I love to make snowmen. Are you any good at it?"

"Actually," he says, laughing hard, "I'm going to create a great snowwoman to go with your man.

"Eric, you don't seem like the type for silly childhood pleasures, so I can't imagine you even making a snowman," I say, laughing back at him.

When we arrive at the park, we find someone has already made a great snowman—in fact, a complete snow family, every character sculpted artistically.

"Wow, I can't compete with that," says Eric. "No way am I going to build my creation anywhere near this Michelangelo exhibit."

"I know where we can build our snowman," I say. "How about the other side of the brook?"

"Good idea, Sue! It will be as if our people will live on the other side of the tracks. They'll be ruffians, the riffraff from the other side of town," Eric says, giving me a wink.

"Will the brook be frozen enough to walk across?" I ask.

"That moving brook never totally freezes, Sue, but we can go across on that dead trunk again. It's probably frozen solid to the ground on both sides by now," he explains.

We walk to the snow-covered dead tree that bridges the brook. A break in the ice reveals rushing water underneath. Eric bounces on the end of the log, testing it, then begins to work his way across the log. Once, his left foot slips on the icy log, but he regains his balance and does not fall. Soon he is able to jump down to the other bank.

"Wow!" he exclaims. "With all the ice on the log, that's a difficult walk. Maybe you shouldn't try it, Sue," he says, sounding concerned.

"I know I can do this," I say, stepping onto the log. "I just have to move slowly."

"Damn, Sue, you be careful!"

I begin, moving two and three inches at a time. It's obvious that it will take some time to inch my way across.

"That's good," says Eric. "Just move really slowly. Yeah, you got it, keep creeping…"

But when I make it to the middle, I suddenly hear a cracking sound as if the dead tree is breaking somewhere just in front me. The tree shifts and I almost lose my balance.

"Sue! Sue! Hold on!" calls Eric. "I'll go get a stick for you to grab on to!"

"No, Eric! I think the break is right in front of me! I think I have to turn back!" In my panic, I am screaming.

Then I hear another voice behind me. "Don't move Sue, don't move!"

It's Gary. He reaches the edge of the brook and stretches his long torso with those very long arms outward across the frozen water. I inch my way back. Finally, I'm able to grab on to him. Soon I'm standing on firm ground.

"You made it! Thanks for helping," shouts Eric, acknowledging Gary's efforts.

"I don't think I should come back that way," Eric calls out. "It looks like it could give way at any time. I'll hike to the bridge. You two have a good day." He turns and heads off into the woods alone.

I wrap my arms around Gary and give him a big hug. "When did you get back in town?" I ask. "I've missed you a lot!"

"About midnight last night. It was starting to really snow. As soon as Mom heard there was a threat of a blizzard, she recommended that I leave. I got on a standby flight and my plane arrived about 11:30 PM."

"That was still Christmas Day," I say. "I'm sorry you had to come home early, but on the other hand I am so glad to see you!"

"I was so full of energy when I got home that I couldn't force myself to go to bed. So I came to the park and made snowmen. I kept thinking how much more fun it would have been if you had been—"

Abruptly I cut him off. "Is that snow family in the center of the park your work?" Before he can reply, I answer for him. "Of course! It's so artistic. I could never have helped you make those masterpieces," I say, shaking my head.

"I got up this morning and walked past your place to see if you were up. I didn't want to telephone because I thought maybe someone was asleep. Anyway, I saw Grey. He said you weren't home and were probably out walking in the snow. So I thought I'd try the park."

I am happy to see Gary, but I also have a lump in my throat. I feel the need to explain why I was with Eric. "When I came outside I went to help Dad and Mark and Grey. They said they didn't need my help, so I thought I'd go to the park and create a snowman. Eric was outside too and asked if he could go to the park with me. When we got here, we saw your snow family, and we knew we couldn't create anything that good. So we decided to build snowmen on the other side of the brook. Eric called it "the other side of the track" and said our snow people would be the riffraff. I thought any attempt at making a snowman should be done far away from your gorgeous creations. My snowmen always look rather funny," I say, laughing.

"Sue," Gary replies, "a snowman isn't about art, it's about fun, enjoyment, and play. I wasn't trying to create art last night. I was just having fun. I have an idea! Let's make a park full of snow angels. There are hardly any footprints in the park. Lets do snow angels all over it."

Gary and I walk to the edge of the park and start making angel prints. We lie down and wave our arms up and down in the snow, forming wings. Then we jump up and fall down to do another, and another, and another. After about forty-five minutes, we have covered most of the park. We are exhausted and lie collapsed in the snow, catching our breath.

"I wish I could see our work from the sky," I say.

Gary points to the water tower at the end of the park.

"Yes," I say, "but how can we get up there? We could get in trouble."

"I know the superintendent of the water district," Gary says. "He's a friend of my father's. Let's walk over to the water plant and see if by some chance he's there."

We hurry through the snow to the water plant where a gentleman is outside, working on a valve of some kind.

"Sir," Gary asks, "could we go to the top of the tower so we can look down on park? We'll only be a couple of minutes, and we will be careful."

"Well, it's Christmas," the man replies. "You youngsters go ahead, but don't stay long."

We slowly make our way to the top. I am a bit out of breath and my legs are aching, but it is worth the effort. The view is simply amazing. We are looking down on the snow-covered field covered with our angel impressions. I wish I had a camera to take a picture. I stare intensely trying to capture the image with my mind, hoping not to forget the sight.

"Wow, Sue," Gary exclaims. "We've made well over a hundred angels."

Gary's snow family looks like small people in the center of the park who are surrounded by the angels. Beyond the park, everything is blanketed with untrammeled snow. Suddenly, I notice something in the woods across the brook. Eric has made a huge snowman. I am excited and want to see it up close. It's much larger than any of Gary's snow people. But I realize I am with Gary. Now I desperately want us to leave before Gary sees it. Most of all, I don't want him to notice my interest in Eric's creation.

"We'd better get going," I tell him, with an edge of panic in my voice. "We made a promise not to stay long, and the man down there is waiting to lock the door."

Going down the steps, I feel relief that Gary has not seen the huge snowman on the other side of the brook. I don't understand why I didn't want him to notice it. Maybe it was guilt stemming from my fondness of Eric, or maybe I wanted to think it would make him jealous. Whatever the reason, I had felt panicked.

As we walk back to the park, Gary comments on the experience. "It's amazing how things look from up high, isn't it? My snowman family looked so little. But it was picturesque with little angels everywhere. Gosh, we did a good job. By the way, Sue, would you like come over to dinner tonight? I'll cook you up something special for Christmas," he says, smiling.

I rush home to find Mom busy in the kitchen.

"Mom," I say, "Gary asked me to come over for dinner tonight. I really want to go because we haven't exchanged our Christmas gifts. And don't forget, there's no school tomorrow. May I please go?" I ask, trying not to sound whiny.

"I guess it will be okay," she says. "You two haven't spent any holiday time together. But I want you home at midnight." I am absolutely shocked; my normal curfew is 11:30. Heading upstairs, I mumble under my breath, "By the way—did I mention that the Walthams are out of town?"

My mind is still stuck on the image of Eric's huge snowman and by noon my curiosity gets the best of me. I head out the door, hike across the park through the snow, and reach the edge of the brook. Finally, I can see Eric's huge snowman and immediately burst out laughing. In the snowman's mouth, Eric has put a huge stick that looks like a joint. It is a really funny-looking snowman, and I am touched, knowing that Eric has made it for me to see. I feel sad that our time together this morning was cut short. Then I see words written in the snow beside the snowman. They read, "Let's party!"

Walking home, I don't know what to make of the two worlds that confront me in the park. On one side of the brook is a perfectly happy snowman family, surrounded by little snow angels. Gary looks at the world with such gratitude and respect. Then there's the other side. A huge snowman smoking a joint and the words "Let's party!" I can't deny it…Eric has me wanting to know more about him.

These thoughts make my head spin. Standing high on that water tower, I hadn't been content to just look down. I had strained to look farther because I knew someone else was out there. I can no longer be content with my surroundings, and I feel pulled to that more distant, unknown side.

That evening, when Gary arrives, I promise Mom I'll be home by midnight and hurry out. Gary rushes to open the car door for me.

"How come I feel like maybe your parents don't know that my parents are out of town?" he asks.

I don't answer his question. "I'm looking forward to your culinary skills," I say. "Have you been slaving over the stove?"

"You'll be amazed at the meal I've pulled together," he says.

His home is warm, and I'm welcomed by a crackling fire in the fireplace, lit candles on the mantle, and a beautiful Christmas tree with muted lights. All its ornaments are handmade, and each is very beautiful.

"Wow!" I exclaim. "What art."

"They're a collection of bulbs that we've painted. We add several new ones each year. Each is dated and signed. The paintings represent moments of our lives. This one was done by my father. It is his childhood, and that's Dad, pushing his sister on a sled. Here is one Mom painted of the meadows behind her grandparents' home, where she played in the winter. I painted this one. It's from seventh grade, a painting of the ice sculpture I made for that contest in the park when I won for my age group. Keep looking, and you might find one that includes a memory of you," Gary says, returning to the kitchen to finish dinner.

I examine each bulb until finally I find it: a painting of me beside a fountain in a courtyard. I remember Gary commenting at the time that I had looked beautiful. "I found it," I say. "That's really a great painting. You and your parents really know how to paint miniatures."

Gary has been busy in the dining room, and I have no idea what he has prepared for dinner when he enters the living room, offering his arm.

"My dear," he says, "your dinner awaits you."

When he opens the dining room door, I am overcome. The table, decorated with fresh pine boughs cradling a beautiful winter arrangement, is set with lit candles on a tablecloth of winter cream. Adding to the romance of it all, Gary pulls out my chair and seats me, reaching to open my napkin. As lovely as everything is, part of me feels as if Gary is too good for me. I quickly remind myself that such a production is not typical in his normal, everyday life, but that he has worked hard to make this night something special. I am moved that it was all done for me.

Gary has prepared a special marinated steak entrée on a bed of pasta and vegetables, artfully presented of course. After the main course, Gary tells me to relax at the table while he clears the plates. He soon brings in a beautiful small dessert dish of crème brûlée. Taking a small cooking torch, he glazes the top. "This dish is an experience to be shared," he says.

There is only one spoon, and he picks it up. Lightly and delicately he dips the tip of the spoon into the crème brûlée, taking only a small amount. Leaning across the table, he silently gestures for me to taste.

"Crème brûlée is to be an experience for the palate; let it be slowly absorbed," he explains, gently putting the tip of the spoon between my lips. The crème brûlée is heavenly. Its sweet taste slowly unfolds in my mouth, an unbelievable treat, and so much more than a dessert. Gary gazes deeply into my eyes, soft classical music plays in the background, and the combination of pleasant sensations is so sensual, so intimate, and so delicious.

After dinner we clean up and then sit beside the fireplace. "I have a Christmas gift for you," Gary tells me. "I hope you like it. Before you open it, I want to tell you its story. It's a small replica of a statue that graces the grand stairway of the Louvre Museum in Paris. It has two names: the one I like is 'Winged Victory.' The other is Nike of Samothrace; 'Nike' means 'Victory,' and the statue was found on the island of Samothrace in 1863. The original stands about eight feet tall. She was found missing her head, neck, arms, and foot. Some believe she was once portrayed standing at the bow of a ship, and the victory she symbolizes may have been in a naval battle around 200 BC.

Looking into the box, I am captivated by my first sight of the statue. I believe I may have seen photos of it somewhere, possibly in an art book and recall a faint memory of its existence. But taking it out of the box is a new experience, especially after hearing Gary's commentary.

"See how she leans forward in her draped garment? How the wind forces the garment to cling to her body?" Gary adds. "The imaginary wind that shapes her garments becomes an intricate part of the sculpture itself. It is that thought of wind that breathes life into her. You can feel her challenging everything. She displays a powerful and seductive strength and courage as she leans forward, welcoming all life has to offer. People have fallen in love with this damaged relic for over 2,000 years. I felt inspired to give it to you because I believe you, too, have to move into the winds of life with courage. I also believe you will survive the raging storms and have great victories that will ultimately help you define yourself," Gary concludes, as he relaxes back onto the floor.

"Oh Gary, I love this so much," I say, thinking how special it is.

"Sue, the way you move about the world speaks volumes. I've been watching you for years. I may not know everything about you, but I do know you ponder everything, restlessly seeking answers about yourself. Everything out there pulls at you. It won't be easy. There are often prices to be paid for such explorations. But people also pay prices for failing to explore. I know that you and I are different, and that sometimes I can be overwhelmed by what life has already given me; that's part of why I am drawn to you. You are everything I am not. I love your curiosity, your strong sense of mystery, and I believe your courage is greater than your fear, your strength greater than your vulnerability. I worry about you, but only because I love you."

I am astounded by Gary's insight, so moved that I am speechless. Tears stream down my face as he takes me in his arms.

"I'm here for you, Sue. You have such a special place inside me. Are you okay?"

My voice cracks with emotion. "You know me so well, Gary. I am overwhelmed that anyone would take the time to know me as you have. I look at you…how you live…and you have such a sense of peace and beauty about life. I wish I could be like you…but I am so far from any such peace. Your presence in my life lets me hope that I might someday find such peace, and I feel afraid to let go of you. The closer I get to the edge of my exploration, the more tightly I cling onto you. But I am still drawn to the unknowns. I want freedom from my programmed life, from my over-thinking and analysis of everything. I want to taste new things without feeling caged up by the moral boundaries I have been taught. Your world of love and beauty is not celebrated in my home, where responsibility and duty come first, where we live our lives less openly. You have been blessed with a family that lives life."

"I am not planning on leaving you, Sue. I'm not going anywhere. I'm not planning on losing you, and if anything, I am planning on you coming to me with a new, profound sense of yourself. I am not encouraging or discouraging you to do anything. I just want to support you with the heartfelt message that I do have much love for you."

"Gary," I say, "I had a difficult time finding a gift for you. It's not as special as what you gave me, but I spent a lot of time thinking about you before I bought this."

"Oh Sue, I love this," he replies. "What a beautiful leather journal! I've spent a lot of time recording my thoughts, but I've never bought a journal to write in. I feel inspired just looking at it. I really love it."

Gary rubs his hand over the leather grain of the cover. Setting it aside, he pulls me to him. As we recline on the floor, I glance up at the clock and see that it is only 11:00 PM. He begins to softly kiss my face. His mouth kisses my lips with gentle intensity. I feel aroused inside, and I want to touch him, so I let my hand move down. He moans in shock. Gasping, he pulls away from me. Now I feel embarrassed—my face flushes, turning red.

"I'm sorry," I say. "I didn't mean to upset you. It's just that I…"

"Shhh," Gary whispers, cutting off my apology. "Its okay. Let's just relax. Shhh, just lie down here," he says.

Now he is trying to relax, trying to pull himself back from the intensity of my touch. A couple of minutes pass, and then he finally breaks the silence.

"I really want to experience everything right now, but I know that's my sexuality screaming. My problem is that I don't want to separate my sexuality from a relationship. I have much love for you. And there is no denying that I desperately want to make love to you. But not like this, not at this time in our lives. I don't want to complicate things. We are on the threshold of life taking us in two different directions, and we agreed not to define our relationship. I don't want to make love until the relationship is defined—a definition that has to include commitment," he says.

I see that he is wiping his eyes. Rather than shocked, I am moved by his words. He has always expressed that making love requires a committed relationship. Now I start questioning myself. Why have I done this? I feel guilty; I know better. Why did I need to violate him like that? He would never have violated me. I remember how he asked permission to touch me under the blanket the last time we were watching the sky. Now I sense a change in him; in fact, he distances himself from me, no longer lying against me. Oh my God! Is he frightened of me? Frightened that he might be weak? Whatever the reason, Gary lies on his back, his arms across his eyes, far from me in body and spirit.

"Gary, please. I am so sorry. I can tell I've upset you. Please tell me what I can do to help you feel better."

"I won't say I am okay when I am not. But it's not about what you did—not at all. It's about what it means. We are so different. I now realize that you need to make love so you can figure out yourself and us. But I need to figure us out *before* I can allow myself the privilege of making love. I long to make love with you. But I love the longings, I love the desires, and they are enough for me right now. I love to savor the yearning, which is evidence of my love for you. But this relationship is not just about me, nor is it just about you," Gary goes on. "It's about us, and we are different,"

What can I say? He is right, and he has defined the problem clearly. The issue is too big for compromise.

"Sue, let's agree that both of us will think about this and talk about it again, very soon. I want to really think about it. You are so important to me, and it deserves to be thought out. Okay?" he asks.

"Sure, that's a good idea," I agree.

"Come here, let's lie here for a few minutes before I have to take you home."

It is comforting being in his arms. The biggest problem we have ever faced now exists, but somehow, being in his arms, it feels as if we can overcome anything. As the clock edges past 11:30, I say that we'd better get going, that the roads are still bad, and so we have to drive slowly. Before we get up, I pull him to me and move my face close to his.

"This was such a wonderful night," I tell him. "Thank you for the remarkable dinner. Memories of the crème brûlée will live on forever. Thank you for such a remarkable gift. I have a lifetime to experience 'Winged Victory' over and over."

CHAPTER 11

Senior Trip

Gary and I grow closer throughout our senior year. We talk about our differences and agree to support each other's journeys, no matter where they lead. We have chosen not to define the relationship. Many passionate moments leave us panting on the edge, but Gary always keeps one foot securely planted, preventing us from going over.

Although it's intense, I love the moments when he is panting and feeling tortured. I love it when he is suspended, gasping, barely hanging on, and fighting that raw lust that rages inside him—an urge he seems almost unable to admit to. It feels cruel that I enjoy watching his difficult moments, when he struggles to fight his way back. But I know why I do enjoy them. My delight in his suffering makes him real, and he becomes a little bit more like me.

I still have my own ongoing internal struggles. I continue to feast on my memories of that one night with Eric. Living two houses away from him makes for constant reminders and I sometimes find myself wanting to run to him. An internal war pulls at me to experience the other side. I am taken away from such thoughts when spring arrives. The time approaches when Gary and I will leave on our senior trip. Although adult chaperones will go along, we will have time by ourselves.

I call Gary so we can match our activities. "Hi, Gary! I need to get my permission slip for the senior trip filled out."

"Glad you called, Sue. I forgot about that slip. Okay, here it is. What should we put down? The only thing I want to check is the 'free time' selections on the second day and evening. It looks like the first day is devoted to mandatory tours, but on the second day, I want to be alone with you. What do you think?" he asks.

"You're definitely right," I reply. "We'll see whether my parents will agree to all the 'free time.' I'm packing right now and can hardly wait to go."

"I have a lesson, and then I'll pack. See you at the bus tomorrow morning at six sharp."

I finish my form and rush downstairs to get Mom to sign it. "Hey Mom, I need you to sign my itinerary form for the senior trip."

She picks up her glasses and sits down at the table. "Sounds like a fun trip. Why aren't you going to these sites listed here?"

"Well, I am planning on going to some of them, but Gary and I don't want to go with the group. Tours aren't very satisfying. Gary is an artist. He likes to really study specific things and not be rushed. He isn't going on the tours the second day because he wants to move at his own pace. And I want to go with him."

"Okay. Just be careful, and don't do anything by yourself. Remember, you are still bound to the rules and curfew. By the way, Sue, would you run an errand for me?"

"Sure! What can I do to help you?"

"I have to go to church for a meeting and the stores will close before I get away. Will you pick up a nice tablecloth that your father and I can take as a gift to Edward and Mary's anniversary party tonight? You know the kind I like, with the rich cream lace, in Willard's department store."

"Sure, I know the kind. I'll go do it for you now."

Walking into the store, I pass through the women's department. I see a beautiful, sensual, silky peach nightgown. It is gorgeous. I stop and imagine myself in it. Surely, something like this will leave Gary hanging on the edge by the tip of his toes—an absolutely delightful thought. Trying it on won't hurt, I decide.

Inside the dressing room, I feel the silky material slip over my body. Oh, it feels as wonderful as it looks! It shimmers in the mirror and highlights my breasts. The mere feel of it makes me want to find a way to wear it for Gary. On our trip, Gary will have a room to himself; he isn't close to other guys in our class. Surely, I'll have an opportunity to visit his room. Yes, I'll buy the nightgown, sneak it home, and sneak it into my suitcase.

The next morning, both of my parents take me to the bus station. As we arrive, Mr. and Mrs. Waltham are speaking with Gary. "You kids have the time of your life," says Mr. Waltham.

"Be careful," my mother says, "and don't do anything dangerous. Watch yourself as you are out and about."

The contrast in the messages from Gary's parents and mine amazes me.

It feels wonderful sitting beside Gary on the bus, holding his hand, my eagerness about the trip climbing. I am excited to see the Capitol and White House. Gary looks out the window, deep in thought. It is so like him to absorb the scenery along the way. Slowly, Gary starts moving his index finger erotically across the palm of my hand.

"You have the need to wake all of me up, eh?" I say, as I slowly open my eyes.

"Oh, Sue," he replies, "it doesn't take much to wake all of you up. Just a breath on you, and you're gone," he whispers into my ear.

Looking up at him, I can't help but smile. He knows he is in trouble—that these next two days are going to pull at every inch of his existence.

We arrive in Washington DC half an hour late. The sponsors collect our permission forms and assign us our rooms. Gary is given a room on the third floor, and I am assigned a room with Mavis Ratcliff, on the tenth floor. Settling in, Mavis and I chat about our plans and unpack until the phone rings.

"Hi, Sue," Gary says. "How would you like to come to my room and start torturing me?"

"Sure! I'll get my swimsuit out. Maybe after dinner we can try the Jacuzzi or swim."

I rush down the seven floors to Gary's room carrying a little satchel that includes my swimsuit, comb, brush, makeup—and the silky peach nightgown. I want to have it in case the night gives way to an opportunity.

Gary closes the door. "Come here, toots! I've been dying all day to give you a kiss." Sweeping me off the floor, he lifts me up and kisses me. Standing me back on the floor, he takes my hand and walks me to the king-size bed in his room. "Oh, go ahead," he says. "Lie on the bed. Feel it, and get your questions answered, 'cause I don't want you pondering what my bed feels like." He is laughing.

"Hey, fella," I reply. "Come here and lie down next to me. After all, you don't want me to leave here wondering what it would be like to lie next to you on this big old bed do you?"

"Heavens no."

As soon as we move into each other's arms the teasing stops. "Gary, are you scared about being alone with me these next two days?"

"It's a nice scare. I've dreamed about it, Sue. I've come to terms with how much I want you completely. I've asked myself whether I'd be better off never tasting full intimacy with you if I knew we would depart from each other later on. This is about many things: my values, my beliefs, my lust, my love. It's not something I want to decide when we are in the heat of passion. But I have my answer, and I'm finally at peace with it."

Gary rolls over to lie on his back and look up at the ceiling. "I know my love for you is not infatuation," he continues. "I love you with all your unique qualities, including your unanswered questions about yourself. You are much more than your unknowns. Actually, your unknowns have nothing to do with your character. That's well-defined. Your unknowns are nothing more than experiences you need to complete. Sue, as you've clearly said, you don't want to receive your knowledge about life through the eyes of others. You need to gather information for yourself.

I am speechless. Gary just keeps unfolding.

"So," he says, "with my questions about myself answered, I now have a big question about you. What would making love mean to you? Would it be just another experience that you long for? You know what I mean—just a moment of information gathering? Or do you really love me? That question haunts me. I don't want to be just an experience."

I am caught up short by his insight and overwhelmed by his feelings. Wiping his eyes, Gary still has more to say. "The way you've toyed with me leaves me feeling like I'm nothing more than a challenge. But then, sometimes I feel authentic love coming from you. Tell me honestly: how do you really feel about me? Sue, I don't need to know where this relationship is going. I just want the truth about how you feel about me, right now."

I feel somber, shaken, frightened, and confused. Yet I respect and appreciate Gary's honesty. Aching inside, I wish I could solidify my thoughts and be clear about what I feel. Gary can talk so straightforwardly about love. He knows it, has lived it all his life. He lives love in Technicolor. My thoughts about love are merely speculative, and all I can do is attempt to let them out. He will have to sort through them. I cannot.

"Wow!" I say. "You really honored me by being so truthful. My world is so gray, unclear, and undefined. You are so clear about love. You breathe love like it is oxygen, free for the taking. You live love, paint love. I respect you, especially the parts that are nothing like me. You say I toyed with you, and looking back I can see that hurt you. You have said many times that everything in your life is enough, that you live in celebration of it. Tell me then, how could I ever feel important or valued, when all that you have is already enough? Toying with you made me feel important because of how you reacted. Seeing you want me confirmed that I had an impact, that I had captured you. I could be sub-missive to your world, and for the most part I have been—like a sponge absorbing the beauty of who you are. You painted the world for me to see. But what did I have to offer you? What did I have that would make your life better? The only thing I thought I had was the fact that my curiosity stirred you." I pause, taking a deep breath.

"Gary, you've told me that everything you have is enough. Well, I represent things that you have never experienced. I am a great intrusion to your peace. Peace is nice, it's something I long for, but I also wonder if I could become bored with it. And if I were to become like you I would have nothing to offer you. I have to know that my differences have some value to you. After all, your differences are so very valuable to me."

As I continue, I feel myself starting to shake. "I loved you deeply, but I don't know if that is enough for you. Most say that real love is forever. That's a nice thought, but I don't know if I agree. It's hard to find anything that lasts forever. I'm inclined to believe that we should breathe in the love that life offers us along the way. If that love is rich and pure, then it will have power greater than my ability to destroy it. At least, the dreamy eyed poet inside me wants to believe that. But I don't know," I say.

"I want to know how you are feeling," I continue, "because your feelings matter to me. Just please tell me: how can anyone can ever feel valuable to you if all that you have is already enough?"

Taking another deep breath, I look at Gary. I can tell I have shaken his resolve. My honesty must have been confusing to him. Now I fear he is in greater turmoil.

"Sue," he says, "don't you sometimes wish you and I weren't so deep, so ana-lytical, so mature? Listening to you, I realize we do have one thing in common. Neither of us has much of a child inside. We don't have a playful, carefree, lighthearted side. We are always dealing with life as if we are fifty years old. I know that's why we were attracted to each other originally. I was drawn to you when you spoke up in class because you are smart and show an awareness about life. You and I probably seem a bit strange to most people our age. You live in your head, always thinking too deeply. You process life like a middle-aged lady who has been through the wringer. I, on the other hand, came from a peaceful existence, not a playful one. My parents taught me reverence and how to appreciate and absorb life. Their mature nature never brought out the child in me. If one of us had a fun-loving child inside, perhaps we could be more simple and playful. Your words made me feel sad. Either I have failed and not showed you how I value and celebrate you, or your low self-esteem and insecurity prevents you from seeing how much you mean to me. Probably, it's a little bit of both."

Gary has hit the nail on the head. Both of us take life so seriously that we can't simply be playful and childlike.

"Sue, you are valuable to me because you force me out of my comfort zone. You have helped me grow and intensified my feelings. You question how I can appreciate anything if I have never felt deprivation and longing. You crave a deeper, richer, fuller kind of love because you felt deprived in your childhood. You've lived through many experiences that have left you sad and in turmoil. But you spend too much time in the trenches of your soul searching and analyzing. I want to support and comfort you, and it pains me to watch you struggle with life. Your victories are too brief, quickly you line up for your next challenge. You are dynamic, and you make life seem fuller, more real, and more exciting. You have said that I help you slow down and breathe in more life. Well, you stir my dormant existence and encourage me to sprint. You make me less complacent about life. We are extensions of each other's world, and that is our gift to each other." Gary seems depleted. Silence permeates the room.

"Gary," I say at last, "thank you for sharing and processing all of this. I feel as if our relationship has matured in the last hour. I have nothing left to say except that I really love you. Our relationship demands such candor and honesty. It's clear how much we both really care about each other."

Gary rolls to his side and looks at me, full of emotion. "I love you, Sue. I think what we went through is probably going to happen again and again. That is who we are together. But it was good for me. Come here. Let me just hold you."

The next morning, Gary is waiting for me at breakfast, where we have fun just eating and looking at each other. The morning at the Capitol is very interesting. Our congressman, Representative Otterman, comes to greet us. I enjoy listening to all the representatives debate issues in session. Gary passes me a note that reads, "Relax, Sue. You are not here to resolve life for these people. They are here to resolve it for you." He is being funny, but his note rings true. I have been evaluating what is missing in their congressional debates.

We leave Capitol Hill about noon and take sack lunches to picnic on the National Mall. It is such a powerful and beautiful piece of land, decked with cherry blossoms whose wonderful fragrance permeates the breeze. Gary stares at me as we eat our lunch. I am playing with my food, carefully examining my sandwich before I take a bite, even rearranging the meat and pickles. "Sue," Gary says, "stop organizing life. Just take a bite and start enjoying it."

In the afternoon we go to the White House. Gary is lost in the great pieces of art that hang on the walls. I, on the other hand, am taken more by the building's history. I get lost in the thought that Abraham Lincoln has slept here, that past presidents had favorite rooms or items in the White House. For me, it is an opportunity to connect with history, not just read about it.

Back at the hotel, I shower and dress for dinner and the concert that evening. The evening goes fast and the concert is terrific. From time to time, Gary reaches out and rubs my hand. We have both agreed to be discreet on this trip, but I can tell it's hard on Gary. I can see his emotion and how certain pieces of music capture him.

When we return to the hotel, we lie down on Gary's bed, and he holds me. His breath softly caresses my ear. He lightly hums melodies from the concert. It is lovely to relax and feel him so close.

Later, I say, "Well, I'd better get going. I have a big day tomorrow."

"You do, do you?"

"Yes. There is this guy I'm going to spend the day with. I don't know if he is a weirdo or what, but I'm going to put myself into his hands, and he has promised me a fun day."

The phone rings about six AM. Gary sounds happy and excited. "Let's not do breakfast with the gang, Sue. Let's go get some coffee and muffins and find a park where we can enjoy them."

"Sounds good to me! I'll be down in a second." I decide to pack my satchel and leave it in Gary's room. I take my makeup, toiletries, and swimsuit, but not the peach nightgown. I've decided that I bought it with the wrong intentions and that I will return it when I get home.

We find a wonderful little breakfast place a few blocks away and buy coffees and a couple of hot muffins. Gary gets directions to a little park. It is a gorgeous morning, with the cherry blossoms full of scent. Gary reaches up to a tree, snaps off a little branch of blossoms, and tucks it into my hair. "There," he says, "I've already created an artwork this morning. I've blended the beauty of the blossoms with the beauty of you." He lightly kisses me.

It is nice being alone together—such a wonderful feeling. Gary reaches over and feeds me a piece of his blueberry muffin. "Taste these huge berries bursting with sweet juice," he says. After I eat it, he reaches across and kisses a crumb off my lip.

"There. Now you have a bit of blueness to your tongue as well. Tell me, what do you want to do today? Be honest. Don't say what you think you should say, just tell me what you would like to do."

"Aren't you taking a bit of a risk, asking that way?" I say. "Let me see...I want to study art and..."

Gary cuts me off. "Great! We can do that..."

"Hey! Whoa there, fella. You didn't let me finish. You did say you wanted me to be honest, didn't you?"

"Oh. Sorry, didn't mean to cut you off. Yes, I want your honesty. Please continue."

"Okay. Now where was I? Oh yeah. I want to study art. That is, the art of, ummm, touching you," I say, looking at Gary and laughing.

"Since you say in the same sentence that you'd like to study both art and me, does that mean you'd like to paint me?" Gary asks.

"Sure, but I prefer painting you in the nude," I say, laughing hard, and Gary laughs too. "I like to study my subjects for long periods of time before I let my crayons touch paper." We both like teasing each other.

"Too bad we didn't bring our art supplies."

"Yeah, I know what you mean," I reply. "My crayon box and coloring book wouldn't fit into my suitcase." I am laughing uncontrollably at him taking seriously the idea of me being an artist. "Seriously, Gary, what would you like to do? I'm game for going anywhere or doing anything."

"Well, for me the Smithsonian Institution is the most important destination. It's very large, so we have to pick an area. I really would love to see the art there. What do you think, Sue?"

"I think that's a great idea!" I say, knowing Gary's passion to go there.

"I know your fondness for Lincoln, so we can visit the Lincoln Memorial as well. Maybe you can crawl upon his lap and chat with him," he teases.

"Don't plan on me noticing you when we're there, 'cause I've always had an eye for old Abe," I tease back.

The morning goes by quickly. At the Smithsonian, Gary studies pieces of art he has been looking forward to seeing. As he shares his insights about each one, I am enthralled by his interpretations that articulate the ambience of each painting. But Gary is a great lover of solitude, peace, and serenity, and I find myself wandering off to look at paintings that rage with intensity. One that catches and holds my attention is of a woman lost in her pain.

Leaving the Smithsonian, we walk along the Mall toward the Lincoln Memorial. Gary is reflecting on art and talking about how artists communicate, how their art speaks for them. As usual, he reflects on van Gogh. "Van Gogh is the painter who most perplexes me. He paints the world as he sees it, always using intense colors, allowing them to speak for him. His paintings are so emotional—such raw, true representations of his feelings." I like listening to Gary talk about van Gogh; he is obsessed with him. After a morning spent studying the paintings of many other artists, he still wants to talk about van Gogh.

After eating, we visit the Lincoln Memorial and then return to the hotel. At Gary's room we both fall on the bed, rather exhausted. Lying there silently, we doze off for about an hour. I wake up and write him a note, saying that I will be in my room.

At 4:00 PM the phone rings. It's Gary. "Hey, why didn't you wake me up? I didn't want to sleep our day away. Would you like me to plan the night, or would you like us to plan it together?"

"I would love for you to plan it," I reply. "Surprise me. It doesn't have to be anything special, as long as I'm with you."

"Okay. Plan on coming down at 6:00 and I'll have something planned. We can always watch cartoons," he adds, teasingly.

I dress up a bit, thinking about where Gary might take me. He answers the door dressed in a nice suit. I am glad I dressed up.

"Let's go," he says, "we have dinner reservations." We take a cab to the restaurant. It is a sweet little bistro in a very old part of town with a warm and very romantic ambience. A violinist plays soft music. I feel myself swell with emotion as Gary pulls out my chair to seat me.

"How did you find out about this place?" I ask.

"Oh, I asked around last night when I went out for a walk about midnight."

"Come on!" I say. "No way would you break curfew."

"You're right. I'd never break curfew. I forgot we had one, really," he says.

The entire dinner is wonderfully romantic. Our expressive waiter sends the violinist over to play a beautiful piece of romantic music. As we are having coffee, Gary reaches into his pocket and pulls out a small package. "I have a gift for you. I want you to remember this trip and how much fun we've had."

"Thank you," I say, "I have memories that will last forever."

I remove the bow and open the box. Inside is a small jewelry box containing a beautiful antique Victorian locket. "I went out this afternoon to a few antique stores looking for a perfect locket that would remind you of this little bistro where we had dinner."

Inside the locket is a small picture of the two of us. Encased on the other side is a pressed cherry blossom. "How did you do this?" I ask.

"Mom and I talked about the trip before I left, and I told her I wanted to get you a locket. She remembered the picture Dad took at Thanksgiving. So she had it made into a miniature. My job was to find the perfect locket here in DC that would accommodate it. I had to do it when you weren't around. I got up right after you left, went out, and found it at an antique store. Remember yesterday, when I put cherry blossoms in your hair? When we got back, I removed them while you rested in my arms. After you left, I pressed them in a book. So the cherry blossom is the one I put in your hair yesterday. I wanted the locket with a cherry blossom petal to remind you of our trip," he explains.

His gesture is so overwhelmingly beautiful. "I love it, Gary. I love it!" My voice is cracking.

"Here," he says, "let me put it on you." He moves around the table and hooks the chain. "It looks great," he says.

I hold the locket out and keep looking at it, then place it on my heart and reach across the table to kiss him. We slowly finish our coffees before we leave.

The night is so beautiful that we decide to take a walk. The air is cool and clean. The sky is filled with stars, with one huge star centered above us. I keep gazing up as we walk; it feels as if the star is following us. We arrive at a small park lit with very old street lanterns. Its beautiful cobblestone walkway is lined with cherry blossom petals. We find a bench and sit down. Gary puts his arms around me and I rest my head on his shoulder. We gaze up into the clear night sky. It feels as if we are suspended in a moment of heaven.

"All of this seems so perfect," Gary says. "I wish we didn't have to go back tomorrow. But we have tonight."

I feel so full of life as we walk back to the hotel. The locket brushes against my chest, and wish I had a gift for Gary. I have no idea what I could have given him. I remember how difficult it was trying to think of a gift at Christmas. Finally, I simply ask him. "I so want to give you something extraordinary. But I can't think of anything. What could I possibly give you that would be special enough?"

"Sue, there's no gift more perfect than the memories I have from being with you." I knew he would say this. I also know he means it. Gary, a collector of life moments, can live on the preciousness of each of them.

"Please, Gary. I *need* to give you something—something extraordinary, something unique. Tell me. Oh please, tell me," I plead.

Gary is moved by my deep desire to give him something and thinks to himself until we reach the hotel.

In his room, he turns on the subdued light of a table lamp. Taking me into his arms, he kisses me. "Sue," he says, "there is one thing I would like from you, but it might make you feel uncomfortable. I would like to light a couple of special candles I brought and delight in you from across the room. Then, should you feel comfortable enough, I would like to slightly drape you and then enjoy the vision of you. You are so beautiful! I want to absorb you, to create art from my vision of you. We must keep silent, so nothing distracts from the visual experience. But if you let me undress you, position you, and slowly soak in your beauty, I can visually enjoy you for however long it takes until I have aesthetically captured you. It might take an hour, maybe a little more—I'm not sure because although I have dreamed about you this way I have never tried it. The times when we've been alone, I have wanted to do it but haven't had the courage to ask. Now that you've offered me a gift, I feel safe telling you that this is what I really want most. Please feel free to say no."

I am speechless. I feel honored—and awkward. Although it is not the kind of gift I imagined, I know it will be undeniably special for him. It might sound risqué to someone who doesn't know us, but we both know his goal is artwork, and not a sexual game. Still, my body squirms at the thought of how sexual it sounds. It will be far more difficult than if he had asked me to make love for the first time. I have low self-esteem about my body, and Gary has no idea how much he is asking me to set aside. Because it will be difficult, I know it makes it the most perfect gift, so I agree without hesitation.

"Gary," I reply, "thank you for asking for something so special. You've chosen what might be the most difficult gift I could give, but I love that and would want nothing less. I wanted you to have something rare and hard-to-find, so please—I'll silently welcome you to take your gift."

Gary takes two large candles from his suitcase, placing one on either end of the coffee table, and lights them. He also produces a large piece of cream-colored fabric that he obviously has been hoping for a chance to use. When Gary gently unzips the back of my dress, I feel myself swelling inside. He lifts the dress forward off my shoulders and it drops to the floor, where I step out of it. Gary hangs my dress in his closet. Not a man ravishing a body, Gary is pure artist, already enjoying an experience he desperately wants to capture.

He stands for a second, looking at me in the candlelight, then kisses my forehead as if in thanks. Ever so gently, he removes my underclothing and beckons for me to sit on the couch. Spreading the fabric over the couch, he positions me laying down with my legs slightly bent, arranging my body in an elongated position. With another piece of fabric he very carefully and artistically drapes it over me, silently shaping the vision he wants. I feel the soft touch of his hand as he drapes the fabric over half of my left breast, leaving my right breast fully exposed. The material lightly falls from my midriff and rests across my left thigh. Gently, he slightly dips the material between my legs, sculpting the material to my body, leaving left leg and feet exposed. He takes his time positioning everything, then gazes with satisfaction before removing his suit coat, tie, shirt, shoes and socks. He steps into the bathroom returns in a pair of tan khakis.

The silence in the room is palpable. Gary comes back to me and tilts my head slightly. He goes to his chair and sits in silence, restfully gazing upon me. At first I feel awkward being stared at, but after a few minutes I start to lose myself in the experience. My worry that I might panic from embarrassment slowly dissipates. I wonder what Gary sees—what it means to him. From time to time, I feel my body reacting to the experience. Taking a deep breath, I feel my breasts heave. The experience allows me to think of my body in new ways.

After thirty minutes, Gary stands up and adjusts my position, giving me an opportunity to move a bit and gain some comfort. No words are spoken. He gently drapes my body again, and when his hands softly touch my flesh, the sensation is like electricity through my skin, causing me to gasp.

Gary moves his chair to a new position from which to capture my candle-lit body. Like a true artist, he notices every detail and pays close attention to the lighting. He is relaxed, lost in the experience, his gaze almost hypnotic. From time to time he tilts his head back and briefly closes his eyes, only to reopen them quickly and return to viewing me.

After about forty-five more minutes of intently enjoying me, he gets up and takes a robe out of his closet. "Oh, Sue," he says, "you are so beautiful! This is wonderful. I will never forget it. May I softly touch you? I desire for a moment, a mere second, to feel what I have visually experienced."

"Yes, please," I breathlessly whisper, desperately longing for his touch.

Gary softly touches my face, my eyes. He strokes my neck, my clavicle, and then my chest, lightly sweeping his fingers downward to feel the shape of my rounded breast. He touches me as if trying not to arouse me but to memorize my shape and texture. He gasps as his fingers explore my body, never touching the parts of me that are draped, always showing respect for my privacy—an artist lost to his art.

At last, Gary gently pulls the fabric to cover the rest of me and hands me his robe. After I am fully robed, he hugs me. We lie down on the couch and he holds me. "I am so full of life right now, Sue," he says. "What you have given me is wonderful, beyond words—I'm not going to ruin it with words that can't possibly describe it. The treasured experience I will hold inside me is the best gift I have ever received. Thank you."

I am silent too, equally overwhelmed by an hour and a half that was both difficult and wonderful. Now that it is over, it feels fantastic to have given him something so special. Finally I rise and say, "We have to be up, packed, and ready for the bus by eight, so perhaps I'd better be getting to bed." I get dressed. He intensely kisses me goodnight, his eyes flooded with emotion and gratitude.

Back in my hotel room, I lie awake, thinking, sorting memories I will never forget and knowing that I have grown deeper in love with Gary. Our talks have taken us deeper into each other. Nevertheless, my mind drifts back to that night with Eric. Why does the power of that one night still tug at me? I find myself thinking about what it would have felt like had I allowed Eric to keep going. Again, my mind wanders back and forth between pleasure and guilt at the thought of it all. When I return tomorrow, maybe I will see Eric—a possibility I can't help but find exciting. Exhausted by conflicting feelings, I finally fall asleep.

CHAPTER 12

Loss and Change

As our senior year flies toward its end, Gary and I continue to see each other, but a new distance arises between us. We each have begun trying to adjust to being without the other. Our dates become less frequent until they are every couple of weeks. By then we are desperate to see each other.

My last big social activity before graduation will be the prom. Gary and I disdain the expensive clothing required, but I've found a nice formal that I can use at college as well.

The anticipation builds until, suddenly, life intrudes one morning. Grandma telephones us from the hospital to say that Grandpa has had a heart attack and is in critical care. The damage to his heart is severe, she says, and she does not expect him to live long. Daddy is more upset than I've ever seen him. When I call Gary and let him know that I will have to miss the prom, he understands completely.

We drive five hours to where Grandpa and Grandma live and rush to the hospital. Only my father may enter the room. He emerges after a long time, and in a broken voice he tells us that Grandpa has passed away while he sat by his side. The pain I feel at the loss of my grandfather is secondary to the pain I feel at witnessing my father's loss. He sits down, trying to hold himself together. My mother comforts Grandma, who comes out of the room crying. I feel helpless anguish, especially because of how my father responds. Although it's the worst I've ever seen him, he merely stands, wipes his eyes with a handkerchief, and takes off walking. I stand up too, wanting to follow him, hoping that he needs me. Mother, who is holding Grandma, shakes her head no, as if to say, "Let him be alone." I know she is right. After all, that is why he walked away. So I sit quietly, a sponge absorbing the pain of everyone around me. I still haven't let myself feel my loss.

My grandfather—a kind man, loved by his community, and certainly good to his grandchildren—had one strained relationship: with my father. Throughout the years I have watched him destroy my father with a sarcastic humor that barely concealed the critical comments ripping at my father. My father never confronted him but would walk away or pretend he didn't hear. I know Dad loved Grandpa deeply, so my grandfather's comments drained the life out of Daddy. What went on in that room before Grandpa died? Dare I ask Mom?

Grandma is being put into a wheelchair and taken to the car. When Mom asks if I am okay, I bring myself to respond. "Did Grandpa talk before he died? Did Daddy get to say good-bye?"

"Grandpa saw Daddy and told him he loved him."

Driving Grandma home, Daddy is silent. Mark says that Grey will arrive as soon as he can get a flight. Grandma weeps all the way home, where Mom helps her to her bed to lie down for a while. When Mom returns to the living room she tells Daddy the arrangements were made ahead of time, and the funeral will be Friday morning. He listens vacantly, looking shell-shocked.

The next two days are difficult. Grandma's neighbors stop by to pay their respects. Daddy stays at the funeral home from the time it opens until it closes at night. Seeing my grandfather's lifeless body is difficult, but seeing my father in such pain is worse.

Walking into the funeral home for the service, I feel less sad than frightened—frightened for my father, who will be giving a eulogy. Dad has not slept for days and looks lifeless. After the minister delivers a message of hope and celebration over the life of my eighty-one-year-old grandfather, I quickly whisper a prayer for Dad as he begins to speak.

"Dear family and friends…Excuse me if I take my time. This is a most important thing for me to do. My father was an extraordinary man who loved my mother dearly. As a child growing up, I watched him work tirelessly to provide for the family. He never complained but was thankful to have a job. He gave much to his community and taught me that life was about giving, not receiving. When I was a child, he was hard on me, something I resented; after all, I just wanted to be a child. His strictness and the urgent pressure he put on me were not easy to understand, and tension grew inside both of us. Later in life, I realized that such tension could not exist without love, and any friction in our relationship came from caring so much about what the other thought.

As beautiful as love is, it comes with its edges. You want the best for the ones you love. When you feel you know what is best for them, often you push and pull at them, trying to help. My father pushed me because he cared, and I never doubted my father's love. But I did spend a whole lifetime trying to figure out his methods. He packed his messages in humor, like giving me medicine but coating it in sugar. That never went down easily with me, because I could always taste the medicine. I so wanted him to respect me enough to talk with me without joking, so what was meant to be sweet only hurt me more. He never could talk directly with me—until the last moments of his life. He said, 'James, you have always been the greatest joy in my life. Never forget, I love you.' Those were the words I had wanted to hear all my life."

"Father left me with a message, and as personal as it is, I offer it to you so that you may offer it freely to your children, who may also need desperately to know what you really feel. I am so thankful he said it to me before he died. Today would be harder without it. I loved my father. I always knew that any pain he cause me was only a part of the undeniable love between us. He is gone, but my love for him will live on. Thank you for your condolences. They mean much to me and my family. Thank you."

I am in tears. I knew that no matter how painful it might be, my father would speak the truth from his heart. Even in his own father's eulogy, his central concern was not for his own pain but for an opportunity to help to others. Descending from the platform, he appears resolved, as if life is returning to his body. When he sits down beside me, he looks at me and—for the first time since Grandpa died—offers me a small smile.

After the burial, we all go home and back to our lives. Grey returns to college. Dad goes back to work, and Mom is as busy as ever with community projects. I go back to school and try to catch up on my class assignments. I talk to Gary on the phone and see him in class. Because Gary goes to the studio every day after school, we agree to catch up on everything the following weekend.

On a beautiful spring day that week as I am walking home from school, I decide to visit the park. The flowers are in bloom, and the grass is a rich green. I go to my favorite spot on the edge of the brook. I sit on the fresh grass, which feels like velvet. Then I see Eric walking.

"Hey, stranger, how've you been?" I call out.

"I've been fine," Eric replies. "Been doin' some things for Mr. Miller, tryin' to make a few bucks. You haven't been around much. How come?"

"My grandfather died. We were gone for awhile," I explain.

"Sorry to hear that. You were also on the senior trip, weren't you? How did that go?"

"Yep. I had a great time. It was fun."

"Well, look there," Eric says, looking at my locket that has fallen open. "You have a picture of you and Gary hangin' on your neck."

"Yes," I reply, holding up the locket. "Gary bought it for me on the trip. This is a cherry blossom from Washington DC."

"Nice gift. So what did you do to deserve it? And what did *you* get the big fella?" he asks, picking on me.

"Well, you don't really want to know," I say, starting to laugh at the thought that Eric would be surprised to learn what I had given Gary.

"Sure, dare to share," he says, laughing, a bit of curiosity in his voice.

"I asked Gary what I could give him that would be special, and he said he just wanted to study me. So he draped my body artistically and studied me for about an hour and twenty minutes," I say.

"What the hell kind of present is that?" asks Eric, completely shocked with what I've told him. "Are you saying that you were basically nude?"

"Yes, I was nude under the draping," I try to explain.

"My God! There's something wrong with a guy who can just sit and look at a person like that. I mean—was any of your body showing?"

"Yes. Part of me was draped and other parts not," I answer.

"Holy crapola!" Eric exclaims. "What's wrong with him? How could a guy just look at you for that long without jumping on your bones? Jeez, I couldn't do that!" Eric is totally stunned by what he has just learned.

"Gary is an artist," I say. "He loves studying things. He must've planned for or hoped for the opportunity, because he'd brought the draping and candles with him."

"Gosh, he is strange. I can't say I wouldn't have enjoyed it, but Lord, I couldn't have lasted more than two to three minutes without begging to take you. Gosh, just the thought of this is making me a little hot here," he says.

I find myself enjoying Eric's reaction. I love the thought of someone begging to take me sexually. Here I am again, tormented by my demons of desiring new experiences.

"Sue," he says, "by any chance, have you been wanting to give me a gift as well? Because I'd like a gift too, but I wouldn't settle for just a look."

I am enjoying Eric's raw, crude teasing. It is as if I'm two people, and he is again tempting my wild side. I feel myself squirm at the thought of him taking me. "Well, Eric, you do stir me up a bit with your outspoken desires."

"You know that deep down you still want to smoke a joint and experience a high, Sue," he replies. "Just remember, I'm a neighborly guy just two doors down, I would be happy to help you out with all that." He gives me a big wink. "I could take you to places you haven't been, where time is suspended and sensations and laughter are endless. You can lose yourself over and over. I know you're a good girl, but gosh, anyone who longs as much as you do should let herself go."

Eric has hit the nail on the head. I live with that longing, suppressed most of the time, but strong and powerful. If I can hold on, I'll soon be at college—away from him and the raging desires he constantly stirs up inside me.

"You sure make me think—and I'll never forget that one night," I say.

"Do you ever think about what would happen if you'd just let yourself go...you know, all the way?"

"Well, I have imagined it. But it is only imaginary, since I have never had sex."

"That guy of yours is way too slow on the good things. Well," he says, getting up, "remember, I am always a willing neighbor who adores you."

We say our good-byes and Eric leaves. Now my head spins with those recurring thoughts and desires about being free to experience life.

I look down and notice that I never closed my locket after Eric pointed it out. The picture of the two of us snaps me back to the reality of how much I care for Gary. I feel tired of the endless pulling inside me. I hate feeling so fragmented.

The next few weeks creep by as I study hard, preparing for my finals. Carrie and I spend time together, sharing our excitement about going off to college in the fall. We rejoice when our application to room together in the dorms is finally accepted. It is exciting to think about being independent—especially for Carrie, who will finally be on her own. Mom and Dad buy us a mini-refrigerator, iron and ironing board, bookcase, bedspreads, bedding, and a radio for our room. Carrie is excited about these gifts, as she is unable to afford the extra things. I don't want her to ever feel like she is borrowing them. She is moved by my parents' generosity.

All at once, my life is changing. With a new sense of trust, my mother and father no longer question me about where I'm going. No one ever mentions curfew. My parents have changed a lot since Grandpa died. I notice that they are not so authoritarian about little things at home. Dad is relaxed and more peaceful. When they bring up the subject of a graduation party, I suggest throwing one for me, Carrie, and Patty. Dad finds my offer to share my special moment with others very kind. He has a two-day conference in Chicago and has begged Mom to go with him. Even though she is busy with preparations for the upcoming party, she finally agrees to go.

Gary is also free that the weekend, except for Saturday afternoon when he will go to the studio. His parents are visiting Gary's uncle in Boston. This weekend will give us the opportunity to spend quality time together.

Gary and I have missed each other. Our dates are now down to every two weeks. Gary has tried to make every date special. We no longer go to movies, because we don't want to waste two hours when we are desperate to be in each other's arms. We have become comfortable with being close, although Gary still controls us, pulling us back from the edge of our sexuality. I have started feeling resentful about it. Sometimes I even fault Gary for my interest in Eric, because Gary stirs up a desire in me that he is not yet willing to satisfy. Yet I know I cannot blame him. I vacillate between respecting and resenting Gary.

On the last weekend before graduation, Gary asks me over for the evening. He loves relaxing there with me, and I feel comfortable listening to the music albums that he loves to play for me. But I know it will be another night of hanging on the edge of passion. I don't know if I can take it and, more significantly, I don't want to. I try to make myself comfortable on Gary's couch, but as my resentment builds I realize I need to be honest about feelings.

"Gary," I begin, "I am not interested in another evening where you and I crawl to the edge of wanting everything, but where you keep us from going farther. It's getting all too hard for me. The tease used to be fun, and I loved panting and wishing, but that's old stuff to me now. I have to tell you that it has started to make me frustrated and angry."

Gary is startled by my words. Sitting back and looking up, thinking about what I said, Gary replies, "I never thought I'd hear you describe our desires as something that make you angry, Sue."

Silence fills the air. The excitement of togetherness has been halted by my honesty. In just one moment I have changed our relationship. Gary loves the closeness, the longings that have stirred us in the past, and the climbing intensity of our desires pushing us—all priceless moments for him. For a while I too enjoyed them, but suddenly I feel vulnerable to anything that offers me the opportunity to fully experience making love. Gary's constant control has taken away my desire to be with him. He is a constant reminder of what I can't have and can't experience. I wonder if I am closing myself off as a means of survival, but I also can imagine Gary never finding the freedom to just let go and to succumb to the moment.

"I don't know what to think, Sue. I'm confused by this huge turnaround."

It's obvious that I have to make what is going on with me clear.

"It's not a huge turnaround, Gary," I say. "Lately, I've changed a lot in how I feel about things. I know I want my sexuality to be a reflection of a relationship, of love and respect. I've had to admit to myself recently, though, that while in being left hanging on the edge once felt special, I gradually have come to resent it. Excitement changed to frustration as the longing stirred up so much in me and made me vulnerable. I was in danger of saying yes to anything that would let me finally unfold and found myself open to taking risky chances. You have no idea what I almost did to experience what you are unwilling to give me. Our relationship has stirred up such a raw desperation inside me that I almost think not seeing you would be better." Now crying, I continue, "Dating leaves me hung out there. It is getting harder and harder to come down after evenings with you. I'm so tired of struggling with desire and desperation."

Gary is clearly shocked and confused. "Sue, I had no idea that all of this would somehow turn to something so painful. It's hard for me to understand. I apologize for assuming that you enjoyed the longing as much as I do. I had no idea that inside it was tearing at you and leaving you vulnerable. My God, Sue, I am so sorry. Please tell me—help me understand what you almost did. I want to know how vulnerable you are because of all this."

"It started early in our relationship. I would leave you and go home, alone with my arousal. I would take a long bath, lose myself to my thoughts, and find some relief. But every Friday or Saturday night we said good-bye I found myself wanting more. Remember homecoming weekend, when you had to be away for your aunt's funeral? Well, I wasn't looking for trouble, but I found myself in a situation with a bunch of classmates who were drinking. It was a party for everyone who had worked on the class float. I was curious about what it would feel like to let go—to be free from my thoughts. I thought drinking would make me mindless, so to speak. Anyway, I drank, hoping to walk to the park, see the sky and stars, and really enjoy them without inhibitions or cares. What I couldn't possibly know was that being impaired opened me up like never before. My sexuality came rushing to the forefront. Well, I'm not going into the details, but I ended up alone with a guy friend who had also been drinking. Together we were both physically raging. The experience of freeing up my sexuality made my body feel so alive. It took me far, very far—but somehow I gained control of myself before it took me all the way. But that was only the beginning. Since then, I've lived with the memories of that night—the freedom, the feelings—and sometimes I find myself wishing I hadn't stopped myself. It wasn't about a relationship, because the person wasn't anyone for whom I had special feelings. But that experience, contrasted with my relationship with you, has left me feeling fragmented. Our relationship is so controlled—with no natural flow of its own. The longer we skirt the edge the more controlling it feels. Our heated moments have stirred me to want the freedom to explore my sexuality."

At last I draw a breath, relieved to have shared my truth. Gary looks as bewildered as I have ever seen him. "My God, Sue, what have we done to you? I should have somehow known you were having a difficult time. It makes sense, because we are so different. When I am left on the edge, I do not feel tormented. I feel so alive. I *like* the feel of wanting. But you are so different—a person who moves quickly through life. I should've known that putting you in a holding pattern would eventually torment and anger you. I am so pained at the thought of you going through all of this. The vulnerability you speak about is scary to me, as well. It makes sense that you would want to pull away. It has been hard not to see you as often as I would like, and I have been dreading the pain we will feel when we go in different directions soon. Remember how we said love was not enough to keep us together? As hard as it is for me to accept everything you have said, I am glad you said it."

"I am really sad, Gary. You are my prince, the one person who loves me for me. You have given me so much and taught me so much. I don't want to let you go. I am not ready to let you go. Let's not define anything. You have always said that we must not define anything, that in time it will define itself. Please," I beg him, desperate that he might end our relationship right now, "don't be conclusive."

"Sue, Sue, Sue, come here. Shhh, it will be okay." He pulls me into his arms. "Sue, my love for you is so complete; I am in no condition to end anything. I have been thinking about us a lot lately. It is strange that I have been ready to make love with you ever since that first night in Washington DC. But I was scared. I needed to understand my fear." He takes a deep breath. "I wanted to talk to you tonight about how I feel. I think I am more afraid of me than of you. I mean, I feared that making love to you might mean more to me than to you. If I felt a deeper connection and commitment and you didn't, I might be left wanting you forever. I know it would be special for you as well, but the difference is that you will let an experience be what it is, while I will long for the ideal, no matter how wonderful the experience itself may be. Strangely, though, I finally feel peaceful about it all. I have longed to make love to you, and I know we will be fine wherever it takes us. I love you, and I want what's best for you, to put you first—even if you grow away from me. No matter what happens, I will always have those moments we have shared up to now—now that making love has become a necessity for me."

I am glad to hear that Gary was ready to make love in Washington DC. I do not want him to make up his mind because of what I said tonight. I do love his honesty and sensitivity.

"Gary, let's talk about making love. There are so many ways to succumb to it. Do you want to plan it—to make it a special night? Or do you want to just let life happen and know that we are okay if it takes us?" I think about how each way would be special.

"Both ways sound wonderful. There have been times I desperately wanted to take you in the moment. It has not been easy to pull back. But I also wanted our first time to be incomparably special. What are your thoughts?"

"I like the thought of getting lost in a moment that sweeps us away, but not for my first time. I am a romantic. I would like to be ready—to create a special night by preparing everything just right. It is funny that you were ready in Washington, because I was too. I had purchased a negligee for the trip and even brought it to your room that first evening. I was ready and hoping, I guess."

"Sue, what if you spent Saturday night with me? My parents trust my judgment so much they will not ask me anything specific about the weekend when they return. You said your parents are out of town also. Well?"

"Yes, Gary. I'll make it happen. I am dying for it to happen. I want it to be special, and this may be the only opportunity we have. Yes, yes! I am so excited! But are you sure that you are ready?"

"Yes, Sue, I am really ready. I have protection; I've had it for quite some time. I'll pick you up about six PM tomorrow.

"I want tonight to end and tomorrow to fly by," I say. "I can hardly wait. I think I'd better go home now and get some things done so that I'm free the rest of the weekend to enjoy whatever happens."

"That's fine. I need to plan tomorrow out. I want it to be so special."

CHAPTER 13

The Pinnacle

I rustle through my closet, my head spinning, wondering what to wear. How should I prepare? What should I take? I've been awake for hours, trying to calm myself down. Despite my excitement, I know the first time might not match the fantasyland of my imagination, which is running wild now. What will it be like to see a man fully aroused? What will it feel like to touch him? How will it feel to have him explore me and enjoy me? These thoughts are so vivid that I can't calm down. Finally, around 3:15 AM, I fall asleep.

When I awaken and look at the clock, it is 6:13 AM. *At last the day has arrived!* My mind now works double-time thinking about my relationship with Gary. I head for Willard's department store, hoping to be there just when it opens at ten, when I see Eric coming down the sidewalk toward me.

"Hey, Sue. Where are you headed in such a hurry?"

"Oh, I have some shopping to do."

"Want to get together later? We could go across the brook and have a little fun." He winks and makes a gesture as if here were smoking.

"No," I reply, without an explanation.

"Okay. Have a good day. Good-bye."

There is no way I can forget about Gary and tonight. It felt great saying no to Eric—as if at last I'm getting beyond all of that. Tonight is so much more important than all the conflicted feelings that have been pulling at me lately. In the women's section of Willard's, looking at nightgowns, I'm amazed by how much my taste has changed since I bought the peach negligee. There it hangs on a mannequin, looking sleazy, almost perverted. I actually gasp at the thought that I ever wanted it. What would Gary have thought of me in it? How could I have changed so much in just a few days?

All afternoon, as I pack a small bag, my anticipation builds. When Mark comes through the door, all hot and sweaty from playing tennis, I have to conceal my excitement. "Hey Mark! I don't think I'll be home tonight," I tell him.

"Okay," he says. "Have a good time."

Later, Mark sees Gary pull into the driveway to pick me up. It feels awkward, but Mark tells me to have a good time and leaves. I get into the car, as excited as I have ever been.

"How are you feeling, Sue?" Gary asks. "I really want to know."

"Great! It has to rank up there at the top," I reply. "How are you feeling?"

"I am so excited, so peaceful and happy. It feels so right for us."

At his house, Gary takes my case and puts it in his bedroom. The room is beautifully lit; music is playing. "I've fixed us a little dinner," he says. "Hope you like it. It's not special, like the last time. We can eat it by the fireplace."

Gary brings in two trays, one holding vegetables, various dips, and hot cheeses, the other bread, muffins, and fruit beside a small, heated fondue pot of chocolate sauce. We dip the veggies into the cheese, the fruit into the chocolate, and we feed each other. Everything tastes delicious and the sensuality of the experience sets the stage.

After eating, we sit by the fire. "It's great that you're spending the night, Sue," Gary tells me. "Lets take tonight slowly and savor every minute. I want to enjoy every aspect of this. How do you feel?"

"Excited," I reply. "I want to experience it all. Now I can I welcome my feelings of desperation, knowing we'll eventually succumb to desire. I feel a pleasant anxiety about it all."

Gary pulls me closer to him. "I felt better after our last talk, Sue. You are right that I have controlled the moments of our intimacy. But I had to, because I wasn't ready. Tonight I want us both to have the freedom to explore and experience each other. What would you like? What is important to you?"

"Hmmm. I want many things, but they can't all be crammed into a single night. Nor am I ready for everything. Since it's our first time, I just want a sensitive exploration of each other. I don't want to create it; I just want to surrender to it and let it take us wherever it may go. I know there may be some awkwardness. I haven't even seen or touched parts of you—nor you, me. I like the thought of a hot bath together; under the auspices of washing you, I get to explore. I can't imagine that we will have to plan much after that," I say, smiling. "So, what are your thoughts about tonight?"

"Well, I like your idea a lot. Actually, I had the same thoughts. Could you give me a couple of minutes?" he says, getting up. "I'd like to prepare the bath."

I lie back, my skin peppered with goosebumps, my breathing so uneven that I must remind myself to take a breath. Gary returns and offers his hand to help me up. We go into his bedroom, which is large and beautiful. He has placed lit candles all around the room. The bedding is cream-colored and welcoming. It is picturesque—not prissy, but artistic and very romantic. Gary leads me into his private bathroom. "Want to change?"

"Sure," I say, reaching for my travel bag. "Be out in a few seconds."

When I come out of the bathroom wearing my gown, the whole house is dark. All the lights are off, and only candlelight remains. Soft romantic music is playing. Gary stands in the bedroom in a white robe. He is beaming. "You look wonderful in that gown, Sue," he says, taking my hand and slowly leading me down the hall to the master bathroom.

The master bath is beautiful. Twenty lit candles surround a marvelous sunken tub filled with a romantic and welcoming cover of rich bubbles. Steam rises into the air. Slowly, Gary slips out of his robe and stands before me, nude. He is a beautiful man. This is the first time I've seen a man nude. It is so different from pictures. Gazing up and down his magnificent torso, I have no doubt about his desire for me; his body is responding to the moment. I am stunned and lost in the vision of him.

Gary slowly slides the straps of my gown from my shoulders, and it falls to the floor. He picks it up and folds it on top of his robe.

"Oh my God, oh my God!" he exclaims. "You are so lovely," he says, more intense than I have ever before seen him.

I am speechless. I try to speak but no words come out. My breath is gone, and I gasp to stay alive. I am lost in a trance, taken by all of this. I reach up, touch his face, and slowly move my hand down his chest and torso. I am not touching him sexually, but I can't help staring at him. Finally, my voice gives way to some words. "This is wonderful," I say. "My God! Thank you."

"Shall we?" he says, gesturing to the bath. "The tub will allow us a place to relax and explore." I step into the tub and slowly glide down under the bubbles. The temperature is hot and perfect. "Sue, please sit with your back against my chest."

The bath feels wonderful, with Gary's warm body pressing against mine. He kisses my neck, and we take our time absorbing each other's presence. In complete silence, he takes a cloth and gently rubs my shoulders and back. Letting go of the cloth, he lets his hand glide against my skin. After a few minutes he pulls me tightly to him. I can feel his arousal. Then, without any words, he turns me until I am lying with my head on the back edge of the tub. Facing him, with my head relaxed, he reaches forward to wash my neck and then my breasts. Eventually he surrenders the washcloth and explores me with his hands. My body becomes more alive than I have ever imagined is possible. I feel myself thrash a bit as my body gives way to his touch. It seems as if he is the artist, and I am his canvas. Ever so slowly, he paints unbelievable sensations inside me that I have never imagined.

Gary leans back, his eyes closed, an expression of satisfaction on his face. A few minutes pass, and strength returns to my depleted body. I so wanted to explore him. Slowly, I crawl up onto him. I reach up to his face and his eyes are closed. I slowly stroke his face, aware that he is lost in the experience. We remain silent, the background sounds of water gently rippling around us and faint music is all we can hear. I continue my pleasure of discovering him. My slow journey down his body stirs him. Reflecting the artistry he has used on me, I slowly and very gently etch sensations into him. I love it when the sensations take him and he gasps and thrashes, out of control at last. When I turn and lean back into his chest, slippery in the water, he wraps his arms around me. After a few more silent moments, Gary says, "Oh, sweetie, I am so lost in you. But the tub is getting cold. We'd better get out."

We step out of the tub together, snuff out the candles, and then hurry back to the shower in his bathroom to rinse off. He towels me dry and I slip back into my nightgown. We go to his bed, where Gary takes off his robe and moves to responsibly protect us. I drop my gown and get under a light sheet. He holds me for a minute, kissing me with a level of passion I have never felt before—so intense and so sexual.

Both of our bodies are escalating. Gary moves down my body, exploring all of me. I am so lost in my body's responses to his breath, his touch, his mouth moving all over me. I feel myself opening and unfolding without any reservation. I want to explore him. I push him on his back and move down his body, exploring every inch. He is gasping and thrashing and both of us are losing control. We surrender to everything. I'm so lost and climbing, and he is, too. Our bodies are sprinting fast. As quickly as we reach one level, we continue escalating to higher levels of intensity and ecstasy. Unbelievable sensations become unleashed as the moment takes us farther and farther. Finally, reaching heights beyond all reason, we are taken over the edge. It's an unbelievable crescendo of release and so beyond anything I have ever imagined. Uncontrollable emotion and exhaustion take over. Gary falls on his back, depleted, hot, steamy, lifeless. I lie exhausted, gasping and trying to calm down.

A few minutes pass. We lie in silence, trying to come back. How can anyone ever describe what must be the greatest of all human gratifications? It cannot be put into words or expressed fully in music or art. It stands alone. Nothing can represent it; certainly nothing can compare to it. I know I will always remember the feeling as something bigger and grander than anything I have ever felt in life, something not to be tainted by impairment nor celebrated outside of a relationship of love and respect. Now that it's over, I feel so connected to Gary by an emotional, spiritual, and physical bond. I am lost in my thoughts about what happened, my memories of something I can't possibly explain. I love the fact that what we shared is outside of any thinking and beyond my ability to describe.

Gary starts to move, still out of breath, and I can barely hear him whisper, "Sue, are you okay, sweetie? Really, are you okay?"

"Sure. I am about as terrific as I believe possible. I'm thinking about how this experience is not something that I can describe."

"Let's just rest and savor all of this," he says, closing his eyes. As I lie in his arms, I see Gary so differently. He looks spent, satisfied, at peace. I watch his breathing slowly return to normal. Soon, I drift off to sleep from the exhaustion of the evening. When I awaken, it is 6:45 AM. I open my eyes and Gary is looking at me. "How long have you been awake?" I ask.

"All night. I had a wonderful time enjoying you while you slept."

Looking around the room, I see that all the candles are gone. Morning sunlight filters through the shutters. Gary pulls me to him. "I am so sorry I fell asleep," I say, "but I was exhausted."

"Shhh. No apology needed. I love watching you sleep and move about in the bed. Did you know that you smile a lot in your sleep?"

"How can I do anything but smile after making love with you? It was unbelievable!"

We let the morning take us. Making love at sunrise is just as wonderful as at sundown. Gary and I lose all concept of time, and the next thing we know it is 10:20 AM. We get up and take a hot shower together. After I help him straighten up the house, we sit on the couch for a few minutes and talk.

"Sue, I want to know if it was as wonderful as you had hoped?"

"I don't have any words that can describe it. It's much more amazing than anything I had imagined. I love you very much."

"Sue, you are wonderful. I was so emotional when we finished, so spent, yet my emotions were escalating with gratitude. I love you so much! I am always captured by firsts. I loved watching you become lost in the experience. I love you."

Gary takes me home. Everything is different now. Everything.

CHAPTER 14

Graduation

With my finals ending, I am at a most pivotal point of life. Soon, my friends, neighbors, and the world as I know it will be replaced by a new environment. But am I really a candidate for change? Although I have been looking forward to moving out of my home and into independence, I still know that I will miss my comfort zone. I have always had hopes that some day my mother will change. I am still perplexed about many things in my family. But regardless of everything, I know I will miss them terribly. I will miss Mom the most.

Mom has changed a lot in the past year. She has loosened up on some of her rules. I have seen her let go of control and allow me to make more decisions. She and I still do not have a relationship where we can talk openly about things. Little does she know how dramatically my life has changed. I wonder how Mom would react if she knew that Gary and I have become intimate. There are so many questions I would like to ask her. Like a lot of girls, I can't talk to my Mom about such things. Why should I still want to after so many years? No doubt, I still remain fascinated by what that shortcoming in our relationship means for me.

We plan for graduation, when my parents will throw a huge party for Patty, Carrie, and me. Patty is now engaged to Hale, but there are complications in the relationship. Patty has lost a tremendous amount of weight. She is so thin and looks so fragile. She has had a difficult time completing high school. Encouragement from her father and my mother, along with all the help Carrie and I gave her with her studies, has helped Patty to graduate. Thanks partly to Mother, she has been picked for the Willard's department store management training position. Mom put herself on the line to encourage Willard's to pick Patty. Had Patty's mom lived, Patty's life would be so different. They had been best friends; she would have intervened a long time ago, and Patty would not have become so thin, frail, and vulnerable.

Carrie is excited about graduating. For her, the beginning of independence means an opportunity to move out of the foster care system and take responsibility for herself. Her fears are far outweighed by her excitement. She and I promise each other that we will have the time of our lives at college. We will head there less than two weeks after graduation so that Carrie can begin her job on the college switchboard and I can start as a freshman dorm assistant.

I am still shaken by the thought of not seeing Gary on a regular basis. He has been accepted at a prestigious institute where he will study art. The distance between our campuses is hundreds of miles. The best we can hope for is to see each other on holidays. It is not going to be easy leaving him. As much as I loved him before we made love, I now find myself loving him even more. I feel transformed; I'm not the same person. I can't really define how I've changed, but I am different—very different.

In college, I'll need to define for myself the new person I'm becoming. No one will know anything about me except Carrie. Finally, I will see how I do without my family and community.

Today I am to pick up my graduation gown, I enter the kitchen to find Mom sitting at the table leafing through a magazine.

"What are you reading, Mom?" I ask, getting coffee and sitting down with her.

"There's an article about thinning out rose beds. I guess they have a root system that spreads, which makes them difficult to control."

"Who would want to control them? They're so beautiful, so why not let them grow freely? Anyway, your roses aren't out of control at all."

"It's not about the roses in the backyard. I'm thinking of the wild roses behind the church. Mr. Farland has suggested that we get rid of them because he thinks they're taking up too much room. I don't want to see them eradicated. They have meant too much to me. Mr. Farland has brought up the subject a lot lately. I thought that if I could thin them out a bit they wouldn't have to be plowed under." She seems greatly concerned.

"Have you talked to the pastor about it?"

"I haven't wanted to bother him with such a small issue. He has been so busy lately."

I know that Mom loves going to the rose garden behind the church, but until now I haven't known how much it means to her. "Well, Mom," I say, "remember: they are wild roses. No one has been able to control them yet. Maybe Mr. Farland can't destroy them even if he tries."

Mom smiles at me with a look of hope that maybe I am right.

"Don't forget to pick up your graduation gown today," she says. "Everything is set for the party. I have to get to a meeting at the community center." She grabs her purse and heads out the door.

I rinse out my cup and look through the kitchen window at all the beauty of my childhood surroundings. Soon I will miss this terribly. I decide that I want to be outside. As I walk across the park I feel a sense of aloneness. No kids are on the swings, and no one is running or playing ball, which feels strange and unusual. Obviously, today at the park is just for me. I spread out my blanket and lie down, closing my eyes, thinking about this special place where I have lived out much of my life.

The memories of the many holidays and picnics celebrated here are vivid. When I was five or six years old, my father used to push me on the swing until his arms tired. One time I cut my knee when I fell off the monkey bars; Mom had to disinfect it with horrible, burning hydrogen peroxide. I have spilled every possible emotion upon these grounds. Patty and I used to hide out here, telling each other our secrets. We would laugh so hard we'd have to hold our aching stomachs. Many, many times I came here alone to cry when I was upset. This marvelous place holds so much of my life—the times I lay with the sun shining upon me and all the nights I spent looking into the stars. When I was little I used to tell Mom that the sky was salting me. I told her the stars were salt coming down to season me. Later, the stars became mysterious and I lay under them thinking about life and God. More recently, the stars have become a romantic backdrop to many evenings of lying under them with Gary.

Many people say their childhood home holds most of life's memories. This is not true for me; they are here in this park where I grew up. I sit up and gaze at the brook, the sight of which is almost overwhelming. When I was a child, the brook had seemed as huge as an ocean that I hoped to someday cross. I had spent hours imagining the trees and terrain on the other side of the brook, pretending that the other side was my island, and hoping eventually to figure out how I could take refuge there. The far side of the brook could represent a better place, somewhere to go when life was hurtful. Other times I had pretended it was an evil place, and I felt thankful that I was safe on my own side. Most of the time it was a mystery, a place I expected to someday explore. As a child, the far side of the brook had power over me because it stirred my curiosity and tantalized my imagination.

Today, I remember all of this, but the brook seems much smaller. Although I am older, I can still feel its pull. This park, the brook, and the woods on the other side are perfect symbols to describe my life. I know every nook and cranny of the soil I'm sitting on. I know the bit of a bump on the ground two feet to my left that makes it uncomfortable to lie down. I also know every place where wild daisies grow in clusters every spring. I know the best place to sit, my spot, with its perfect view across the brook, where I can lie back and look up with no trees blocking the sky.

Gary and I had come here on our first date and many more dates as well. We would lie on our backs, look at the stars, and talk. It's also the place where Eric and I came the night I first felt the effects of alcohol, when my impairment unleashed my raw edges. As I look into the woods across the water, I find myself excited about the life experiences I am about to embark upon. The brook and the other side represent life's mysteries that tug and tease me, an unknown that has always made me feel alive. I take a deep breath and stretch, feeling excited and overwhelmed. The events, feelings, and experiences I associate with this park make it the most important place in my life.

I fold up my blanket and head across the park. There, leaning against a tree, watching me, is Eric.

"Hey, Toots," he calls out, "what you're up to?"

Eric has caught me off guard, as I have just been thinking about him. "Nothing. Just waiting until afternoon to go get my graduation gown. What are you doing today?"

"Not much. Helped Mike Nichols pull a transmission this morning. So have you been over to the woods on the other side lately?"

"No. I've only been there that one time with you."

"Well, I was over there last week, and not that I'm a nature lover or anything, but there were some flowers popping up all over, and I thought about you. Actually, I think about you a lot. I guess it's because of that one night."

Thinking about what he's saying, it's apparent he's been kind of pursuing me. I want to deal with this, so I decide it is time we talk.

"Gosh, Eric, you used to pass me a thousand times throughout the years and never spoke to me. Then after one night of drinking by some chance I ended up with you. What is it about that night that has opened you up to being so friendly with me now?"

Eric seems stunned by my directness.

"Gosh, I didn't know I was so rude before. See, you were always someone I admired. You were like this innocent girl who was smart and kind. I have dated tons of girls—actually, I'm not bad-looking, and I've had the fortune of having most girls pursue me. I've had a lot of opportunities and have enjoyed many of the ladies completely, if you know what I mean. But that night was different. When I found myself with you—it was so strange—my first thought was protecting you. I'm a man who generally takes advantage of opportunities, so that is not like me; personal satisfaction is indeed my goal, if you know what I mean. Anyway, I did not want to take advantage of you. Damn! It was the first time I ever felt like that. What's even more amazing was that I have never wanted anyone as much as I wanted you." He looks down and seems surprised by his own honesty.

"Thanks for sharing that with me, Eric. How can I help but feel anything other than special after that," I say, not expecting such a confession. "I am so thankful you took such good care of me that night. I believe we all have special, life-altering moments, and that night will always be one of mine. I shudder to think of what might have happened instead. I had no idea that my sexuality would come rushing to the forefront. The really neat thing is that because of you that night remains a good memory, not a tragedy. If it had been anyone but you, it might've been a nightmare that I would have to live with. Instead, I look back on it as the awakening of my sexuality, so I have no regrets about it. I am glad that it ended when it did because my sexuality is tied to more than my body."

Eric has been sitting and listening attentively. "You are so neat to listen to! You really think things out. That night is still so alive inside me. I've had a lot of encounters in my lifetime. Hell, I've had a lot of encounters since that night. Not much lives on inside my old brain, but that night, that one damned night, is so unforgettable. I remember how you smelled, how you felt, the silkiness of your skin. God, Sue! It's still a powerful memory."

Eric seems so lost in recounting that night. I feel sad that he has such an attraction to me. I can't tell him that the importance of the night for me has nothing to do with him as a person. I have expressed my appreciation for his caring for me and for his restraint, but I am now way beyond what happened between us. I am deeply in love with Gary, and our experiences are far beyond anything Eric could possibly understand.

"Well, Eric," I say, "thanks for opening up with me. See? Even a rough old calculated soul like yours has a big piece of puffiness to it. I want you to find someone who's special and not wrapped up in her own moment of self-exploration, as I was that night. You deserve someone great. Well, I'd better get going. I'll be leaving for college in a couple of weeks. Mom said she sent you an invitation to the graduation party. Please come."

"Sure," he replies, "I'll try to make it. But a guy like me has to leave things open. Can't tie myself down with commitments. You take care now. Bye."

Walking away, I feel horrible. As painful as it was to dismiss his feelings, he needed to know I'm not a candidate for anything more than friendship. I am flattered by his being so drawn to me. Putting it into perspective, I feel sad that the relationship we had, such as it was, is over. Something about Eric still lies dormant inside me.

Gary arrives, and after we go pick up our gowns, we head back to my favorite spot in the park. I ask him about his feelings about graduation.

"I'm glad to be moving on. However, when my life is over, the highlight will not be high school graduation. I think maybe that one night with you will rank up there in first place," he teases. "I'm still coming down from that night. I may never get over it; actually, I hope I never do. It means everything to me. I feel so connected to you. I know you'll be leaving in a few weeks..." he says, looking down, almost broken.

"I don't want it to be hard for you," I say. "We can write and call from time to time. I'm scared about it, too. I started thinking about leaving home today. I don't think I'll really know how much everything means to me until I'm away. But I hope leaving you doesn't hurt more than I anticipate. It's already unbearable."

"Come here, Sue. Let me hold you. I found out that making love to you connected us more. That night has left me wanting you so. I never expected it would stir me up as it has," he explains.

"I think about it too," I reply. "I am different somehow, as if that night has calmed me down. I don't feel desperate or vulnerable, but more complete and whole. I'm no longer panting and wondering what it would be like. That's not to say I don't wish for more. I wish we could make love now. I do love you."

I can tell Gary wants me. He is kissing my neck in a rather feverish way. It is sexual and wanting. I can hear his breathing pattern change. Finally, he pulls away and falls back onto the grass.

"Oh my God! I could get so lost in you. Is there anywhere we could go tonight to enjoy each other?" he asks with desperation.

"Oh, I would love to, but I can't because my grandmother is coming to visit. I have an idea! Why don't you come to dinner? Afterward we can go out for a ride. It won't be everything, but then again, we could enjoy each other."

"Are you sure your mom won't mind me coming to dinner?"

"Yes. She's told me over and over to feel free to invite you. She cooks a lot in case we have last-minute dinner guests. In the past I've brought Carrie or Patty home at the last minute."

"Great! I'll take you home now, and I'll be over later."

Gary drops me off. Grandma and Dad have returned, and Grandma is lying down.

"Hey Daddy, tired from that long drive?"

"Yep, but I am so glad your grandma will be with us for a few days. She is looking forward to your graduation. What have you been up to?"

"Oh, just enjoying the sunshine at the park and spending some time with Gary."

"How are you going to handle being away from him? The two of you are pretty close now."

"It's going to be difficult, but we can do it."

"I have no doubt that you will get through it."

After dinner Gary and I go for a drive to be alone. I recommend we take the Old Mackenzie Drive that overlooks town. We have never been parking. Turning the car lights off, Gary pulls me to him. It feels icky—sleazy, not romantic, and not right.

"Gary, I don't like how this feels. I only like cars for one thing: transportation. It feels awful in here. This is not how I picture you and me ever making love…this isn't us. I don't like it." I sit up and move back to my side.

My words surprise myself because I have fantasized about being sexually wild in a car. Yet I never envisioned it to be Gary; he isn't like that. He is about beauty, art, and poetry, and now he is my first experience. I find myself not wanting to do anything that would tarnish the memories of that one magical night.

"You're right. I hate the thought of being in a car, hiding in this wooded area. I don't want this either."

We drive in silence to the park, both of us thinking. Walking across the park feels natural and wonderful.

"Sue, can we plan one more special night before you leave?"

"As much as I want to, I can't think of any night when mom and dad are away. After graduation I have only days before I go to college."

"I know the time is quickly going by. As much as I want to make love, we will always have that one very special night," he says.

Resting and gazing at the stars, he's thinking hard. Obviously making love has taken him deeper, leaving him wanting me even more. To him it feels like his wife is about to leave him. I feel very different: peaceful, finally free from my raging curiosity about what it's like to make love. I no longer feel desperate. The beauty of that one night brought it all together. I feel completed in every sense of the word. As much as I love Gary, I am preoccupied with the excitement of graduating and going off to college. Now that one great mystery of life has been solved, I'm ready to move on to other life experiences.

"Gary, are you okay? How insensitive have I been? The night before we made love I was having a difficult time dealing with our controlled intimacy. I remember telling you how angry and vulnerable it left me at the end of each date. Thinking back, I recall you being concerned, but eventually you said you were ready to make love to me. My God, only now do I realize you sacrificed yourself and your beliefs. You gave what you considered the ultimate gift between two people. I think you put me first because of your concern for me."

"Sue, come here." Pulling me into his arms, he continues. "I love you more than you know. Making love with you was necessary. It was the right thing to do. I knew it that night, and I have not changed my mind. I have no regrets, only awesome memories. Yes, you are right that I believe that making love is about commitment, a union, a lifetime together. That was the me before I grew in love with you. Real love transforms me beyond my idealism."

I tremble as he speaks, trying to get control of myself.

"Please calm down, Sue. Let me explain it to you. Everyone has ideas about love. Mine were very idealistic, perfect, and unreal. My love for you forces me to be more realistic. It opens me up, and slowly my ideas are not as important as understanding and loving you. Love is not a 'me' word. When it happens the 'me' part no longer exists; all I want is to be there for you, to love you, to care for you. Eventually the wide-eyed dreamer in me has to wake up and realize that love is about putting the other person first. Look at you. Right now you are pained at the thought of me being sad, and you want to do something about it. You have abandoned yourself to take my sadness on. That's love. Sue, making love to you was not a rash decision. I'd been thinking about it for a long time. Remember the night before we made love, when you gave me your honesty? I didn't like it that you were so angry and vulnerable. I felt responsible. I failed to realize that I had controlled you by controlling me. The one thing I knew for certain was that I wanted you to have your first experience with me. I am someone who loves you. I will treasure that moment for the rest of my life and will never forget the first time you gave yourself completely to me. Listen, please, please listen. On that night I was ready to give you whatever you wanted—whether it be a lifetime or just that one unbelievable night. I've always told you that whatever I receive in life is *always enough*. That does not mean I wouldn't like it to be more, but my parents taught me to have a deep sense of gratitude. I'm excited for you and your journey in life. Your happiness, joy, and peace are essential to me. I'm fine, Sue. I like the fact that I'm going to miss you. Those feelings could not exist if I didn't love you so."

I'm in shock. I can't remember feeling so loved by anyone. Yet I feel guilty. Although I love Gary, my love is not equal to his love for me. I don't know how I feel about sacrificing one's self for the sake of another. I'm not able to disregard myself or my dreams for his sake. But it's clear, too, that he does not require me to be like him.

"Gary, I don't know what to say. I have never felt so loved. I love you. I will also always treasure and never forget what you said about our first experience of making love."

Gary is holding me tight. The breeze is caressing us under the stars. We are at peace and emotionally exhausted. After a period of silence under the stars, he speaks.

"Just think, Sue. When you feel lonely, all you have to do is lie under stars. It will be like I'm there with you. I'll be looking at the same stars, and they will keep us connected."

I take in his words, knowing I will recall them another time.

"Well, it's late, and I better get home soon."

Gary pulls me to him and gently kisses me. After a few special minutes of unbelievable closeness he takes me home.

The morning of graduation day finally arrives. Lying in bed, I hear my parents and grandmother downstairs in the kitchen. Walking through the living room, I noticed how perfect everything is for the party. "Good morning everyone," I say, beaming.

"Sue, today's the day! Did you sleep alright?" Grandma asks.

"Okay, sort of. I was kind of too excited to sleep well."

"I wonder why the Walthams aren't throwing Gary a party." she says, looking puzzled.

"Gary's been a loner and not that social with anyone. They asked me to come for dinner tomorrow night to celebrate our graduation. I can take his present then."

The rest of the morning goes by quickly. The doorbell heralds Gary's arrival, and I leap from my chair to greet him. "I'll see all of you at graduation…got to run." Mom rushes from the kitchen to wish us well. Driving to the school, Gary reaches over and takes my hand. His warmth and gentleness help me relax. As we line up for practice, I look across the auditorium at Gary, and he winks. He alters everything about me with his smile, touch, or the infamous wink. I remember him telling me that he never used to wink before he met me.

We relax in a classroom, waiting for parents and guests to arrive. Finally our moment to move out into the auditorium arrives. The graduation march starts, and the first students take their place leading the rest of us in. Gary and I meet at the back and march together. Overtly I take his hand. I don't care what others think; it's not about them.

The ceremony is filled with great music. The governor delivers an uplifting message of courage. Superintendent Hobart goes to the podium to announce the recipient of the Douglas Farlington Scholarship. He clears his throat and begins:

> *This recipient is a student who has always achieved high grades. She not only works hard academically, but she participates in every school charitable event. She did all that while working at the Bella Reed Senior Home. She has taken on many odd jobs throughout the community to save for college. She is not as priv-ileged as most of her classmates; she has never had the security of a home or a family. As a matter of fact, she has been shifted to three different foster homes while attending our school. Her teachers have been moved by her determina-tion to prepare herself for college. She maintains excellence in her studies while facing obstacles in life that most of us can't imagine. This is the first time since the inception of this scholarship twenty-five years ago, that both the faculty and community committees reached a unanimous decision to award the Dou-glas Farlington Scholarship to Carrie Ann Dougherty.*

Our class rises to its feet applauding, and I am so proud of her. I can tell she's stunned. She never expected to receive a scholarship. Crossing the plat-form to receive her award, she is emotional. Mr. Hobart hands it to her and asks her if she wants to say anything. Wiping her eyes, she steps to the micro-phone:

> *I want to thank the faculty and committee that chose me. I know there were others who deserved it just as much as I did. When you grow up in the foster care system you can survive if you learn to be grateful. You always know that you're just one of 'those' kids, and in time you surrender the hope of ever feeling very special. I never imagined that someday there would be a moment such as this when I would be acknowledged for my own merits. Today, right now for*

the first time, I finally feel special. It feels remarkable. Thank you for giving me this honor.

Everyone rises, giving Carrie a standing ovation. Tears running down my cheeks, I hug Gary. I can't wait to hug her after the ceremony. I see my mom wiping her eyes. It feels unbelievable that a room of students and community are saluting a girl who for the most part went unnoticed. I'm so happy for Carrie.

Finally it's time to receive our diplomas. As the students cross the platform, they move their tassel from one side to the other. My name is read: "Susan Elizabeth Martin." As I walk across the platform, I look for my family and see Mom brush the edge of her eye. I can't recall a time that she has shown emotion over me. I look back quickly as I shake the superintendent's hand and take my diploma. As we march out of the auditorium for the last time I'm filled with one thought: now my life begins.

It's fun welcoming people to the party, and Mom and Dad are gracious hosts, directing the guests to food and punch. Patty, Carrie, and I move about the room talking to everyone. People rush to congratulate Carrie on her scholarship. Greeting family, students, teachers, and neighbors, I'm on automatic pilot, moving quickly from person to person—until I see Eric standing in a corner. Immediately, I make my way to him with a glass of punch.

"Here's some really good stuff," I say, laughing at the thought of him drinking punch. "Wow, you sure know a lot of people. I am glad I get to see you for a minute. I want to wish you the best and everything. I got to get going."

"Sure, Eric, thanks for coming by." I give him a hug before he goes.

Just as he leaves, Gary comes in, and I rush over to greet him. I take his hand and am now dragging him through people. Hale finally arrives and joins Patty. It's a lovely party. After three hours of socializing, we open the gifts. We receive many lovely cards and presents. I especially like the special notes people write. One unsigned envelope I open has a homemade ticket that reads "One Ticket: For a Ride to the Other Side." I know who it must be from. I am the only one who understood Eric's little joke, and it made me smile. Eventually everyone leaves, including Gary. Patty, Carrie, and I put on our pajamas and spend the rest of the night laughing and recalling our school years.

The next day, Patty and Carrie leave early. I help rearrange our home back to normal. Dad takes Grandma home and Mom finally relaxes with a cup of coffee.

"Mom, thanks for the best graduation party."

"I am glad you enjoyed it," she says, not looking up from her newspaper. Her postures never leave room for me to share my heartfelt appreciation. She walls herself off so fast, as if using the newspaper to shield her. I go to my room, put away the piles of gifts, and spend the rest of the day writing thank-you cards.

That evening Gary picks me up for dinner at his house. As I get inside the car, I'm overcome with a desire to kiss him. When he turns his head to back out of the driveway, I shout "Stop!" He hits the brakes, and I lean over and kiss him really passionately. I can tell he is caught off guard.

"Gosh, you could give a man a heart attack with a kiss like that," he smiles. I don't respond, letting the kiss speak for itself.

Before dinner we chat about the graduation ceremony. Gary and I exchange graduation gifts. I give him a paperweight with our picture in it. He really loves it. He gives me a new charm for my bracelet—"1st." I certainly don't have to ask what it symbolizes. Gary always buys me charms that are symbols of great moment. After a lovely dinner with the Walthams we go to the family room, where Mrs. Waltham plays the piano. Afterwards, she passes out flutes of imported juice and Mr. Waltham offers a toast.

"To Gary and Sue, two people who love each other enough that they are able to step back and watch the other soar. Congratulations not only on graduating, but, more importantly, on becoming two very wonderful individuals."

The sincerity of the toast is deeper than its words. Everything they say is sincere, every word always heartfelt and honest. Mr. Waltham says they will always be there for us, and I know it is true. Mrs. Waltham offers her toast.

"To each of you. Open yourselves up to this wonderful world. There are many ways to grow. I wish you the medium that best takes you deeper into your understanding of yourself and life."

Another beautiful toast. The words remind me how much I love being in their home. Not one breath goes unnoticed. In my home it is hard to get anyone to listen; everyone is wrapped up in their own thoughts or projects—including me. The Walthams are different. Tears fill my eyes. It's ironic that although I'm looking forward to leaving my home, I'm terribly sad at the thought of leaving them.

"It is so important for me to tell you what you mean to me." I say. "I will miss you both so much. Your home has been such a place of joy for me—a place of love, sensitivity, and kindness. All three of you live your lives with such passion and goodness. Thank you for being so nice and for letting me be a part of it. I am looking forward to the excitement of new experiences. It will be hard without Gary. I do love your son. I don't know what that will mean for us, but I know it is true. I am so fortunate for everything. Thank you."

Mrs. Waltham gets up and hugs me. Mr. Waltham follows, affectionately kissing me on the forehead like a father. Both of them wish me well and leave Gary and me alone.

Gary and I go to the back yard and lay in the big hammock swing. It's wonderful being so close. The stars pepper the night sky. The crickets are chirping, and the fireflies—their magical, minuscule lights going off all over—spread around us like pixie dust. This feels like heaven. As we quietly lay in each other's arms, my chest fills up with sadness at the loss of such moments with Gary. I start to cry, and he pulls me to him. Softly he whispers in my ear, "It's okay to cry." Together in the most tender way, we hold each other.

We move past our emotions and regain our composure, but remain silent. The moment is one of the most powerful times we have felt, when the beauty of our love and trust for each other are strong enough that we can be real. As the night grows chilly, Gary reaches down, takes a blanket from a basket, and covers us. We never share any words; we don't need to. I feel safe. My exhausted body grows limp, and I fall asleep in his arms.

We wake the next morning at sunrise. It feels wonderful waking up in his arms, although we didn't plan for it to happen. It is like a gift from God, a moment I never could have dreamed could be so perfect and wonderful. We kiss each other, and then I suggest I call my mom to let her know what happened and to explain that I will be home soon.

As we enter the kitchen, Mr. and Mrs. Waltham are having breakfast.

"So you two decided to wake up, did you?" Mrs. Waltham teases. "We got home about eleven and saw you asleep. It looked so special and wonderful that I called your mom and told her you had fallen asleep. I asked her if it would be okay to let you sleep until morning. Your mother said yes and thanked me for calling."

Gary's parents are extraordinary people who see the innocent beauty of our night together and didn't read more into it than what it was. Rather than disturbing us, Mrs. Waltham took it upon herself to call my mother for me. I could tell she wanted us to have the memory of one of our last nights together.

We eat breakfast and Gary takes me home. Busy in the kitchen, Mom seems fine and says little about it. All in all, my graduation week is wonderful—full of nostalgia as this period of my life comes to a close.

CHAPTER 15

Transition to College

The evening before Carrie and I leave for college has come, and Dad has been packing the station wagon all day. I'm feeling anxious about leaving home, yet filled with excitement. I'll miss Patty and worry about her. I spend a lot time with her the week before I go, but our time together is interrupted every time Hale shows up, reminding me that things change, people change. Life brings people to us, and then we grow in different directions.

Gary and I have spent a few hours together every day all week but find no opportunities to make love. We talk about making every effort to see each other, but the promise feels like a Band-Aid, just something to cover the wound until the pain goes away. It's not the end of our relationship, yet we can't know what will happen. Our lives will be drastically altered when daily conversations are impossible. Tonight I see him one more time.

As the sun starts to go down, I hear the doorbell ring. I hear my father talking to Gary.

"You are always welcome here. Don't forget us, because we promise we aren't going to forget you," he tells Gary.

Gary takes my hand and we head for the park. Every moment seems so heavy. What should I say? How should I express my love for him when I have no idea if my love can sustain the distance and time? My heart feels like it's being ripped out of me. How can I leave him? I can hardly breathe as we sit. Looking directly at him instead of the sunset, I want to remember every little detail in his face. He's looking back intensely. Neither of us says a word. We absorb all we can of one another before the light from the sun fades into the earth.

Our emotions too large for words, we keep silent. Words are too empty to offer comfort to this kind of sadness. We must trust God for whatever will be. Lying in his arms, I must come to terms with saying "So long." I won't say good-bye—that feels too final. But I can barely speak at all. Finally I say the only thing I know to be true: "I love you."

"I love you too, Sue."

He's kissing me, and we hold each other tightly. After fifteen minutes we roll on our backs and stare into the sky.

"Let's look at our connection, Sue. See that one star, centered just below the Big Dipper?"

"Yes. Yes, I see it."

"Okay, that's our star. If you ever want to feel my love, just go out and look at it. There's always a possibility that I will be looking at it at that moment too."

"Yes, it will be our love reflecting back."

"May I touch you? I want to touch you so much."

"Yes, please, I want to touch you as well."

Gary pulls me to him and slowly touches my face. His hand gently moves about me. I'm so alive with every touch. Slowly I roll him over on his back. Even though there can't be a moment when we could soar, we love feeling the raging desires inside of us. All of this is a reminder of how alive we are with each other. Gently I roll off him and relax in his arms. Together we lay there for some time, allowing ourselves to slowly return to the reality of the moment.

"Gary, it's getting late, and I've to go. Mom reminded me to be home early since we will be leaving before sunup."

"I know," he says, helping me off the ground. "Sue, we have much to be grateful for. Let our last kiss end with smiles: no more tears, just the best wishes for each other. How's that?"

"Absolutely perfect."

I fear a prolonged silence would reveal I was collapsing inside. He walks me to the door and pulls me into the light from the porch.

"Thanks, Sue. I wish you the very best of everything. Never, ever forget I love you." He kisses me one last time.

I look back at him, determined not to blink, but holding back tears. I force a smile. "Thank you for everything. You are in my heart, and I love you."

Quickly we turn away from each other. He walks away as I go inside and collapse on my bed.

Mom wakes me at 5:30 AM. I'm still dressed in my clothes from the night before. Quickly I shower, and we leave. At Bella's place, Carrie is waiting at the front door. Bella hugs her and wishes her the best. It's strange seeing their good-bye. No "I'll see you at Thanksgiving" or "Call me..."—just a final-seeming closure. It is obvious that Carrie is used to it. She is now on her own, and her smile speaks volumes.

Driving away, I look back at my house one last time. When we pass the park, my eyes flood with tears as I think about the night before. I try to remember Gary's smile. Surely that will help.

"Hey, do you know what our dorm looks like?" Carrie asks.

"Yeah, we are going into a really nice dorm on the east side. It is a little far from classes, but it sits upon a hill that overlooks a little stream."

When we arrive, Carrie and I rush to the front desk and get the keys to our room. Our new home is very humble, but nonetheless it's all ours.

As Dad makes trips back and forth from the car unloading things, Mom helps us unpack and organize the room. Suddenly Dad comes through the door with two guys helping him.

"Hello, I am David Mitchell, and this Keith Saunderland. We're sopho-mores. Welcome to Broctren Harbor College."

"I am Sue Martin and this is Carrie Dougherty."

"Gosh, guys, thanks for rescuing me," laughs Dad. "I almost dropped that refrigerator as I pulled it out of the back of the wagon."

"Nice meeting you," Keith says. "If you have any questions, here's our phone number. We live in Langton Hall. Don't hesitate to call," he adds, smiling at Carrie as they leave the room.

When Mom and Dad finish helping us set things up, Dad sighs. "Well Eliza-beth, we better get back on the road. It's a long drive home." Dad puts his arms around me. "Sue, call us weekly, or any other time. If you need anything, let us know. We love you and will miss you. Have fun, but don't let fun get in the way of studying. Remember, I love you," he says as he kisses me.

Mom tells Carrie our home is now her home. Then she comes over to hug me. "Don't forget me. I will always love you," she whispers. I hear these unprecedented words, but for some reason I don't respond. Carrie and I walk them to the car and watch them drive off.

We rush back to our room, excited. We make our beds, put our clothes away, and decorate our walls. Carrie hangs a special poem she loves. I hang a van Gogh reprint that Gary gave me and place a picture of Gary on my desk.

Carrie notices me do so. "It must have been hard leaving Gary."

"It was hard and still is, but I can't allow myself to stay in my sadness. On second thought, maybe I'll put this picture in the drawer for right now. It keeps me too connected to the sadness."

After everything is in place, we lie on our beds and go through our packets of information. Carrie decides to visit her supervisor and set up her training schedule for the campus switchboard. I head off to the dean of students' office to get my training schedule.

The campus is gorgeous: rich, green lawns edged in flowers, old buildings with years of ivy growing up them, majestic, large oak and maple trees everywhere. As beautiful as it is, I feel out of place walking across campus. Students rush from class to class, all of them looking so engaged in campus life. At the dean's office, I don't see his secretary, but his office door is open. He looks up.

"Can I help you?"

"Yes, I am Sue Martin, a freshman and soon-to-be dorm assistant. I'm here to get my training schedule."

"Welcome Sue, come on in. You are going to love Broctren Harbor College. Please have a seat. I have the schedule right here. I am the dean of students, John Morrow. I have been dean of students at Broctren Harbor College for two years, after having moved here from Austin, Texas, where I was born and raised. Now tell me about yourself."

"Well, I am from Beckenburg, Ohio, a small town on the eastern side."

"Well, Sue, this is a special place: nice people and one heck of a faculty." Just then someone knocks on his door. "Excuse me for a second."

He steps out, and quickly I gaze around his office. On his desk is a picture of a very pretty little girl. Behind his desk are many plaques describing various awards and accomplishments. One reads "State of Illinois, Dean of the Year."

Returning to his chair, he settles back in. "So, what do you plan on majoring in? Do you have any career goals set yet?"

"No, I'm leaning toward social work, but I am not sure. My high school counselor encouraged me to relax and said in time I would know what I wanted to major in."

"That is so true, but for some reason I bet you are the type of individual who likes to know exactly where you stand at all times so you can keep pushing yourself. Am I right?"

"Wow, how did you guess? I love pondering the unknown, but only from a fairly comfortable position. Right now I am out of my comfort zone. At least I am here with a friend who is also a freshman. It is nice to be sharing a room with her."

"Oh, that's great. What's her name?"

"Carrie Dougherty. We have been friends for years."

"Well, please ask her to stop by and introduce herself. I try to get to know as many students as I can. That's one of the nice things about being on a small campus. I know that adjustment away from home can be difficult, but I am here to help."

I leave Dean Morrow's office feeling good. In some ways he already feels like an old friend—someone I can turn to. I explore campus, looking around the bookstore and then coming upon the campus church—a huge place compared to the little country church I was raised in. On my way back to the dorm I run into Carrie."

"Sue, this place is amazing. I stopped by the registrar's office, and my scholarship has been posted to my account. It looks like I might not have to take out any loans my first year!"

"That's great, Carrie."

"I am so excited. I have an idea. In forty-five minutes we can go to the dining room and have dinner. Tonight let's hang out at the student center. Let's get to know a few students. This might be the only time we are free from studying. Working this summer was a great idea; we can have fun and work. We only have two weeks before classes begin."

Carrie is bursting with an enthusiasm that I have never seen in her before. In the past, she always had to live someone else's agenda. She now owns the right to live her life.

We can hardly contain our exuberance as we enter the cafeteria. The food selection is great, and when we find a table with three girls we ask if we can join them.

"Please sit. Welcome. My name is Lea. This is Sarah and Michelle."

"Thanks, I'm Carrie."

"I'm Sue. This is our first meal here."

We enjoy the conversation that develops. They talk about faculty and staff, share stories about professors, and go over a few rules, curfew times, and repercussions for missing classes. Our first dinner leaves Carrie and I feeling like we have already made some friends. We head off to the student center, where Carrie sees a sign reading, "Poetry Exchange Tonight." I encourage her to go.

Later, as I leave the center, I notice clouds moving across the darkening skies. I sit on a bench and look upward. Through the clouds I can clearly see the Big Dipper. Below it lies one shining star—our star. It's powerful, it's bright, and it makes me feel close to Gary. Closing my eyes and resting, I feel a tear running down the side of my cheek.

"Sue, are you okay?"

Startled, I open my eyes to find Keith Saunderland, one of the students who helped dad move our refrigerator. I try to regain my composure.

"Oh, hi Keith," I say, hoping I remembered his name correctly.

"Sue, I see you're sad. Sorry for intruding. Are you okay?"

"I will be in time. Just those first day adjustments," I say.

"It's understandable. I had a difficult time adjusting at first, but that quickly changes as you make friends and get into the pulse of college life. I am rather shy, as a matter of fact. If David hadn't gotten me involved with helping your dad, I probably wouldn't have met you. Let me be your first friend. It would make me feel good. How about it?" he says.

"Thanks. That would be nice," I say.

"Let's get a soda at the snack bar," he offers.

"Sure, lets go," I respond, walking beside him.

I enjoy talking to Keith. He is nice, and it is easy to see his shyness, but I admire how he forces himself to open up and share. I feel comfortable with him. After we talk a while, I return to my room, where Carrie is already ready for bed.

"Where have you been?" she laughs, playing the mother hen.

I explain what happened and how Keith came by.

"Wow, Sue, you already have a new friend on your first day. You have got to teach me how to do it," she teases. Then she tells me how much she enjoyed the poetry exchange.

The rest of the week I am swamped with my training program and meet many students. I become friends with Sherry McClain, a freshman in Wade Hall. She and I are so much alike: deep, over-thinkers, risk takers who are curious about everything. Sherry comes from an upper class home. Her father is the mayor of Burlington, Missouri, where she was raised. She is flying high now that she is free to explore life. I find myself feasting off her excitement and energy. Carrie works shifts on the college switchboard. Exhausted by the first weekend, we decide to sleep in on Saturday morning and skip breakfast.

The second week is even more fun. All of the new dorm assistants spend a day working individually with the dean of students, dean of academic affairs, dean of women, dean of men, and the chaplain. I am assigned the first day to work with the chaplain, Reverend Raymond Ayer, who appears very young for a pastor. I arrive at his office early, and he goes over his schedule with me. I am to shadow his day and understand his duties to gain insight into his role. First, there's a prayer service at Langton Hall, the men's dorm. David Mitchell later teases me that on that day guys held back on prayer requests for dates because I was there. Next Reverend Ayer teaches a religion course on Old Testament history. During lunch, Reverend Ayer asks about my spiritual needs. His warmth opens me up, and before I know it I am pouring my heart out about my spiritual struggles. After lunch I attend the Faculty Governing Board meeting. Finally, my day is complete.

The next day I am assigned to the dean of students, Dr. John Morrow. We start out by chatting over coffee and doughnuts, and he openly shares details of his life. He's a single dad of six-year-old Katie. His wife had been killed in a car accident two years earlier. Over the morning I spend with him, he responds to at least twenty-five calls from students. His responsibilities encompass so many areas of student life. In between calls, he and I talk. He asks personal questions about my family, dating, and my philosophies on everything. We laugh a lot, and I find myself intrigued by everything about him. In the afternoon, we attend the Dorm Advisory Council, a committee that handles nonacademic student discipline problems. At the end of the day, I feel like Dr. Morrow and I have become close friends.

The third day I spend with the dean of academic affairs, Dr. Willard Snow. His entire day is spent in various academic meetings. At the end of the day we talk about my academic plans, and he offers some suggestions.

The fourth day is fun. I shadow the Dean of Men, Dr. Samuel Lowe. We meet with the men's dorm advisors to review dorm issues. The big issue of the day turns out to be a few guys in Langton Hall who are harboring a fugitive dog. No dog has been produced, but campus security has been hearing barking from indoors every night. None of the guys owns up to it. Dr. Lowe is a rather intense individual who feels compelled to find the dog and dismiss the responsible student. All in all it is interesting.

The final day of the week I spend with the Dean of Women, Dr. Sarah McBride. I am intimidated from the moment we meet. She is much older than the other faculty. She has been in this position for thirty-one years and speaks quite gruffly. As I enter her office, she is quick to set the tone. "Well, let's get going. We don't have the time for idle chitchat. I am Dr. McBride, and I take it you are Susan Martin."

One of the first things she does that day is confront a female student about her clothing. According to Dr. McBride, the student has worn a sweater that is too tight and a skirt that is too short. Next, I attend a meeting where she is quick to criticize Dr. Lowe for being too easy on the male students, allowing them too much freedom in the dorms at night. Apparently, they are noisier than she feels is reasonable. We return to her office, where she does dictation and makes phone calls, the whole time acting as if I am not present. She never asks anything about me but is cold and distant with everyone. I can't understand how she can be the Dean of Women.

She dismisses me for lunch and tells me to be back at one o'clock. I go to the dining room to eat with Carrie.

"Are you still having fun?" Carrie asks.

Laughing, I tell her how cold and intimidating Dr. McBride is. "I am going to crack that shell around her if it's the last thing I do while I am here at Broctren Harbor," I add.

As the afternoon progresses, I sit in her office while she continues to write letters. It is easy to understand why her waiting room is empty. She calls people to her; it appears that no one comes into her office willingly.

"Okay, you can go. I hope you learned something today—especially what *not* to do while you are a student. Good-bye."

I suppose anyone in my position would run off, thankful that the day is over. But I refuse to be comforted at being dismissed. Slowly, I walk to her desk, taking her by surprise. "Thank you for allowing me the privilege of spending a day with you," I say. "Spending time with the faculty has been great, but I enjoyed today the most. Thank you so much." Smiling, I turn and walk out, feeling her stare boring through me.

Walking back to the dorm, I find myself feeling challenged by her. I'm curious about who she is. How can anyone be a dean for so long with a personality like that? Maybe she has changed throughout the years. Maybe life dealt her some kind of trauma. Or, maybe something is going on just today that has left her cold. She is definitely a mystery I want to solve, a fascination perhaps connected with my many years of longing to be close to my mom. I know that Mom's cold nature doesn't represents the truth about her. Here again, in an even more extreme example of the same phenomenon, is Dean McBride.

At dinner, as I'm telling Carrie about my thoughts regarding Dr. McBride, two students sit down next to us. One of them is the student whom Dr. McBride confronted.

"Hi Sue, do you care if we join you?" she asks. Her name is Lynn Brock.

"Not at all, please have a seat."

"Sue, am I dressed okay for dinner?" Lynn asks me, laughing.

"You look perfect," I say, laughing back.

Lynn introduces herself to Carrie and then says, "I can't help but want to eat with Sue because she was in my session today with Dr. McBride, who chastised me for what she said was outrageous clothing." She laughs again, adding, "Everyone knows that Dean McBride is cold and heartless."

"Does anyone know why she's that way?"

"Once, during alumni weekend, Amy Rannier, a graduate of Broctren Harbor College fifteen years ago was visiting the gals in our dorm. We were asking her questions about everything, and someone asked about Dr. McBride. Amy said that Dr. McBride was stern even back then. She said that there were stories that she was a woman scorned and that she had been raised in a violent home. Basically, these were made-up stories, though. Dean McBride's grandfather is the largest benefactor to the Broctren Harbor College Foundation. He served eight years as the college president and had only retired one year before she attended Broctren Harbor College. He has since passed away. Anyway, how did you enjoy your day with her, Sue?"

"I was intimidated, but as I got further into the day my curiosity grew. Her personality is a mystery," I say. Then I change the subject. I don't want to share any more of my thoughts about Dean McBride. She is someone I want to get to know on my own terms, not through rumor or stories.

It's Friday night, so Carrie and I walk around Broctren Harbor, a beautiful little town whose small harbor opens up to Lake Michigan. Little harbor restaurants and gift shops overlook the shoreline. We have dessert as we look out at the lake. Carrie tells me again how excited she is about being independent as we walk back to campus and dusk turns to darkness. Carrie gets cold, so I encourage her to go inside. Alone, I look up into the sky. I find the Big Dipper and, looking harder, find the star beneath it. Tears run down my cheek as I stare at it. I miss Gary so much. Maybe he too is looking at our star right now.

I wake up in the middle of the night, restless and with much anxiety. At home when I awake in the night, I write, read, or open my window and study the sky. Now I feel trapped in my bed. I don't want to turn on the light and wake up Carrie. Thinking about the week, I conclude it has been a good experience, but when tears stream down my face I finally admit I am homesick. I miss Gary so much. More than that, I realize I also miss my mom and dad.

Rolling over and quietly sobbing, I realize this is probably normal. How can anyone not be affected when everything changes overnight? I get out of bed in the dark and feel for my purse on the dresser. I put on my robe, slowly open the door, then quietly close it. Walking down the corridor, I feel like I can barely breathe. Tears blur my vision. At the pay phone, I open my purse and pour out my change. Dare I call Gary's house and wake up his parents? He is always my special place to land when I'm sad. Thinking now, I know it's wrong; after all, we are going in different directions. I think of calling my mom and dad, but I can hear my mom telling me to pull it together and face life. Crying harder, I put my change back into my purse. This is my moment to deal with life. I feel so alone, so unbelievably alone. I slide down the wall, landing on the floor in the hallway.

What is this about? Am I missing the life I left behind? Is it about a specific person—my mom or dad? Or is it Gary? Is this about loss or about fear? My head rests against the wall, my eyes are closed, and my tears continue to fall.

"Sue, are you okay?"

Opening my eyes, I see Kathy Miller, the dorm advisor.

"Oh, just having a bit of trouble going to sleep," I say, wiping my eyes.

"Why don't you come down to my quarters for a cup of hot chocolate and talk?"

As nice as her offer is, something inside me wants to gut this loneliness out. I need to resolve this for myself.

"Thanks for the offer, but I am fine, really. I am on my way to bed." I get up, pulling myself together.

On Saturday morning I don't feel like eating breakfast. I stop at the snack bar for a cup of coffee and get my mail. There's a letter from Gary. We agreed to give each other time to adjust. We decided two weeks would be adequate time, fearing that anything sooner might pull on us. I planned on writing him today, realizing it would be two weeks today. Obviously, he planned on having his letter arrive exactly in two weeks.

Quickly I bounce down the streets of Broctren Harbor. The skies are clear and, feeling the sun, I walk the shoreline until I find a quiet spot. Taking my shoes off, I sit on the sand. I open Gary's letter:

ᘒ

Dear Sue,

First of all, it goes without saying that I miss you so much. I imagine you found someplace special where you are reading my letter. I can just imagine you sitting there, with your shoes off…relaxed. Of course, my heart is racing as I write you. I am always filled with you.

How are you doing? I know you are a trooper, probably absorbing everything. No doubt you are overwhelmed. Are you making new friends? I hope so—you have such a wonderful personality. I ran into your father at the gas station last week.

We talked a few minutes. He said that he misses you a lot. He also told me that your mom won't talk about it, but she obviously misses you too.

So, have you visited our star? I have been to the park quite a few times. I sit in your spot and I look at our star, hoping maybe you are looking at it as well. We don't need to pretend we're strong. There were lonely nights when I missed you so much it took everything in me not to call you. I have crazy thoughts of throwing everything aside so we can be together. But we are better than our desperation. And we're more able to soar now that we have filled each other with so much life.

My life is changing. I will be leaving tomorrow. I have enclosed a card with my new address. Each day I seem more alive. You gave me so much. The memories of you are like keys that have unlocked parts of me. You planted a ton of treasures inside me. I am discovering so much thanks to you. Excitement fills me, and I feel more alive than I have ever been. Thanks, Sue.

Now about how much I love you. You didn't think I would forget that, did you? I'll finish my letter with what I want you to remember the most. I love you dearly. You are and will always be loved by me. My love is not fickle; it's as real as the air I breathe. It does not exist for you to ponder what it means, nor should you waste time wondering where it will take us. Instead, let it be the source of comfort, strength, and joy. It exists as a result of where we have been. No one has the power to change our history. Maybe life will take us away from each other, or maybe not. Either way our love is something we will always have. Remember, we cannot require it to be more than what it is. Never forget that what we have is always enough…

Love, Gary

Feeling the sun bearing down on my face, I press his letter to my heart. It's a comforting letter. As much as I miss him, his letter left me feeling renewed. I feel excitement returning inside me. I especially love how he ended it.

Now, opening my case, I pull out paper to write him.

෴

Dear Gary,

I just got your letter. It's great hearing from you. I miss you a lot. There have been so many times I wanted call you as well. You were so right about giving us two weeks before writing. I miss you, but this will not be a letter of desperation. I am so glad you held us back from doing anything out of desperation. You were so right about that. When we finally made love it was out of love and readiness. I will always be grateful for the lessons you taught me.

I like college a lot and have had some wonderful experiences through the training program. It has given me an opportunity to get acquainted with key faculty members. I have met a lot of students and am getting to know a few of them a little better. Having Carrie here is wonderful. Her adjustment is far better than mine. It's sad that she has no one to miss in life. She is totally focused on her new life. It is fun watching her be all excited about everything.

I am glad you are doing well and—as you said—"coming so alive." I don't know exactly what that means. Maybe you can write more about that in your next letter. Once you are settled in and adjusted to your schedule, please feel free to call me sometime. I am generally in the dorm by 10:00 PM during the weekdays. We have an 11:00 PM curfew. Weekend curfew is midnight.

Now about how much I love you. Aw yes—bet you thought I forgot that, eh? No, I have decided to save it for last so you don't forget it. Yes, I love you. I miss not touching you and being physically close to you. I feel such a loss from not being with you, and I love what you said about love. It is something that can't be taken away. I promise not to smother it with my over-thinking. I need to let it fill me and support me. It meant a lot—what you said about our love being always enough…

In closing, I can't help but imagine your beautiful face. I hope I made you smile while you read this letter. Yes, I have been with our star a lot. Gary, I love you…always.

Sue

I drop the letter off on the way back to campus. I feel so renewed and at peace with everything.

I decide to enter campus through the back way. Walking past the faculty and staff homes, I see Dr. Morrow.

"Hello, Sue. I am glad I ran into you. How are you doing?" Just then a front door opens. The cutest little girl rushes out, saying "Daddy, hurry so we can play."

"Okay, honey," he hollers back. "Would you like to meet my daughter, Katie? I have a wonderful lady who lives in and takes care of us. She bakes the best things. Come on in and let's see what she has whipped up today," he says.

As we enter the house, a matronly woman greets me with a smile. "Welcome. My name is Hattie. Come on in. I'll get you two something to drink." Dr. Morrow goes to find Katie. "Here are some cookies that most of the students like. John is always bringing students by. I love to bake, so I hope you enjoy them."

"Thanks, they are delicious. They remind me of my mom's. She uses extra brown sugar in the oatmeal."

"Yeah, that's the secret. Your mom taught you right." Eating the cookie, I think about the fact that mom never taught me *anything* about baking.

"Okay, Katie, meet Sue."

"Hi, Sue. Glad to meet you. Are you new here?"

"Yes, this is my first year. What grade are you in, Katie?"

"I'm in first grade. What do you think of Hattie's cookies?"

"They are terrific, and the lemonade is good."

Katie takes off into the living room. Hattie excuses herself to go fold the laundry. Somehow it feels as if both of them know what they are supposed to do when Dean Morrow brings a student home.

"Sue, I want to talk to you about last night. Your dorm advisor, Kathy Miller, came to see me this morning and mentioned that she found you distraught and sitting in the hallway last night about three in the morning."

"I was just missing home a bit. I didn't want to wake Carrie, so I went out into the hall to think. Ms. Miller was nice and offered to talk with me, but it was necessary for me to work through it alone."

"How do you feel today?"

"I feel great. It's important that I be my resource for comfort. I could have awakened Carrie, who is a dear, trusted friend. I could have called my parents or other friends. But I needed to wrestle with it myself, and I did. Today I feel great."

"Great. So tell me, Sue. What are you all about? What is it about you that I should know?" He appears so caring and sincere that I feel comfortable talking with him. Maybe it's the sensitivity he shows me. Maybe it's because I feel renewed and fresh after reading Gary's letter. Whatever it is, he has asked a question that I want to answer truthfully.

"Okay, let me take a stab at answering your question. I am a person who ponders life. I feel things more intensely than most people do; however, I don't make decisions based only on my feelings. I value frankness, evidence, and truth. Small-minded people should run from me. Yet I am very sensitive to others. The reason I get up every day is because I am just plain curious. From time to time, I escape from my ivory tower and walk on the edge of life. On a rare occasion, I will step over to experience the other side. Be assured I am not self-destructive; I love life. Life offers me many mysteries that keep my mind racing. Last but not least, you should know that I generally sleep from exhaustion, not peace. There, did that answer your question?"

Now I'm laughing. I can see that Dr. Morrow is intrigued. "Sue, you really make me smile. You remind me of my late wife. She was spicy and loved to ponder everything in life. She would go on tirades about issues she was passionate about. Tell me, if you only get to accomplish one thing in life, what will it be?"

"I want to know when I die that I made a difference. I don't care about what kind of difference. I just need to know that my life profoundly changed something or someone."

"I bet you have already done that a thousand times by being a daughter, sister, or a friend."

"I need to know that I did something no one else could have done except me. Every time someone dies I ponder that person's purpose and importance on earth. What was it about them that altered or changed something in a way no one else could have?" Dr. Morrow listens quietly, thinking. "Dr. Morrow, what tugs at you? That is, what is your personal great challenge right now?"

"Sue, since my wife died, I bury myself in anything that keeps me busy. My challenge is to walk up to the starting line and take off running again. I need to open up. I need to feel life again. You kind of tugged at me earlier when you described yourself. You remind me of how alive I was when Rose energized me with her passion about issues. Now I need to step out and start breathing life in."

"Katie is another reason to step up to the starting line," I respond. "Kids are so observant."

"You are so right. Katie is wonderful. She has had a difficult time ever since Rose died. I put my own grief aside and spent all my time either doing my job or being there for her. We are very close. No doubt Katie is the joy of my life."

"Well, you need a piece of life for yourself. You can't just be a dean and dad."

"Sue Martin, you are a wise counselor. Thank you."

"Well, I better get going—so much to do today. I am registering for classes, and I know the lines will be long. Anyway, you have a lot to do as well. You've got to get to the starting line. Thanks so much for stopping me, but please don't be concerned. I am doing fine," I say.

"You take care Sue, and remember I am here if you need to talk."

CHAPTER 16

Home for Thanksgiving

The first months of college quickly pass. By now I know most of the freshmen and have developed a few close friendships. Carrie and I have grown very close. Carrie has such a deep passion for writing poetry and stories. She is definitely leaning toward a writing career. She is an inspiration to me.

I am busy with all my classes and hardly have time to look back at the life I left behind. Mom and Dad call once a week. Still, late at night I think about Mom. I really enjoy watching her live her life. I think about the many times I saw her behind the church sitting in the rose garden. At Mrs. Williams's funeral she had told me it was her special place where she could go to think. As a child, I'd hide behind a big, old oak tree to watch her among the roses.

I miss Gary, but not as much as I did the first month. Gary writes faithfully, and I enjoy his letters. We have talked on the phone a couple of times, but it was so unsatisfying, having other students around who were waiting to make calls. At first Gary enjoyed college, but now it is secondary to the enjoyment he takes in painting. Apparently, one day his passion was so strong that he was compelled to paint and the experience of doing so was amazing. Now everything rushes from inside of him. His letters are filled with excitement, and I am glad he is happy being consumed with painting. After seeing an exhibit in New York featuring the works of French painter Jean-Louis Pacquet, Gary has asked to become his student. Impressed with Gary's work, Jean-Louis agrees to take him on. Gary will finish the semester in December and move to New York in January. I am happy that he will be home for Thanksgiving and Christmas

The new experiences in my life are very diversified. I love philosophy and psychology, which keep my mind speeding. Being a dorm assistant is fun as well. Dean Morrow and I have grown close. We spend a lot of time working on campus issues. I encourage him to get back into life.

I have a new friendship with Sherry McClain. She is so happy to be away from home. Being the daughter of a city mayor is difficult. We can be laughing one moment and in tears the next. Sherry has a lot of repressed anger. She is intelligent and insightful about herself. Both of us are excited and curious about life. She fears her curiosity could quickly lead her down the wrong path. I share some of my experiences with her but omit my first sexual experience with Gary, which I want to hold onto as something that only he and I will ever share. But when Sherry asks me if I have gone all the way, I am honest that I have. She is more concerned about her welfare than I was when I harbored such curiosities.

Then there is my relationship with James Barrington, Jr., a freshman from New York. He is the son of James Barrington, Sr., the well-known founder of Barrington Industries. He comes from a very privileged home, yet he is so untouched by all of it. His father is disappointed that he did not attend Harvard, his alma mater. James really hates his family's greed. When he was seven years old, he was sent to a Christian boarding school, where teachers and ministers raised him. He felt love and unbelievable peace and grew spiritually. He is passionately committed to helping others.

One day in philosophy class, I challenge the professor's statement that evidence provides a greater truth than anything that is merely reasonably probable. "Evidence, in and of itself, is void of process or history. Therefore, it is nothing more than a tangible fact that doesn't clarify how it came to be," I explain in class. Of course, the professor's point made sense, but part of me wanted to challenge everything said in this class. My challenge may have been nothing more than a form of semantics, but I wanted to show how ambiguous some of his ideas seemed to me. After class, James and I go to the snack bar and talk. From then on we are very good friends.

One day crossing campus I notice Carrie sitting with Keith Saunderland. They look rather cozy and intimate. Keith is looking at Carrie so intensely. As I turn the corner, I run into Dr. Morrow.

"Hello, Sue. Glad I ran into you. Are you going home for Thanksgiving?"

"Yes. I am leaving Wednesday morning."

"I am glad you are finally going home. Hattie makes a ton of food, so I always invite a few students to celebrate and thought you might like to come over. I suppose Carrie is going with you?"

"No, she has to work on Friday and Saturday."

"I will call and invite her. It will be nice to have her over. Now, you have a great time at home, but don't get so comfortable that you forget how much we will be looking forward to seeing you return."

As I turn and start to walk away he hollers back.

"Hey, Sue! I need to talk to you about something. It's important but not urgent. I would like to spend some time with you at your convenience. It doesn't have to be before you leave, but maybe we can get together when you come back. How's that sound?"

"Well, you have my curiosity piqued. I have classes until late."

"Well, I am booked solid today and tomorrow. Don't worry about it; it is just something I want to share with you. We can talk when you get back. I've got to run now—have a good day."

The rest of day I do research and think from time to time about Dr. Morrow. I have a bit of a crush on him that I know is inappropriate. Quickly, I push such thoughts away. That evening at dinner Carrie tells me of her invitation to Thanksgiving dinner at Dr. Morrow's. I ask about her relationship with Keith. Carrie says he has approached her a couple of times about doing things together. She says he's a very nice person and that she feels drawn to him.

On Tuesday, I'm consumed with classes. I stay late at the library, finishing up a paper so that I won't have to do it at home. When the alarm goes off at 6:30 AM, I quickly get ready, grab my suitcase, and head for the train station. My suitcase is so heavy. All of a sudden, Dr. Morrow drives up.

"I take it you're headed to the train station. Let me take you."

"Thanks. This was heavier than I thought. What are you out doing this early in the morning?"

"Well, a student got picked up by the police. I went over there, but they aren't ready to release him until they hear from his parents. But hey, I get to rescue you! Glad I can help you with this suitcase. Let me carry it."

"Gosh, such service. A gal couldn't ask for much more."

We sit in the station sharing idle chitchat. He talks about Katie decorating the house for Thanksgiving. Finally, my train arrives. He hands the conductor my suitcase and hugs me. I am rather shocked that he gives me a hug, but it feels warm and caring.

"What time does your train get back on Sunday?" he hollers, as the train starts to move. "Four thirty in the afternoon," I holler back. He is still waving as the train pulls away.

For the first hour, I keep thinking about the morning. Dr. Morrow is a caring person, and I shouldn't read anything into his kindness. I enjoy the train ride. The trees are almost bare, and the leaves are dancing from the force of the train sweeping down the track. Halfway home I fall asleep.

"Next stop, Beckenburg, Ohio," the conductor announces.

I strain to see who is standing at the station. Through the steam I can see Mom and Dad. I am flooded with emotion. I am home.

"Was your train ride okay?" Mom asks.

"It was great."

As we drive by the park, I think I see someone in my spot by the brook.

"Dad, Dad, stop. Let me walk home, please. I want to go through the park."

"Okay, sure. We'll see you in a bit."

As I walk across the park, I can tell the person is tall. Oh my God, it's Gary. He beat me home. Now running, I scream.

"Gary, Gary!"

"Sue, you look terrific. I miss you."

He takes my face in his hands and really kisses me. It is so intense, like he desperately needs it to sustain himself.

"Come, let's sit and talk for a bit. I almost came to the train station. I looked up the schedule when I came in late last night. But I didn't want to ruin your parents' excitement. I'm dying to kiss you. This is perfect. I had the idea that if I came here you might see me on your way home."

I love the fact that every detail about everything is so important to Gary.

"Oh, I am so happy." I say, reaching over and kissing him again. "What have you done to my calm fella? You look so excited and alive."

"Well, I am about as happy as ever. After you left, it took me a few days, but then you gave me so much that all of it came rushing out at me. It was a transformation like no other. I had a new level of intensity and passion inside. You helped me overcome my shyness, and my confidence soared. All of a sudden I wanted to express it on canvas. The next thing I knew I was painting with such unbelievable passion, and somehow I finally had the skills."

"I love your letters. I can feel your new sense of intensity and joy. At first when I got to Broctren Harbor College I felt empty. The memories of you encouraged me. Slowly, I just kept doing what I was supposed to. Now I enjoy college very much. I have made new friends and my life is moving on."

"Hey, I have an idea. I will pick you up later so we can come back here. We need to discuss that star of ours," he says.

"That's perfect."

Gary takes me home. "Hey, that was Gary in the park," I explain.

"I knew it was, Sue." says Dad. "I could tell he missed you. Before he left for college, I ran into him a couple of times. It is easy to see that he really has strong feelings for you."

It is nice that Dad was so sensitive to Gary. Mom's in the kitchen fixing dinner, and it feels wonderful seeing her there. It feels great being home.

"I really miss not being around you. Mom, I missed you more than you can imagine."

She looks up from stirring her pot and smiles an incredible smile that speaks volumes about how she feels. I feel myself becoming emotional.

"Dinner will be ready in about ten minutes. Your father put your suitcase in your room." Going upstairs, I know she has pushed me away because she was moved by what I had said.

At dinner I ramble on and on about college. Both my parents ask a lot of questions. Mark updates me on the whereabouts of my acquaintances and then catches me off guard.

"Eric is asking about you. He wants to know how you are doing. He asks me every time we pass each other. I didn't know you and he were that close."

"Eric and I have always been friendly to each other. Remember, when I was little we played together? Ever since we have been friendly, even though we are very different."

When Gary picks me up and we return to the park, the sun is diving into the earth. "I know that everything has changed. Being in this park feels so normal."

"Things have changed so much in such a short period of time. Sue, how do you feel about the changes? I know we walked away from each other to see what was out there. Even though my life is pulling me further from you, nothing has changed when it comes to my love for you."

"I love you dearly, but I have to admit my love is reshaping its place in my life. Something as special as what we have is not going anywhere. Our relationship is a huge part of where I came from. I will love you forever. It is still powerful and very important to me. I know I have to keeping moving, as do you. Finally I am at peace about that," I say, trying to explain how I feel. I no longer feel desperate or fearful about my relationship with Gary. Yet I do still love him. Gary holds me as we look at the stars.

"So, how many times did you visit our star?" I ask.

"After you left, it felt like our star was all I had of you. I came to the park every night the first week. Then I started remembering everything, and the memories became very special. On the last day before I left for college, I was at the studio and all at once was overcome with the need to paint. Since then, I have felt you more than ever. In college I would visit our star once or twice a week. I no longer go there longing for you. I feel great knowing you are alive in my paintings. Sue, tell me about everything about college. What is pulling at your curiosity now?"

It's a great question. I have been moving so fast that I have little time to think about my new life. "Well, I am overwhelmed with the changes in Carrie. She is so alive—like a new Carrie. I enjoy seeing her soar. I love my classes; nothing is too hard yet. I like philosophy the most, especially the abstract nature of the material. I really push the edges of my professor's calm nature, as I am quick to question everything. Let me see…oh yes. Many new people have come into my life. I am intrigued by Dr. McBride, the Dean of women. She is cold, calculating, and she pushes everyone away. That fascinates the heck out of me. I want to crack her shell and get to know her. Then there is Dr. Morrow, the dean of students. He and I have become close. Slowly I am making a family away from home," I explain.

Gary listens so attentively. "Why do you think Dr. Morrow is so intriguing?"

"He's the person I report to for my dorm assistant position. He is the first person I got to know on campus, and he has worked hard helping me to adjust to campus life." I know my interest in Dr. Morrow involves so much more than that, but I have not allowed myself to analyze it yet and can't say more. Maybe I don't want to know, or maybe I like the fact that my feelings about him encompass something a little mystic.

Gary is respectful and does not push for more information. "I am so glad you are adjusting and liking college," he says. He pulls me to him, and it feels great having his arms around me. The night's coldness is starting to set in.

"Tell me about Jean-Louis Pacquet and moving to New York."

"I met him at his exhibit. Actually, I had the weekend free, and Mom and Dad sent me a plane ticket to meet them in New York. I almost didn't go because I am so lost in painting now. However, I felt the need to see my parents, and they had mentioned Jean-Louis Pacquet. I ended up going to his exhibit alone after mom came down with the flu and dad had to stay with her in the hotel. It was a marvelous exhibit. I am fascinated with his color integration. His paintings are such emotional, rich, visual stories that come to life. I wondered where his visions came from, so I approached him, and we talked. It turned out the paintings represent real life moments that he splashes upon canvas. He explained how he paints his vision, how the emotions are just there. Anyway, I feel so connected to his style. He said he wanted to see my work, so when I got back I shipped him a couple of my paintings. A couple of weeks later, he shipped them back with a letter. He said he would like to work with me and offered me the opportunity to study under him. Immediately, I knew it was right. My parents were supportive, and Mom and Dad found me an apartment in New York. So I'll go to New York in early January."

It's wonderful hearing the excitement in Gary's voice. Finally, the coldness of the night becomes so uncomfortable that we decide to leave. In the car, Gary says he has to return to college on Friday because he has a huge term paper due. We make plans to spend Thanksgiving evening together.

That night, sleeping in my bed feels wonderful. I think about my relationship with Gary. We still have such a love for each other. Maybe we will always be the great loves of each other's lives. I can't imagine ever loving anyone the way I love him. Our love fuels us to openly walk out into life. It continues to give us comfort and support.

As I am falling asleep, my thoughts drift to Dr. Morrow. I wonder what he needs to talk to me about. My thoughts about him are hard to unravel. There is something about the way we look at each other. I know he has something more to say to me. He has strong values and self-discipline, so I can't imagine he would ever cross an unspoken line with me, or even be open to anything closer than what we already have shared. Yet I am very attracted to him. Am I seeing something that is not there? My wild imagination and curiosity often take me to places in my head where I can never go in reality. Probably this is just another of those times when I let my thoughts run beyond the border of rationality. Finally exhausted, I fall asleep.

It's a beautiful Thanksgiving morning. Mom is having the time of her life fixing the most unbelievable meal. I spend the morning trying to reach Patty. Mom says she has become very thin, but Patty tells me she is fine. Mark is busy with all of his senior year activities. Grey and I talk about the academic challenges of college.

As always, Thanksgiving dinner is marvelous. Mom's sweet potato pie, cranberry salad, and, of course, her special stuffing and gravy are terrific. I am stuffed when I finish. I decide to start cleaning. I'm not going to ask if I can help because I already know the answer. Finally, everything is off the table. I go back to the kitchen and help with the dishes. Within fifteen minutes everything is done. I am surprised that Mom let me help her.

"Mom, thanks for a wonderful meal—and thanks for letting me help you clean up," I say.

"It's nice having you in the kitchen with me. I miss not having you home."

I am stunned that she has opened up. I have never heard her say she misses me.

"I miss you more than you can know," I respond, and have to leave the kitchen.

I spend the afternoon talking more with Dad, Grey, and Mark. Gary picks me up early and says his parents decided to drive to Sholam, Ohio, to see a play about the first Thanksgiving. "Sue, let's talk about us," he begins. "Let's talk about how we feel. I don't think we are as fragile as the last time we left each other."

Gary is so right. As much as we will miss each other, we know now we will be fine.

"I know you are right. Last time, it was like we were walking away into a great unknown. Now it's different because we know where we are going. You found a wonderful world in painting, one that obviously has changed everything about you. I have changed as well, in that I am more open to new people and experiences. I don't feel desperate the way I did when we parted the last time."

"Sue, nothing has changed about my love for you. It continues to grow. However, I have reshaped how it exists in my life. Before, I needed your presence to fill me and make me feel alive. After you left, I was lost, but days later I put it in perspective. At that point I realized that what I was left with was enough. It will always be enough. Gratitude made it more than enough. All of sudden I was overwhelmed with all that you had given me. Everything turned into colors splashed upon canvas. Our love has given me the one thing I so longed for. Memories poured out of me into my art. Maybe I had the skill but never the right picture to paint. Whatever it was, I came alive. Our love continues to fuel my art. I know all of this may not make sense to you, but it is my truth."

"I think I kind of understand. But do you miss me physically? That is, do you miss touching and loving me physically?"

"Of course I miss you completely. How could I ever stop wanting you? I have let that one night run wild in my thoughts and exhaust me a million times over. I'm always thinking about making love with you again and again.

The thoughts are always toying with me, but nothing can ever be as powerful as the first time we made love. I have read that the first experience is the most captivating and powerful. That is not saying it is the most sexually satisfying, although I do believe ours was. It is rarely repeated. Nothing is as special or electrifying as the first time you experience something. The first touch, the first taste, the first time your body opens up to be taken…I will never forget the first time my body went over the edge in ecstasy. I remember everything—how you breathed, how you got lost in my touch. I remember the overwhelming exhaustion and satisfaction. It was as powerful as life gets."

"What are you going to do if I get wild and hot and want to take you? Are you telling me that you are going to stop because you don't want anything to take away from that first time?" I tease.

"I am about as weak as they come. I will gladly surrender to your wild desires," he laughs, knowing I am toying with him.

Then Gary recommends we check out our star. We go into the back yard. Gary brings a heavy blanket to cover us. We get into the hammock and into each other arms. He covers us to keep warm. Looking up, we see the stars are covered by moving clouds.

"Do you think that maybe someday you'll find someone and fall in love with them like you did me?" I ask.

"I am so in love with you I can't imagine it. I know that in the end we may not be together. But I have you, I really have you, inside me. I am full of you. My sexual desires are attached to you."

"Gary, you aren't going to tie up the rest of your life in that one night are you?"

"Sue, sometimes one moment can sustain me for days. That one night might sustain me forever. That one night gave me more than most people get in a lifetime."

I knew I would also remember that first time forever, but it could never be enough to sustain me forever. As much as I love Gary, I am slowly opening myself up to others. No one would ever be able to replace Gary in my life. But I am so different…

Slowly he kisses my face, gentle and nurturing. "Sue, you don't need to understand me; you need to go out there and be who you are. I will always love you—always."

As he kisses me more passionately, a tears run down my cheek. Everything he says fits into my life. I have his love and his support. In the sky, the clouds move off, and the Big Dipper and our star glisten. Gary kisses me feverishly now and asks to touch me. I so want him to. His hand gently caresses me under the blanket.

"Sue, will you be my canvas?"

With great care, his hands etch sensations that take me away into unbelievable ecstasy. Both of us tired and depleted, we hold each other. I know his intimate act was for me and that he wants to pleasure and somehow satisfy me. Even though he is still on the edge holding on, it is enough for him. After all, he always has those memories of the first time. Once again we fall asleep in the hammock and don't awaken until about four AM. His parents are sleeping. He takes me home. Standing on the porch, we kiss each other.

"See you at Christmas."

"Yeah, see you at Christmas."

As in the spring, we both walk in different directions, but this time it's different. I am okay—I really feel okay. I tiptoe to my parents' bedroom door.

"Mom, I am home. Sorry—I fell asleep, and that's why I am late."

"Its okay, Sue. You don't have a curfew any more. Good night." Everything feels so different. In just a few short months, everything about my life has changed.

Saturday I spend the day with my parents and brother. My mother invites the pastor and his wife to dinner. Afterward we play board games. Eventually, I excuse myself to go to my bedroom early. Lying in bed, thinking about the weekend, I mull over the painful realization that nothing ever stays the same. Time changes everything. It is now apparent that my home is college. Carrie once said that a strong person creates a home within herself—that way you always feel comfortable anywhere. She learned to do that after being tossed from one foster home to the next; her survival was due to her ability to create a sense of belonging inside herself. Before I fall asleep, I realize I have learned that love has different meanings and that people love each other differently. Passion transforms your life, I tell myself quietly. Passion that consumes you can give you a satisfaction that no one can take away. Gary is transformed by his passion for painting now, a practice that defines everything about him. I crave something in my life that will consume me, too.

I love the morning walk to Willard's department store to see Patty. She is working on the floor, helping people. Finally I make my way through the crowd, and we hug each other. It is hard to have a conversation while she responds to customers. We agree to plan something at Christmas. On the way home I feel down: tired and emotionally drained. Being home for Thanksgiving has been hard on me. I love Gary, but I have come to see how our love is different, how it has been reshaped by our changing realities. He is consumed by his painting, and I am happy for him. Then there is Patty. As great as it is to see her, I know both of us have changed. It's quiet at dinner. Afterwards I visit with the family and then turn in early for the night.

The next morning I awake, excited to go to college. I rush downstairs and get a cup of coffee, telling Mom I want one last visit to my spot in the park and won't be long.

"Okay, but your train leaves today at noon. I know your father and brothers still want to spend time with you. Grey's train leaves for college fifteen minutes after yours, so all of us will be going to the train station."

Walking into the park, I feel renewed. Sitting by the brook by myself, I smell the fresh air of the morning. Thinking about returning to college is exciting. I can hardly wait to hear about Carrie's Thanksgiving at Dr. Morrow's house. I am still curious about what Dr. Morrow wants to talk to me about. My thoughts turn to Dr. McBride. I can't wait to get to know her.

I spend the rest of the morning with my family. Finally, Grey and I pack our bags, and the family takes us to the train station. Again I feel myself well up over leaving. In spite of the changes, there were many special moments—especially the times Mom let me help her in the kitchen and told me she misses me. Now looking at Mom standing beside Dad, I notice for the first time that she looks more fragile than I have ever seen her. I can see that my parents are aging.

When the train arrives, I hug my father and brothers first and then Mom. "Mom, you mean the world to me. Thanks for everything. I love you."

"Don't get so emotional. We will see you in a few weeks. I love you too."

As I get on the train, everyone is waving. Emotions sweep over me as the train slowly leaves town. Relaxing, I close my eyes. All at once I hear a familiar voice.

"Well, if it isn't that charming gal of my dreams."

"Eric! What the heck are you doing on this train?" I ask, as he takes the seat beside me.

"Gosh, I thought maybe a hello or a 'Hey, I miss you' might be your first words. Or a 'Gosh, my dreams are coming true because you're here!' Oh well, I do have a hopeful imagination. I am on my way to Fayetteville, just forty-five minutes up the tracks. I'm going to help my aunt bring her kids to our house. She hates driving alone, so I volunteered to take a train and drive them back. I thought you might be home for Thanksgiving. I went to the park on Saturday hoping to catch you there, but I guess the old park isn't good enough to hang out in anymore, eh?" Eric loves to tease me.

"Well, I spent most of my time with the family. I didn't do much but rest up."

"What happened to that boyfriend of yours? You know, ol' Mr. Prince Charming?"

"He had to get back early."

"What the hell is wrong with that guy? After all these months, you'd think he'd be pouncing all over you. The man is crazy to leave early."

I enjoy his banter. He is the one person who always makes me feel better. It's so strange, because we aren't close at all—except for our very special secret connection. Eric always makes me feel so alive.

"So tell me: how's college life? Are you partying? Are you taking a little piece of life from the other side?" he teases.

"No, I spend a lot of time studying." It feels good talking with him, for once finding something that feels unchanged. It is vintage Eric.

"So, Eric. What's up with you? Have you been picking the wildflowers on the other side of the brook while you read poetry and think of me?"

"Let's not make fun of the finer things in life. I do like looking at those cute little flowers, but generally it's not when I am reading poetry. No, I generally enjoy them through a billowing smoke with a robust smell," he says, inhaling deeply while pretending he is smoking a joint. He doesn't miss a beat. He knows I am curious about marijuana.

We laugh so hard about everything. He has taken a full-time job at the mill, because his family needs his income. He lives at home and supports them. He admits he still parties and loves it, but his work schedule keeps him from doing it as often. We enjoy sharing our lives with each other.

"Well, Eric, is there a lady in your life?"

"Oh there are many who seek me, but I think I will always be pining away for that one neighbor girl who I can't get out of my head." He smiles at me.

"You're special, and I suspect that neighbor of yours thinks about that night too. But gosh fella, you're a vital man with needs. Don't lie away pining for someone who has her nose in books," I say, smiling back.

Just then the conductor says, "Next stop, Fayetteville, Ohio."

Eric has made my day. Even though our conversation might seem insignificant, he has made me feel special, and I am laughing. I so want to say something special to him without it leading anywhere.

"Well, Eric, your stop is next. I am glad I got to see you. You are always an amazing surprise out of nowhere, and I always leave feeling great afterwards."

"Well, I hope I am around the next time you need your spirits lifted. I can't think of anything I would rather do. It's great seeing you. Take care of yourself." He stands up and turns to go. I cannot let him walk away. Immediately, I stand up too.

"Eric, you are not going anywhere without hugging me."

"Oh my God, heaven must be looking down on me," he says, throwing his arms around me. I reach up and kiss him on the cheek. I can tell it means a lot because as he turns back and looks at me from the door I hear him say, "Thank you"—this time not joking, but speaking from the sincerity of his heart.

As the train leaves, I lean back, thinking about what has happened. Why does Eric make me feel good? What is it about him that's special? Maybe Gary is right about "first time" experiences. Or maybe it is just that Eric makes me laugh, with ability to tease me and toy with my curiosity. He represents experiences that pique my interest.

Nearly asleep now, I am startled by a sudden thought. Suddenly, it makes sense. Eric is special because he puts me first. Gary makes decisions based on his standards, his ethics, his goals. That always feels so controlling, and it disregards who I am. But Eric is different. Everything he ever did or said is based on putting me first. I think back to our one night together, when Eric could have taken advantage of me. After all, I was impaired, and it was not beyond his morals. But he didn't. His main priority was taking care of me. Although he is attracted to me, he never steps over the line. He talks with me and never pushes me. Smiling, I fall asleep.

CHAPTER 17

Shock and Loss

When the train pulls into the station, I am shocked to see both Carrie and Dr. Morrow waiting for me. Quickly I exit the train. "Hey, thanks for coming to get me," I say. "But really, you didn't need to."

Both hug me, but I see that something is wrong. Carrie has been crying.

"What's going on? What's wrong?" I ask, panicked.

"Sue, let's go inside the station and talk," says Dr. Morrow. I feel my body start to tremble. Carrie has not said a word. "Sue, two hours ago, Carrie received a call from your mother saying Patty had died."

"Oh my God…no, no!" I start crying. "I saw her on Friday. She looked thin but not sickly." I can hardly speak. "Carrie, oh no. Please—this can't be…Oh God, no!"

Carrie is crying hard and holding on to me. I gasp, finding it hard to breathe. Carrie has not been able to say anything. My body is now trembling with denial, resisting acceptance of the news. There is no way of getting around or beyond it. I feel death's power pulling me to that horrible place where I have no option but to be engulfed by this all-encompassing pain.

Carrie is trying to say something. Finally, I hear her whisper, "Sue, there's more. Patty took her life. After spending all day with Hale, she went home. Sometime late last night Patty took a whole bottle of pills and went to sleep. Her father couldn't wake her this morning."

I am devastated, full of the most unbelievable pain. I feel my body convulse. I am thrashing my arms against Dr. Morrow.

"Why, why, why?"

I am going into shock. Dr. Morrow helps me up, and Carrie lifts me from the other side. The next few minutes are a faint awareness of being in his car. Both of them help me to the infirmary, where Dr. Madison checks me out. Shock is a strange thing. It is like your body protects you by removing you from the impact and placing you in a protective, incoherent void. He gives me a pill to relax me. Although tears continue to fall, I feel my body calming down. I am starting to remember the horrible truth that Patty is dead.

I can hear the doctor tell Dean Morrow that I will be okay for the trip home. Somehow, four hours had passed since I got off the train. When I look up, I see my mom and dad coming through the door. Mom rushes over to me.

"I am so sorry, Sue. I am so sorry." Now I am crying harder in her presence. I lose all control. Raw pain is cutting through me. There is not much anyone can say to comfort me. I feel myself alone, empty and lost amid everyone around me. Death takes away everything—the rawest of all reality. I am angry that I let this happen. Certainly, I could have prevented it. I hate myself. I have been irresponsible in friendship, and now she is gone—not just dead, but from the worst kind of death: suicide. Feelings of unbearable loss and overwhelming guilt are choking me. My focus ought to be about Patty's family. Cutting off my emotions, I sit up.

"Mom, how are Mr. Williams and her brothers, Jim and Dale?"

"Mr. Williams says it hit the family terribly hard. He is having a rough time. The pastor is with them and is helping with the arrangements."

"We need to get home. I want to be there for them," I say, now getting up.

"Are you sure you're ready to leave?" asks Dr. Morrow.

"Yes, it is so important I get home." I can feel myself moving into that "don't talk, don't feel" mode—and "just do what you need to do" way of coping. Although I am not sure what it is I need to do, I know I need to get home and be with Patty's family.

"You girls do not need to worry about your classes or jobs right now. I will take care of everything. Our prayers and thoughts are with you. If you need anything, call me." Dr. Morrow hugs us.

The first three hours of the ride home are in silence. Carrie and I hold hands, a way of connecting when neither of us is able to talk. We feel like we let Patty down. Mom is quick to remind us that Patty took herself away from us. Mom talks about Patty's life and how she never recovered from her mom's death. All of us would have tried harder or tried different things had we known what we know now. When death occurs, everyone looks back with regrets about what could have been done differently.

We arrive home and Mom puts Carrie in the guest room. I go to my room to finally be alone. A few minutes later mom comes in with a tray.

"Sue, I know these next few days are going to be harder than anything that you have been through. Now is the time for you to find comfort in your faith. No one can take this pain from you. In moments like these, we must find comfort in God."

I can feel myself getting upset. I didn't feel like rushing to a God who could let this happen. Although God had been my greatest source of comfort in the past, my faith is now shattered and unavailable. I listen to Mom but feel myself closing off to what she is saying. She kisses me and says to wake her if I need to talk. It's strange how I am acting—like I'm outside myself. Here is the love and caring I always wanted from my Mom, but I'm angry that it comes at the expense of Patty's death.

I spend most of the night thinking about Patty. It is late when I fall asleep. The sun wakes me as it streams through the blinds onto my face.

"I need to go to the Williams home to spend time with them," I say. Carrie decides to stay at our house and do some things for Mom, who is very busy helping with all the funeral arrangements.

Arriving at their home, I find a lot of cars. Many people from the community are stopping by to see Mr. Williams. I feel like I am on automatic pilot, going from person to person, and nothing feels real. I see Patty's brother Dale outside sitting on a bench by himself. I feel myself choke with emotion. As soon as Dale sees me, he stands up to hug me. It's like we are family, and only we can understand each other's pain. After a few minutes, both of us wipe our eyes and sit.

"Sue, I can't believe she just took her life. I talked with her in the morning. She seemed happy to be going over to Hale's family's home. Hale says everything went okay; they had a barbeque and played yard games. He said that on the way to our house she appeared fine. Dad remembers she took a glass of water when she went to her room, but he didn't think anything about it. Who would? When her alarm went off in the morning, dad heard it ring and ring. He went to see if maybe she left it on and went to work. But she was lying there with the empty bottle of pills and a note beside her. Sue, the note said: *To everyone, there was nothing you could have done. As selfish as this is, I need to find my own peace. Forgive me. Remember, I love all of you. Patty.*

I had not known there was a note. I am lifeless as Dale puts his arms around me. Jim drives up, still visibly shaken. "I don't want to go inside with all those people," he says.

"Patty loved you so much, Sue. Her whole childhood was about you gals playing and laughing. She had a few other friends, but it was never anything close to what you meant to her," Jim says, now holding me.

"Well, I loved her. She was my world as a child. I shared every feeling, every secret, with her. After your mom died, she pulled away, and I let her. Now I am so angry at myself," I say, choking through my tears.

"Sue, listen, all of us tried to reach her. Patty was changed by mom's death; she was inconsolable. She stopped taking care of herself and barely ate. She started drinking a lot, and I think the autopsy may show alcohol as well as pills. I think she ran to Hale to hide from all of us who wanted to help. Hale didn't know Mom, so he offered her a world without any memories of Mom. I am no psychologist, but she really kept her distance from anyone who kept Mom's memories alive," Jim explains.

After a while we go into the house. The pastor says the funeral service will be Tuesday at 10:00 AM, and burial will immediately follow. He asks if anyone wants to do a eulogy.

"Dale and I want to speak," Jim says. "We would like Sue to speak if she would like to."

"Yes, I want to speak at the funeral," I say.

In the car I tell Mom about the note that Patty wrote. Mom says it makes sense. She believes Patty isolated herself in her depression. Mom talked to her about getting counseling, but Patty refused. Mom encourages me to take time reflecting on the good memories and special qualities about Patty. Those memories will help me write my eulogy.

I decide to go to the park and think. There I can write out my thoughts. I am still in this huge fog of emotions. It's strange how death suspends the life you are living, encapsulating you in a dark abyss where you are ravaged with such excruciating pain. I think how horrible Patty's pain was when her mom died. It's sad that it took Patty's death to help me understand a little bit more about the pain she suffered over her mother's death.

Relaxing by the brook, I have no idea of what to say. Rolling face down onto the ground, I sob my heart out.

"Sue...."

I look up. Eric is sitting on the ground nearby. He reaches for my hand, pulling me into his arms.

"I know about Patty. I am so sorry. I used to watch you two play here in the park when we were kids. She was the one with all the laughter and energy. She was great for you, because you were too deep about things. It was Patty's sweet, simple ways, pulling at you, making you laugh," he says, reaching up and gently wiping away my tears.

"I know. You're right. No one made me laugh like her."

"Remember those stupid Easter egg hunts in the park? Remember when she snuck into the community center the night before and wrote on every colored egg 'Property of Sue & Patty'? The next morning they hid them and explained to everyone to disregard the message written on them," Eric recalls, laughing.

"Yeah. I also remember how when she didn't like one particular song they sang in church Sunday after Sunday she snuck into church and cut the song out of every hymnal. She was so pleased when the minister finally stopped praying for the hymnal phantom," I laugh.

Patty and Eric weren't close, but they had grown up together in the park and at school. It felt good talking with Eric. Finally, he had to leave for work. We hug again for the second time in two days, but after two very different exchanges. Our talk helps me decide what I need to write in my eulogy. Quickly, it pours out of me.

Walking home, I think how death is so all-encompassing. Even though I'll survive the next two days, my loss of Patty will last a lifetime. The more I think about life, the more it feels cruel. We are born free of burdens. From that point on the burdens progressively increase, as life dishes out events that pile pain and loss on top of pain and loss. Maybe we don't age from physical conditions but from the endless sadness of death stealing what we love the most. Certainly, I watched Patty age after the death of her mom. Now I feel like I have aged a lifetime.

The following day I am shaking as I walk up the sidewalk to the funeral home. Mom, Carrie, and I walk together. Inside people are up at the casket looking at Patty. It feels so wrong. Most of these people don't really know her. They are somehow "showing respect" by staring at her dead body. This all seems too cruel. I wish Mr. Williams, Jim, Dale, and I were here with her alone. That is what she would want.

Jim and Dale walk over to hug me. Each of them takes an arm and we approach the casket. Looking at Patty's body is devastating.

"She looks like she is asleep and peaceful," I hear a neighbor say.

No, she is dead, I think to myself. Patty is not asleep. I know how she looks when she's sleeping. No matter what people say about how nice or peaceful a body looks, the person is dead, and I'm not in denial. This is not a featured moment or highlight in Patty's life. I feel angry. But I need to remain reverent and respectful of Jim and Dale. We don't say a word. I turn and Jim and Dale walk me down the aisle.

"Would you like to sit?" Jim offers.

"No, I think I need to get some air, and you have other people. I am fine."

"No, Sue, now we only have you," Dale says, wiping his eyes. Both of them walk me outside to sit on a bench under the shade tree.

We talk again about Patty, and it's obvious all of us are having a difficult time. After a while my mom comes and takes me home for lunch. Afterwards I come back to the funeral home to be by myself with Patty.

That evening, I receive a phone call from Gary. His mom has just telephoned him about Patty death. He wants to know how I am and wants to come home to be there for me. Unfortunately, there are no trains until tomorrow, and even then he wouldn't arrive in time for the funeral. I assure him that I am doing fine. Carrie and I return to college on Wednesday, so there is no reason for him to come home for a few hours.

The next morning at the funeral, the church is full. Dale asks me to sit with his family up front. I am relieved that the casket is closed. I don't want to see Patty the way I did the day before. I want to think about her life and what a gift she was to me.

The minister opens the service with prayer. He reads comforting scriptures that call on us to reflect on our relationship with God. Finally, it's time for the eulogies. Dale goes first and speaks about Patty being the little sister who kept him on his toes. His words are beautiful and very personal. Jim talks about the joy she gave to everyone, sharing story after story. I feel shaken as I walk to the podium.

ꙮ

Good Morning.

I am happy to say that Patty was my sister and my friend. She and I met in kindergarten, and together we took on the world. Not just any little girl, Patty was fueled with extra energy and adventure. As a child she had a huge imagination.

Anyone can find a friend. But Patty was so much more to me. I lived in books and spent too much time thinking and processing life. Patty took it upon herself to rescue me. She taught me much about girl things, especially about fashion and hairstyles. We told each other our secrets. Patty had a soft heart. She was sensitive to others and always found positive words to speak about everyone. She offered me an extension to her way of looking at life, and that brightened everything up about the world.

Sadly, Patty's world was dimmed when her mother died. The two of them had been inseparable. Her mom's youthful nature and carefree heart were so inspirational to Patty. After she was gone, it seemed like life was drained from her. Today, I know what it feels like to lose a piece of your heart, and now I understand how Patty felt after her mom was gone. I know Patty would want all of us to remember the energy and zest she had as a child. Don't let those memories fade, for when they are gone so are vital parts of each of us. Let us remember to celebrate each other, not only today but forever. There are so many things I wish I had said to Patty, so many things I wish I had done, like writing or calling her more often. Please take heed and open up to your loved one. Nurture love and never take it for granted.

In closing, I want to share a conversation Patty and I had once about God. I was quick to tell Patty what I thought about God. I shared scriptures about God's love and mercy—things from various religious books. Patty listened to everything I had to say, and then I asked her what she thought. She apologized for not being open to any of my insights. She said she could not afford to let anyone define God for her. To do so would be too limiting. She said that God was indefinable. By faith, she simply believed. She assumed that God was bigger, greater, and better than anything on earth, that God's love was beyond all understanding. But otherwise, she just lived by faith. That had an amazing impact on me. After that discussion, my spiritual confusion brought on by conflicting books and various interpretations of the scripture disappeared. Patty changed everything about what I thought. Now, I too walk in faith. Today, her life has taught me one more lesson. I need not try to figure why she is gone; instead, she would remind me to simply trust God and to celebrate the life she lived.

The pastor says a closing prayer and invites the congregation to the burial service. At the grave, when her casket is lowered I feel so empty inside. After the closing prayer, each of us passes by the casket to lay a flower. As I lay my rose, I see a stalk of wild roses cut from behind the church. I know they are from my mother. The service ends, and everyone leaves except for Mr. Williams, Jim, Dale, and me. We stand as they lower her casket further into the grave. Then we leave.

When I get to the sidewalk, I can see my parents and Carrie are waiting. Off to the side behind a tree, Eric is standing. I walk over and he gives me a hug.

"If you need anything, don't forget to call me," he says.

I thank him.

❧   ❧   ❧

Patty has been laid to rest, but she will never be forgotten...

CHAPTER 18

Adjusting

Back at campus, I have much to do. I am still shaken and obsessed with Patty's death. I sit in class, not listening to what's being said, remembering little. My mother has told me to keep moving and eventually it will get easier. After three hard days of going through the motions, I decide to stay in bed. It isn't worth moving about the world when I feel so dead to it.

Carrie is concerned and tries to get me to open up and share. On the third day of staying in my room and missing classes, I receive a call from the dean of women's office. Dean McBride has been notified of my non-attendance and wants to talk with me. As much as I am intrigued by her, I am not in any condition to deal with my curiosity right now. I tell her secretary I will call back when I have my schedule in hand. I assure Carrie that I will go back to classes on Monday.

On Friday afternoon, Dr. Morrow calls. "Sue, would you like to have dinner with Hattie, Katie, and me?"

"Thanks for the invitation, but I am tired and really not up to socializing."

"Sue, we need to talk. I won't take no for an answer. Remember, I know exactly how you are feeling." As I'm getting ready, I feel like I am moving in slow motion. Carrie watches me.

"Sue, I am not going to let you fall into the same depression that took Patty. I won't leave you alone. I am going to push you and push you until you start living again."

As I turn around, Carrie is crying, not afraid to show me her sadness. I am shocked at her concern and deeply moved by it. Immediately, I want her to feel better. It's strange how we can change when it is for the good of someone else.

As I walk to Dr. Morrow's house, I feel some life returning inside me. Katie greets me at the door and takes me to the living room to meet her friend Ellie, who is spending the night. We talk and laugh and then have dinner. Afterwards Katie and Ellie play, and Dr. Morrow asks me to come into his study.

"Sue, I know the pain that you're in. When I was immobilized by my wife's death, I didn't care about anything for quite some time."

He opens up and spares no details, telling me about his anger and rage at God for taking her. He shares the pain and difficulty he had at the funeral and burying her. But then there was Katie, and he was forced to get beyond the horrible pain and be there for her.

He talks about the day Carrie rushed over to tell him of Patty's death. She had asked for his help in telling me, fearing correctly that I wouldn't be able to handle it. Carrie had shared how close Patty and I were. He said he was devastated for me and that he knew it was going to be difficult. "Sue, looking at your pain takes me back to the day my wife died. I know the gamut of feelings rushing through you—the sadness, pain, and anger."

Listening to him helps me understand a bit more about my own thoughts and feelings. Finally, he mentions that he has talked with Carrie the day before and sees me spiraling into the same kind of depression he went through. I listen—really listen. Both of us wipe our eyes from time to time. I open up and tell him my thoughts, pouring out my pain as I feel it.

"I hate myself and feel guilty for not being a better friend," I say, now crying. Everything comes rushing out: the raw, the ugly, and the hateful masked in a lot of self-pity.

"I knew there was something wrong with Patty, but I always pushed it aside. I feel like I did not care enough to intervene." I cry and cry and until finally my emotions are drained from my body. He puts his arms around me and pulls me to him. With him holding me, I feel depleted and tired, and I feel my eyes close. I fall asleep. When I awake, it is daytime, and I am covered up. Hattie is sitting beside me in a chair.

"How are you Sue? You were so exhausted that you fell asleep last night. John covered you up and let you sleep. I called Carrie and let her know we were going to let you sleep. John's at work, but he told me to call him when you awakened," she says.

"Oh, don't bother him. I feel fine. I feel much better."

"Well, I will fix you a nice breakfast." She calls Dr. Morrow after all. A few minutes later, he comes through the door.

"Good morning, Sue. How are you feeling?"

"I feel pretty good. Better than I have in days," I say, with a hint of my old smile. After breakfast he walks me across campus before heading back to his office.

The second week flies by as I study for my finals. Time and time again I find myself deep in sadness, but I push to work through it. I make an appointment to see Dr. Morrow. He is my outlet to work through my pain. Also, I remember he wanted to talk to me about something when I got back from Thanksgiving. With everything that had happened, he never told me what it was about.

"Dr. Morrow, do you remember when you took me to the station for Thanksgiving? You told me you had something you wanted to talk to me about when I got back. Because of everything, I am sure the timing hasn't been right. But now that my curiosity has returned, can you tell me?"

"I don't really have the time right now to go into it, and I would rather talk to you in a more comfortable setting. Maybe you could come over for dinner tomorrow night. We could talk afterwards."

The following night, I am nervous when I arrive at Dr. Morrow's home. As we are eating, I start to worry. After dinner, he asks me if I would like to go for a drive. That is surprising, but I love the idea of getting away from campus. While driving, he appears nervous. Finally, he stops at a small roadside park area. We get out to sit on a picnic table.

"This is hard for me to talk about, but I feel it is so necessary. Where do I start? Katie was really small when her mom died. She doesn't have any visual memories of her mom. However, other people on campus do remember her. Many of them have pointed out to me that you look a lot like Rose. Here, let me show you."

He gets his wallet out and shows me a picture of her. It is amazing how much we resemble each other. Now, taking a big breath, he stumbles over his words.

"When I saw you, I was so taken…Not only do you look a lot like her, your personality is a lot like Rose. Slowly, I found myself drawn to you. It is so inappropriate of me to let things get out of control. But you cared so much about me, and it really helped me get back into the swing of life. Now, I find myself slowly obsessing about you. One of my close colleagues picked up on all of this. He was kind and talked to me about it. He made me look at it for what it was. I wasn't being fair to you. You deserve the right to be a student in my eyes, not a fixation. I want to apologize and explain that I am working hard to put this into perspective. You have done nothing wrong and have been a wonderful friend. I want to apologize for the inappropriate ways I have been looking at and relating to you."

I am shocked over his confession, and I had no idea that I resembled Rose. I am sad as well. I had thought all our special exchanges were about us, but they were merely moments that reminded him of Rose. As upset as I am, I understand it. I know how the pain of losing someone can make us vulnerable. But I have to be honest with myself. He has been a highlight in my college days so far. This is just another moment in life where I got dished someone's reality to live with. Feeling disappointment, I still want to help him feel okay. Most of all, I want to get through this and get back to my room.

"Well, thanks for telling me. It makes sense. Don't be hard on yourself. I do understand. Well, I think I need to get back. I have a few things I need to get done tonight."

Now Dr. Morrow is looking at me strangely. Suddenly I wonder whether he is looking at me or at Rose. Once again, nothing can ever be the same.

"Sue, I fear I have hurt you. Please tell me what you are thinking about this."

"Oh, I will be all right. After all, this is nothing compared to what I have been through lately. Please, I will be fine. Can we go now?"

He can tell I'm closing off. I don't want his pity. I need him to take me home.

"Sure, but I feel maybe if we talk a bit more it will help."

"Help who—you or me? You have had plenty of time to think about all of this before you shared it. Please give me the courtesy of some time. I will be fine."

As we drive home, I talk about the trees along the route, pretending to be fine. When I get out of the car, he asks me if I would like to come in.

"No, I have got so much to do. Thanks. Bye."

By the time I get to the dorm, Carrie is on the phone in the hall. I know it is Dr. Morrow talking to her about his concern for me. I am seething at the thought of him taking such liberties. Carrie comes to the room, and I like how she handled it.

"Dr. Morrow called and asked me to be sensitive to you tonight. He wasn't specific and asked me not to mention he called. I told him I couldn't do that. I also said he didn't need to remind me to be sensitive to you. What the heck was that about?"

Carrie doesn't know it, but she has made my day. She has respected our relationship by being unwilling to be secretive about his call. I tell her about the whole conversation. Her honesty and openness mean everything to me. Carrie and I are growing very close, and it feels good that we can depend on each other.

The next week I take my finals and prepare to go home for Christmas. I keep moving, doing what Mom told me, and she is right: each day gets a little easier. Walking back to the dorm, I come upon Dr. McBride.

"Sue, you have not made an appointment when I requested that you do so."

"I am so sorry. I will call your office at once and schedule an appointment."

"Be at my office at 3:00 PM tomorrow."

Arriving at Dr. McBride's office the next day, I am a bit nervous, challenged again by the desire to figure her out. I sit across from her and notice a few Christmas presents stacked up behind her. "So, Dr. McBride, are you staying on campus for the holidays or spending it with family?" She looks shocked that I would feel comfortable enough to ask a personal question.

"I haven't made up my mind, but let's get back to you. Dr. Morrow reports that you lost a friend, and that that was why you missed chapel and classes. I later find out that you are back on campus and still not attending class. My job is to decide if you should go to disciplinary review for your absenteeism. Dr. Morrow wrote a letter on your behalf. But what do you think?"

"The days I was off campus were for services, and they qualify under student bereavement policy. However, after I got back on campus, the classes I missed do qualify for disciplinary review. So I recommend you follow the policy on that. I understand that the outcome could be many things, including suspension, and I respect the seriousness of all this."

"Are you telling me that you feel you should receive discipline for not attending classes that week after you got back?"

"Oh, I did not mean to imply that. I merely agree that such behavior is regarded as a violation of policy, and therefore you should process it accordingly. Now, regarding what I feel about that week, the truth is that I was so pained I couldn't feel anything. I was numb and beyond myself. No matter what the outcome of a disciplinary hearing were to be, I know that I was too numb to cope with anything. If you and committee did not see it that way, I am obliged to follow whatever you decide. I won't ever be upset with myself. Under the circumstances, I did the best I could, and I can live with that."

It is amazing: I feel good answering her questions. She can't touch me; I am not a candidate for anyone to mess around with. I have been through hell these past few weeks. Nothing can compare to that pain. I can't be shaken by this moment or by Dr. McBride. She needs to do whatever she needs to do. I will be fine with it.

"Well Ms. Martin, you make a lot of sense. How are you feeling now? I do hope better."

I am startled by her sudden sensitivity. It is obvious that her inability to frighten or terrorize me removes the wall she hides behind. Apparently, she intimidates others to keep them at a distance. No one gets close to her, out of fear. That's her way of controlling life—so she doesn't have to feel or connect. Now she sits without her wall of intimidation.

"Thank you for asking. I am doing better. I have learned not to deny my pain. Sometimes I do well, and other times I succumb to it. But I am no longer frightened by it. I'm learning how to cope." In a matter of minutes I have changed everything about this conversation. No longer was Dr. McBride talking *at* me; she was talking *with* me.

"I see. Well, I am glad you are doing better, and it sounds like you have the right perspective about it. Well, I think we are fine here. I certainly hope things get easier for you."

"Dr. McBride, I am sorry I did not make an appointment. At that point I wasn't a candidate to talk to anyone about anything. Please, I meant no disrespect to you. Today I feel like I made a friend, so I am glad you kept after me. Thanks."

She looks shocked. Probably no one has ever thanked her or referred to her as a friend. People run from her in fear, and that is what she expects from me. She stands up and comes around her desk to walk me to the door. This is big. I remember how she says, "Bye," and people leave while she goes back to her paperwork.

"Dr. McBride, I hope you have a great holiday. Thanks again for caring so much."

"You have a nice holiday, too," she says, now shaking my hand.

Walking back to my room, I feel terrific. I am getting back to my old self. I tell Carrie that I cracked the shell around Dr. McBride.

The next day Carrie and I take the train home. Mom and Dad are waiting at the station, and it's great to see them. As we are driving home, I glance toward the park but don't see anyone. Gary will be home for Christmas and then move to New York to study under Jean-Louis Pacquet. Gary has written me many times. His phone calls are nice reminders that he cares. I have not written him nor anyone since Patty died.

I start to think how life slowly takes away our laughter and smothers our dreams. All the pain forces changes. I still love Gary, but inside I am no longer as excited about seeing him as I once was. It is not his fault that he wasn't there for me at the worst time in my life. He tried hard to comfort me in phone calls and letters, yet I feel distant and removed from him. Patty's death has changed me. I am different, and he is not part of my transformation. I have learned the blatant truth that nothing stays the same.

Walking in the house, I can see the traditional Christmas decorations, yet I don't feel the Christmas spirit. Being home, I'm shrouded in my memories of the last time I was here. Fearing to show my sadness, I speak about the beauty of all mom's work.

"Oh mom, you really did a great job as always at decorating."

Carrie is happy to be at our home. I know she appreciates being with people who care about her. I don't want to bring anyone down with my sadness. I know I can give the performance of my life for my family's sake. After all, this is the most joyous holiday of the year.

"Is Grandma coming for Christmas? When will Grey be home?"

"Well, Grandma is not feeling well, so Dad and I are going to go spend a few days with her after Christmas and before New Year's. Grey will be home tomorrow. By the way, Gary called earlier this morning asking when you would get home."

Carrie goes upstairs to relax. I decide I need some fresh air. "I am going for a little walk and will be back in a bit," I call out. As I go out the door, I suddenly realize the park is no longer the place I want to visit first. I need to go to Patty's grave. As I cross the street to enter the parking lot of the church, I can see someone in the cemetery. As I walk closer, I am shocked to find that it's Gary.

"Gary, why are you here?" I ask, puzzled.

"I knew it would be the first place you'd come. I wanted to be here for you," he says. I am touched by his sensitivity. I hug him and walk over to her grave. A stone marker reads: "Patricia Anita Williams/April 3, 1951–November 28, 1969/Never To Be Forgotten."

I feel my eyes well up. Gary pulls me to him. We stay for a minute and then walk back to his car. It is cold, and we sit inside and talk.

"Sue, how are you really doing?"

"I'm in a much better place today than yesterday. Each day I do a little bit better. For a while all my enjoyment in living was suspended."

Gary holds me, and it feels good in his arms. He speaks of nothing about himself. He simply remains with me as I open up and share. Finally, I suggest I get home. I didn't want anyone to worry. Gary and I make plans to spend Christmas evening together.

After I get home, I talk with Mom about Christmas.

"Mom, I haven't done any shopping because I haven't felt festive."

"Sue, you and Carrie can go shopping tomorrow. It's important that you push yourself to get the old you back."

For the first time, I sleep completely through the night. After breakfast, Carrie and I head out for shopping. It is a beautiful, cold, sunny day. It is so hard being in Willard's department store, where I talked to Patty for the last time. I buy something simple for everyone, unlike in years past when I would look forever for the perfect gift.

On the way back, Carrie drops off chocolates for Bella while I continue on the path home. I think about Eric and how much I appreciate him, how he had helped me by talking about my childhood days with Patty. I decide to walk past my house and knock on his door. His mom answers and says he is working.

I spend the rest of the day wrapping presents and visiting with Carrie. Christmas morning everyone gathers by the tree. Mom has some great Christmas music playing, and Dad passes out the gifts. Carrie enjoys being part of the family. We have a good time opening identical gifts; it's like we are twins. Mom fixes a great Christmas brunch. We spend the afternoon at church, where the choir performs an abbreviated version of Handel's Messiah.

That evening I feel good about being at Gary's home. His mother fixes a lovely dinner, and we open gifts and talk. His parents are sensitive to all that I have been through. Afterwards they leave to look at the decorations in town.

Lying in Gary's arms, I feel at peace.

"I am sorry I am so silent Gary, but being with you is more powerful than spoken words."

"Shhh, just lie here and know that I love you."

Midnight comes quickly, and Gary takes me home. It will be the last time I see him during this trip; Carrie and I must return early to campus.

"Gary, I'm excited about you studying in New York. I want you to continue to write me and keep me updated. I am getting back to myself, and I'll be writing you regularly."

He walks me to the door and backs me up against the side of the house. Looking me straight in the eye, he makes sure I know how much he cares.

"Sue, I'm in love with you. Nothing has changed in me. I am sorry I wasn't there when you needed me the most, but don't ever doubt my love."

"I love you too, Gary."

We kiss one more time and again walk in different directions.

The next day we take the train back to Broctren Harbor College. I feel good to be back on campus. Carrie is busy working many shifts at the switchboard. I spend a lot of my time on library research and writing a make-up paper. As I stop by the student center to pick up my mail, I run into Dr. Morrow.

"Good to see you, Sue. I heard you came back to campus early."

"Yes. I had to finish a paper to wrap up last semester."

"What are you going to be doing for New Year's Eve?"

"I am going to finally relax. Carrie has to work, so I plan on staying in and reading a new novel I got for Christmas."

"Why don't you spend it with us? Katie and Hattie will probably go to bed early, and you and I could ring the New Year in."

"Thanks, but I think I better relax."

"Don't say no. Think about it. If you change your mind, the offer still stands. I'd like to spend time with you."

"Don't plan on me, really…well, I've got to run. See you later."

I am quite confused by his invitation, which feels inappropriate. Was this another opportunity for him to remember being with Rose on New Year's? Thinking about it makes me feel icky. My feelings for Dr. Morrow changed immediately after his disclosure that I look and act like Rose. All of his invitations have little to do with me. Walking back to my room, I am fingering through the mail. Right under a letter from Gary is a letter with a return address reading, "The Other Side of The Brook." Shocked, I rush to my room and open it first.

༄

Sue,

Hello there! Mom said you stopped by to wish me happy holidays. I couldn't believe it. I was also a little concerned, thinking maybe you needed to talk or something. By the time I ran into Mark, you had just left for college. I decided to take a chance and send you this note. I don't know your address, but I know you are at Broctren Harbor College in Broctren Harbor, Illinois. Hopefully, this got to you. So. how are you doing? I am confused as to why you went back to college so fast. I don't know Mark well enough to ask such a question. He always looks a little strange when I ask anything about you. I know you have been through a lot. Please write me and let me know how you are doing. Anyway, if you get lonely let me know. I like riding that train and wouldn't mind coming to check in on you.

Hope you didn't think that was a weird offer. I do care. I think about you and miss you. It felt good that you stopped by.

Take care, Eric

I am pleased to hear from Eric. Even though we barely have a relationship, he is special to me. I like the fact that he went out of his way to write, and I can admit that I miss him, that he even means a lot to me. I can hardly believe his offer to take a train just to visit me. Eric is a constant surprise, and I like his unpredictability. I take out a sheet of paper and write him:

∾

Dear Eric,

It is nice hearing from you. I am doing fine. Sorry I missed you at Christmas, but I wanted to wish you happy holidays. About the fact that you like to ride trains, if you plan on coming this way I would be very happy to see you. My schedule through the week is impossible. But I could forgo the excitement of doing my Saturday laundry <wink>. I would have to know in advance. Thanks for writing. It is great hearing from you.

Smiling...Sue

Next I open my letter from Gary:

∾

My Dear Sue,

How are you? I am filled with the specialness of you. I so love you and hope you are doing well. It is hard to know how to help or be there for anyone, but I do need you to know how much I care.

I have moved into my apartment in New York. It is perfect. Tomorrow I have my first day at the Jean-Louis Pacquet Studios. I owe much to you. The rich realities you gave me have enabled me to paint. I knew how colors looked, but you taught me how colors feel.

Remember that I am with you in thought. Never feel alone. Call me or write when you can. Most of all, know that I celebrate you every day. I love you dearly.

Love, Gary

It's a wonderful letter: vintage Gary, so passionate about life that it is hard to relate to him. He is always up. Everything he says is so abstract, so hard for me to touch. Gary fits in well with my dreamy-eyed romantic soul, and that's great when I am flying with him. But when Patty died, I found out that I needed something tangible and real to grab onto. Gary has never experienced anything that painful. After Patty was gone, everything I was left with wasn't enough. And although I am doing better, still I am at a loss. Maybe that's why I am a bit drawn to Eric. His father left him when he was a child, and his life has been filled with hard knocks. When he sympathizes, it comes from such a real place inside him. I have such love for Gary, and whatever happens, I doubt that I will ever stop loving him. But now I find myself intrigued with the idea of Eric someday coming to visit. I write Gary a letter, too, and mail both letters at the student center. Also getting her mail is Dr. McBride.

"Hello, Dr. McBride. Did you have a nice Christmas?"

"Sue, it is nice seeing you. Yes, I did. I was able to finally relax and catch up on my reading. And how about you?"

"It was nice being home. I had to get back early to finish a paper."

"Take care, and have a nice New Year's Day," she says with a soft smile.

About seven PM, a dorm acquaintance named Betty comes running to my door.

"There is this guy on the phone. He says that he has been calling every dorm trying to find you. His name is Eric."

"Great, thanks," I say, running down the hall to get the community phone.

"Hello, Eric. I just mailed you a letter. I got yours."

"Gosh, I didn't think I had the right address to find you. Then I thought I would call each dorm on campus. Anyone who had met you wouldn't forget you," he says, now laughing.

"I missed not seeing you at Christmas, but I was home for such a short time."

"How are you doing, Sue? I really want to know."

"Oh, better. It was really rough for quite a few weeks, but I am feeling better."

"Has your laughter come back?"

"I haven't had much reason to laugh, but I am smiling right now, and that feels good. Eric, if you get bored and want to visit some time, that would be great."

"What? You're not kidding, are you? You would make time to see me? Gosh, I feel honored!" He is even more taken back by my invitation than I had expected.

"So, Eric, what kind of a party mess are you getting into tomorrow night for New Year's Eve? I hope you stay safe."

"Gosh, Sue. I have been working so much I forgot to plan anything. How about you? Are you going to live it up with the frat guys?" he teases.

"Actually, Dr. Morrow wants me to spend the evening with him. He is dean of students. I used to enjoy spending time with him, but recently everything turned weird, so I turned that down. I guess I will curl up in bed with my book."

"Hmm…in bed sounds exciting, but not with a book."

"I know, but when the chips are down a good book means a lot."

"Sue, thanks for talking to me and writing me. I know you and I are different. But I care about you and consider you a friend. You take care of yourself. Maybe some time real soon I might take a train ride, so take care."

As I hang up, I realize how talking to him made me smile. Bouncing down the corridor, I feel so much better. I am left trying to figure out what I find so special about Eric. He doesn't put anything between us, and he looks directly at me when he talks. Gary's passion of art and beauty are always in front of him. It's like he is always looking around for visions of life. I never feel like *I* am his vision.

The next day I relax. About 1:30 PM, I receive a phone call. I think it might be Gary or my parents checking in. Much to my surprise, it's Eric.

"Hello, Sue. I can't imagine you spending the whole day and night in bed with a book, so I thought I would call you and make you get out of bed," he says, laughing.

"Actually, I wasn't in bed. I am getting ready for a red-hot date for New Year's Eve. How's that?" I say, teasing him right back.

"*Really?* Oh my, then my stupid little plan backfired. Oh well, I took a risk," he says, now sounding very dismayed.

"What do you mean? I'm only teasing!"

"Really? Well, I thought about you not having anything to do tonight, so I hopped a train and am at the train station here in Broctren Harbor. Halfway here I thought it was stupid of me to come without calling, although my intention was to surprise you."

"What do you mean—you are here?" I say, shocked and happy.

"Yep. I just thought New Year's Eve was a time to party, and I couldn't stand the thought of you lying in bed reading. Listen, I don't want you to feel pressure. It was stupid of me to just come like this."

"No way. I am happy you came. Gosh, I could use a night out. When are you going back?"

"Well, I can catch a 1:35 AM train out, so I'll be with you until next year, see? Well, that's if you can stand me that long."

"Great! Can you give me about forty-five minutes to get dressed? Listen, you can come to the main lobby of Brea Hall and look for the bell system. Just push 303 to ring my room and I will be down in a couple of minutes. You can enjoy watching some of the pretty girls of Brea Hall until I get there."

"Nah. It's strange, but I never could see anyone except you. See you in a bit."

I feel my spirits lift. I feel happy that Eric made such an effort to see me. Hurriedly, I get ready and leave a note for Carrie.

Eric is on time, and I feel myself come so alive at the thought of seeing him. Rushing down to the lobby, I can hardly wait for the last door to swing open. There he stands. Eric is a very attractive guy. He's dressed up, not his typical jeans and leather coat. I rush to hug him.

"Gosh, it's great to see you. You make my day," I say, wanting him to know I am excited.

"Being with you makes my New Year's Eve special. You are so sweet-looking. Mind if I hug you again?" he says, now pulling me to him.

"It's too cold outside, so let me give you some ideas of where we can go and what we can do tonight. You can decide; I am just happy to be with you. There's a big party that starts at eight and lasts through the ringing in of the New Year. Or, we can go to the student center lounge, but that is generally packed. There really isn't any place that is very private. I can sign off campus, but I have to be back by 1:00 AM," I explain.

"I want you to do whatever you want," he says smiling.

I'd want a quiet evening with Eric, but I don't want him to misinterpret anything. "We can have dinner somewhere and then find a special place where we can hang out."

"Sure, I want to do whatever you want," he repeats, taking me seriously.

"Eric, you're such a very special friend. I am trying hard to not get involved with anyone beyond friendship right now. I like seeing you and talking with you so much that I don't want to ever hurt you. Gary and I have a lot of love for each other, but that relationship is changing. Patty's death has left me feeling vulnerable right now. You don't know how much I enjoy the fact that you are here. I feel kind of selfish and needy, and I don't want you to get hurt. Part of me fears I could give you the wrong message. In all honesty, I'd like to get a room at the Broctren Harbor Inn. I want to be alone with you to talk and just enjoy each other, but I know that I am vulnerable and needy. I fear that you might feel used later on or like I misled you. Gosh, this is hard to admit, but you are the only one with whom I feel real right now. I don't have to pretend, and you are able to take my truth. Do you kind of understand what I am saying?"

Eric has been attentive. It is strange that I am so able to lay it all out there so easily.

"Sue, I am glad you can be honest. I know we are very different people and that you're in a place where you need to stay open to life. I know that I am a friend, and I don't play games with making it any more than it is. For some reason, I feel like your protector or—this may sound stupid, and I can't believe I am saying it—your angel. I am someone who wants to take care of you, someone you can be real with…I am not denying that I am attracted to you and have feelings for you. But I am no fool about the fact that we live very different lives and are only friends. Don't worry, I won't read anything into anything. I'm a pretty wise guy and know the truth. But I do feel honored that you feel safe with me. I won't be disrespectful," he says.

"There is this inn on the shoreline," I suggest. "This is a college community and most of the students are gone for New Year's. So I bet we can get a room, relax, and have privacy to talk and enjoy our time together. Maybe we could pick up some food on the way there. How's that sound? By the way, I want to take care of this; after all, you came all this way."

"No way are you paying. I am man of means, and I want to take care of everything."

"Eric, this is a very small, conservative town. Since I am a student, how about this? Why don't you go to Broctren Harbor Inn and get a room? Call me and give me the room number. I will be over within twenty minutes. I will bring some food."

"That's great. I will call you in a bit."

I go to my room and pack a small tote bag. I have no preconceived notions about the evening but feel good about being with Eric. When the phone rings, I rush down the hall to get it, and Eric gives me the room number. On the way to the inn, I stop for sandwiches, chips, pie, and sodas. Coming out of the deli, I run into Dr. Morrow on the sidewalk.

"Sue, glad I ran into you. I was going to give you a call to see if you changed your mind about coming over tonight."

"I'm sorry, but I have other plans. Thanks anyway, and have a nice New Year's Eve."

I finally reach Broctren Harbor Inn and find the room—a cute little room with a balcony that overlooks the lake. We can see the sunset from the balcony.

"Sue, how are you feeling about being here, really?"

"Great, I am so glad that I can relax with a friend."

I spend time telling Eric about campus and all the craziness I have experienced. I tell him about Dr. Morrow and Dr. McBride. I open up about my classes, especially philosophy. It's fun opening up and trusting him with my life. Then I make Eric tell me about his life. He shares a lot about his work and how he has matured, taking on more responsibilities. Now a supervisor, he feels strange giving directions and overseeing people. He talks about his family, especially his mom, who has been sick this winter. He says he doesn't party much any more.

It's fun talking. After a while, we both lie back on the bed and relax.

"Eric, I love this evening with you," I say, moving over to him.

He puts his arms around me, and it feels good to be held by him.

"Well, I am enjoying this a lot. Would you mind if I kiss you? Or would you rather we lay here and I give you space? I don't want to offend you in any way," he says.

"I would love for you to kiss me. You can really be with me tonight if you want to. I shared my truths with you earlier. I did that so I could be free tonight for whatever happens. I want to be held, and I want to make love." I barely finish before he pulls me to him and begins kissing me.

It is wonderful unfolding with Eric. We kiss, and I feel myself give way to a sweet passion that takes me.

"Sue, I am so happy to be with you even if it is for one special night."

He is unbuttoning my blouse and I unbutton his shirt, and no more words follow—just a sweet permission to enjoy each other. I see him reach into his wallet for protection, and I relax. The next minutes are spent with him delighting in all of me and I him. Nothing fast, but a growing passion that takes us completely and most satisfyingly over the edge, and it is wonderful. Eric knows how to approach everything. He knows how to move and turn and give a woman the ultimate pleasure. He is unbelievable in how he drives my body to ecstasy. It is so intense and electrifying. No awkwardness, just amazing natural movements from a very experienced man who knows how to put a woman first. It is awesome.

Now, lying in his arms, I feel so appreciative of the moments we share. It is the best I have felt in a long time. After a couple hours of resting and silently enjoying each other, we slowly and intimately move into another moment that sweeps us beyond ourselves. This ends with us hearing sounds of fireworks outside. Exhausted and depleted, we open the curtain to see fireworks majestically fill the sky. They are beautiful off the shore of Lake Michigan.

"Sue, this is wonderful. Thanks for a terrific evening. Don't worry that I will read anything more into it than it being one very special night."

"You have restored life in me. Thanks for making me feel special. Tonight has moved me beyond my sadness. I like how natural it feels to be with you. Thanks for understanding where I am right now. This was terrific and very special."

The clock reads three minutes to midnight. We count down the last seconds of the year and kiss at midnight, wishing each other a Happy New Year.

CHAPTER 19

Second Semester

The second semester opens up with the students attending the annual Christian Mid-Year Seminar. This year's topic is "Survival: Testing One's Strength of Character." All faculty members participate as facilitators of small groups. As I sign up, I see that Dean McBride is a group facilitator. I feel this will be an opportunity to get to know her.

On the first day of Mid-Year Seminar, I enjoy the morning lecture. As I arrive for my small group, Dr. McBride smiles as I enter the room. Everyone opens up and talks about the life experiences that changed them. Dr. McBride is rather quiet and only speaks up to redirect the conversation from time to time.

"Dr. McBride, please share with us what happened in your childhood that brought about the most significant positive changes to your life," I ask. I can tell she is a bit uncomfortable with my question. I know I am the only one with the courage to ask her anything.

"Sue, when I was fifteen years old I became very ill. To make a long story short, my grandparents took me to the doctor, and I was told that there was little to no chance that I would survive. A couple of days later an experimental drug created by a physician in Germany but yet to be tested on humans was suggested. With special permission from regulators, I was given the drug. One morning when I woke up my temperature was gone, and energy returned to my body. I am here today because the medicine worked. That revelation shook the core of my existence, and I came to realize the power of healing. I am here because of God."

It's amazing how every student listens attentively. Her personal disclosure silences the room. As students leave for the day, many stop to thank her for sharing her story. She is moved by their appreciation. I am the last to leave.

"Dr. McBride, what you shared was so powerful. Thank you so much."

"Sue, thank you for asking about me."

That night I tell Carrie about my small group. She says she heard I was the only one who signed up for Dr. McBride's group. The other students were forced into the class because the other classes were full. I feel especially thankful that I was there to hear her tell her story. Maybe this is a fleeting moment for the other students, or maybe it is a beginning. Either way, she finally has fifteen students who listened and cared about what she was saying. There was no wall between any of us. At the end, all were left overwhelmed with the healing power of God.

On Thursday, Dr. Morrow asks to see me. After my group meeting, I comply with the request, feeling manipulated by his power to summon me.

"Have a seat, Sue. I want to talk about your abrupt change since our last talk. I didn't share everything that day because you said you need time and wanted to leave." I could not understand my anger, but I found myself seething as I sat there. I certainly knew why I had the right to be disappointed, but the anger was coming from someplace deeper.

"I really miss you a lot. It is not Rose I am talking about. You did not give me time to explain. Sure, my attraction toward you in the beginning was because of your resemblance to Rose. After a bit, however, I became very drawn to you. As a matter of fact, I still am. I don't know how appropriate that is, but in any case it is true. I hope you allow our friendship to grow. I feel good talking and sharing with you. You make me feel so much more alive."

"What do you want me to say, Dr. Morrow? I feel that all of this talk is about what you want, what you desire. Little of it has to do with me. You have become just another instance in my life when I let myself feel like I am valued only to find out that the relationship is more about how well I fulfill the other person's needs or dreams. Well, I haven't heard anything as to why I am special. What it is about me that you find intriguing? Have you asked me how I feel? Also, I don't like that looming reality of what's appropriate and what's not. I get the idea that you want me to stay open to our rather unique friendship because it gives you the illusion of being close to someone. I don't want a pseudo-relationship that doesn't offer me intimacy and closeness. I don't want to dream and pretend, and—as you implied—anything beyond fantasy is not appropriate. I am a real person who has real needs."

He looks upset and sad. "Wow, you are upset, and I feel bad about it. But you are wrong about me liking you because it meets my needs. I like you because..."

Immediately I cut him off. "You can't be there for me, Dr. Morrow. You can't walk over a line. I don't want words where you tell me how much you care but can't touch me or show me. I won't settle for a token experience. I am not a desperate college kid who is vulnerable to you. Any previous feelings are gone, and I now see you as just the dean."

"Sue, I want to talk more about all of this, but not here in the office. Please, just allow me one more talk. I promise it will be the last if that is what you want."

My first thought is, "No way: this is ends now." But I must have some feeling for him. Otherwise, why am I angry? The most predominate feeling underneath my anger is helplessness. I feel helpless because this situation is defined by his conditions and history, and I have no control."

"Okay. I will meet you to talk it out."

"Good. Thank you. On Friday night, how about we leave campus and find a comfortable place away from here to open up? Would you like to come over for dinner tomorrow night?"

"No dinner, but how about I come at seven. We can leave then."

Walking back to the dorm, I find myself angrier than when I went. Later that night, I share my feeling with Carrie.

"Sue, do not go off campus with him until you understand yourself. I worry that you may be vulnerable. I don't want you hurt."

"Right now, I don't feel anything special for him. I can't imagine being vulnerable."

The next day is our final day of Mid-Year Seminar. In the group meeting, we share how the experience impacts how we feel. As we get toward the final minutes, I realize Dean McBride had not said much, so I ask her a question.

"Dean McBride, how has that situation of being so ill at the age of fifteen affected how you live your life today?"

Just as she starts to answer, the bell rings. I hear her say, "I believe I will be healed." As I walk out of the room, I wonder what she means. She spoke in present tense: "believe," not "believed."

That evening I meet Dr. Morrow at his house on campus, and we drive out of Broctren Harbor. "Sue, I thought we'd go to Mason."

"That's fine. How did you like the Mid-Year Seminar?"

"I enjoy the small group process. I was hoping you would sign up for my group, but I noticed you signed up for Dean McBride's group. You are amazing. Most students fear her."

We stop and get a couple of root beers and go to the park. We park in a rather private place and make ourselves comfortable in the car. Dr. Morrow turns so he can look at me.

"Sue, you are wrong about how I feel about you. I am really taken by you."

I cut him off, not wanting him to go any further. "Yes, Dr. Morrow, but all I am ever going to be allowed to call you is Dr. Morrow. That really doesn't allow for much, now does it? Anyway, my feelings for you have changed."

"Sue, please don't think I am following you or anything, but I know you were with a man on New Year's Eve. I saw you walk back to the campus with him sometime after midnight. I saw you walk into the Broctren Harbor Inn earlier in the day. Is this person someone special?"

I am shocked he knows so much. I feel paranoid; maybe he *is* following me. "How do you know so much? Anyway, yes, it was a wonderful evening of intimacy and celebration. Something I could never have with you, Dr. Morrow."

"By intimacy, do you mean you were totally intimate with him?"

"That is really none of your business and an inappropriate question," I say, with a tone that is as cutting as I can be. Silence fills the car. I wonder why he is confronting me with this. After all, it had better not be because he's the dean of students, as I am presently off campus and in his car.

"Sue, I care about you. I don't know how to handle my feelings. Sometimes I think I shouldn't hold back and instead let myself be true to what I feel inside. I have very strong desires for you. But it could be dangerous for you and for me. Everything about it has warning signs going off in my head. How do I deal with my obsession of desiring you?"

I am shocked. I had no idea that he feels this strongly about me. At first it feels so flattering. Quickly, though, my thoughts change, and I believe I'm only a reflection of Rose. I recall Carrie's warning that I might be vulnerable to him. In spite of my curiosity, which normally pushes me into exploring things, I feel the need to move beyond all the mysticism of this moment.

"Dr. Morrow, please. We need to move out of Disneyland and back into reality. Our relationship has nowhere to move. It's inappropriate under the auspices of student-dean relationships. Let's just honor who we are right now." I can tell he is emotionally stretched, hanging out there on hope.

"Sue, please let me kiss you. Please, call me John for this one night. Please don't close off until we have allowed ourselves at least one second of real intimacy," he begs in desperation.

I am shocked that he wants to cross that line, even if only for one night. I am confused because I know it is wrong and because I am nevertheless intrigued and can't deny I want him to do it. My head is spinning: am I merely Rose coming alive for him? I do not respond, and the silence is choking us both.

He moves over and puts his arm around me. Obviously, I need to take control of this situation. But I don't. I stay silent as he pulls me to him. I let him kiss me. It's tense, passionate, and I respond to it. I can hear the emotion by how he's breathing. Pulling away, he looks at me and still I say nothing. I can see he is wrestling with himself. I know he longs for so much more. I neither encourage nor discourage him. He is not going to blame any of this on me. He is raw with desire and fighting himself to get control. Suddenly, I feel like I am watching a movie. I feel myself disengaged from him completely. I know I want him, but I won't let myself believe in anything that's happening. My responding to the kiss has taken him.

"Please, Sue, please let me hold you. Tell me you want me to hold you," he says, begging.

"No, Dr. Morrow. I won't have you blaming me for your own desires."

"Please call me John, please," he says, now moving over again and pulling me to him. He kisses me again so passionately, so intimately, with such desire. I respond, but suddenly I feel toyed with and annoyed. Yet, I want to push him to the edge, unravel him, and wreak havoc with his reality. While he is kissing my neck, I take his hand and put it on my breast. I need to know if he is playing around or open to real intimacy. His fingers rub me, but then he abruptly pulls back. I can see he is deeply shaken by his actions.

"Sue, this is wrong, really wrong. You are right, we need to get ourselves into perspective. I am sorry if you are hurt by this," he says, now distraught.

I stay silent. I have protected myself by not trusting any aspect of this encounter. I feel used, but I realize I volunteered for his experiment. He is playing with a fire he can't afford to play with. He is lucky that I am somewhat reasonable because I could have tormented and toyed with him until he was unable to stop. His regrets could have been bigger than they are right now. I feel sorry for him, though. He is embarrassed and upset. However, I do not want to make it easy on him. I gave him logic and reason all night, and he chose to keep pushing ahead. I count the transgression as a personal victory: I did not abandon my reason, nor did I give way to my curiosity, proving that I've matured. I only feel responsible for forcing him to go beyond his surface game of kissing. But I am right; it snapped him into realizing he was playing with fire. I know I wouldn't let myself be party to anything else.

"Dr. Morrow, we are fine. I am sorry you are having difficulty, but this is over now. I am really clear about my relationship to you. You need to get yourself together, and I am no longer the person you need to talk to. Now please, can we get going?"

"Sue, I am so sorry about everything. Please forgive me."

"You are forgiven—but don't push any more. I am not open to anything beyond an appropriate student-dean relationship."

We drive back to Broctren Harbor in silence. As we arrive on campus, he apologizes one more time, and I assure him I am fine.

The next few weeks pass quickly. It is time I pick my faculty advisor. It is an important decision to make. Even though I am not completely comfortable with Dean McBride, I feel it opens up an opportunity to get to know her, so I register her as my advisor.

Carrie and I take a class on aesthetics. Our semester project instructions are to:

> write a paper that details your personal experiences where the elements of contrast significantly change the way you viewed a situation in life. What activating event or sequential experiences occurred that changed how you view a specific outcome? Detail the contrasting sequence of events that brought about the change...

Carrie knew right off what she was going to write. Her whole life was filled with contrasting realities as she moved from one foster care arrangement to the next. For me, it was much more difficult. I thought how Gary's way of thinking is such a contrast to mine. He lives in the present, where everything is enough. I can't live without thinking about tomorrow or the next day. He has such peace and satisfaction in his life. I, on the other hand, am restless and live off the energy of my curiosity. The way Gary lives clearly challenges me, and the contrasting differences provide me with a different outlook on life.

Then there is my mother, and the huge contrast in how she relates to others as opposed to how she relates to me. I had spent my childhood feeling confused by the contrast between how warm and caring she is with others and yet cold to me, leaving me feeling insignificant. That contrast—the stark disparity between how she treats others and how I am treated—contributed to my childhood feelings of worthlessness and low self-esteem. I decide this would be too painful to write about.

I could write about the contrasting lives of Eric and myself. He is an extension of everything I am not. He is "carefree" and so risk-taking. His grabs life at all costs, ignoring danger or consequences, seeking immediate gratification and surrendering impulse control while staying open to the moment. He makes every minute of life important, as if each were his last. He lives his life with no regrets—a huge contrast with how I live mine. I am so calculating about everything. I measure everything before I do it, except for what I do when I am with him. I had to abandon my standards and moral structure to taste the edges of life. This would be a great paper to write, but it would be too revealing and certainly could have consequences as to how I would be viewed by whoever read it.

I think about the huge contrast between Carrie's life and mine.—another excellent potential paper topic. But I know that Carrie is writing about her life experiences, and I don't want to write anything that would parallel any of the details in her story. If anyone has the right to analyze the contrasts in life, it's Carrie.

I decide not to be hasty in determining what experience to write about. I have the whole semester before I have to hand in my paper to Dean McBride. Thinking about all of this, I suddenly get a great idea. The great contrast I can write about is how Dr. McBride is viewed by other students versus how she is viewed by me. I'll focus on how others fear her. I can include my first encounter with her, when I had to shadow her for a day. She was cold, distancing, and barking out directions. Now I see a very different woman. Why the contrast?

I'm excited because I have the whole semester to gather more information. My encounters or interests in Dean McBride derive first and foremost from my wish to know her, not because I am doing a paper. With this clear in my mind, I feel it's a great paper to write. She will be the only one to read it, and it will be an opportunity for me to say things to her that I observed.

I share my thoughts with Carrie and ask that she never tell anyone what I am writing about. She promises, but she has reservations about it, suggesting that it could be offensive to Dean McBride. I might end up being targeted by her wrath. But that is the kind of fear that keeps students from getting to know her. Dean McBride has a wall around her, and I want to know what she is hiding from or why she is walling out the world. Either way, a significant barrier has not been penetrated.

The next day I call to make an appointment to see Dean McBride. Her schedule is open except for three hours from two to five every afternoon because she has to be someplace, according to her secretary. So I make an appointment for the following Monday. I make a notation in my notebook: "what does Dean McBride do for three hours every afternoon?" Later that day, talking to Sherry about her classes, I tell her how much I enjoyed the Mid-Year Seminar. She says she was in a boring small group and had not enjoyed her experience. I told her I was in Dean McBride's group.

"Sue, you should have signed up early so you didn't get stuck with her."

I explain that I chose Dean McBride's group. Sherry says that when Dean McBride saw her sitting on a guy's lap and kissing him, she warned her that further behavior of that kind could result in discipline. Since then, Sherry signs off campus to go have fun, refusing to be in a place where she can be seen by Dean McBride. I can't figure out why Dean McBride is so cold when she deals with students. Taking out my notebook, I make a notation of what Sherry said.

Monday quickly arrives, and I have classes all morning. At lunch I sit with Carrie and Sherry. Carrie reminds me of my appointment with Dean McBride.

"Why did you get called in by the witch," Sherry asks?

"I made the appointment. She is my advisor," I explain.

Sherry is completely shocked that I have elected her to be my advisor.

"Sue, you're crazy! Why would you have anything to do with her?"

A girl named Jenny is at the table and she speaks up. "Dean McBride is not human; she's void of all human features. Are you writing a science fiction book and using her for a character?"

Another girl, Mindy, says, "I know of two students who left Broctren Harbor College because they clashed with Dean McBride and they hated being confronted by her."

I quickly eat my lunch and go outside to write a few more notes. Off I go to Dean McBride's office, and for the first time I feel a little queasy. Her secretary says she will be ready in a minute.

"Clara, how long has Dean McBride been at Broctren Harbor College?"

"She's been here for fifteen years, and I have been pleased to be her secretary all those years." The phone buzzes, and Clara says I can go in. Dean McBride is seated at her desk. It's strange that such a small woman seems so huge. Perhaps it's because of how those big eyes appear through her thick glasses. I sit down, and she looks up with a rather perplexing look.

"What is it that brings you here?"

"I chose you to be my advisor, and I want to talk about my future curriculum."

Reaching into her drawer, she fumbles for a brochure on requirements and prerequisites.

"It is wise to read this in its entirety. You have plenty of time to plan your course work, but certainly this brochure will answer your questions. Now, is there anything else?"

Shaking from fear, I want to get out of there. Still, I push myself beyond my comfort zone. "Yes, I want to get to know you. It's important to know the people who work so hard to help me," I say, forcing a tone that warrants a response.

"Ms. Martin, what is it that you want to know?"

"Have you enjoyed your years at Broctren Harbor College, and are you pleased at your own career choices?"

Sitting back into her chair, she seems to relax. "Gosh, no one has asked me those questions in quite some time. Broctren Harbor College is not only my career but a way of life. I was raised by my grandparents, and my grandfather was a past president of Broctren Harbor College. I grew up on campus. I went to college here, left for a couple of years to do graduate work, and returned to become the dean of women. My grandfather encouraged me at a very early age to think about working here. Growing up, I looked forward to my pending role here. Now, years later, I have some regrets. I wonder what life would have been like out there? As a child, I found this campus huge. Now, as the years come and go, it gets smaller and smaller, offering less and less. I have enjoyed being the dean of women. In the last few years, though, it has been less fulfilling for various personal reasons that I don't care to go into. Well, I hope this helps answer a few of your questions. I do need to move on with my day. Have a good day, Ms. Martin." She brings the conversation to an abrupt end.

"Thanks, Dean McBride, for talking with me. I do look forward to talking with you in the future. Have a nice day." I can feel her staring at me as I leave.

I feel good that I didn't cower in the midst of feeling uncomfortable. In the end, I had taken another step toward Dean McBride. Always there seems to be something that encourages me. She did not avoid my question and gave a very honest response, even if it was not that disclosing. On the way back I stop at the library for history on the presidents of Broctren Harbor College. Why was she raised by her grandparents? Where were her parents? After some research, I come across a clip announcement:

January 4, 1905

President Albert Wayne McBride, his wife Elma, and granddaughter Sarah moved into the Broctren Harbor College president's estate today. President McBride comes to Broctren Harbor College from Freeman College in Helpena, Alabama, where he served as president for five years.

I keep looking through the clip file…

September 29, 1911

Obituary

Elma Louise McBride passed away at home. She is survived by her husband, Albert Wayne McBride, president of Broctren Harbor College, and by granddaughter Sarah Ann McBride. Funeral services will be held Friday at the Broctren Harbor College Church, and burial will immediately follow at the Broctren Harbor Cemetery.

That obituary clearly shows no other close relatives. I am left wondering what happened to Dean McBride's parents.

Walking back, I feel my curiosity crawling. I sit on a bench and go over the notes I have composed:

1. Where does she go every day for three hours?

2. Get to know her secretary of fifteen years, whose name is Clara Winston.

3. What "various personal reasons" have caused her last ten years to be problematic?

4. Why didn't she leave Broctren Harbor College? What keeps her here?

5. Obituary of grandmother does not state any other living relatives, other than her husband and Dean McBride. So what happen to Dean McBride's parents?

6. What about that childhood illness that almost took her life?

All of this seems like a mystery. I really want to get to know Dean McBride. Something about her is sad. I find myself caring about this cold, completely withdrawn, not terribly likable woman. Why is she hiding in her own self-imposed tomb? Besides the mystery surrounding everything she has said, I dearly care about her. For some reason I feel connected to her. I have no idea why.

CHAPTER 20

Curiosity Growing

I continue my pursuit of information about Dean McBride. I decide to go to her office because I know she leaves at 2:00 PM. I talk with Clara Winston, her secretary for fifteen years.

"Clara, I'm a resident assistant, and I want to get to know faculty and staff. Since you have been at Broctren Harbor College for fifteen years, I bet you have a lot of insight. What was it that brought you to this campus in the first place?"

"My mother worked here and loved her job. Mainly, I wanted to work for Dean McBride because she treasures professionalism. I take pride in my work. Our philosophies and work ethics are compatible." Her phone rings. "Hello, I am glad you called. How was it today? Okay, sure I can do that. Do you need anything else? Are you okay to be alone, or would you like me to stop by? Sure, I can find it for you, but it's generally in your left drawer. I'll be by in a few minutes."

It sounds like she is talking to Dean McBride. I am concerned by what she says. What did she mean by "How was it today" and "Are you okay to be alone?" The whole conversation sounds like Dean McBride is sick. I can tell Clara is busy after the phone call, so I leave. I sit on a bench outside of the building. A few minutes later, I see Clara leave through the side door. I watch her head for the campus faculty housing area. I walk in the same direction, but she doesn't see me. She rings the doorbell, and Dean McBride opens the door. Dean McBride is dressed in a robe, but other than that I can't see much. Clara reaches in her purse and hands her a bottle of something that looks like pills. They speak for a few seconds, and Clara leaves.

I turn and walk in a different direction. Now thinking, I review the facts. Dean McBride must be sick. Clara asked if she needed help. I feel shaken and very concerned. Dean McBride must be doing something that weakens her or makes her sick. Maybe she is doing something that drains her energy. I want to know what is going on. All at once, I recall what she said in Mid-Year Seminar as the class bell went off on the last day. When I had asked her how that childhood illness still affects her today, the bell had almost drowned out her words, which were something like, "I believe I will be healed."

Walking home, I feel very sad. Dean McBride is a very special person. It's like she is a family member who is difficult to deal with, someone you still love despite her ways. As I reach my room, I fall on the bed. "Why God, why?" After a few minutes, I sit up, thinking. I will give Dean McBride space. I will never share what I heard or suspect. It's obvious that this is a very personal and private matter. Even though I want to know what was going on, I will respect her privacy.

Later that evening I tell Carrie that I am thinking about doing my paper on the contrast between Gary and myself and how that impacts my outlook on life. Carrie seems relieved that I'm considering something other than Dean McBride to write about. I still have a whole semester to think about the paper. But for now, I am unwilling to consider Dean McBride as my topic.

The next few days I focus on my classes. As the week comes to an end, I am ready to relax. As I finish my last class for the day, I stop at the post office and pick up the mail. I sit in the sun and read my letter from Gary.

ॐ

Dear Sue,

As always, you are in my thoughts. Things are going great here. Jean-Louis Pacquet is a very interesting man to study under. His techniques help a lot. He is careful not to taint my visions with input. He will have an exhibit in Chicago during spring break. I was thinking you might be able to meet me there. I would love for you to meet him and see his work. Of course, I would love to see you.

Although he and I have not developed a relationship outside of paintings, I do consider him a friend. He talked about the importance of each of my paintings and how I must see them as possessions of value He has moved me beyond my hobby mentality into being a serious painter. I want the two of you to meet.

How has your world changed? Are you now more settled and feeling part of the college community? I do so want to hear from you. I know you must feel distant from me. Your nature is based on the tangible reality that surrounds you. I under-

stand that's part of you. I, on the other hand, will always be filled with your beauty. You are constantly in my thoughts and an inspiration to my works. I love you dearly. What you have given me will always be a vital part of my life. Please know I love you. Let me know what you think about meeting me in Chicago for the Jean-Louis Pacquet exhibit. Feel my love, it is always there. I am here for you. I love you, Sue.

Gary

It's great hearing from Gary. Sometimes I find myself holding on because I know he sees more in me than I do myself. Returning to my room, I lie down and think about that ever nagging question regarding the purpose of life. I have experienced the rapid pendulum swing of changing realities. From those wonderful times of loving and celebrating life with people I have been suddenly flung into the lowest pits of despair over death.

My thoughts run wild thinking about everything, especially Dean McBride. I'm sad at the possibility of her being ill. In some ways, I want to run away from dealing with Dean McBride. I don't want to own my truth of being afraid to take on more sadness. I rationalize my truth to make me feel better, concluding I must walk away out of respect for her privacy. Before her illness, I did everything I could to get close to her, and to hell with her privacy. I became challenged by her coldness, which reminded me of my childhood relationship with my mother. I have never been able to confront issues with Mom, but I will not let another person dismiss my existence. Dean McBride is an outlet to confront the misery I still hold inside. Why should I care about this cold and terribly unlikable old woman? It's always the shattered pain of yesteryear that becomes the catalyst of my actions today.

It all starts with that never-ending curiosity of mine. I always want to know whatever is being kept from me. Dean McBride keeps people away as if she is hiding something. That piques my curiosity. Also, I like the challenge of trying to get to know her. Her cold and insensitive ways repel others, and that intrigues me. But now, looking back at everything, it occurs to me that this is all about me, with little regard for her. It is rather sickening to think that I engage in games that toy and play with others without any regard for how it affects them. Maybe I'm growing up; maybe now this realization of my inappropriate behavior will bring about change.

The following week I go out to dinner with James Barrington, Jr. We have become good friends. We leave campus and go to his exquisite apartment building. He lives in the penthouse in a very expensive and unbelievably decorated apartment. Freshman are not allowed to live off campus, so his parents rented this place for him to get away on weekends. He hasn't shared this with others, fearing he would be seen as a "little rich boy."

We go down to the garage, which holds a beautiful Corvette convertible. He keeps the top up until we are out of the area, but then he puts it down for us to enjoy the fresh air and sights. We go to a small town with a lovely Italian restaurant. Everyone there seems to know him. After dinner we return to his place and relax as we talk the night away. About ten PM, he asks me if I would like to spend the night, as he has a nice guest room. I call the main campus switchboard and tell Carrie I will be out for the night and not to worry.

"James, what do you want out of life? You seem so sad and so lost."

"I want to know that I am loved for myself, not because I'm a Barrington. I watch my family be loved for the millions they give to charities and see how they are celebrated for being Barringtons. All that doesn't have one thing to do with me as a person. The only thing this privileged life has given me is mistrust and paranoia. I don't share anything, fearing I will be consumed for the wrong reasons."

"James, I know I can't possibly understand everything you are saying, but I do care about you as a person."

"Oh Sue, I am so slow at getting to know and trust people. But you have always been very kind and sincere in your efforts to get to know me. It's always refreshing when you fight to pay for your soda because you don't expect or want me to. It's like you have a need to be responsible for yourself. The other thing I love is that you don't cut me any slack when you confront me. You are genuine and never sell yourself out trying to placate me. Instead, you will cut my legs out from under me when you are defending your position on things. The fact that I am a Barrington has no effect on how you treat me. Even bringing you over here, I knew, wouldn't affect how you feel about me. I know you aren't changed by any of this. Come Monday, you will fight again to pay for that damn soda. I have come to trust you immensely. Now, relax and tell me about your family and your life. What is it that no one knows about you—you know, that thing you hide inside?"

Feeling totally relaxed, I start to share about myself. "I have a nice, middle class family, who are pillars in our small town. On a much smaller scale than yours, I often feel like I am popular only because my last name is Martin. My parents are the president and chairman of everything. No decisions in the community are made without their input and, generally, their leadership.

Now—about what I haven't shared with anyone. Hmm. I feel comfortable sharing it with you because you don't have a relationship with my mother. I have many friends back home, and Carrie is a friend from home. They adore my mother—and rightfully so because she is so wonderfully giving to them. My mother makes everyone's world a better place. Of course, everyone thinks I am fortunate that she is my mother. Most of the pain I have felt is from my relationship with her. When I was a child, she pushed me away, never allowing herself to engage with me. She gave me good, basic care, but she had nothing to do with me other than caring for me. I was never allowed in the kitchen. She didn't teach me to cook or clean, always pushing me away. When she spoke to others about me, she called me 'poor ol' Sue' and went on to say something that implied how much she loved me even though I wasn't up to speed. It certainly contributed to my poor self-esteem."

"Gosh, Sue, do you mean that no one knows how you feel about your mom?"

"Yep, no one except you. My mother is a wonderful human being, and I have watched her all my life with total amazement about how she gives to others. But anyone who could have seen how cold and distant she was with me would have wondered why. She was like a second mother to most people. I don't know what the problem was, but something was terribly wrong. She has changed as I have gotten older, so now I feel like we have grown much closer. I still have haunting memories of cruel acts of pushing me away. The memories come back when I am in a bad place."

"How did you survive while you were going through it?"

"I always had my faith. I believe God will not allow me more than I can bear. I trust God has some purpose in all this. Somehow whatever happens will make me stronger or give me insight that will be valuable in life. I have to believe my relationship with my mother has a purpose, or I don't think I would have survived it. I am not saying it is worse than what others go through, but it was traumatic to me. I think that life is nothing more than a journey of faith. We are all tested beyond reason. When we humble ourselves and realize we have no control over certain things, we come to trust God. I believe our purpose on earth is our journey to God. Ultimately, we have a choice about our soul."

It's a great feeling letting it all out. James has become so special—a real friend whom I trust. We stay up talking, and he shares many of his childhood memories. The more we talk, the more we understand and care about each other. About 3:30 AM we turn in for the night. I sleep so soundly I do not wake up until ten AM. James is in the living room working on a college paper. I have some coffee but feel the need to get back on campus. James drives me to the campus entrance. As I get out of the car, I see Dr. Morrow walking down the sidewalk. I quickly say hello but keep walking.

Carrie is in our room working on a paper. I share about my evening and explain that James and I have become great friends. In many ways, he feels like a close brother. I study for a while and then answer Gary's letter.

∾

Dear Gary,

Thanks so much for your letter. I would be happy to meet you in Chicago to attend the Jean-Louis Pacquet exhibit. Chicago is so big, so it is a bit scary for me. Maybe you could arrange to be at Union Station when I arrive. We could spend the day together and attend the exhibit. We'll catch a late train out for home. It would be fun riding home on the train with you.

I still have two weeks before I am done with classes. Jean-Louis Pacquet's exhibit is the second day of our spring break, so I will stay on campus until I leave for Chicago. I will arrive at 9:45 AM on the day of exhibit. Then I will put myself in your hands for the rest of day. We can take the 11:45 PM night train home. Let me know how that sounds.

I do miss you and think about you. I have finally found comfort in my college life and made some great friends. I am really looking forward to meeting Jean-Louis.

Please know I love you. Write or call and let me know if these plans work for you.

Love, Sue

It feels good thinking about seeing Gary again. I no longer feel pressure about our relationship, and I still have a rich love for him. The fact remains that his peace and happiness is important to me.

As I am walking across campus, I hear Katie hollering at me. I turn around and she and her father are walking down the sidewalk. I stop and wait for her.

"Sue, I miss not seeing you," Katie says. "I got a puppy and named him 'Harold.' He is a mutt—you know, a blend of many dogs. When can you come over to see him?"

It's great to see Katie. "Can I come now, since you look like you are on your way home? That is, if it is okay with your dad?"

"Sure, Sue. You are welcome to stop by and visit Katie any time." I notice him put the emphasis on Katie, as if to show me that he has moved on since we last met.

I can hear the puppy barking inside the house. As we walk in, Hattie looks frazzled.

"John, you're going to have to do something. He is chewing the edges of the furniture."

"Katie," I say, "get me a newspaper. I will show you how to train your dog." I roll up the paper, and every time the dog goes to chew on the edge of the chair I hit him hard on his nose with the paper. I explain that the blow does not hurt, but the noise has tremendous impact, and that it's the best way to get the attention of the dog. Hattie offers us some refreshment, and I sit and have some lemonade with Dr. Morrow and Katie. The phone rings, and Dr. Morrow takes the call.

I hear him say, "Thanks, Clara. Tell Sarah not to worry. I will take care of everything. Tell her to get well and hurry back."

"I overheard what you said. Is something wrong with Dean McBride?"

"Sue, I am not allowed to say anything. I won't deny that I was talking to Clara about Sarah McBride. She'll be leaving for about a month, but that is all I am at liberty to say."

"But you said to tell her to get well and hurry back. That means she is ill. Is she going to be okay? Please, I want to know. I promise never to say anything to anyone."

"Okay, but this must be kept confidential. Sarah has had leukemia for years. She's been in remission until her recent checkup. Now she needs more treatments. In the past, they have put her in remission. Let's pray they work this time as well. Please, no more questions. I beg you to keep this to yourself."

I am shocked at the severity of her illness. "Dr. Morrow, is she at home or in the hospital?"

"Sue, please do not go to the hospital to see her. Surely she would be upset that you knew any of this."

Obviously, she is in the hospital, then. I feel shaken, and tears well up in my eyes. Katie has taken Harold to her bedroom. Dr. Morrow can tell I am upset, but he knows better than to step over the line by being personal with me.

"Well, I must go. Tell Katie I said good-bye."

"Please take care of yourself. Thanks for talking with Katie. She asks about you."

The next week, I do not hear anything about Dean McBride. I know the students won't miss her. I stop by her office, and Clara tells me she has taken time off. When I ask if she is on vacation, Clara says Dean McBride does not allow her to comment on her personal life. I am out of the loop; all I can do is pray for her.

James and I spend a lot of time together studying and just talking. On Friday he invites me over to spend the night at his place. That evening we talk about our past relationships. James says his parents have arranged many situations where he is forced to meet wealthy socialites whom his parents feel are perfect for him. He hates their pushiness about him finding someone. I share about my relationship to Gary. I explain how he has been there for me and gives me so much. James can tell that Gary means a lot. He also says it's obvious that Gary and I do not connect at an emotional level. His insights are on target.

I ask James if he has ever met anyone who he feels is that special person. It's strange that I'm framing my language without a definitive gender. James picks up on that.

"Sue, promise me that you will never divulge what I am about to tell you."

"I promise," I say, thinking I know what he is about to say.

"No one knows this, and I have never ever shared it with anyone. My parents would not be able to handle this should they find out. I am not attracted to women. I'm attracted to guys."

"I am your friend and would never ever reveal that to anyone. Also, I am a very open thinker. I don't think this world is as defined as the moralists do. I believe in diversity and find most people too rigid in their thinking. Have you been in a relationship yet, or have you met anyone that you have been attracted to?"

"I have been attracted to a couple of guys, but I haven't stepped toward anyone and defined myself. My parents are very outspoken about gays and have said that homosexuality is an evil and a curse. I have let their outspoken ways dominate my thoughts, and I am immobilized out of fear. I hate that I am the way I am. I have dated girls and found them to be wonderful, but I have no desire to be with them beyond friendship. All of this has left me fragile, and I stay hidden in my secret hell, fearing it will destroy my parents if they know."

It is obvious that James lives a somewhat tortured life hiding the truth about himself. My heart is overwhelmed with his honesty and pain. What can I possibly do or say that can help? "James, I certainly can't relate to your situation, but I can tell you this. I had a lot of misery and discontentment in my life because of my mom. The pain was often so unbearable as a child. One day I realized that I did not have to live in the shadow of that pain. I had to be willing to step out and claim my life. I opened myself up, and I have taken chances at trying to find out who I am. I know that I have done things that would devastate my parents if they found out, but I did them anyhow, with no guarantee that it might not blow up in my face. I have taken leadership over my life. Should anything happen in my relationship with my parents, I will be fine because I now have myself. I am not that vulnerable anymore, so now I am able to look at them with appreciation, not out of neediness. I do know that my life is so much different from yours. But you can't hide and give up your life for your parents or anyone. You are entitled to live your life as you see fit."

I can tell James is feeling better just having someone to talk with.

"Sue, I started rebelling against my parents at the age of eight. My father tried to use his money as a means to control me. I chose to go to a Christian boarding school instead of the Premier London Academy, where he went as a child. He wanted to me to go to Harvard, but I chose Broctren Harbor College. When they picked friends for me to associate with, I chose other individuals as my friends. Each of these disputes came with huge fights and horrible words. Looking back at those things and trying to imagine what would happen if they saw in me one of the things they detest most in society is almost more than I can bear. Do you see what I mean?"

"You're right; this is huge. I find your heart putting them first. Excuse me for putting you first. You can't live out your parents' ideas at the cost of everything you are. I am not saying you are ready to do anything, nor am I able to assess whether you could handle their disappointment or possible rejection. Surely you have to weigh those things. Someday, though, you have to taste freedom and know how it feels to soar and be yourself. You have protected others, and that is an aspect of love, but their love should not require you to be what you aren't. You understand what I am saying?"

"Oh Sue, I can't believe I am talking about this. You are so easy to talk with, and I so need to do so. It is a huge step for me to say it out loud. I hope I haven't burdened you. I never let myself feel too depressed over things; after all, I am fortunate and have a wonderful life. I have much to be thankful for."

It's amazing how James enjoys life and has a sense of gratitude. I believe in time he will explore and grant himself the right to his life. Tonight has been a huge night for him.

The following day, I notice Carrie is getting ready to go out. At first I assume she has to go to work. Finally, she confesses she has a date with Keith Saunderland. They have been talking a lot, and a couple of times he has taken her to the snack bar after work. She is really enjoying his friendship. I can't help but tease her.

"So, Carrie, when I am to expect you home?" I ask, playing the dutiful mother.

"Keith is taking me to a movie and we will probably stop to eat. I'm excited." Carrie has never been on an official date. This is a big moment for her.

"I am so glad for you. When did you notice that you really started liking him?"

"He really stared at me when he and David helped your father move the refrigerator in on the first day. It's nice that someone finally noticed me. I never considered he would ever ask me out. Oh, look at me rambling."

"I want you to have a terrific time."

Keith arrives, and Carrie takes a couple of last-minute glances in the mirror before she leaves. So many times I wished Carrie would be treated special by someone. If ever there was a real-life Cinderella, it is Carrie. She was raised without family. No one ever wanted to adopt her. She went unnoticed by most people. She did not grow up with a normal girl's life. I start thinking how difficult it was for her in high school. Most of the kids in school knew her plight and avoided her. They all had families, and I believe some thought less of her because she didn't. Families are such a big thing in our community. Here at college she was equal to all of us. Our families are not a part of the college experience. Here it is about independence and growth. I have watched Carrie soar. She is more equipped to handle college independence than the rest of us. After all, independence has been her way of life.

As the evening approaches, I decide to go for a walk and look at the sky. There's a campus trail that covers two miles. Hiking between the beautiful buildings, I stop and enjoy the patterns of the aged moss and vines. As I turn into the faculty housing area, I notice the lights are on at Dean McBride's home. I can see her silhouette as she moves about the room. Obviously, she is home and now recovering. I stop for a second and then resume my walk. I continue the pathway leading back to Brea Hall. I feel exhausted and sit on a bench.

Looking up into the sky, I see the Big Dipper, centered beneath it that one bright star. I think of Gary and how our lives have changed. I close my eyes and think back to the first and only time that we made love and how it was so magical. I have so many memories of feeling special. Walking back to the room, I feel exhausted and lie down. I doze off and am awakened by Carrie's key in the door.

"You didn't think you were going to sneak in here and not tell me about your date?"

"Oh, Sue, I had a great time. It was fun—he is so nice. I really enjoyed myself."

"Did you go to dinner? What did you do? How did he make you feel? Tell me, Carrie! I'm dying to know."

"Well, we decided that we didn't want to go to a movie because that took too long, and we wanted to spend the evening just getting to know each other. So he suggested that we go to a cafe on Lake Michigan and watch the sun go down. It was that beautiful little outdoor cafe by the inn. After our soda, when the sun was just about to dip, we ran along the coastline to a little cove and sat down to watch. It was such a beautiful, private place to sit and talk. Anyway, we really got close."

"Mmm-hmm…so how close, Carrie?" I egg her on.

"We kissed, if that is what you're asking. It was nice, sweet, and very exciting. After it got quite dark, we went to Belgos for dinner. It was wonderful seeing the reflections of his eyes in the flickering candle. I don't want to forget it, ever. Then we came back to campus and found this special area on the other side of Langton Hall where this romantic little gazebo is surrounded with lilacs. They smell heavenly. We stayed there until he brought me home."

"I am so happy for you. It sounds terrific."

"Is it okay if I keep this little light on for a bit? I want to write about my evening?"

"Absolutely. You keep it on and write until you have it all captured."

Turning over to go to sleep, I am excited that Carrie had such a wonderful time.

CHAPTER 21

Spring Break Arrives

As spring break approaches, I feel excited about the Jean-Louis Pacquet exhibit and seeing Gary. We will have just a day together before he returns to New York to attend a lecture given by French painter, Benoit LeBranche, the mentor of Jean-Louis Pacquet. I think about Dean McBride. I decide to write a note and take her flowers before leaving for spring break.

Dean McBride,

I have been thinking about you. I miss you. There's a notice on the bulletin board saying you are on a leave of absence. There are no explanations as to why. I wonder if you might be sick. I want to get to know you better and wish to support you in any way I can. I know your nature doesn't allow students to get close, but I feel close to you.

Here are some flowers for Easter. Please know that I do want to see you again soon. Don't hesitate to call or write me if you feel up to it. I care about you...a lot.

Warm regards, Sue Martin

I head to the florist. On the way I see James in his car. "Hey Sue, what are you up to?"

"I need to get some Easter flowers for someone. What are you out doing?"

"I went to the cleaners. How would you like to get something to eat?"

"Okay, but I need to drop off some flowers before I can go out."

"That's fine. I can take you to do that, and we can leave from there."

I know there will be questions about the flowers. I find a lovely bouquet of fresh flowers. When I explain they are for Dean McBride, James is shocked. He drops me off in front of Dean McBride's house. I ring the doorbell and Dean McBride answers the door. She is fully dressed and looks to be herself.

"Hello, Sue. How are you? Please come in."

"Dean McBride, I have missed you. I didn't want to leave campus for spring break without stopping by and dropping off these Easter flowers."

"Thank you so much. They are beautiful. I have been waiting for you to stop by and visit. I thought maybe you found out how sick I am and got frightened, like most people do."

"What made you think I would be stopping by? What do you mean about me finding out how sick you are?" I ask, surprised by her insight.

"Sue, let's see if I can explain. First of all, you have taken steps to get to know me. Clara has informed me of the questions you've asked her. Ah yes, then there is the day I called Clara after one of my treatments. She later told me you had been sitting there, and I know you are intelligent and would figure it out. Also, I saw you out of the corner of my eye when Clara dropped off my medicine. Let's see, ummm…oh yes. I understand you looked up the history of my grandfather at the library. Then there was one other night when you walked by my place; security notified me. There are many things that I have noted but can't seem to recall right now. Why don't you tell me why you are so interested in me?"

Sitting in a comfortable chair across from Dean McBride, I am in shock. I take a couple of breaths and realize I have to get myself together. This is my opportunity. "I find you fascinating because others are so quick to run from you. I believe there are stories behind faces, and from the first time I met you, I have wanted to know your story. I have asked others why they run, and generally it is because they are fragile and can't handle your curt nature. I find that aspect of you most interesting. I am excited about people who challenge and stretch me. Remember that day I shadowed you for training? Well, it was so nerve-wracking, and yet it stirred every inch of my curiosity. The more I learn about you the more questions I have."

Dean McBride listens attentively, then responds. "I told all the students in the Mid-Year Seminar that I am ill, but only you heard what I said. Only those who care and were listening to me would have understood. When you heard I took a leave of absence, I'm sure you put it together. I am a very private person, but I treasure the fact that you have tried to get to know me. Thank you. I have not hidden myself from you. I need those around me to be courageous and not back down, and clearly you were. Please ask anything you want. I do not wish for you to get to know me through research or talking with others. I welcome you and look forward to us getting to know each other." I feel my eyes tearing up. This means so much more than I thought it would.

"Dean McBride, you say you are ill. Can you share what's going on?"

"Sure. That medicine I took as a child kept me alive but later affected my body. I developed leukemia and have been fighting it all my life. I have lived with the threat of death since I was fifteen, and I am still here and fighting fifty years later. From my understanding, there's no other case like mine. People fear death and run from it. I found out early on that people get close to me until they discover my health problems. Then they pull back and abandon the friendship. My illness is too painful for them, and they run. The distancing by others has had quite an impact on me. So I have chosen to be somewhat reclusive and do not engage with anyone beyond my responsibility as dean. That way no one else has to suffer when I go through periods of treatment. For the most part, it works. No one on campus has missed me except you and Clara. I didn't want Clara telling you what was going on. I wanted you to find the courage to ask me. I need people who can handle the tough times my health often creates. I fear my illness can be difficult for those who are too fragile. I know it took a lot for you to come knocking on my door, but I am glad you did."

Just then a woman enters the room.

"Sarah, it's time for your medicine. You need to rest. The doctor does not want you up beyond an hour at a time."

"Okay, fine. Sue, there will be plenty of time for us to talk, so please feel free to stop by. Here is my home number. It would be better to call ahead of time because they have me on a schedule. My medicine makes me sleepy, so I have to lie down for a while. Anyway, thanks for caring so much. It feels good that you went to such effort to get to know me," she says, with a soft tone of sincerity.

"Thank you for seeing me. I will be off campus for Easter. After I return, I do want to talk more," I say.

As I walk down the street, James is parked waiting for me.

"Wow, you shouldn't have waited. I would have called as soon as I got to my room."

"Are you okay?" he asks.

"It is such a long story, and I will tell you while we eat. I am starved. This has to be kept in the strictest of confidence. I can't tell you everything, but I can tell you that I am a friend of Dean McBride, and I care a lot about her." That evening I told James about my strong desire to get to know her. However, I did not tell James about her illness.

Tuesday morning arrives, and it's a beautiful morning. The sun has yet to edge the horizon as I walk to the train station. I relax and think about my past train rides. I recall the time I rode the train with Eric. Then there's that memory of getting off the train and being told of Patty's death. Here will be one more trip, this one offering new insight into Gary's world. I sleep most of the way and awaken to the conductor saying, "Chicago Union Station." As the train stops, I see Gary standing there.

"Sue, you look wonderful! Gosh, I want to hug you and never let you go."

"I am so happy you invited me. I'm excited to meet Jean-Louis and see his work. Have you seen the exhibit yet?"

"Yes, his work is marvelous. One of the paintings is very recent. I was able to enjoy watching its creation from beginning to the end. It took Jean-Louis about a month to perfect it. His techniques are amazing, but I will say no more and let you judge for yourself. The exhibit opens up at two and stays open until six. Jean-Louis has dinner reservations at this quaint little bistro. We can take our time at dinner and afterwards return to the train station for our late departure home."

The cab driver weaves through traffic, dropping us off at a small cafe near the exhibit. We have about an hour before it opens. Gary shares his new insights into composition, color, and texture. It's exciting listening to him as he gets lost in some of his descriptions.

Arriving at the gallery, we find a line of people waiting to get in. Everyone is excited to meet Jean-Louis Pacquet. Although the exhibit will last a week, Jean-Louis will return to New York, where he will host French painter Benoit LeBranche's lecture. As we go in a side entrance, I feel excited as I enter Gary's world. There is a large picture of Jean-Louis Pacquet on an easel outside of the exhibit area. He is a very nice-looking man in his late fifties. His face has wonderful features that showcase much intensity and passion. Gary points him out as we move into the exhibit area. He is busy talking with guests.

Gary starts to walk me through the exhibit. It is amazing how Jean-Louis captures the beauty of life. The first painting, a group of people having a picnic in a picturesque landscape, is so beautiful. Gary quickly asks where my eyes are drawn. I point to a lady who stands out because of how the bright color of her dress conflicts with the pastel colors worn by others. He smiles and makes a note of that in a little notebook he is carrying. We move to another, then another, all scenes of people in the most amazing scenic settings. Gary explains that these are not imagined scenes by Jean-Louis, but real places and people in Paris. Jean-Louis loves the outdoors and sets up his easel and paints scenes of life. Gary talks a lot about Jean-Louis' ability to see light so perfectly. He points out the exquisite shadowing that contrasts the sunlight.

Moving about the exhibit, I notice a huge painting of a woman looking down, as if she has lost something or is trying to cope with something. It seems so out of place. I point out the painting and ask Gary about it. He encourages me to ask Jean-Louis about it at dinner. Each painting has an engraved plate listing a title and date. The titles are fascinating, and I find myself wanting to know why he named certain paintings as he did. First looking at a painting without knowing the title, I find myself lost in my own experience; then, looking at the title, I ponder what Jean-Louis' world has been like. I become more and more lost in many of the paintings. It's exciting to experience life through this medium. After two hours we are near where Jean-Louis is greeting people. As the couple ahead of us leaves him, Jean-Louis turns to me.

"Ah, this is the light from which you see your world. She is filled with such intensity, I can tell," he says, reaching to give me a hug.

"I am so glad to meet you," I say, struck by his eyes and smile. "I have heard so much about you from Gary."

"Let me formally introduce you two. Jean-Louis, I am pleased to introduce you to Sue Martin. Sue Martin, this is Jean-Louis Pacquet," Gary says, beaming.

"Oh, I am so glad to meet the woman who awakens the artist and gives him visions," he says, glancing at Gary and then back to me. "Sue, I am looking forward to dinner tonight. We have a lot to talk about. Thank you so much for coming to the exhibit."

Many people are pushing to meet him, so we quickly move on. Gary and I go to a small park and I talk about each painting. Gary exudes a passion that is beyond what I remember. His voice, which was always clear and steady, is now filled with an influx of emotion. His body has become animated with his arms and hands moving as he talks about painting. Gary is so different and so much more alive.

We arrive at the restaurant as Jean-Louis arrives. "Oh, sorry I'm late, but it has been a wonderful day," he says, giving us a hug. We are seated at a very private table. The waiter takes our order, and we relax into conversation.

"Sue, tell me. What is it about Gary that you find the most fascinating? You know, that special part that makes him different from anyone else?" I love the quality of Jean-Louis' question.

"There is much about him. He is so alive to all the things around him. The thing I find most interesting is his strong sense of gratitude. He is always saying that what he has is enough. That haunts me because I am a restless person, always pushing and wanting more. I find it hard to enjoy the moment because my mind is entertaining thoughts about what I don't know, what I can't see, what I have yet to attain. Having Gary in my life makes me stop and enjoy what's before me," I explain.

"Yes, yes. I see what you mean. Gary, what is it about Sue that makes her so special?" Jean-Louis is looking squarely into Gary's eyes with such intensity, as if he is pondering what the answer will be.

"Sue gave me the edges of life that I hadn't experienced. She has a level of intensity that awakened me. I have replaced my idealistic thoughts of love with a real love. She makes my life so much more. She is the inspiration behind the scenes that come alive on canvas."

"Ah, Sue, you must know how much you mean to this man. I am fortunate to work with him, and I see how alive he is. You have given him much."

I love hearing Jean-Louis speak with his dialect and intense passion. I am completely fascinated by his presence. I finally get a chance to ask him about his paintings. "So tell me: what is it about painting that gives you life? That is, what would be your loss if you couldn't paint again?"

Jean-Louis' face changes quickly, his expressions now formed by his emotions. He seems so pained. "Sue, oh Sue, to make me think about such a thing is devastating. I think my life should end with my last painting. I don't think my life could exist without it."

I am taken by what he says. It's as if my question transformed him into a dying man. I have forced him to look at what would be his greatest loss. It is clear that painting is his oxygen and that, with the last stroke of his brush, his life will end.

"You have shocked me. I couldn't possibly comprehend one thing in my life that would be so powerful that I couldn't exist without it. I can't understand how something can be so all-encompassing," I say. Jean-Louis' eyes are filled with emotion. I can tell I have taken him to a place that is haunting. Part of me wants to explore this, but I need to respect the sincerity of his disclosure. I decide to ask him about his paintings. "Could you tell me about the lady in the painting called *Disbandment*? Where did the vision come from, and what is the painting really expressing? Surely this is a painting that you had to get out of you. It appears haunting and painful and not like anything else in your exhibit."

Jean-Louis' eyes widen in shock. I can tell he is shaken by my observations and my directness. He looks over to Gary as if to acknowledge something, but I don't catch it. With an influx of intensity in his voice, he speaks with a shaken tone.

"Sue, no one ever asks about that painting. Most people quickly move by it, not wanting to take it in. Gary said that was the painting you would ask about. I am glad he prepared me, because you could have caught me off guard. I have to give you a bit of background. I generally paint the exuberance permeating from within me, as I see beauty in this world. That leads to about fifteen major works a year. This is the only painting that took everything out of me for over a year, beginning in 1938." He takes a deep breath. "The painting is of Felicia Anne Houzet. I fell in love with this lovely woman in 1936 when I was twenty-two years old. I met her while I was painting in a park. She stopped by and asked about my painting, questioning the details of a large tree filled with branches of lilacs. I loved how she pointed at specific details and commented about their value. Before the end of the day I had her sitting at the edge of the water, and she became part of my painting. After that day I became a bit distracted by her, and my painting slowly got pushed away. That was the beginning of a wonderful period in my life, and we were very close for the next year. I grew so in love with her. She was a scholar in sociology and was researching cultural differences. She made it clear from the beginning that she was moving to Germany in a year to continue her work. All that seemed so insignificant, as I was willing to move anywhere to be with her. Then one day I met the famed painter Benoit LeBranche. I became fascinated by him. He was fifteen years older than me and had a huge studio set up in Paris. His paintings were sought around the world. I started to spend time with him in his studio. I became inspired again and returned to the seriousness of my painting. Well, it finally came time for Felicia to start preparing to move. She assumed I would be going with her; after all, I believed I would as well. However, Benoit was impressed with my work and offered me an opportunity to work with him. By then my soul was alive again with painting. So I had to tell Felicia that I was staying in Paris. It was so painful to say good-bye. It would be the last time I saw her, for she died in a bus accident in Germany a month later. I was pained beyond anything I had ever experienced. Out of all the wonderful moments we had, I was left with this painful image of the last time we talked—the moment I told her I could not go with her. The image of that painful moment tormented me for months, until one day I had to get relief. The pain had devoured me. I had not been able to paint and had become lifeless in my grief. I took out my canvas and forced myself to paint the one haunting memory of the last time I saw her. I titled it *Disbandment*—as in dispersing, or parting company. That is how she looked when I told her…broken, dark, gray, tormented, and lifeless." He wipes his eyes before he continues. "Sue, that painting was my grieving process. It took forever to complete; it was like I was bleeding on canvas. When it was done, I realized that painting had given me a new sense of life. After purging that awful pain, I saw beauty like never before. Suddenly, I was contrasting the beauty of light against the dark pain of death, and it opened me up to a greater level of intensity. It is amazing how that painting freed me inside. The painting is a cleansing of the loss of her. After it was out of me, amazingly, all my great memories of Felicia returned. It was my most life-altering experience. Anyway, I look at it today knowing it is my most important painting—not the best nor the most beautiful, but surely the most important one." He wipes his eyes again and takes a deep breath and a drink of water. I must share my thoughts.

"As I walked through your exhibit, I found myself glancing back at *Disbandment*. I knew it was the most important one of all. Few people take the time to give meaning to pain. It seems pain far outlives the joys in our lives. I work hard to give meaning to everything that impacts my life. What happened to the first painting of her by the water's edge, the one you painted the first time you met her?

"I originally gave it to Felicia, but upon her death it was returned to me. It now hangs in my apartment in New York. It was not one of my better paintings, but it is invaluable to me. I must say Sue, you are intuitive and so wonderfully rich with insight. Gary is right about you."

He glances at Gary with a smile. Gary is silent as Jean-Louis and I talk. I was curious about the man whom Gary found so amazing, and Jean-Louis is clearly interested in knowing me because of things Gary shared with him. I feel thankful for the opportunity to meet him. Now he is a friend of mine as well.

We spend the rest of dinner talking about many things. Jean-Louis is finally able to share more about Felicia and why he was so attracted to her. We talk about the paintings in his exhibit, and I share my rather simplistic thoughts about each of them. He seems fascinated by what I have to say. Before long, we need to get going.

"Sue, it has been such a pleasure getting to meet you. What Gary says about you is so beautiful, but even words pale in comparison to meeting you in person. Thanks so much for coming to Chicago to meet me and see my work."

"Thanks for taking time out for me. I feel honored I got to spend time with you as well."

We grab a cab, rush to the train station, and board the train for home.

"Gary, I hope I didn't embarrass you. I was so wrapped up in talking with Jean-Louis that I forgot to breathe. I was embarrassed when I heard myself gasp a few times."

"I really enjoyed listening to the two of you. Jean-Louis was really taken by you. He had told me the story of Felicia and said that no one ever commented on that painting, but I knew it would be the first painting you would ask about."

Gary talks a lot about Jean-Louis' personality and shares many stories about Jean-Louis' life experiences, which shaped who he became. He is excited to meet Benoit LeBranche, who is the most powerful influence in Jean-Louis' life. We talk for a couple of hours before I start yawning. Gary pulls me close, and we sleep as the train rolls down the tracks. When I awake, Gary is sitting there staring at me.

"I love watching you sleep. Did you know that you smile a lot?"

"I had good dreams, and I am sure they do make me smile. How long have you been awake?"

"I woke up about half an hour ago. As I hold you, I wonder about your life now. How are you doing at college, and what interesting things are going on?"

"I've grown to love it there. I feel like I have grown up a lot. I have so many wonderful friends. I am challenged by all of my classes. Probably the most fascinating thing in my life is getting to know Dean McBride." Gary listens attentively as I tell him everything about Dean McBride. The time flies by, and soon we arrive in Beckenburg.

Gary says he will call later in the day so we can plan a little more time together before he returns to New York. Getting off the train, I see Mom and Dad waiting for me. It feels like I have been away for a long time.

"I love you, Mom. I have really missed you a lot."

"Sue, it feels like you have been away forever."

On the way home, I can feel the exhaustion from not getting much sleep. As we drive by the park, I can see the sun starting to grace the earth with its wonderful morning light. Part of me wants to stop and enjoy it for a moment, but

I'm too tired. I talk with Mom and Dad and then go to bed. Eventually, I'm awakened by talking, and I rush downstairs to join in.

"Sis, how is it going at college?" asks Grey.

"Great, I love it. It feels like its home. It took awhile, but I am really comfortable now."

"How is Carrie doing, and why isn't she here for Easter?"

"Well, take a deep breath, gang. Carrie is dating one of the nicest guys on campus. His family is coming to meet her on Easter. She is so happy and excited. I think it's serious, but I don't think Carrie allows herself to admit it. She is not so trusting, which is understandable when you look at how she has been treated in life. I would never want her to get her hopes up. She has been through too much. However, there is no reason for such thinking because it is apparent he adores her."

Everyone, including Mom, sits around the table and talks for over an hour. Grey has been happily dating the same girl for five months. Mark's been accepted at Ohio State University and is having a good time. Mom's been working hard in the rose garden at the church. She had to take a stand to keep them from being plowed under. Apparently, my parents took it upon themselves to get the wild roses under control. Dad says he was battered with thorn pricks all over his body, but now the roses are growing beautifully on a trellis he made for them. It was important for him to get involved because of Mom's love of them.

Before I take my normal walk to the park, I decide to visit Patty's grave. Coming upon the cemetery, I see the beautiful wild roses now entwined with the elegant trellis Dad made. I think about life and death and how this place is so special. I kneel at Patty's headstone as I feel the loss this grave has taken from me.

Heading back, I think about Eric and wonder how he's doing. He's so sensitive and has helped me cope with homesickness and Patty's death. He always shows up at the right time to bring me out of the doldrums. Eric makes me feel special and celebrated. He has given me pleasure beyond anything I could imagine. No wonder I continue to be stirred by the thought of him.

The park seems the same, yet different. It appears smaller and simpler. It's strange how things seem bigger when we are children. I sit at my favorite place by the edge of the brook and rub my hand into the grass. It is so velvety. Looking across the brook, I have memories of how it pulled at me as I was growing up. Its mysticism keeps me stirred, but now it look less vast and scary. I laugh thinking about the huge snowman Eric made with a joint in its mouth. Now the brook seems dried up and shallow. Things change, I think…I lie down with my back against the earth and my face toward the sun. As the sun warms me, my thoughts drift to Dean McBride. I can't imagine living with the diagnosis of leukemia. It's sad to hear her talk about how others reacted to her illness. Now she pushes people away, protecting them from having to suffer through her ups and downs. She is determined to stay detached from others, sparing them pain.

It's hard to imagine living a life that's supposed to end anytime. How can someone cope or come to terms with it all? Obviously, Dean McBride is strong and has coping skills. She came into my life for some reason. I remember how I ran from Patty, turning my head when I knew there was something wrong. I'm like the people Dean McBride spoke of who run because they are uncomfortable with illness. She represents my opportunity to care about someone who is living a painful reality. She felt honored that I went through so much to get to know her. She has made it clear that she welcomes me coming closer.

The sun is getting too hot. I sit up, blinded, and dust myself off before I start home. The park that served as my spiritual home for many years is now just a place to visit.

I tell Mom all about Dean McBride and everything that's happened. She listens.

"Sue, make sure that you are getting to know Dean McBride for the right reasons; that is, don't do it as a reaction for feeling bad that you weren't able to help Patty. Only do it because you want to get to know Dean McBride. Make sure this is not about you. She has probably seen all kinds of phony acts of charity from others. What she needs is love and genuine caring."

I am moved by the depth of what my mother says. I know she reaches out to a lot to people, and it's never about her. This is good advice, and I receive it without resentment. I feel my relationship with my mother is growing, and I really appreciate her insight. Soon Gary arrives, and I hear him talking with my brothers. I barge in on them and joke, "Okay fellas, I've got to break this up.…I have only a few hours to be with this guy."

On the drive to his house, Gary says his parents are at a concert. His mother has left us a lasagna and salad for dinner. Quickly, we eat and clean up so that we can head outside to the hammock. The sun is going down.

"Gary, what do you think about the story that Jean-Louis told regarding him and Felicia? Do you think there are similarities between them and us?"

"I feel we are very different. Let's suppose Jean-Louis had given up his opportunity to return to painting and his opportunity to study under Benoit. I believe that as much as we think someone else can fulfill us, the truth is that we can only fulfill ourselves. People can support, love, and encourage us. I do not believe we can be fulfilled by surrendering ourselves for someone else. Remember when Jean-Louis said they parted knowing it was the last time they would see each other? What he meant was, he knew she had closed the door. She only wanted him the way she needed him to be. To her, he had not passed her test of love, which meant laying down everything for her. This was a horribly painful situation that almost destroyed him."

"Gary, you're right. If their love required such a sacrifice, it could hardly be considered love. On the other hand, when we love, we do make sacrifices and put the other person first."

"Yes, Sue. You've sacrificed by letting me go, and I have sacrificed by letting you go. And why? Because we want what's best for each other. We hold a special love that requires us to let each other go. Jean-Louis is so moved by our love for each other. Also, we never require that our love be more than it is. What makes it so beautiful is it's already enough. If I have nothing beyond what I have, I still have everything. Jean-Louis said Felicia told him when she left that he was dead to her. For her, it was everything or nothing. We have never put conditions on our love; we just simply love each other."

"I feel that I am not very insightful when it comes to art. I felt inadequate talking about it and didn't always understand what you two were saying. I enjoyed being with both of you. I found his paintings beautiful. I'm sorry I don't have a better understanding of art."

"Sue, the role of the viewer is to enjoy the art for whatever reason. Jean-Louis and I treasure your comments. You are so special. You see things with your own intensity and life experiences. The things you shared were so important. Sue, I keep falling in love with you over and over…for a multitude of reasons. You are so much more than most people."

I close my eyes and let myself feel what he has said. I wasn't sure what it meant, but I knew it was more than just words to Gary. "Thanks for making me feel so special. I love you and I'm never alone because of it."

We kiss and slowly become lost in each other, taking satisfaction in the wanting. We are in no position to let ourselves have more.

"Sue, I want to make love with you again under the right conditions. I am hoping that you will spend a few days with me in New York. I have a nice comfortable apartment."

"Oh, that would be nice," I say, now closing my eyes and resting in that thought.

Slowly, I fall asleep engulfed in the warmth of his body. The next thing I remember is waking up about 5:30 AM with the birds singing. Gary's face is about three inches away. He's sleeping, and I listen to the beautiful rhythm of his breathing. His face is wonderful. It's moments like this when I enjoy him so. He looks so gentle and sweet. My mind drifts to Jean-Louis and Felicia and how sad it was that their love ended with such pain and disappointment.

Slowly, Gary opens his eyes. A smile arches itself across his beautiful face. "I love waking up to you like this. It is always my greatest vision of beauty," he says, kissing me. "I knew we would fall asleep in each other arms. Are you glad we did?"

"Absolutely. It is wonderful. I love sleeping in your arms." The sun now rising out of the earth is so bright.

"Let's have some breakfast. My train leaves in a couple of hours," he explains.

"Take me home now. You must need some private time with your parents."

Gary takes me home and walks me to the door. "I love you and never forget I am always connected to you," he says, kissing me.

"I love you too, and thanks for everything." Again, for another time we turn and walk away from each other.

Mom is sitting at the breakfast table having coffee. "Did you have a nice evening—or should I say night?" she says with a tone of uneasiness.

I feel comfortable telling her about it. "Yes, we had dinner and just talked. We laid outdoors in their huge hammock and fell asleep. It was nice just being together."

"Gary is one of the nicest young men I have ever met. I feel comfortable about the two of you being together."

I hurry and get ready to surprise Gary at the train station. Getting out of the car, I see Gary with his parents. Not wanting to intrude, I wait for a couple of minutes.

"Sue! What a surprise," Gary says, putting his arms around me.

"Sue, it's so nice that you came to see Gary off....I think we will move on and let the two of you say good-bye. Don't forget, your father and I will see you in a couple of weeks on our way to Boston. Good-bye son."

The train is about fifteen minutes late. Finally, we hear the horn as it moves into station.

"I love you, Sue, really love you, and I never forget that. Never." He kisses me so intensely.

"I love you too. Take care of yourself."

He boards the train, and I see him take a seat. The train starts to slowly move. I wave and wave with Gary waving back. Finally, I can't see him, and for some reason it feels like he is gone forever, leaving me unbelievably sad. As the caboose turns the corner, I have an inexplicable feeling that my world is gone. I tell myself I must not think that way.

I wonder why I am so different. I love everything about Gary, yet he doesn't know some things about me that I have kept to myself. Our last couple of days together have been very intense. Jean-Louis Pacquet was intriguing. Then, the last night with Gary was like so many other times I have loved being with him, yet somehow I feel drained, as if I am performing. Yes, that's it. I love those moments, but they require me to be attentive. It's like I have to perform, requiring myself to fit in and be what I think is appropriate.

All at once, my thoughts drift to Eric. Eric knows me, quirks and all. He knows my need to be self-indulgent, carefree, and risk-taking.

Coming upon the park, I feel so alive with desires of just wanting to let go. I love being with Eric because he brings all of that out in me. Most people live their life balanced pretty much in the middle. They are stable, consistent, and steady in the way they live. But then there are others like myself who live with the high-highs and the low-lows. That contrasting intensity flings us from one end of the pendulum to the other. We live with great emotions and feel everything much more intensely than the rest. We become crazy people who risk much to find a little piece of mindlessness and laughter. In our desperation, we involve ourselves in risk-taking behaviors. We rush to the edge, panting.

I know such desires are only momentary. After the risk-taking and exuberance, the guilt sets in. Thinking about all of this is painful. I feel fragmented—like I'm two people. I have been like this most of my life. I remember being told things as a child that made me feel less than normal, and I tried to figure out what "normal" was so I could act accordingly. Never have I felt integrated and whole. All this thinking has given me a headache. I go home and take some aspirin.

That evening Eric calls and asks me out to dinner on Saturday night. I am excited to hear from him, but I know it will be hard to explain to my parents why I am going out with him. I think about how I should approach the subject. Going downstairs, I find Mom.

"Mom, I am going out Saturday evening with Eric, so don't plan on me for dinner."

"Eric Barnett? For heaven sakes, why?"

"Eric and I have always been friends. When Patty died, we talked in the park, and he really helped me. Anyway, we just renewed our friendship. We agreed someday we would go out and just talk about the good ol' days. So he asked me to have dinner tomorrow night. It's only as friends, and I feel good about it," I say, hoping that somehow this rather strange answer will be enough.

"Sue, I don't really understand. I do caution you as to how others look at Eric. He is known to be wild. You are old enough to make your own decisions, and I do hope this one doesn't cause you any regrets."

"Mother, Eric and I have spent time together throughout the years. He's been a friend, and he treats me with respect. Anything less would not be acceptable to me."

"I know that, Sue, but thanks for reminding me. You have a nice evening Saturday." This exchange clearly shows we can talk about life now that I am older.

The next day goes by fast and I hear the doorbell ring. Dad answers the door.

"Eric, nice to see you," he says, as I finally make it downstairs.

"Hi, Eric—great to see you. I am all set to go."

"Great. Have a nice evening, Mr. and Mrs. Martin, and don't worry. We are going out to dinner, and Sue will be home early. She's an old friend I have missed since she went to college."

Mom comes in from the kitchen. "Good evening, Eric. It's nice to see you. Have a nice dinner."

As we get into the car, I can tell Eric is nervous. "So you survived the ol' family greetings," I laugh.

"Yes, it was kind of scary for me. I am used to picking up my women at hot spots where I rarely meet any of their families. Your parents are so well-known and respected in the community. I hope they didn't say anything horrible to you about going out with me."

"No, they didn't. I explained to my mother that you have always been a friend and that you always treated me with respect. And she was fine."

Eric drives out of Beckenburg to a country restaurant. We get a nice booth in the corner and slide in close to each other. It's a nicely dimmed, private dining area—intimate and perfect.

"I'll bet with Gary you probably pick at food, not enjoying it, because you need to look all feminine. Well, you are with me, and I want you to really enjoy your food. I want you to lick your fingers and smack your lips with enjoyment. This place has the best barbeque in the world."

We order ribs, corn, and kettle beans. As we are eating, I get barbeque sauce on my nose.

"I'd like to lick that sauce off your nose, but I do have my manners," he says. I just let go and laugh, and marvel at how fun it is to feel this free. After dinner, we go for a ride to a beautiful area overlooking the valley. In the distance, we can see the few lights of Beckenburg below. As he turns off the car, I quickly slide over to him.

"Thanks so much for not forgetting me," I say. "You really are special. I have been thinking a lot lately about my life. I am like two people. One is that girl who loves and appreciates Gary, a girl who's very passionate about college and her career. Despite her, the other girl inside me wants to run off and retreat with you. It's sad—neither of those girls really gets what she wants. I seem so fragmented and confused."

He pulls me closer. "Sue, you're just fine. You are complex and intense. I know there are parts of you that I cannot relate to. You are my dearest friend. When I am with you, I am stretched to be the best I can. We have a friendship that offers a special place for each other. I love whatever time we have together. I loved it when we spent New Year's Eve in Broctren Harbor at the inn. I love making love with you. That New Year's Eve will be the main feature on the highlight film of my life."

We kiss and let ourselves be tortured with growing urges. It's amazing how six hours of being with Eric has cleared my head. I am so relaxed. As we get about a block from my house, he pulls into the park.

"Sue, if you ever need me for anything—to talk, to laugh, to play," he says with a wink, "then please call me, write me…Never feel like you have to be sexual with me. I of course love that, but I want you to know that our friendship is more than that. I am going to give you a goodnight kiss here in case your family is up."

The next morning I attend sunrise Easter service at the park. We have a special breakfast afterward, and then my parents take me to the train station.

CHAPTER 22

Everything Changes

I'm glad to be back on campus. Carrie and I talk the night away. Carrie says her "fondness" for Keith is growing. I talk about my trip to Chicago and my meeting Jean-Louis Pacquet. I am comfortable sharing the details. Hopefully, someday she can share with me her feelings about Keith. I never mention Eric, who remains my one hidden secret, that private indulgence that I protect. Or is our relationship the one thing I am most ashamed of?

After being back for a day, I finally get into the swing of classes. I stop off at the student center to get the mail and find a letter from Dean McBride.

Dear Sue,

Thanks so much for the lovely Easter flowers, I have enjoyed them so. I am feeling much better and hope to be back on campus in a few weeks. I want to invite you to spend Friday evening at my country home. Clara filled out the necessary paperwork for you to get a school car and will get you a map with directions. Should you not be able to come, we will plan something again soon. I do hope you had a wonderful spring break. Look forward to hearing from you.

Regards,

Sarah McBride

My head is spinning. I planned on contacting Dean McBride on the weekend. I continue to go through the mail and find a card from Jean-Louis Pacquet. It's lovely, hand painted with a watercolor scene of a lady looking into the sky.

ॐ

Dear Sue,

Thank you so much for attending the exhibit and having dinner with me. You are so wonderfully expressive and insightful about life. Do not keep yourself from us. Gary says you plan on coming to New York soon. I do hope I get to see you when you are here.

Warm regards, Jean-Louis Pacquet

The rest of the week goes by quickly. Finally I am on my way to Dean McBride's home. Driving on old Highway 81, I admire the lush trees arching over the roadway and fields rich with crops. I pass a couple of farms and all of a sudden come upon a beautiful plantation home set far back from a majestic, open gate. The long driveway leads back to the huge, beautiful home. I ring the doorbell and a butler answers.

"Come in. I am Jessie. Sarah is waiting for you in the southern parlor—off to the left. Let me show you there."

Inside is a large entrance area with an exquisite chandelier. A huge, double winding stairway artistically arches upward. The floor appears to be some special kind of marble. Jessie walks me into this beautiful room full of light and wonderful colors. Dean McBride greets me.

"Sue, I am so glad that you were able to come. Did you have any problems with the directions?"

"No, they were fine. You have a beautiful home. Thanks so much for inviting me."

"This home has been handed down from generation to generation. My grandfather left it to me. Although it is huge and maybe too much for most people, it holds a lot of family history. It was built in 1817 by my grandfather's grandfather. He was the owner of the largest plantation in this area, and he had many crops. Today I have farmers who work the land, and the farm is the most satisfying aspect of my life. When I get healthier, I will take you out on a tour of the farm. I'd love to show you the animals and the beauty of this place."

It's exciting to see Dean McBride light up as she talks. She seems like a different woman in this setting. She looks a lot better, with color returned to her face, and it occurs to me that this is the first time I have ever seen her smile. She is warm, personable, and so charming.

"Sue, did you have a nice spring break? How is your family? Tell me about your mother. Are you close to her?" I am shocked by her question. I feel myself starting to close down, and I feel uncomfortable. A few seconds go by. I need to be respectful and say something.

"I have a good relationship with my mother now, and I love her dearly. But when I was a child she pushed me away. She took good care of me, but she said things that tore at my self-esteem, leaving me feeling anything but normal. I heard her talk with others about me as if there were something wrong with me. Mom referred to me as 'poor ol' Sue'—words intended to express love and concern, but words I detested. They conveyed the message that I wasn't normal. She treasures all my girlfriends and is like a mother to most of them. I admire her giving nature and how she cares. But the more I saw her capacity to love others, the more I felt rejected and insignificant in her life. Something about me affected my mother so that she constantly pushed me away. I haven't talked about it, but it tore at me. Even today it has some power over me," I explain, feeling my eyes tear up.

"My dear, I am sorry that you had such a difficult childhood. You have come from a difficult past, but it has made you who you are today. You don't appear to me to have low self-esteem. Perhaps that is a testimony to your ability to overcome those messages. I too had a difficult childhood. My mother was a troubled, rebellious young woman with very strict, conservative Christian parents. At the age of fifteen, she ran away and was legally listed as missing. At sixteen she became pregnant with me. She had no idea who my father was because she had been selling herself in New York. My grandparents took her in, and when I was born they chose to raise me. Seven months later she was found beaten to death in a New York City alley. I did not learn any of this until around the age of twelve. My grandparents raised me, and I felt very loved by them," Dean McBride explains.

"I am so sorry. I can't imagine being raised without a mother. Surely I am lucky that I have a mom who loves and cares for me. Mom never abandons me, but there is something terribly wrong that I still don't understand even today. My mother has changed as the years have gone by, and she and I are growing closer all the time. Today I feel her love. How have you been affected by your mother's rejection?" I'm not afraid to ask because Dean McBride seems so open to honest disclosure.

"I had wonderful grandparents who did everything for me, so I did not feel disadvantaged. As a matter of fact, I felt like I was their world. When I was fifteen and became so sick, I remember thinking about my mom. I was raised to believe I would someday be in heaven. I remember praying to God that somehow in the last hour or minute of her life my mother had asked for God's forgiveness. I hoped she would be in heaven waiting for me. A couple of days later, though, I snapped out of thinking that way, and I just prayed that God would see fit to heal me so I could be with my grandparents. From that day on, I haven't had many thoughts regarding my mom. I never felt responsible for whatever went on with her. I never considered what my mom did as having anything to do with me. Maybe your mother was going through a difficult time when you were a child. I am glad that she has changed and now you feel close to her."

Listening to Dean McBride, I realized how lucky I am to have a mother who has always been there for me. Whatever happened in the past no longer exists today. I am fortunate that mom and I have a good relationship.

Eventually Jessie announces that dinner is ready in the dining room. In the large and beautiful room a huge dining table has been set at one end for six people. Jessie comes back in and sits with his wife, Bertha. Clem, who oversees the animals, and Betsy, the housekeeper, take their place at the table. Dean McBride introduces all of us, telling me these people who have overseen the farm for years are her family. They always eat together, something very important to Dean McBride. After dinner, she and I sit on a beautiful sun porch to watch the last minutes of the sunset.

"All the people here seem so happy and so close."

"Oh, Sue. They are all wonderful people who have taken pride in this farm for years. Most of all, they have given me so much. Their spirits and love pull me through the difficult times when I have been so sick."

"How long have they been with you?"

"Jessie's parents were dear, dedicated people who were here with my grandparents. Jessie and I grew up here. We are like brother and sister. He's a couple of years older than me. Soon I hope to show you the land and the other houses where they live. My grandfather had special homes built on the grounds. He did not like the original 'servant quarters' that were part of this large plantation. He tore down those small buildings and had lovely homes built on the grounds for them to live in. From generation to generation, they have been loyal to my family. They are all remarkable people."

Dean McBride shares openly about her childhood and the difficult times when she was sick. Jessie and his family had always tried to keep her spirits up. She says her grandfather made it possible for Jessie to go to Broctren Harbor College. After Jessie got a degree, he did not want to leave the farm; he loves the life here. College introduced him to Bertha, who is a teacher at the elementary school in Broctren Harbor. Clem's family has farmed the land for years. There is so much more about Dean McBride that I am curious to learn, but I can tell she is tiring. Nevertheless, she is quick to invite me back.

"Sue, I am here for you. Don't hesitate to call. Clara knows where I am at all times."

I feel great as I drive back to Broctren Harbor College. Dean McBride is nothing like anyone on campus thinks. She is an amazing woman. She is very caring and full of love and joy. It's understandable why she remains distant from others. She doesn't want to put others through her health scares. I now know she is never alone but has a wonderful family of friends. I am thankful she felt comfortable enough to explain everything.

The following morning, I run into Dean Morrow.

"Hello, Sue. How are you? It's been awhile since we had that talk, and I still feel horrible about it. I hope you have forgiven me. I still want to be your friend, and Katie misses you."

"I feel fine. I'll make a point of calling Katie. I need to get going. Bye."

As I walk to James's place, I feel upset over what has happened between me and Dean Morrow. I want us to be friends and nothing more, but the way he looks at me still feels creepy.

"Sue, it's good to see you," James greets me. "How was your dinner with the mean old dean?"

"It was wonderful, and she is nothing like the person everyone on campus thinks she is. She has a marvelous home in the country with many people who work for her and who are like her family. I really enjoyed myself a lot. How was your Easter with your family?"

James is excited to tell me that he mustered the courage to tell his mother that he's gay. He says she was devastated and said she could not tell his father, who couldn't handle it. He felt so good about owning his truth. She cried but said she had long known something about him was different. He is shocked that she didn't demand he change.

I tell James about my time with Jean-Louis Pacquet and Gary. Eventually, I feel so comfortable that I tell him about Eric. James is a good listener, and we trust each other with our secrets. He shares with me his struggle to repress his sexuality. As a young kid, he had hated the thought that he might be gay. His father had pushed him into strong masculine activities like football and base-ball. The only thing that had kept him sane had been his church group. He became a Christian at a very young age. His Christian friends had appreciated and loved him. He says God's love sustains him, and he is at peace.

As the weekend comes to an end, I realize how intense and fulfilling it has been. Carrie gets back to our room early. She talks about Keith and says she is concerned their relationship is moving too fast. After we talk for a while, she realizes she must find the courage to trust his love for her. This is her moment to let go of her history and walk openly into the future. We talk until we are exhausted and finally turn out the lights.

Monday, as I'm leaving class, I run into Keith.

"Hey, Keith, can I speak with you for a moment?"

"Sure. Let's go outside. I will walk you back to Brea Hall."

"Listen, Keith, this isn't any of my business, but I love Carrie like a sister, and I don't want her to get hurt. She's been through too much."

"Sue, I respect your need to talk to me. I haven't felt this way before. In fact, I'm in love with Carrie. I see her pull back when she is feeling too good. It's as if she's trying to protect herself, not trusting in the moment. I understand why she does it. It may take a lifetime of loving her before she trusts me. I have no history of running from one girl to another. I haven't dated much because I take it so seriously. But Carrie is right for me, and I plan on giving it everything I've got. If she closes the door because she's afraid, well, I'll just be there wait-ing for her to reopen it. I am not going anywhere, and my love can be trusted." It is obvious that he loves her so much.

As the weeks pass, everyone is looking forward to the campus festival, which will involve games, music, outdoor theater productions, and a big dance. I ask Gary to it, but he's in the middle of a painting and says he must stay focused. I think about Eric, knowing he's the one I really want to invite. Finally, I weaken and give him a call.

"Hey, babe, what's happening there? Need a little laughter?" he says, laugh-ing.

"Yes, actually. We have a fun festival coming up, with games, music, and a big dance. I thought you might enjoy it."

"I am sure I will, but not as much as I will enjoy attending it with you."

"I could get a reservation at the inn. You could spend Saturday night here and go back Sunday. How's that sound?"

"It sounds great. I'll get my ticket and let you know what time my train comes in. I could come to your dorm so you don't have to walk to the train station."

"No way—I will be waiting at the station, all excited to see you. I need to have a little fun."

The next day I tell James that he will get to meet Eric. James says he will be staying on campus that weekend and offers us his apartment. "Please, you are like a sister! Damn, can't a brother do something nice for a sister? Please stay in my place. I have the best wines and tons of food here, so you won't need to go out. Please, let me do this. If it helps you to decide, we'll make it a tradeoff. In return, you can let me use your sociology notes because you take everything down verbatim."

"You can always use my notes; you don't have to trade for an elegant apartment," I say, flattered. "Still, I don't know how Eric will feel about it. For now, let me get a room at the inn."

"Well, don't be surprised if it is full. After all, the alumni are coming this weekend. If you can't get a room, just remember you have your answer."

He is right. I call but they are sold out. With much appreciation, I agree to using James's rather luxurious apartment. I wondered what Eric will think. When I tell Carrie about my plans, I can tell she is concerned about my being with Eric. I tell her that Gary can't come and that Eric is only a friend.

When Saturday arrives and the train pulls into the station, I can hardly wait to see Eric. I explain that the Broctren Harbor Inn is full but that we can stay in an apartment of James Barrington. Of course, he knows the Barrington name, and he is confused about how I can be so close to James. I explain that we are the best of friends, emphasizing James's phrase: like brother and sister. Eric respects my privacy and does not push for more information.

When we arrive, James greets us with wine.

"Eric, please feel free to help yourself to anything and everything here at my home. I can't stay here this weekend because the college requires us to stay on campus at least one weekend a month. My parents got this place for me to get away and relax. Sue and I are close; she's like a sister to me. I love it when she comes over, and we relax. What I am about to say I don't share with many people. I am gay. So be assured that I look at Sue as nothing but a sister."

Eric begins to relax; soon James says he must get going. After James leaves, Eric and I get comfortable and talk about things. As we talk, I feel the wine kick in, and it feels good. Finally, we change into casual clothes and head off to campus to attend the festival. As we move about the crowd, we see students performing as street artists, doing magic and being mimes.

"Sue, Sue. Come here!"

I turn around to see Katie standing at a booth selling tickets to dunk her father in the dunk tank. How I would love to do this, I think. Instead, I encourage Eric to give it a try.

"Okay, Katie, let's see if we can make him go splash." Eric takes the three balls. His first throw misses.

"Oh let me try," I say. With all my might, I throw it with precision. Wham! Into the water he goes.

"Sue, you did it!" Katie screams. Getting out of the water, Dean Morrow hollers back, "Bet you can't do it again!"

I take the last ball in hand. Once again, concentrating with all my might, I throw it hard and hit the spot again. Off the bench he goes.

"*Wow*, Sue, you are really good!" Katie says. "Want to try again?"

"No, two dunks are good enough."

Dean Morrow gets back up on the bench. Again, he hollers "Bet you can't do it again!"

"I know I can, but I have proven myself already. Bye."

"Gosh, Sue, you shock me," says Eric. "I would have bet you couldn't do that. It's hard."

"Remind me to tell you about that man later. You'll see it wasn't skill as much as anger." For some reason, I feel so much better after that.

As we get a hot dog, Carrie and Keith join us. I explain that Eric is a childhood friend. Eric explains in detail the surgery I performed on him at the age of six. He also mentions that I dunked the man in the cage. Carrie smiles, knowing it was Dean Morrow. As we move about the festival, I see Clara and Dean McBride.

"Dean McBride, I am so surprised to see you out. How are you feeling?"

"Actually, I feel good. I need to get myself back on campus. I am going to start back at work on Monday for half days. How are you, my dear?"

"I am great. Let me introduce you to a friend from back home who is visiting me."

"Glad to meet you, Dean McBride."

"You too, Eric. I better keep moving. I can't stay out here long. Sue, do come by soon."

Eric and I attend the afternoon concert. It's fun sitting on the ground under a shade tree and listening to the music. Afterwards, we go back to the apartment and relax. Both of us are so tired that we fall asleep. About 6:30 PM we head out for the dance. It is a lovely evening. The air smells great, and we hear the music as we walk onto the campus.

"Thanks so much for sharing this day with me. It's always special being with you."

Finally, a beautiful slow song is performed. Eric asks me to dance. As we're dancing, I can see my dorm friends staring. In the middle of the song, the singer calls out, "trade partners." Mindy cuts in to dance with Eric. As I am about to move out of the dance area, Dean Morrow taps my shoulder and immediately takes me into his arms to dance. He is gracious and does not pull me too close.

"I hope you enjoy dancing with the cleanliest guy here," he says, commenting on being dunked all day in water.

"Yes, you are clean. I think I helped in that process."

Peace sweeps over me, and I finally feel reconciled with Dean Morrow. Gazing across the dance area, I see Eric looking at me while Mindy tries to get me to notice that she's dancing with him. As we catch a glimpse of each other, Eric winks.

Finally, Eric and I dance one last time. He whispers in my ear, "I want to set you free tonight." I want that too. As we walk back to the apartment, it's nice feeling Eric's hand in mine. The further we walk, the fainter the music. Arriving at the building, we finally are alone.

"Eric, I am so glad you came. I wanted to see you. I know you understand my confusion about everything; nothing has changed. I did so enjoy being with you today. As always, you somehow transport me to a better place, where I am carefree and lighthearted."

"Shhh, Sue. Let yourself relax and be free. I understand where you are, and I don't expect anything. Yet I treasure everything. Let me just be with you tonight. Let yourself be free to enjoy it."

We go to the bedroom, and I dim the lights. Immediately, Eric takes me in his arms and passionately kisses me. I am lost in it. My hands move about him, and my mouth is drenched with his kisses. We unfold quickly, my inhibitions lost to the wine. He unbuttons my blouse, pushes it off my shoulders, and then continues to remove everything. His eyes now consume my nakedness. Swiftly, we come down on the bed, locked in an embrace that demands so much…Finally, at the edge of ecstasy, the momentum takes me, and I am out of control. Maybe it's the wine, or maybe it's because I am fully relaxed and without reservations or concerns. Whatever it is, it is remarkable—totally indescribable. As the night continues, we climb to the edge and soar over and over until we are lifeless and exhausted.

We awaken a little after ten the next morning. As the morning sun slants through the shutters, Eric pulls me to him, whispering, "Thank you, thank you." We enjoy each other one last time. Afterwards, we talk until it is time to walk him to the train station.

"Eric, thanks for coming. It was the best time. Thanks for making my weekend."

"It feels good that I can make your weekend special. Sue, you are terrific."

After his train leaves, I go to the apartment and clean things up. I start thinking about my life. I have to admit that coming off the weekend I'm filled with ambiguity. Remembering the unbelievable freedom and physical release, I feel completely rejuvenated again. Why have I slowly let myself evolve into two very different persons? Who gets to have it any way they want it? Although I love Gary, I still have to deal with the fact that I've been sexual with Eric on three occasions. Eric is always about the moment: he's my Disneyland. But no one lives in Disneyland. I visualize my future with Gary. I won't think about Eric until I am exhausted and tired of living my structured and intense life. And then, feeling like I deserve it, I will justify being with him instead of dealing with the real issues.

What's my relationship with Gary all about? What led to my promiscuous behavior? I use to believe that making love was a privilege of commitment and that, most of all, it was exclusive. Now I allow myself to misuse it for pleasure. I justify it with my own self-indulgent reward system.

Thinking about this is so draining and painful. If I allow intrigue to dominate my life, it will only be a matter of time before I run into someone else who intrigues me. I could spiral into a vicious cycle. Surely, most things in life require commitment and discipline. It's imperative that two people have the strength of their convictions and remain committed to each other. Yet the drudgery of routine pales in comparison with the experience of meeting new people, and my curiosity and intrigue make me vulnerable. I am letting my moral compass erode, surrendering my control for meaningless pleasure. I fear where I'm headed, and it's painful owning my truth. All of this is a result of my low self-esteem. It all started as a child, when I tried so hard to be noticed. No one meets all my needs, so I treasure the parts of people that supplement the gaps in myself. My challenge is to make peace with me. All of this craziness only exasperates the problem. I am starting to deviate from all that I believe.

What can I do? How do I straighten all this out before I self-destruct? I must find someone to talk with who can be objective. I need someone who has a good moral compass and yet is not judgmental. I will not talk with the campus pastor. I need someone I can confide in, but I have no idea who. Sadly, I know it takes times like these to remind us that God is there. I hate calling upon God out of desperation instead of in thanksgiving and celebration.

CHAPTER 23

Freshman Year Ends

As my freshman year comes to an end, and I am busy studying for finals, I am thankful that Dean McBride is back on campus and that we have grown very close. Her wisdom and insight are invaluable to me. She is a deep thinker, and I enjoy our debates. Her communication style and sensitivity mean so much to me. I'm desperate to open up and share my most unsettling realities in the hope that she can shine a light on my darkness.

It has been a while since Gary and I talked, although we write each week. He has invited me to New York for the summer, but I am unable to go. My life is spinning with constant change and I welcome it.

Carrie is working a lot. She talks about Keith and their relationship in significant terms, saying they are serious and committed. Carrie is frightened of the word "love." She doesn't have a point of reference from which she can measure the depth of her feelings.

As I walk out of my final class of the year, I feel the tension and stress leave my shoulders. This is a moment that I want to remember. I sit on the grass under a huge oak tree. Taking a deep breath, I think about my freshman year coming to an end. I wonder what my life is going to be like in five years.

I think of Eric and how I would like to unwind with him. He would be my reward for all of this struggling and hard work. He is the only person who can take me away from all of this. If I called him, I know he'd come. He is my escape, or more like my fix. However, I can no longer toss aside the foundation of everything I believe. Maybe I should visit James and try to drink myself into oblivion. It not exactly what I want, but drinking would provide some diversion, celebration, and relief. Sadness is welling up inside me. At the dorm I find a message from Dean McBride, and I call her.

"Sue, I'm glad you called. I know you just finished your last class. I thought maybe you'd like to spend the weekend on my farm. It would be a nice way to let yourself relax. I'd love to visit with you, and we could enjoy the beauty of the outdoors."

"Yes, I would love that very much. Thanks for asking me."

"Good. Pack a few things and meet me at my office in about thirty minutes. I am looking forward to the weekend. See you in a bit."

She sounds so happy, and I feel excited. My dark thoughts start to dissipate. Surely she's God's answer to my prayers. Yet I can't imagine opening up and sharing my dark side with her.

Jessie drives us to the farm. It's fun listening to them pick at each other.

"Sue, I don't know how appropriate this is, but I am tired of hearing you call me Dean McBride. Please continue to call me that on campus. But out here, please call me Sarah. I want you to be part of our family...and I am your friend."

"Sue," Jessie says, "There are other names we call her if you don't like 'Sarah.'" Dean McBride reaches over and playfully hits him, laughing.

Dean McBride takes me to my room. I can tell she is still struggling to get her strength back. It's a huge, elegant bedroom with a private sitting parlor and private bath.

"This is your spot. If you look off your balcony, you'll see a field of wild flowers with the wind rustling the land. I will leave you to unpack and relax. I need to catch a nap to keep up my strength. Dinner will be served in an hour and half."

I walk her to the corridor. As I unpack, I feel like I've been transported to another world. The fresh breeze sweeps through the balcony doors and windows. The room has Victorian furnishings, including a large canopy bed and tables rich with gold gilt and wood inlays. Marvelous oil paintings hang on the walls. One large painting is of a young girl, and I wonder if it is a young Sarah. As I walk onto the balcony, the breeze sweeps my hair. The vision is breathtaking, and I am captured by the grandeur of all I see.

Only a couple of hours ago I was contemplating indulging in behaviors that are contrary to my character and beliefs. Now, breathing in this panoramic beauty, it's easy to see how Sarah is able to experience ongoing healing in this setting. I close my eyes and start to think about my life. What is it all about anyway? We are born to live and then die. In between, we are to figure out our

purpose. I think about Sarah's life and how important she is to so many people. It's sad to think that I am not that close to anyone in my family. I love my
mom and dad dearly, but not one member of my family really knows me.
Sarah knows more about me than the combined insight of all of them. Gary,
who I love, doesn't know the other side of me. He has no idea that I indulge in
meaningless pleasures, surrendering everything—including him. Suddenly, a
breeze sweeps over me. My thoughts dim as I fall asleep.

When I awaken I realize it is time for dinner. As I reach the dining room,
Sarah, Jessie, Bertha, and Betsy are preparing to eat.

"I am so sorry I'm late. I just woke up," I say, taking my seat.

"Oh, please—no apology necessary," Sarah says. "We eat everyday at the
same time, and sometimes one or two of us chooses not to eat. It's no problem.
Are you feeling all right?"

"Oh, yes. I was sitting on the balcony with my feet up, and the way the
breeze swept over me let me fall asleep, and it was wonderful."

"Good. I am glad you rested. Now, let us pray:

*Dear Lord, bless this food, and bless Betsy who prepared it. Bless Jessie for his
labor in growing it. Be with all of us as we live to honor you, Lord. Thank you for
letting Sue be with us. Help her to feel part of our family. Always show us your
way. Thank you for your love and mercy. Amen.*

Everyone reflects on the events of the day. Bertha describes her students and
the fun things they say in class. Jessie asks if I would like to go horseback riding
in the morning with him and his nephew Samuel.

"Put Sue on my horse, Freckle, because he is gentle," says Sarah.

"I would love to go," I answer.

"Sue, I want to take you to our lake and teach you the therapeutic value of
fishing," Sarah adds. I am surprised she's up to such a thing. She explains that
Jessie will drive us there in the jeep and come back to get us. We make plans to
fish after my early morning horse ride. After dinner, Sarah and I sit on the
porch and watch the sun go down.

"Sue, I am so happy that you are here. There is something special about you
that beckons to me and tells me I ought to get to know you even better. How
are you doing, really?" It's as if she knows there's something more going on.

"It's strange that I beat down your door to find you, and now you have opened it so wide. I'm afraid I might say something that might make you wish you hadn't gotten to know me."

"Please Sue, don't be afraid. I am not judgmental. Nor am I without experiences of my own that I regret. Let me tell you a story or two. When I was eighteen, I found myself so angry at everyone, including God. I was tired of living with a death sentence always hanging over my head. I decided that if God was going to toy with me, then I would venture out and experience life before it was taken from me. I started drinking. I loved being impaired because it took away the painful truths in my life. I'd sneak out on Freckle and ride to a part of the farm where I could pull out a flask of whiskey and not be seen. I'd lie under the sky until I passed out. Eventually, I got involved with a married man who bought hay from us weekly. We had clandestine meetings at a vacant building outside of town. We met a couple of times a week for three months. One day his wife followed us. She came in with a gun and shot him in the leg. My name ended up in the papers, humiliating me beyond all belief. My grandfather was very disappointed in me, but he stood by me through the ordeal. Even after that, I found myself wanting to be with men, so I continued my reckless behavior. Jessie found out everything. He got so mad at how disrespectful I was toward my grandparents that he threatened to tell everything. I knew my grandfather would be upset, as I had him believing that my bad days were behind me. Finally, I was able to put someone else ahead of myself. I struggled to keep myself on the straight and narrow. Now, I am not suggesting that you are going through anything like what I did, but I know you are going through something. I care, and I am here for you," she concludes.

Sarah speaks with such softness. Shaking, I start crying, partly in disbelief that she has shared so openly about her life. I certainly could relate to parts of her confessions. Sarah moves beside me and puts her arm around me.

"Sue, just let it out."

I know she is holding me to make sure I understand that she cares. I can't remember any time in my life where someone cared this much.

"Sue, as pained as you are right now, eventually you'll give value to all this emotional suffering. It's necessary for us to be overwhelmed by our pain. It forces us to look at life differently. Without such moments, we would spiral deeper into our darkness and become even more lost. This pain offers you a chance to change things in your life."

I know she's right. I feel so weak—yet relieved, too. Finally, I have someone I can talk with honestly.

"Thank you for being so open and so caring. As sad as I am about my life, I'm even more overwhelmed by your warmth and concern. I can't ever remember anyone caring so much. Thank you. I don't know where to begin. I may be rationalizing, but I must say it as I see it. As a child, I was so pained because I didn't feel like I was good enough. I was vulnerable to anyone who would say anything nice to me. I was so needy and believed myself somehow disadvantaged. To cope, I fantasized and pretended a lot. I thrived on intensity and curiosity. My thoughts were always about what was out there, what I had yet to experience. I didn't live in the moment, because whenever I did, I had to deal with rejection and an overwhelming feeling of low self-worth. I grew up living in my head. I read a lot and mentally matured much too fast. I was a deep thinker, so when other kids were talking about silly stuff, I was contemplating life and the purpose of mankind." Now out of breath, I take a drink of lemonade.

"Just take your time Sue, and don't feel pressured," Sarah says, wiping away a few tears.

"As the years went by, I was saturated with intensity about life and issues. I had a friend named Patty whose mom drank a lot and eventually died of alcoholism. Early on, I remember, Mrs. Williams said drinking was the best way to relax because it took the edge off her problems. She said it helped her become mindless, and she felt so free. I couldn't wait to try alcohol. Then one day when I was a senior, I went to a party where they had alcohol. This was not the group of kids I normally ran around with. The party wasn't far from my home. Since I was walking, I thought it was a perfect time to try alcohol. They made me a couple of drinks, loading them with alcohol, and it wasn't until I had drunk them down that I realized they would hit me so hard. At first, it felt amazing: my nagging consciousness was gone, and I was giddy and free. Leaving the party, I decided to walk to the park and lay under the stars. Eric, a neighbor who was concerned for my safety, asked to go with me. In the park, we started kissing, and for the first time my sexuality was unleashed. Next thing I know, my clothes are partly off and we are physically escalating. I was a virgin and had never been intimate. As a matter of fact, I had a steady boyfriend—not Eric—with whom I shared strong beliefs that sexual intimacy was for marriage only. Being impaired disengaged from everything, though—everything except my raging sexual curiosity. Although it was not intercourse, I experienced a lot. I snapped when I felt him move over me fully aroused. I was able to stop myself, and he was respectful of my decision. But that night was the beginning of my sexual curiosity." I take a breath…

"Sue, you're trembling. Relax for a couple of minutes. Don't push yourself too quickly. I understand completely what you have shared. Although my experiences are different, there are many similarities. I found out early on that sex was a powerful thing. It took me away from my reality and actually felt therapeutic," Sarah explains.

"Yes, I know what you mean. I didn't tell anyone about that night. Sex became a focal point in my thinking. I realized Eric could be trusted and would not tell anyone. My relationship with Gary, my boyfriend, continued to grow. I had a lot of love for him, but it remained undefined. Gary is such a gentleman with high morals. I believe his character and values are perfect. Unfortunately, I am flawed. Gradually I developed a longing for sexual exploration, until I put pressure on Gary, teasing him and trying to get him to take me sexually. He was definitely stirred, but he did not like to be toyed with. After some time, he decided that I was close to the edge. He wanted our first experiences to be with each other, no matter how life panned out. It was a difficult decision for him, but he loved me. Ultimately, I know he sacrificed his values to provide me with my first real experience. It was magical, perfect, and beautiful beyond anything I had imagined. He made sure it was the most unbelievable, safe, and romantic night. He's gentle, caring, and slow to create; both of us were fully completed when it was over. We made love only one time. Gary made it clear that once was enough for him. He didn't want that kind of ongoing intimacy at that level, not at this time. At first it was enough for me, but I overanalyzed it until I began to long for sexuality in a different context. That first night had been about us, our relationship, and our love, but as time went by I longed to be taken to the edge for pure physical reasons—no attachment, just sexual lust and being out of control. My memories of my night with Eric dominated my thoughts. I loved the thought of being out of control and raging. I liked how it made me feel. Slowly, a form of teasing and seduction developed between Eric and me. Eventually, we were fully intimate. He became my fix. Afterwards, I would be remorseful and would distance myself from him. Eric understood and accepted that it was nothing more than indulgence and reckless play. Always, after a long period of exhaustion and pressures, I sexually turned to Eric to transcend my reality. I always enjoy it, but afterwards I feel horrible about myself."

"Sue, is that the same Eric to whom you introduced me at the festival?"

"Yes it is. That was the last time I saw him. Ever since, I have been trying to deal with all of this. I feel like I am fragmented—like I have two lives. I love Gary, and I am not sure where our relationship is going, but he is very important to me. I don't have those kind of feelings for Eric. I only think about Eric when I am exhausted and want to escape," I explain.

"The earth is a trying place," Sarah begins slowly. "It's not heaven. What we do wrong is not as significant as how we move beyond it. No one is perfect, and life's potholes are there for us to learn by. You can neither wish your problems away nor act as if they don't exist. You must reroute yourself on this journey to a place where you can find peace and comfort. Surely, your moments of pleasure and release are fleeting in comparison to the aftermath of pain that follows. You are frightened that your behavior is taking you further from the foundation of everything you believe. I know how that feels; I was there. I can't tell you how to get where you need to be. That is your journey and for you to discover. However, the discomfort and pain you are experiencing is necessary to move you in a different direction. I care about you deeply and do want to be here for you."

Her words are so powerful. She is right about the fleeting pleasure being no comparison to the aftermath of pain. Talking with Sarah has lifted an enormous weight off my shoulders. Saying it out loud made me own it. Although I have no real answers, I feel a lot better. It's late and Sarah needs to go to bed.

"Thanks, Sarah. I can't tell you how much I appreciate your time and concern. It's late, and I don't want you to stay up any longer."

"Well you are right; I do not last as long as I used to. Sue, we will talk more. This is just a beginning." Sarah hugs me.

I sit on the porch and listen to the crickets. I feel calm. More importantly, I have faith I'll eventually be okay. There are so many stars in the sky. All at once I see the Big Dipper—something I haven't looked for in quite some time. Centered below is the brightest shining star of all. It's amazing that I feel so good—as if a small part of me is coming back to life. I think of Gary and hope he is looking up. Smelling the fresh air, I feel chilled.

As I walk down the corridor to my room, I notice a huge, beautiful painting of a picturesque scene: three ducks floating on a stream while a young woman sits at the water's edge. She is beautiful and has a parasol that matches her dress. She looks lost in the beauty of the moment. It's very intimate, and as the sunlight filters through the trees, the light creatively intensifies the feeling of romance. The wonderful painting makes me think about Gary and Jean-Louis. How they would love this painting! All of a sudden, I see the name in the corner: LeBranche. Isn't he the painter who was a teacher and mentor to Jean-Louis?

Yawning, I turn in for the night.

I awaken early and the sun has yet to appear. As I look from the balcony, I see Jessie talking to a young man. I dress and hurry downstairs.

"Sue, here's Freckle, Sarah horse. She's a pretty calm horse, but every once in a while she has a bit of spice and will take off on you. Just remember to pull back on your reins a few times, and she will slow down," explains Jessie. "This is Samuel. He just graduated from high school and will go to Broctren Harbor College in the fall."

We take off riding, Jessie and Samuel and I. Freckle likes to trot but eventually steps up the pace. The cool morning air sweeps the rolling fields and huge woods. We ride about twenty minutes until we get to a stream. Jessie suggests we get off and rest a bit. He has hot coffee for us. Samuel tells me about Sarah—her generosity and what an inspiration she has been to him. Then he asks, "Sue, is it true that everyone on campus is scared of Sarah?"

"How do you know about that?"

"Sarah has always been part of my family's life. She is so nice and giving. Once when we were talking she said I would find out that she is viewed differently on campus. She says the students are frightened of her. That's so mind-boggling; don't you think she's wonderful?"

"She presents herself differently on campus," I answer. "She appears cold and to the point. Students are frightened of her, but I saw her as a challenge and wanted to get to know her. Eventually, she couldn't keep that false front up. Yes, you're right, she's wonderful."

"Let me tell you two why Sarah's that way," Jessie says. "This is not my story to tell, so I ask you both to keep it to yourself. Sarah has been sick on and off all her life. She had many friends, but each time she became deathly ill, they became awkward and did not know what to do. In time, people became so uncomfortable they stopped coming around. She became hurt by that, so when she turned twenty, she moved to Paris and lived there for a little over a year. Eventually, she had to come home when she became ill again. It had been the happiest time of her life. She had fallen in love and kept her illness from the gentleman, not wanting his pity. Before she left, she told him she was dying and that she did not want him to watch her die. She demanded that he accept reality and not complicate her last days. Now, any normal man who loves a woman would not let her fade away without being there for her, but this man never contacted her again and probably assumed she died. It was cruel. I could tell she was hurt that he had not fought to stay with her. Back home, her treatments worked. Sarah has had five major periods in her life when she was told that she would not make it. She has always lived with the knowledge that she's dying. After Paris, she pulled away from all people except those of us here on the farm who love her. She had made a commitment to her grandfather that she would serve Broctren Harbor College. I doubt he'd imagined she'd live so long. People don't know that she is the mental giant behind most of the successful growth on campus. She works tirelessly to make sure campus life is full for students. She does all of this without allowing her name to be recognized for her efforts. She has told me that she needs to distant herself from students for her own emotional welfare. In return, she gives to them in ways they have no idea. I can't tell you how many times I have had to take money and mysteriously put it into certain students' accounts to keep them from leaving college. Those students mistakenly believe it comes from some supplemental college fund. The irony is that those students probably don't like her. She can be theatrical and cold, but that way at the end of day she doesn't feel so emotionally drained. Sarah is not that strong, and she can't handle students pulling on her. I do understand why she is choosing to protect herself. She has found peace in her life here on the farm. She loves her flowers, animals, and,...and Lord, can that woman fish. It's amazing that she opened herself up to you, Sue. I don't know how you got through that wall of hers. She has told all of us that you are special. I have shared pretty frankly here, so I ask that the two of you honor your promise to keep this information to yourselves. Please do not mention to Sarah that I said any of this. My Lord, she would kill me," Jessie adds.

"Uncle Jessie, how am I to be on campus with her and know that she is so wonderful when I hear kids talking about how cold she is?"

"Well, you have to respect the students because what they are describing is true. She does keep her distance. Just remember to respect to respect her need to be who she wants to be. You know you are always welcome to go see her. She will always be there for you because she loves you. The same is true for you, Sue. You are part of her now. Both of you need to respect her privacy and not share any of her personal information. She has no need to be seen any differently than she is now. Sarah has peace and doesn't need the adulation of others."

I am amazed at what Jessie shared.

"Samuel," I say, "I will be on campus for you as well. Don't hesitate to come to me if I can help in any way. I look forward to getting to know you."

We ride back to the farm. Entering the house, I hear Sarah laughing in the dining room.

"How was your early morning ride?" she asks.

"I loved it. Freckle was the perfect horse—gentle but frisky. I am going to run up and change my clothes. I will be down in a few minutes."

"Put on your fishing clothes, because I am going to show you how to catch fish," Sarah hollers.

I hurry and change. Jessie helps us in the jeep.

"Now, Sue, all the fish know Sarah, and they only have eyes for her hook. You are going to be humiliated by her talent," he laughs.

"Oh, stop it Jessie. Just because you have no knack for fishing doesn't mean Sue will have the same problems. Sue, as you can tell, fishing is a point of contention between Jessie and me. When we were kids, he was the lousiest fisherman in the area. As he got older, he became even worse," she says, laughing and teasing him.

The ride is beautiful over the lush acres of the farm. Jessie takes us on a tour of the homes that Sarah's grandfather built for each family. They are lovely ranch homes, large and sitting in beautiful picturesque areas. We pass through rather thick woods and come upon a beautiful natural lake. Jessie hands Sarah a can of fresh nightcrawlers and leaves. Sarah takes my pole and shows me how to hook the worm. The water is so peaceful. It's fun watching Sarah in her fishing gear. She's bouncing around the rocks at the edge of the water. After a couple of minutes, she reels one in, then immediately sets it free. "Too small."

Surrounded by nature, Sarah reconnects with the beauty of life. I can't help but feel anything but sheer gratitude. We fish for about an hour. Sarah catches five fish and I catch two. She suggests we lay our poles down and have a snack. The basket Jessie has left us is full of fruit, muffins, and hot coffee.

"Sue, are you enjoying yourself?"

"Oh yes—more than I can explain. I can see how this place is a force in your healing. How are you feeling today?"

"I feel great—or should I say, as good as anyone my age *can* feel. Sure, there is still a bit of weakness and stiffness, but gosh, for my age that's pretty good. I do wish I could have gone horseback riding with you this morning. Those days may be behind me now. I say "may" because I am not someone whose behavior anyone can predict," she laughs.

We talk more about her health. Each time she is out of remission, the possibility of death returns, but so far her body has been receptive to bone marrow transplants and other treatments. She says eventually the time will come when she won't make it to remission, but she adds that she won't bet against herself.

"Sue, how are you feeling about what you shared last night?"

"It's amazing how this wonderful place transcends the confusion and problems. I haven't thought about it at all since I went to bed. I slept so well."

"Well, let's focus on pleasant things. Tell me about this wonderful man named Gary. Tell me what he is like and why he is so special to you."

"I met Gary at school. Actually, we have known of each other since kindergarten, but he is rather shy. We never really talked until high school. He is a very quiet, peaceful man, always filled with gratitude about life. I have never heard him talk about being unhappy, disappointed, or upset. He is respectful of all that he has been given. He and his family celebrate life through the arts. His mother is a pianist and composer. His father is a craftsman who makes furniture and creates inventions. Gary is saturated in art, but his passion is painting. He is an only child who was raised in the most loving home I have ever seen. They all care so much about each other and share such mutual respect. My junior year, Gary asked me to a dance. Then we dated throughout my senior year. Being with him gives me so much. He is like an extension to a new world and a new way of thinking. He has added so much more to my life. Still, we are indeed very different," I add.

"Tell me...you speak of loving him, but you have not said what you think love means. Can you share what you mean?"

"Well, I am not sure if I can. He has helped me feel complete and more secure. He has reflected about how he sees me, and that has meant the world to me. Unfortunately, I was very insecure when we first started dating. I felt awkward about myself and feared I was so flawed and abnormal that no one would find any value in me. Gary changed everything about how I felt about myself. He made me feel beautiful, smart, and so alive. I slowly recovered from all that deep-rooted negativity. He is so verbal about my qualities, and he knows how to celebrate them. He credits me for illuminating his world. Even today he says his passion in painting is because I awakened that part of him up. I love this man who has elevated everything I feel about myself."

"How do you feel about him romantically, intimately?"

"We have the most romantic times together, and I love being in his arms and close to him. He has defined boundaries and I respect them. Yet I ponder how he is able to have them. I don't think it is control. I think he is clearly defined and at peace with his values. I am much more emotional, intense, and fluid. I don't like definitions, which are limiting and take away the natural flow of life. Because I love him, though, I am respectful. I know I love him because I am willing to surrender parts of me. He is just as loving and encourages me to walk openly in life. He doesn't want me contained. Both of us want what's best for each other—even if that might not be each other. Yet we love so deeply that we are still hopeful we will end up together."

"Both of you sound mature, and it does sound healthy. No relationship can exist in perfect harmony because no two people are alike. A relationship is the blending of two people. Love does not guarantee that two people will be together. Love is love, and it can take people in different directions, yet it remains love." Sarah says.

Somehow I think she is now reflecting about her life and the man in Paris.

"Sue, a person full of passion for life such as your Gary has to be free to capture those visions. Some have said that a person's passion is his real love in life. And although such a person may love someone, it's hard to be committed to a relationship if it draws him away from his passion. Not every human on earth will find a person to love. Love can come through other means of living one's life. Many artists, musicians, and scientists are lost in the passion of their craft. All of the finest works come from people who put their passion above everything else. Some of them have a disastrous marriage and are horrible parents because their families come second to their passion. Now, I am not implying that you and Gary will not be together. Surely, what you have is very real. Nevertheless, how the relationship is lived out could be different from the traditional family. You are right to just stay open. Too many people have defined things that ended up smothering their possibilities."

What Sarah says is very interesting. Felicia had boxed Jean-Louis in, and the relationship ended. Sarah had drawn a line with the man in Paris, and that relationship ended. Surely her wisdom comes from the painful realities of her own life.

Jessie drives up to check on us. Sarah hands our fish to him and says to come back in an hour. Pouring coffee, Sarah asks if I'd like to return to talking about last night. It's good timing because I'm not as vulnerable after sharing so much.

"Sure. As painful as it was opening up last night, it felt good getting it out and saying it. There isn't a lot more about the details. I know I use Eric for sexual release. It's all about my restlessness and stress. It's about my intensity and longing to just let go and be taken by something. I find myself craving it. But afterwards, I walk away feeling empty and embarrassed by my behavior. I feel so out of control and confused. I'm frightened when I think about the double life I live. For the most part I am stable, structured, and organized. But there is a part of me that craves the intensity of the other side," I explain.

"Sue, don't fragment yourself or believe for one second that you are two different people. You are one person with diverse thinking and desires. I too was like that when I was young. There was a terrible, carefree, reckless side to me. I wanted to run. I hated the fact that I was supposedly going to die at any time. I needed, wanted, and craved to forget everything. Sex was an unbelievable high for me. It transcended everything, and my body never felt as good as it did in those moments. Now I believe I misused it. I have come to terms with all that, but I won't deny the pleasure it gave me. You are as normal as anyone can be. We all have issues. Trust God to give you the strength to work through them. It won't be overnight, and you may struggle in the beginning, but in time you will find your way to peace about everything. Please let me be here for you," she says.

We continue to talk, and Sarah shares more about how she used her illness to justify her immature, wild behavior as a teenager. Fishing with Sarah has been so much fun. Not only have I gotten to see her so alive and enjoying herself, but we both have opened up. As we return to the house, Sarah becomes tired and goes to lie down. I take a walk through a beautiful wooded area. Wildflowers and berries are everywhere, and the hummingbirds are in paradise as they suck the nectar from within the petals. Butterflies are floating and fluttering amid the heavenly floral aromas wafting off the bushes. I sit on a large rock and think about everything Sarah has said.

I feel like my life has taken a huge turn. I no longer look at myself as fragmented; my actions are merely a result of personal weakness. Sarah has said that ownership of one's behavior is part of the healing process. No longer can I see myself spiraling out of control because of external conditions or other people. I must stop blaming everything and everyone outside myself for my feelings. It's time to start taking responsibility for how I act. That "pseudo-victimization" buys me my pathology. Sarah's explanations have been enormously eye-opening revelations. When I stop seeing myself as a victim, I will become responsible for my behavior.

As I walk back to the house, I think about this place. It's a paradise and—most of all—a happy home. The weekend has been huge: everything has changed for me. I have learned so much from Sarah, who is my friend and mentor, and I feel ready to return to my life.

The following morning, my parents arrive and call me from the Broctren Harbor Inn. They ask Carrie and me to come to their room, since there's no real place for us to visit alone on campus. They greet us with excited hugs, and we talk about everything.

"Sue, it feels like it has been forever since I saw you last. I couldn't bear it if it were much longer," Mom says. Even though it has been only three months, it feels like years. Mom looks a little more fragile and smaller. Dad looks tired, but clearly he is excited to see us. My parents ask Carrie a lot of questions about Keith, and I feel glad that they care so about her. She openly answers everything. Dad asks to meet Keith. Carrie blushes and says she hopes they can meet him while there are here.

We walk to an outdoor cafe on the edge of Lake Michigan and have lunch, continuing to talk about everything. Dad invites us to dinner and tells Carrie to invite Keith. Eventually, Carrie leaves, saying she'll contact Keith and that she looks forward to dinner later on. I spend the rest of the afternoon with Mom and Dad talking about everything.

That evening we have a great time with Keith and Carrie at dinner. Keith is not hesitant to explain how he has grown in love with Carrie. He talks forthrightly about their future. I can tell Carrie is moved both by his love and the love of our family. Keith promises not to let us down in his love and loyalty to Carrie.

The next day, I'm excited that my parents and Sarah will meet. That night while we drive out to Sarah's farm, I tell them about Jessie, Bertha, Clem, and Betsy, and how they are family to Sarah. As we pull up, we see Jessie outside working on a piece of equipment. He drops everything to meet my parents.

"Well, it is indeed a privilege to meet you. Sarah is really looking forward to this evening. I will see you in a bit at dinner. I better get cleaned up."

As we approach the front door, Sarah opens it to greet us. "Mr. and Mrs. Martin, come on in. I am so pleased to get to meet you." I quickly introduce them to Sarah, who takes us into the formal living room. Immediately, Mom comments on a huge bush of roses outside the house. Apparently, they resemble her wild roses at the church. It's strange that I had not noticed them.

"Those have been there as long as I can remember. They are so naturally beautiful. Throughout the years, Jessie has tried to control them, but they have always been more determined than he was. I love them and bring large bouquets in the house. Jessie says they stick the nonsense out of him, and yet whenever I go out there I have never really been stuck by them," she laughs.

When Betsy announces dinner, we make our way to the large dining room. After Sarah says grace, everyone starts helping themselves to the feast.

"Tell me," Sarah says, "What was Sue like growing up as a child? She is so full of energy that I imagine she was a handful."

"She was a very independent child—always inquisitive about everything. She read a lot and stayed to herself, which could have been because her two brothers were always quite busy. She wasn't very social, but she was kind, sweet, and cared a lot about people," my mother explains.

My father adds: "She was a challenge for me because she studied issues that were quite adult. I'd encourage her to get more involved with her friends, but she carried a tablet around that had a million questions about life. My work required me to travel, and I knew that when I walked in that door Sue would have a list of things she would want to talk about."

"Who is Sue most like, her mom or dad?"

"Well, Elizabeth and I have talked about that a lot. She's truly her own person—not really a reflection of either of us."

"It's fun listening to all of you talk about me like I wasn't here! Dad's right, I am not like either of my parents. I do wish I had more talent, like Mom, and I wish I could let go of things like Dad."

Sarah immediately picks up on these words. "That's quite an insight, Sue. Your wish that you could more easily let go of things, that makes me smile. Sue has been pretty determined to get to know me. I am rather cold and distant with students on campus. I have chosen to be that way because I have had bouts of illness throughout my life. In the past, it was hard on students when I became so sick. It broke my heart to see them so pained about my condition and not be able to do anything. I made a decision to distance myself, as a way of protecting them from the ups and downs of my health situation. As students graduated, eventually there were no students left who knew my history or health problems. Stories of my rather cold nature would be passed on to new students. When Sue arrived, she became terribly inquisitive as to why I was so distant. She made it her mission to try to get to know me. Her persistence and determination meant a lot. Most students fear me—not from anything I do, but more from those myths that have been handed down. Each year, the stories become more embellished and farfetched. At any rate, it's given students the necessary space so that they don't have to cope with my bouts with sickness. Sue's determination and unrelenting ways clearly made me notice her and endeared me to her. Now I feel so fortunate. I don't tell many people this, but I have leukemia. I have been out of remission several times, and death is always a possibility. That is tough on those who care so deeply about me. Therefore I choose not to let people get close to protect them from the difficult times" Sarah explains.

I can tell my parents are moved by Sarah's openness. "Well, I am the way I am because I have been fortunate to have a mother who is a pillar of strength. She has showed me the importance of being there for people at difficult times," I explain.

"Sue has lived in a home where we are very open about life and death," Mom explains. "We have always been there for others and count it a blessing to trust God to see us through. I can't think of anything more special than loving people, no matter what is going on in their life. Sue has lost quite a few people close to her already. She lost Mrs. Williams, to whom she was very close, as well as her grandfather whom she adored. Most tragically, she lost her best friend Patty. As difficult as those times were, I saw her stay firm in her faith and grow."

"You have a wonderful daughter. I am so glad that she was courageous enough to fight through the myths and stories about me and push ahead to get to know me. I have been fortunate that the Lord has seen fit to keep me around. There are so many blessings in life, and finding someone as determined as Sue has been in reaching out in friendship is priceless," Sarah concludes.

After dinner, Jessie takes my father and me on a jeep ride to show us the animals and crops. Mom and Sarah stay behind and go for a short walk. Everyone seems as if they've known each other for years.

CHAPTER 24

Looking at Life Differently

As I begin my sophomore year, I have matured emotionally and spiritually. No one has played a bigger part in my personal growth than Sarah. We spend time together on the weekends, and we have grown close to each other. Her health is better than it's been in years. I no longer run or escape the stresses of life, nor do I blame the unfairness of life on my childhood. Carrie and Keith have grown deeply in love. It's beautiful watching them celebrate each other. Carrie finally trusts what she's feeling. Keith makes sure she knows he loves her. All she can focus on is how much she appreciates what God has given her. On Carrie's birthday, Keith proposes to her. They quickly set a date, and I am so happy to share in their excitement and plans.

Gary and I are still trying to communicate by writing and calling. He always says that he misses me deeply. Before I return to college in the fall, we have the chance to spend time together briefly in the hammock at his parents' home. Gary tells me that Jean-Louis has been going through a rough time now that Benoit LeBranche, the inspiration in his life, has passed away. Jean-Louis is going through a dark period of grieving. Gary tells me about his only meeting with Benoit. When Gary had asked Benoit about his remarkable paintings, which seemed to sequentially tell his life story, Benoit had told him more about his life. Apparently, as a young man Benoit had met a woman from the United States who was an exchange student. They had dated feverishly for six months, and Benoit was lost in her. She had been full of laughter—intelligent, deep, and very playful. Benoit had come alive in ways he never knew possible. She had stirred him with her ideas and given him a new way to look at life, helping him work through the pain he held inside from his childhood. He had started painting from this new sense of existence. She had freed his emotions; for the first time he could feel everything with greater intensity. Then one day she became ill. She had to return to the States for treatment but had insisted that he stay in Paris to paint. She had begged him to stay there—for her sake. He had wanted instead to join her, but she would not allow it. Out of love and respect for her request, he had continued to paint, as she had asked. She had made Benoit promise that he would always put his passion for painting first. Benoit soon received an unsigned telegram from, he thought, a family member, telling him that his lover had died and had already been buried. After years of great pain, Benoit eventually forced himself to celebrate her through his paintings. For the rest of his life, all of that emotion and love had come out in his paintings. Gary had said no artist has ever painted love or the reflection of love so beautifully. Benoit sold many paintings throughout his lifetime but saved his masterpieces and left them to Jean-Louis.

My weekend with Gary made it clear that he was fascinated by Benoit's life and needed to share it. Gary related to Benoit, saying he too was awakened to existence by a powerful love. So many times, Gary has said that I awakened the painter in him. While telling the story of Benoit's life, Gary implies that our love stories are parallel. The weekend with Gary also shows me that I am no longer a needy girl who craves affection and romance. Gary commented on the change in me. I have become responsible for my own happiness. I am no longer needy or desperate for intimacy, which has taken a proper place in my life: as a gift and a celebration. Gary and I relax more in the presence of each other. When the weekend ended, I had no need to figure out what it meant beyond the fact that I enjoyed being with him. I still love him.

On campus, much has changed. My relationship with Dean Morrow has grown in a healthy and respectful way. I tell the whole story about our inappropriateness to Sarah, who sheds a lot of light on why I shouldn't be so quick to judge him. Sarah confirms that many faculty members had been amazed at how much I looked like his first wife. Although Dean Morrow inappropriately reached out to me, Sarah says that my resemblance to Rose has awakened and revived him. After Rose died, Dean Morrow had gone into a deep depression. Everyone had done everything to pull him out of it. The campus had been frightened that he wasn't there emotionally for Katie. The board of directors had even met to consider asking him to take a leave of absence because he had become so distraught. When I had come to campus, a huge transformation had occurred in him. Sarah says I gave him hope. This year he has begun to move outside his pain and become alive again. Now he is dating a woman who owns a boutique in Broctren Harbor. Sarah says I was the only person capable of reaching him, as if Rose had come back to tell him to get on with his life. Sarah says she believes we are used as angels in other people's lives.

My relationship with my parents is growing in different ways. Mom and I talk weekly, and I enjoy our talks. She has been having problems with severe headaches, but the doctors don't seem to think that it is anything. She gets some relief from medication. My dad, now fully retired, is writing a book about management systems. He loves keeping busy and still does a rare lecture when he is asked.

I love the weekends, when I can get away and enjoy the farmlands. Most of all, I love my hours of talking with Sarah. She is so wise and insightful. She has helped me clarify what's important in life. When we first talked about death, it was frightening, but Sarah has helped me see that dying is just as important as living. There can only be peace at the time of death if the individual doesn't fear it. Sarah shares her stories about each time she became sick and how she learned so much about herself. She does not profess to know what death will be like, but she does indeed have peace. Not fearing death, she lives each day filled with gratitude.

Looking forward to my next weekend on the farm, I stop by the student center for my mail and find a letter from Eric. I feel my heart drop from overwhelming guilt. Eric has no idea of the changes in my life. So much time has passed. I always knew that my thinking about him had been inappropriate, but now it seems strange that I used him and never cared about him. My wild days of recklessness are over, and I need closure.

༄

Dear Sue,

Gosh girl, what's going on in your life? I do hope you remember me? Aw, come on now, you know I am that guy who takes you out for a fun time. Anyway, just did not want you to think that I had forgotten you. That would be impossible, you know. Call me. I'd love to come for a visit. I'd even be willing to do an ol' dance or two if you ever have another one of those festivals. Take care, and hope to hear from you.

Just a-whistlin' Dixie, Eric

Eric makes us sound like yesterday, and yet I am far beyond the last time I saw him. I almost hoped he would have forgotten me. Yet I know this has a purpose in my life.

After dinner, Sarah and I sit on the porch. Eventually, I bring up the letter I got from Eric. I explain that I thought no contact would somehow end things. She reads the letter and smiles. "Gosh, he does sound like a lot fun. He has such a sweet tone, doesn't he?" I like the fact that she always sees the best in people. "Now, tell me Sue. Did he mean anything else to you besides a good ol' fun time? Did you ever have real feelings for him?"

"Sad to say, I did not really think of Eric as anything but a good time—a safe place to explore and taste the edges of life."

"How did Eric see you? Why did he think you were with him on those occasions?" Sarah never looks at anything from one side. Here she is caring about a man whom she does not know. She is not about to lecture me about what's best for me. "Tell me honestly, Sue. Do you really think that all Eric wants is to be with you sexually? Is that really all he cares about? If so, you simply have to tell him that you have decided not to use your sexuality as an escape or an adventure any longer. Explain that it is something sacred and special, and therefore you aren't open to such activities anymore. That would be both definitive and factual. However, by saying that, you would only be defining yourself with no regard for his feelings, making him nothing more than a pleasure object."

Sarah is right. I knew somehow she would say this. I have never really cared what Eric thought, never considered how he felt about anything. Here I was, in a much better place in my life. Yet I had to clean up the mess of my past behavior.

"Sue, this is an opportunity to give to Eric. Taking the time to apologize and explain how you have changed shows him that you value who he is. It is like saying he's important and has the right to know the truth. You didn't lie, but you did use Eric for selfish reasons without any concern for what it meant to him. You need to give him respect and bring closure to your past behavior. It's up to you both whether you remain friends."

As always, Sarah makes so much sense. I already chose the easy, selfish way by ignoring him and hoping that he would stay away. I almost wish Sarah would tell me to write Eric a letter saying that I no longer indulged in sexual irresponsibility and that would be that. I should have known, though, that she would be concerned for Eric. I am ashamed at how selfish those moments of indulgence were. It feels awful thinking about what I was like back then.

"Sue, may I suggest that you write him a letter, or call him and tell him? Tell him you have found peace and are more responsible in life. Say you would be happy to explain this in person if he wants to visit you sometime. Apologize for not contacting him sooner. You are welcome to invite him to the ranch for horseback riding and a picnic if you think it will help him better understand."

Her recommendations sound so noble and healthy. Still, I found myself not wanting to open the door to seeing him. Maybe it is because Eric represents the side of me that is so embarrassing. Maybe it would be awkward—or maybe I deeply fear how I will react to seeing him.

"That's a good idea," I respond, "but for some reason I fear seeing him."

"Do you feel weak—that you couldn't hold Eric off, or something like that?"

"No, not at all. Eric has never been aggressive or pushy, and he takes all of his cues from me. I have been very clear that I would not choose to indulge in such behaviors. Oh, Sarah, I don't know what it is, but I don't want to see him," I say, wiping my eyes.

"Maybe you don't want him to become real to you. You seem to have made him a nonperson—a man without feelings or a pulse. To see him now would require you to finally acknowledge him as someone who probably cares about you deeply. You would have to deal with his feeling for you. You'd have to come to terms with the fact that you have been intimate with a real person who had real feelings. Could this possibly be the problem?"

My God...that must be it. She is so right. I haven't allowed Eric to become human in my thoughts. I treat him like a fix, a fun moment. During all those times, I never considered how he really felt. I know seeing him and talking through things requires me to let him come closer. To do so would be far more intimate than the playful physical sex we've experienced. I feel vulnerable to hearing how much he cares for me. I was never attracted to him intellectually, but seeing him will force me to deal with the fact that he has been attracted to me. It would require me to listen and care. Once again, I have been thinking only about myself. Sarah is asking me to care about Eric and do the right thing.

It's getting late and Sarah goes to bed. I sit on the patio and think about Eric. Finally, I write him.

ᢙ

Dear Eric,

I am sorry I have been so long in contacting you. College is much more encompassing now that I am a sophomore. I have grown so much in so many ways. I am no longer reckless or aloof as I was back when you were so nice and kept me safe. I have changed much. I would be happy to explain this in person, as writing it in a letter seems so inadequate and impersonal. I spend my weekends on a large farm owned by one of our deans. She said I could invite anyone to the farm to enjoy it. Maybe you could come down, and we could do some horseback riding and have a picnic so I can better share how I have changed. Eric, please know that I appreciate your kindness and friendship.

Warm regards, Sue

I mail the letter the next day.

The next weeks are exciting, as Carrie prepares for her upcoming nuptials. I am the maid of honor and my parents will give her away in a small wedding at the campus church.

I soon receive a letter back from Eric.

ᢙ

Dear Sue,

I received your letter and am glad you are doing well…That's all I ever wanted for you. I understand that you have changed. You are an inspiration to me in so many ways. I would like to take you up on the visit to learn more about what's going on in your life. I could come down on a Saturday and leave that night. I don't want you to feel obliged to do this if it is uncomfortable in any way. But I consider you a friend and care. Just call, and if I am not here, leave a message.

Thinking of you, Eric

His letter seemed okay and suggests he understands. That evening I call him.

"Sue, I look forward to seeing you. I do understand that you have changed. Good for you;"

"Well, I could meet you at the train station and we could go to the farm and have a picnic. Or, we could just stay here in town and pick up some food for the beach. What do you prefer?"

"I think the beach would be great. I wouldn't get there until 11:30 AM and would leave about 10:00 PM. Do you think you can stand me for that long?" he teases.

"Sure—I have a lot to tell you. I want to catch up on what *you* have been up to," I say.

"I'll see you in a week. If something comes up, please let me know. We can always plan it some other time."

I tell Sarah that Eric is coming next weekend. She suggests that Eric and I come to dinner at the farm.

To get my mind off things, Sarah and I go fishing. I am getting better at it and have even become competition for her. On Sunday, after I get back to the dorm, Gary calls to ask if I can come to New York the following weekend. He says he really wants me to see his paintings and feels it's time for me to get to know the painter in him.

Because of my plans to see Eric, I tell Gary that I can't come. I feel bad that I can't go and wonder why I haven't asked to see Gary's paintings myself. Perhaps I should cancel my weekend with Eric, but I want to bring closure to our past. After all, I will have many other opportunities to visit Gary and see his paintings. I decide to stick with my plans.

The week goes by quickly. Before I know it, I am meeting Eric at the train station, despite my ongoing uneasiness about seeing him. We go to a café, pick up some food, and head to the beach. It's a beautiful day.

"It seemed like a long ride today," he offers, "Maybe it was because I was a bit unsure about coming."

"I was afraid it might be awkward for you. I am sorry you're uncomfortable."

"Oh no, Sue. I did not say 'uncomfortable,' nor did I mean to imply I was. I just felt unsure whether you really wanted me to come. I didn't want *you* to be uncomfortable. My concern is for you; I am fine. I am hoping you aren't doing this because you feel obligated."

I can see that Eric is sincere. All of sudden it hits me: I know why I did not want to see him. Since I haven't let myself think of Eric as a person, I can't know how I will react to this very kind, captivating man. Thinking of him as a "playful experience" and nothing more has kept me from caring about him, and now I fear I could care too much. Opening up and sharing for even a moment now sounds so difficult, because I have come to see Eric as a very sweet and kind guy who always treats me really special. More importantly, he really cares about me.

"Thanks for caring about me, Eric. I need to apologize and explain a few things, though. Where do I begin? This is not easy for me to talk about. I am embarrassed by my truths and actions. After the last time I saw you, I started to think about my behavior in terms of my values. Ever since the first time you and I connected after the homecoming float party, I have found myself slowly opening up the door to ongoing experiences with you. You were safe, not pushy, and always willing. You were my means to sexual freedom. You were well experienced and knew how to take me to a world of enormous sexual highs. I always walked away from you feeling so completed—an awesome feeling—but a feeling that was only ever a high from the sex. Afterwards, we would have no contact and would go on with our lives for a time until my life would get a bit stressful. Right away I would start thinking about being sexual with you. My desire tugged at me, and I wanted it…even talking about it now makes me think how much I enjoyed it," I admit, reaching for my soda.

Eric listens attentively, gazing at me with a softness that makes me feel comfortable. "Are you okay, Sue?"

"Yes. After the second time I was with you, I started thinking how easy it was to escape into these moments of pleasure. I was able to disregard my moral compass. By allowing myself to indulge in such experiences, I was making sex a fix, a high, a way to let go. I found myself craving to be out of control and taken by sex. Well, months would pass by, and whenever I was alone I became preoccupied with memories of those times together. They became powerful and pleasurable to recall. Gradually, I started to feel as if I were two people: the moral me and the carefree-in-the-moment me. I say that because morals require thinking, planning, and responsibility. Being carefree and in the moment required me to die to my conscious reality. That got easier and easier to do. In time, I hated the way I had come to use love and define love. I started thinking about my love for Gary—how making love with him had been such a sacred moment. I didn't blame you; you never instigated anything, of course. If anything I am so thankful that you kept me safe and have never set out to destroy my reputation. You have been nothing but a wonderful friend."

"Thanks for saying that…I would never do anything to hurt you."

"I know that more than anything, Eric. I prayed that God would give me someone whom I could talk to confidentially, someone who wouldn't moralize but who could help me examine my fragmented self. Sarah—the dean I told you about—became my friend, and our relationship grew. One day I opened up and told her what I was dealing with. She confronted my misuse of sex, saying that I could not allow myself to destroy the moral fiber of what I believe. I have grown much, and now I don't find my inappropriate thoughts pulling at me. I have learned how to better cope with stress. I don't want to divert or run," I say, completing my confession.

"I am happy for you. I wouldn't want you any other way, and I am glad you feel like you can share this with me. It means a lot, and it helps to know that I didn't do anything offensive that kept you away. I know we only had a few moments of reckless fun. I am not going to say I didn't enjoy it, but I knew that you would move on and that you were just experimenting. Nothing you've said shocks me. I am just glad you are okay."

"You're a great friend. I like your humor, your fun ways, and definitely your silliness. Eventually, I have to come to terms with our relationship. I guess it means more to me than I imagined. You're not easy to forget. If that first night had never happened, I don't believe that we would have grown together in friendship. For that I am grateful."

"Sue, because of you I decided to get my life together. I have moved into a steady job and now am a supervisor. I don't play around with drugs or drink like I used to. After being intimate with you, I found myself wanting more from a relationship than I had with other women. Your sense of humor and outlook on life has made me a look at life differently. You have had a good effect on me. If you can grow from all of this and walk away without any scars, then I will be fine. I never wanted you to become like me. I wanted to be more like you."

We talk for the rest of the day until evening arrives. Sarah greets us at the farm. At dinner, Jessie tells Eric stories about the first time I rode a horse. He and Samuel had been covering their mouths trying to keep from laughing. He said I would be gutsy and say, "Giddy up" until Freckle started to gallop; then I would panic and say, "Whoa girl, whoa girl." Freckle had been so confused by my commands and must have imagined two different people were riding her. Sarah shared our fishing stories with Eric, even confessing that I had beat her in the fish count. After dinner, Sarah asks Eric to go for a walk with her in the flower garden. Eventually, I see them sitting on the patio, and I join them. Soon it is time to go. Eric and I said our good-byes. I look him in the eye and tell him he is a special friend and not to stay away.

CHAPTER 25

Violence Darkens Beauty

Carrie and I spend the next weeks planning her wedding. Keith is busy coordinating flights and train connections for family members, while Carrie and I are busy discussing the details of the ceremony and reception. Once all the catering and reception details are finally completed, I find myself feeling almost as excited as Carrie. I can't remember ever being this happy. Both of us find it hard to sleep at night as we count down the days: only four weeks to go.

I am so busy I don't find time to see Sarah after Eric's visit. As I approach my dorm room, I see a message sealed in an envelope attached to my door.

> *Sue,*
>
> *Please come to my faculty residence as soon as possible. I desperately need to talk with you. It is imperative that I speak with you as soon as possible.*
>
> *Sarah*

The note includes a time, indicating that it has been written within the last thirty minutes. I am alarmed, my mind running wild with the thought that she may be desperately ill again. What could it be? I rush out the door and walk as fast as I can toward her residence, trembling. Rushing up her steps, I ring the doorbell.

"Sue, please come in. Please have a seat." Sarah sits beside me on the couch. She looks fine, but I can tell she is shaken.

"Sue, I don't know how to tell you this, so I am going to just say it. I received a call from your mother. She and your father are on their way here. Your mother received a call from Gary's mother. Gary was brutally murdered last night on the subway in New York."

"No, no, no—please, my God, no!"

Sarah throws her arms around me while I cry despairingly, uncontrollably, my head swimming in pain beyond all reason. Gasping, coughing, and crying, I am thrashing and hitting my knees and screaming.

"This can't happen to him—not him! Not him...*not to him!*"

Sarah tries in vain to console me, but I can't hear a thing. I am consumed with anger and hatred. How could someone harm such a beautiful human being? Gary, who would never hurt anyone, was the most kind, sweet, gentle human I've ever met.

"Why? Why? *Why?*" I scream. "*God, you screwed up this time!*" I scream, even louder. "Why did you have to take him, and so violently? God, why didn't you protect him and save him? Why? *Why?*" I am lost in a hell that is darker than anyplace I have ever been.

Up on my feet and out of control, I run for the door with no idea what I am doing. I faintly hear Sarah beg me not to go, but I run out and down the sidewalk, screaming and crying, in an unbelievable state of hell. This is more than I can bear! Running across the grass, I trip and fall, then beat the earth with my fist. Losing someone unexpectedly to violence is too horrible for words, and my fists viciously strike the earth over and over.

"Murder? Murder, you bastard! Why? Why? *Why?*" My hand bleeds from the blunt blows. Exhausted, I lay my head on the ground, murmuring and sobbing. "Why, why...my God, *why?* I just want to die. *I—want—to—die!*"

I don't know how long I've lain here, but Sarah is now sitting on the ground rubbing my back. Carrie is holding my hand. I slowly try to muster the energy to sit up.

"It's not fair. Gary is the greatest...it's just not fair..."

Somehow, Jessie appears too. "Sue, honey, let me help you up." Jessie and Carrie lift me from the ground. We go back to Sarah's place, where Dean Morrow and the campus physician have arrived. The doctor gives me something to help me sleep and cleans and bandages my bleeding hands. Mentally, I resist the shot, but physically I am in no condition to push him away. I drop off to sleep.

When I open my eyes, Carrie is still beside me, and my mom and dad are standing nearby. Another trip to campus to collect the pieces of me for a funeral, I think. My head aches, and I'm still not thinking too clearly. I want everyone to go away. My pain is too unbearable, and I tell myself, "I want it to end." I am not sure what I mean by that, but I don't want anyone to tell me I will be okay or that, in time, things will get better. Any attempt to comfort me would insult the devastation that I feel.

Everyone leaves the room except Mom. "Sue, I am so sorry. I am lost for words." She takes my hand and rubs it. I pull it away. "Is there anything I can do for you?"

I say nothing. There are no more words inside me. I have poured my voice into the earth, damning everything and everyone for my pain. I can't speak, nor do I want to. I just stare at her. I'm just not able to exist in their reality with them…not right now, anyway.

"Sue, please talk to me. Is there anything I can do?"

I roll over with my back to her. What could anyone do? Tears continue to fall. It's amazing how much suffering a human can go through. I knew my pain at that moment was only the beginning. How could I cope with this? God wasn't a resource I could call upon this time. After all, I couldn't understand how he could let this happen to Gary. I am devastated that Gary died violently, and all at once I must hear the details of his murder. When I roll over, however, Mom has left the room. Trying to stand, I find my body lifeless and hard to manage. I have no strength. Slowly I walk to the doorway, outside everyone is talking. Mom says she fears this is too great a loss for me to bear. Hanging onto the doorway, I force myself to speak.

"I…I…I…I want to know the details," I say, now trying to return to bed. The next thing I know, I'm waking up. Obviously, I fainted. Sarah is sitting beside me.

"Sue, you have been sleeping for about twelve hours. How do you feel?"

"Better than I did. But this isn't a nightmare that will go away, is it?"

"No, Sue, it isn't. I wish it were."

"Are my mom and dad here?"

"They went to the inn to catch a little sleep. They will be back in a bit."

"Sarah, have you slept? You need your rest," I say, now concerned for her.

"Yes, I had a nap. I'm fine"

Strangely, I've calmed down from the devastation and shock but not from the horror and pain. My body feels drugged and sluggish, but the intensity of the sadness cannot be altered.

"I am glad you are here. I need to know what happened to Gary. I want the details…please Sarah, please," I say, begging her to tell me.

"Okay, but this will be difficult for you. Gary went over to Jean-Louis Pacquet's studio and was on his way home at about 9:30 PM. He was on the subway when two men pulled a gun and a knife and started robbing people. An elderly man said no to the robbers, and they shot him. Gary tried to help the elderly man by putting a compress on the wound. The police believe that Gary thought the two men had gone, but witnesses said that one of them came back into the car, walked up behind Gary, and slit his neck. By the time the subway car stopped, Gary was dead. That is all I know. They believe he was killed for trying to save the elderly man."

Hearing how he died horrifies me: Gary, who celebrated beauty and only believed the best about people, had died in such a horrendous act of violence. As the tears fall, I close my eyes and lie back on my pillow. Sarah sits with me in silence.

"Sarah, I am glad you told me. I needed to know. I'll get dressed and sit in the living room and wait for Mom and Dad."

"Okay. I will get us some tea and something to eat while we wait."

Although I have slept a lot, I still feel weak. I can't imagine how I will ever cope with all of this. It is still so hard to breathe. I make my way to the living room. Everything seems so surreal. I hear Sarah in the kitchen. I think about how Gary wanted me to come to New York. Regrets, such horrible regrets, fill my thoughts. Why didn't I call him more, write him more? I loved Gary—there was never a doubt about that. I refused to define our love, and now the tremendous loss of him will do it for me. Not only will the pain smother me, but I'll be forced to see how terribly important he was to me.

Sarah brings a tray and pours tea. "Sue, please drink this and eat a piece of muffin."

"Mr. and Mrs. Waltham must be devastated beyond everything. He was their only son and the focus of their life. Then there is Jean-Louis, who was so close to Gary. Jean-Louis is still trying to cope with the loss of Benoit LeBranche." Sarah looks startled when I say that name.

I try to drink the tea, but I am too numb to taste it. My mother and father arrive. As Mom walks in, I throw my arms around her.

"Momma, he's gone—what am I going to do?"

"I love you, Sue, I love you," she answers. It's so powerful hearing her say those words. I hug her tightly for a long time.

"Sue, we don't know what we can do for you, but we love you," my father says.

"I know, I know…I am so out of it. It seems surreal…but I know it's real. I am in a fog, rejecting it…unwilling to accept it. I go in and out of dealing with it. Maybe this is the process that the body uses to help us through it. We take in only so much reality before disbelief and denial take over, giving us a moment to breathe and get our heart beating right again. I don't know. I feel so unstable, and parts of me want to end the pain at any cost," I admit, crying and trying to explain what I am going through.

"We want you to take your time. Stay at your pace, whatever it is. We will all just be here for you," Sarah says. "Carrie called. She wants to be with you if you want her to. She said she wants to be respectful of whatever you need."

My mind quickly thinks how unfair life seems. Only yesterday I was filled with such joy about her upcoming nuptials. "Well, as much as everyone wants to help, I really think I need space and time. No one can make this situation better. It's a hell I must go through. I am going to be profoundly changed by it; I already am. It's not only about death but about injustice and violence. Gary illuminated my world like no one else. Now, in the most disgusting, horrible, ugliest way, he was taken from me. I feel the deepest sense of hatred and anger. What I am going to do with all that? It scares me. I have never known these feelings before." The intensity of my rage abates for a moment. "I love you all. I'm sorry I am unable to find my way around this. Unfortunately, you have the pain of watching me go through this unbelievable hell. I can't make any promises. I feel empty of resources to counteract all of this. God is on hold—and I do not welcome any defense of him from any of you," I say, feeling my anger rising up inside of me again. I am full of despair, hopelessness, cynicism, and unbelievable anger.

Everyone listens silently with respect as I slowly deplete my thoughts. They know that as long as I stay angry I am shielding myself from dealing with the loss. I know we play mental games when we are unable to face reality. We deplete our emotions and project everything onto the situation or onto others.

"I am going to lie down," I say, wanting to escape all of them. Alone in the bedroom, my thoughts turn on me. Gary's tragic death isn't the only reason I am plummeting into darkness. Most of all, I am angry at myself. I loved this man but took him for granted. He loved me dearly, and I never feared he would stop loving me. He gave me my freedom to walk openly in life, loving me so much that he required nothing in return. His love was all about giving. My love was all about me—about wanting more than the awesome gift of what he was. I delighted in his love for me, but never did I accept him as enough. Yet in all truth he was more than I could ever comprehend. It was as if I passed up a diamond to frolic in cheap glitter. I hate myself for not loving him in the way he deserved to be loved.

Thinking about his qualities, I know that it wasn't that he wasn't enough for me. I was just insatiable about life. I had no loyalties because that would tie me down and make me define myself. I grew up dreaming, hoping, and wanting. I can't remember a time when I was satisfied. No one could have been enough for me. Now I have lost the greatest love I will probably ever have the opportunity to experience. Why, oh why, was I so foolish?

Gary had peace and savored everything about life. I will never forget how he was captivated by that uniquely shaped pinecone, how he watched it grow until it freed itself and fell. Even then he had taken it home to appreciate. He loved to smell the air, to touch the dew on grass, and to admire the beauty in the various shading of light on nature. I will never forget how he delighted in me when we made love. It was like he was discovering a new world, and he was emotional and sensitive to everything. Oh, how I will miss his touches and how he looks at me. I will miss his warm, sweet breath on the back of my neck as I lay in the hammock, watching the sun go down. I will miss his long arm pulling me into him and his sweet, calming voice saying "Shhh, it's okay—you are always safe with me." How will I ever be able to delight in the night sky again, with that one bright star centered below the Big Dipper glaring at me? I am so tired of the tears that fall. I realize the memories will be everywhere, reminding me of how foolish I was to think he was never enough. Emotionally drained beyond reason, I fall asleep.

When I open my eyes, Carrie is sitting next to me. "I love you, Sue, I really love you," she says, holding my hand.

"I know, Carrie. Thanks. I just don't know how to move through this horrible pain. I am sorry I am so out of it."

"I can't imagine how you feel, but I am here, and so is everyone else."

"I think I better get up and make my way home. I know I have a lot to face, but I have to do this for Gary and myself. Carrie, promise me that you will not postpone your wedding. I couldn't live with the thought that my hurt stopped the one thing I want so badly for you. I need your wedding to force me to feel something other than this horrible pain. Please promise me that you will have it exactly as we planned it—promise?"

"Sue, I *was* thinking of postponing it. If you want us to continue, of course we will, but I have no problem postponing it."

"*No,* please. It would be another thing that I couldn't live with. Please, I will be there and honored to stand up with you."

Carrie and I walk to the living room.

"I am better now. I need to get home. I need to be there—it's important."

"Okay, Sue," says Mom. "I have packed your things, if you are sure you're ready."

Sarah says, "Sue, may I have a few words with you alone in the bedroom?" She closes the door behind us. "I know there is not a stable feeling inside you right now, and you are just pushing ahead. That is to be expected. I know this is an enormous tragedy you face. After you have been through the services and burial, you will need time for yourself. I want you to come immediately to the farm for at least a week. There you will have space to think and heal. Of course, I will be there the whole time with you. Would you do that? Please?"

I don't have to think about it. I know it's a place of peace and a refuge for healing. "Yes, it is exactly where I will want to be after I get through these next few days. I love you, Sarah," I say, as I hug her.

"I have talked with your parents already. They think it would be a good place for you to come as well."

I say good-bye to Carrie and Sarah. Carrie and Keith will attend the funeral. Sarah hugs me tightly. Before I go, she whispers in my ear: *"Choose to feel better."*

CHAPTER 26

Remembrance

The next morning, I go to see Mr. and Mrs. Waltham.

"Sue, please come in, how are you doing?" Right away I see the pain in Mrs. Waltham's eyes.

"It's a horrible shock. I'm still numb and pushing myself at this point. I go through the motions of what I need to do, but inside I am drained and numb. I know you and Mr. Waltham are devastated beyond all reason," I say.

Mrs. Waltham wipes her eyes. "Sue, it is so unbelievable...totally bewildering. I talked to Gary the night before. As always, he was so full of happiness and joy. The next day, to be told that his life was taken in such a horrible way...well, it's too hard to even talk about."

"I know. I am so sorry. Gary loved you two more than life. He believed he had the greatest parents in the world." I put my arm around her.

"Thank you. We know he loved us. He was not shy in telling us or showing us. You know, Sue, you were his great love. He would have never dated anyone after falling so in love with you. You gave him so much. Really, you are responsible for inspiring his paintings. You changed him. His passion for painting was like an internal fire that swept over him. Thank you for loving and giving so much to our son."

Mr. Waltham joined us. We cry as we talk about Gary. It is necessary: we cry with no pretense and no holding back. After a while, Mr. Waltham suggests we go to the patio and have some tea. Sitting, I look at the hammock where Gary and I used to lay and watch sunsets. I sob, remembering how wonderful it was.

Mrs. Waltham tells me not to run from the memories. She says that in time the memories will help me heal.

The service is on Wednesday. There will be no viewing of Gary. He was about life and living, and his parents want to be left with those memories. Also, they didn't want to display the horror of how he died. Mrs. Waltham will play a piano tribute she composed.

"Sue, we know Gary would not want the service to be long and drawn out. He would want everyone to step outside and smell the air and remember that life is still good," says Mrs. Waltham."

"You know he would be quick to tell us that whatever he had in life was enough. He lived with the richest sense of gratitude and appreciation," Mr. Waltham says.

"Sue, we have chosen not to speak at Gary's service. He knew our love for him. He would not want to be the focus of anything, and he would rather we shared something that offers others a glimpse of the beauty of life. That is why I have wrote my piano piece. Jean-Louis Pacquet will speak about Gary's passion for painting. We don't want you to feel pressured about the service, yet we want you to know you are welcome to be a part of it," Mrs. Waltham explains.

"I agree that Gary would not want anyone standing in front of people talking about him. He walked this earth quietly, lovingly, and peacefully. He never needed nor wanted to be noticed. By the way, do you still have the curved pinecone from three years ago—the one he put in the cornucopia on the table at Thanksgiving?"

"Why, yes. It sits on the mantle of the fireplace in the family room," Mrs. Waltham responded.

"May I borrow it for the funeral? I would like to share a story about it. I will speak for only a couple of minutes, but I want to honor Gary by sharing that story."

"Why, that's lovely Sue. Of course. I don't think we have ever heard that story, so it will be special a moment in his life we have yet to learn about. All I remember is that he brought it home and kept it until the holidays, when he added it to our basket of plenty."

I spend the rest of the morning with the Walthams. We feel better sharing our memories. Jean-Louis will arrive that evening and stay with the Walthams. I leave their home feeling life returning to me again, just as Gary would want me to. At home, Mom can tell right away I'm doing better. Jean-Louis calls later to ask if he can meet me for lunch the following day, and I agree.

That evening I stay in my room thinking about Gary and working on what I will say at the service. Rather than a eulogy, I plan to offer up a simple moment of sharing a story that clearly captures Gary better than any other. From time to time, I am in tears, wondering what it will be like to never be with him again. He would want me not to suffer one moment of loss but rather to focus on what we will always have.

After a night of sleep, I finally feel more stable and competent to deal with things. The morning goes by quickly. I go to the Walthams around lunchtime. Mrs. Waltham greets me at the door and leads me to the living room. Jean-Louis stands to hug me.

"Sue, I am so glad I get to spend time with you," he says. Mrs. Waltham excuses herself. "Sue, I am so sorry. I am yet to come to terms with it. How are you doing?"

"I was beyond myself, initially collapsing in despair. My family and friends have been there for me. I constantly recall Gary saying that no matter what happens we will always have each other."

"You are so right, Sue. That is exactly what he would tell you."

Mrs. Waltham lays out a lovely lunch for us.

"Jean-Louis, how are you doing, really? Gary told me about your recent loss of Benoit LeBranche. Now, we have lost Gary. Certainly all of this must be so very difficult for you."

"Sue, a lot of me has been weakened and I feel quite drained, but I have rich pieces of Benoit and Gary inside me that will sustain me. They both have instilled much in me that death can't take away. I too am like you—I know that my sadness is about my own loss, but I am trying to step away from my selfishness and move into a celebration of both their lives."

"Gary talked a lot about you," I say. "He was so honored to study under you. It's amazing how his passion and excitement took flight when he got to New York to study with you. It was his dream. He started talking faster and had such an influx of emotion in his voice when he shared stories about you. I remember him saying, 'Jean-Louis doesn't tell me how to see things. He works hard not to affect my vision...He simply wants to aid me in my techniques.' I remember it meant a lot to him that you valued his vision of things."

"Sue, the reason I wanted to see you is to explain how important you were to him. Gary loved you so much that not even an hour could go by without him bringing up your name. He told me that he was working on getting you to New York because he was ready to show you his work. I know you have not seen any of his paintings. I am not going to tell you anything about them. You need to know that they are essential to your life. In the upcoming weeks or months, somehow you must make an opportunity to see them. It is imperative that you see them. So do promise that when I contact you in the near future you'll come," he concludes somberly.

"Absolutely. I will be there—you can count on it."

"Remember, Sue. You were more than you know to him," he adds, hugging me.

That evening I write the story of the pinecone. It's so special because I don't have to think about it. I simply write the story, remembering how truly wonderful Gary was.

The next morning I hear the doorbell ring. A few minutes later, I'm surprised to see Sarah and Jessie sitting in our living room having coffee with my parents.

"Sue, how good it is to see you!" Sarah says, hugging me.

"I didn't know you two were coming to the service. It's nice to see you both. Oh, come here, Jessie. Let me give you a hug too," I say.

"Gosh girl, it's good to see you. You've been in our prayers."

A few minutes later the doorbell rings again. It's Carrie and Keith. We sit and talk for a bit. I can tell they are all relieved that I'm doing better.

Eventually we all make our way to the church. Lovely piano music is playing, uplifting melodies so different from what I'm used to at funerals. It is definitely music of beauty and celebration. Mr. and Mrs. Waltham give me hugs and take their seats. Jean-Louis Pacquet comes in a few minutes later and asks me to sit with him and the Walthams. In place of a casket there are only fresh flowers. Instead of funeral bouquets, they are beautiful, fresh, potted flowers ready to be taken and planted. In the middle of flowers is a painting portraying three hands reaching into a wooded area of grass. One hand is a woman's; a butterfly flutters on it. The second is a man's, lifting a tree branch that has fallen to the earth. The third hand, a more youthful hand, cups a wildflower. The painting only shows what these three very different hands are doing. I can see Gary's signature in the corner. It is beautiful, with sunlight and shade filtering through the wild plants of nature.

The minister opens the service by reading a beautiful Psalm about rejoicing. He speaks for a few minutes and then offers a prayer of thanksgiving for the life of Gary. Mrs. Waltham plays the piano tribute to her son. The music is almost triumphant. Next, Jean-Louis goes to the podium.

We all have questions about life. But not Gary. He simply lived it. Whatever it brought him was always enough, for he truly lived with gratitude. Being so full of joy, happiness, and love, he poured himself into his paintings, letting the colors splashing upon canvas express his peace and love of life. He was the richest man in the world because he knew how to capture every moment and value it. Painting offered him a way to express the specialness of everything. I was fortunate because he chose me to share in his passion. He would be quick to tell you that he was my student. But I must set the record straight: it is I who learned the greatest lessons from him. It is hard not to be transformed in the presence of one who only sees the beauty of life, as Gary did. As a painter I always had my visions, but when Gary came into my life his presence gave me a new way of looking at the world. He would find it difficult to understand why I am saying anything that makes him appear a hair bigger than a simple man. Beauty to him was not in status, or importance, or in achievement. He didn't understand why humans elevate things, making one thing more important than the next. Beauty was equalized to Gary, for he was able to see it in everything and everyone. This was his first painting after he came to New York. I would classify it as his first painting, although he would say, "Why does something have to be first?" Mr. and Mrs. Waltham, you have not seen this painting until today. It was intended to be a gift to you from Gary.

Jean-Louis opens Gary's journal and begins to read:

I remember how they taught me about beauty...Mom would be quick to say "shhh, listen to the butterfly whip his wings in the wind, hear the rhythm, see the movement." Then later that night she'd sit at the piano and capture that moment by writing a melody. Dad was reaching down to the earth at the same time, in the same area, to pick up a tree limb that he later laid in the rock garden. When I asked him about it, he said it had been struck by lightning. He showed me the split in it and talked about how beautiful it was. He called it a reminder that in devastation you can still see beauty. I remember reaching down at the same time they did to cup the wild lily and smell it. Three hands reaching down to celebrate the gifts of life. My family taught me to celebrate life through the acknowledgement of beauty.

Closing Gary's journal, Jean-Louis looks up. "Gary never got over that moment and captured it on canvas. He loved his parents and felt fortunate to be their son. He also loved a young woman who he was quick to say awakened the painter in him. Sue, it is you who gave him his palette of colors. So with the gifts of celebration and gratitude given to him by his parents and the wonderful palette of colors inspired by his great love for Sue, Gary would be quick to say that what he had was always enough. Thank you."

As Jean-Louis walks off the platform, I make my way to the podium. I feel strong and ready to share my story. I place the pinecone on the edge of the podium for all to see.

Gary and I spent most of our time outdoors. We didn't want to be confined to manmade walls. Gary always saw nature as his home. After school, we often went to the park to talk and enjoy the beauty of being outside. One particular day, Gary said he had something to show me. He took me to a large pine tree and pointed up, saying "See that uniquely shaped pinecone?" "Yes, what about it?" "Well, it's just so unique; it's shaped differently. Some would say it's odd or deformed, but I think it's beautiful because it's different" Day after day, as we walked though the park Gary would walk over to the tree to see how this pinecone had changed. Slowly, it grew bigger and even more unique. It was as if he were watching some unusual natural phenomenon when, to me, it was just a plain ol' pinecone. After a few weeks, he seemed to have forgotten about it. Then, one day I was alone in the park and was drawn to look at it. It was gone—everything had fallen to the ground. I got on my knees and pushed through the leaves, trying to find where it fell, but there were so many leaves and, of course, it could have rolled anywhere. I gave up and forgot to mention to him that it was gone. A couple of weeks later I went to the Walthamses' home for Thanksgiving dinner. In their family room, right in front of me on the coffee table, sat a huge cornucopia basket with leaves, berries, nuts, and that pinecone. I was shocked, so I asked him about it. Gary said he had gone to it everyday and waited for it to naturally fall to the earth. He said its beauty was so special that he had to put it in his family's basket of plenty, a cornucopia filled with things collected all year long on nature walks. Gary saw beauty in everything: the odd, the different, the unique, and the ordinary. I was so fortunate that he helped shape a better vision of life for me. He taught me so much. To him, there were no such words as bored, empty, or lonely. Gary was captured by the world he lived in, full of all that surrounded him. He was never lonely because whatever he had was always enough.

The minister says a closing prayer, and we go to the cemetery for the burial. The minister reads scripture while the casket is lowered into the grave. After a closing prayer, everyone goes to the Walthamses' home.

I introduce Sarah and Jessie to the Walthams and Jean-Louis. After most of the people leave, I say my good-byes to the Walthams, assuring them that I will stay in touch. Jean-Louis and I hug. He reminds me again that I will be hearing from him soon.

Sarah, Jessie, Carrie, and Keith return to my family's home. We visit for a while before I pack to leave with Sarah and Jessie. Mom hugs me so hard, telling me that she loves me and to call if I need anything. Sarah, Jessie, and I say our good-byes and start the long drive back to Broctren Harbor. Sarah and I share the back seat.

"It was a very special service," Sarah says. "Gary was obviously a remarkable person. How are you doing?"

"I still feel numb, but it was good to spend time with Mr. and Mrs. Waltham. They helped me celebrate Gary's life. Now I can better deal with the loss. Mrs. Waltham says that if Gary believes what we have is enough, then out of respect we must appreciate what he has already given us. It would be wrong to selfishly despair about what might have been."

"The words you and Jean-Louis Pacquet shared were quite lovely."

"Jean-Louis is having a difficult time because he recently lost his mentor and friend Benoit LeBranche. Gary was there for him as he dealt with his grief. Now this. It's almost too much for him. Jean-Louis has been through a lot of terrible losses in his lifetime. By the way, he made me promise that I would come to New York as soon as he could arrange some things. I wasn't sure why, other than that he wants me to see all of Gary's paintings. He says they will be important to me and that I will understand when I see them."

"Yes, Jean-Louis and I talked a bit. He is a very kind man who loves talking about you and Gary. He told me how rich and wonderful your love story was. He asked me to encourage you to come to New York. Does he have family, or is he dealing with this alone?" Sarah asks.

"I know he has thousands of art fans around the world, but as far as anyone being close to him...well, I don't think so. I want to keep in touch with him."

Resting my eyes, I wonder how Jean-Louis would deal with all of this. I hope he doesn't pull away from his painting. Yet I know every stroke of his paintbrush will remind him of loss.

We arrive in the early evening. Sitting at the table with Clem, Jessie, Bertha, Betsy, and Sarah, I feel relaxed. It's amazing how I have come to feel like this is my home.

After dinner, Sarah and I relax on the patio. She tells me a story about when her grandfather died. She said he was all she had as family. After he was buried and everyone was gone, she felt like life was not worth living. Also, she was racked with guilt for not being a good granddaughter. Her depression kept her immobilized for awhile. Eventually, she had suffered enough. She became determined to make it up to him by doing what would have made him proud. By doing something to learn more about him, she became fascinated by the very same things. She wouldn't have found joy in life had she not taken the time to celebrate and understand who he was.

The next day I sleep in until noon. Sarah wakes me to make sure I am okay. I feel so exhausted. She says depression does just that: it depresses our energy and desire to push ahead. She encourages me to get up and enjoy the beautiful day outside. I spend a lot of the next three days walking the grounds and riding Freckle. The fourth day something snaps inside me, and I collapse in tears as I sit by the lake. Everything finally comes to a head. I start thinking about the horrible violence that took his life. I wonder how Gary must have felt the moment his life was leaving him. I wonder what he thought about. Did he finally come to grips with the fact that not everything and everyone is beautiful? I hate the grotesque image of him dying in such a horrific way. His death was such a contrast to how he believed and lived his life.

I experience a deep sadness that I didn't spend more time with Gary. I'm upset that I didn't go to New York and see his paintings. How tragic that I took everything for granted. Now I want to give meaning to Gary's death—but how? I know he would want me to keep moving.

Pulling myself together, I ride back on Freckle. I want to stop all this self-pity and get back to living my life. Carrie's wedding is in a week. I should be getting back to campus to help her with the last-minute details. Now is not the time to stay selfishly away trying to comfort myself. Sarah is right. Just as she picked herself up after her father's death and forced herself to look at the value of his life, I want to do the same. I want to be there for Carrie's wedding. After that, I will contact Jean-Louis and the Walthams and view Gary's paintings to understand his passion.

CHAPTER 27

A Last Name With Meaning

When I return to campus, I try to focus on what Sarah told me: *Choose to feel better.* Although my thoughts are filled with sadness and loss, I continue to push forward and help Carrie with the wedding. It gives me a momentary focal point. My parents arrive the day before the wedding. I have dinner with them and we talk about how I'm doing.

The day of Carrie and Keith's wedding arrives, and the weather is beautiful. Carrie is excited as she is quietly memorizing her vows. Keith's family has arrived. "Carrie, I am so happy for you. I couldn't wish for a more wonderful thing to happen to anyone. You are so deserving of this day."

"Thanks, Sue. I keep thinking that tonight I will finally have a last name that means something. I will know why I have it, I will be connected, and I will have a real family. It has been strange having a name that means nothing. I am so excited." I had never thought about the fact that Carrie's last name, Dougherty, had no meaning or significance to her. Now she will be related to others and share their name.

As the morning progresses, the excitement grows. We arrive at the church about forty-five minutes before the ceremony so Carrie and I can get dressed. Mom's waiting for us and gives us the final touches. Looking at the clock, I see it is already time for us to make our way to the back of the church. Carrie and I give each other a hug. Carrie is so beautiful and excited.

As the doors open, I see Keith waiting at the altar. He is dying to look past me in an obvious and charming attempt to see Carrie. Finally, it's her moment. As the piano tempo announces her, everyone stands to their feet. My father has her by the arm and is walking her down the aisle. Arriving at the altar, Dad puts her hand in Keith's hand and takes his seat.

The service and music are moving. At last, Carrie and Keith share their personally written vows to each other. Carrie goes first:

My dear Keith, I give you a family of one. I offer you a dowry of nothing. I humbly stand before you with only myself and ask that you know it is everything I have. Many people have shared their lives with extensive families, rich histories, inheritances, and legacies. Each of them belongs to the many who surround them, who are called family. I stand before you alone, simply a woman who longs to love you with every fiber of her being. I do not feel less than those who come from so much. I feel full and bursting at the seams to share all my dreams, wanting to give them to someone whom I can call family. As others have distributed their love to the members of their families throughout their life, I come tanked up, overflowing, and ready to heap a lifetime of love upon you. I pledge my honesty, for I have nothing to hide. I pledge my simplicity, for I have learned to survive with only the most basic necessities of life and want nothing more. I pledge my laughter, for I learned it was the only thing that gets me through unbelievably trying times. I pledge all my effort and loyalty to our union to secure it from any harm that life may throw our way. Most of all, I pledge to you my heart. The richest sense of love exists inside of me. I will not settle for the love I have today, for I know I have only touched the edges of what it can be. I promise to exploit its every possibility and overwhelm you with its endless potential. I promise my love will be evidenced by my actions, my loyalty, and my faithful commitment to you always. On this, our wedding day, I offer you the simplicity of who I am and the endless potential of what our love can be. I love you.

Carrie's vows are overwhelming. She has not shared them with anyone, so this is the first moment they have been spoken aloud. She and Keith had no rehearsal, as they agreed to make their marriage ceremony a real moment, not a production. Everyone is moved by what Carrie said. Now Keith offers his vows to Carrie:

My dear Carrie, I stand in front of you more alive than I have ever been. I was a very shy kid, never wanting to be seen by others. How is it that today I want to stand in front of the world and scream to everyone that I have found the richest gift life can offer: you. I was also not the sharpest kid in town. I couldn't have dreamed a dream as lovely or wonderful as you are. Your presence in my life has drastically altered who I am. I find myself feeling like I am on the top of the world. You have offered me an extension of everything I am not. You are more than a woman; you are a new world opening up to me. You always speak of yourself as simple, thinking of yourself as coming from such humble background. You are so wrong: you are the richest human I have ever met. You possess a beauty and knowledge that only come from standing alone in the world and surviving it on your own true terms and qualities. You ride on the coattails of no one. You are shadowed by a history that defines who you are. No, my beautiful Carrie, you are self-made, self-driven, and most of all self-determined. We talk about courage a lot in this world. Well, courage is not in numbers; courage stands alone—fearless in the midst of uncertainty. You embody what courage is all about. You have triumphed, you have risen above others, and you stand as a testimony to human endurance. Now, today, I pledge to you a world that not only celebrates who you are but offers to surround you in love. I ask you to relax and know you are no longer alone. I pledge to be there with you as you face the challenges of life. I pledge to warm you when coldness causes you to tremble. I pledge to hold you when you momentarily weaken, as we all do from time to time. Never are you to ever feel alone, disconnected, or that you don't belong. I pledge to be a husband who surrounds you with as much love as I possess. I promise to keep true only to you. I love you, Carrie. I now am your family.

I glance around: not a dry eye in the place. They are remarkable vows written from the hearts of two people who love each other. The minister offers them communion. Finishing the ceremony, he says, "I want to introduce you to Mr. and Mrs. Keith Saunderland."

Tears fill my eyes. It feels wonderful to be this full of happiness again. Carrie, who lived with fourteen different families throughout her childhood, whom no one ever wanted to adopt, has found her family. She always had to fight the feeling of not being good enough. Now smiling, she stands at the pinnacle of happiness, wanted by a man who loves her more than anything else. This will always be a most memorable moment because I love Carrie so much.

The reception is quaint and elegant. Keith and Carrie rarely take their eyes off each other. They do their wedding dance never looking away. After much music, food, and celebration, we wish them the best as they leave for their honeymoon.

I spend the evening with my parents at a local restaurant. We talk about the wedding and how wonderful it was to see Carrie so happy. I needed today to counter my overwhelming sadness. It seems to have brought a momentary balance and hope back into my life.

As the semester ends, I call Sarah and let her know I'm going home and will return to Broctren Harbor in a few days. The next morning, my parents take me home. Coming into Beckenburg, Mom says my brothers are home and Grey's girlfriend, Marcia Batten, is spending the weekend. Immediately I decide to go to the cemetery. Mom offers to go with me, but I want to be alone. As I'm walking, I begin to tremble. Behind the church, I pause momentarily by an overwhelming vision: the magnificent wild roses covering the trellis Dad made.

I reach Gary's grave. Its headstone reads "NEVER STOP CELEBRATING: WHAT YOU HAVE IS ALWAYS ENOUGH." I sit beside his grave, overwhelmed by the memories rushing through me. He was the first person who made me feel like I was enough. I didn't have to pretend or resort to theatrics like I did with others. He was my place to just lie still and feel good about myself. I lie on the grass beside his grave and look up at the sun. "Thanks, God, for Gary. Please forgive me for my anger when he died." It's a time for healing. I want to make my life right again. In Gary's honor, I want to celebrate and make whatever I have enough. It feels cathartic lying here. God gave Gary to me at a time when I felt unappreciated and damaged. Gary restored my belief in me and made me feel beautiful. He rejuvenated my dying energy by awakening my senses to the beauty of the world. He was a lifeline at a time when I so needed one. He was a gift from God. What I received was enough—surely it was enough.

As I wipe my eyes, I kiss his headstone. I walk away from his grave, passing Patty's grave and then the wild roses. These grounds hold my deepest emotions and memories. On my way home, I see Eric step out of his front door.

"Hello, Sue. I saw you walk by earlier and figured you were probably going to the church and cemetery. I didn't want to disturb you. How are you doing? I am sorry about everything."

"It's tough. Had you asked me two weeks ago, I would have said unbearable. Somehow, God has given me strength. It is a terrible loss. Thanks for asking. How are you doing?"

"Oh, not much has changed in my life. I think about you, and I do appreciate the time we spent together the last time I saw you. You are right about Sarah. She is so caring. How is she doing?"

"She's doing fine. She's been such a help and comfort to me. Maybe after I get through some of my rough spots, we will have you come back to the farm so I can check out your horseback riding skills," I say, wanting Eric to know that he is still my friend.

"I'd like that, but give yourself the necessary time. Take care of yourself."

I spend the next days with my family. This has been an important trip home. It was necessary that I go to Gary's grave to renew my faith and ask God's forgiveness for my anger and wavering. It's strange how quickly life moves. Suddenly tragedy and pain engulf us, and we find ourselves lifeless and unable to move. The pain becomes so great that we are compelled to work through it to find relief. I know it will come again, but for now I move back into the realm of trying to live.

Jessie is at the train station to pick me up. Sarah had called my house and found out that I was on my way back. It feels good being back in Broctren Harbor. The farm is my real home now. Sarah greets me with a tray of food on the sun patio. We talk about the wedding, and I share how I enjoyed being with my family.

"Sue, did you go to the cemetery?"

"Yes, oh yes, and it was good that I did. Gary's headstone reads, "Never stop celebrating; what you have is always enough." That is exactly what he would be telling me. It was his way of life. I know I have to move on. It is what he would want. I also prayed and asked God's forgiveness for my anger and for turning from him. I want to make things right and heal."

"While you were away, Jean-Louis Pacquet called. I explained you were at home. He said he did not want to bother you there. We talked for some time about his adjustment to life. He seems lonely and appreciative to have someone to talk with. I listened as he summed up his life, saying he was pushing ahead to give meaning to the life of Benoit and Gary. Anyway, he wanted you to know he is sending a letter and an invitation. I encouraged him to send it here, as I knew you would be with us. It arrived today. Here—I will give you time alone to read it."

⌘

Dear Sue,

I hope this letter finds you doing better. We all have to move on into the celebration of what Gary's life stood for.

I need to tell you some things that were not appropriate to discuss when we were planning Gary's service. Mr. and Mrs. Waltham know I am writing and have asked me to do so. Gary's apartment will remain exactly as he left it for now because the Walthams want you to have an opportunity to visit it.

I'm writing because Gary had a last will and testament. In it, he named you as a beneficiary, along with his parents. The will is in the hands of an attorney and will be read when you come to New York. Mr. and Mrs. Waltham would like you to come for a few days. Enclosed is an invitation to an exhibit. It is imperative that you come at that time. Attorney Bateman said he could do the reading of the will any time during your visit.

I have asked Sarah McBride to come with you for support. She said she would be happy to do so. Please read the invitation and let me know if you can come. As always, my thoughts are with you. Never hesitate to contact me should there be anything I can do for you. I am always here for you...

Warm Regards, Jean-Louis

I open the invitation:

French Painter Jean-Louis Pacquet

&

Mr. & Mrs. Walter Waltham

Cordially Invite You To The

Opening Reception

of

The Garrett D. Waltham Exhibit

On July 16, 1973, at 7:30 PM

at

The Jean-Louis Pacquet Gallery

7737 Mercer Avenue

New York, New York

RSVP

I am surprised by the invitation. I'm being forced to look at the most important aspect of Gary's life and realize I never was part of it. We never really talked about his paintings. I feel sad that I have been so selfish and do not know this side of him. Nevertheless, I am excited to confirm that I will be attending. I am glad he invited Sarah as well. I call Jean-Louis and leave a message that I will attend the exhibit and stay for a couple of days. Sarah comes back into the room.

"I am glad that you will attend, too," I say. "I do want you to go with me."

"Well, you think it through. I would be pleased to go. Jean-Louis thought it would be nice for you to have someone with you," she explains. "I let him know I thought you might want to go to the exhibit alone with no one there distracting you. I feel strongly about that Sue, this needs to be your moment with Gary's work. I will come to the exhibit later that evening when it opens up to the public. Anyway, we have plenty of time to work out the details. It isn't for three weeks."

Finally I will see the paintings of the man who captured my heart.

CHAPTER 28

Overwhelmed at His Life

Jean-Louis greets Sarah and me in the airport terminal. "My dear Sue, I am so excited to see you. Sarah, it's wonderful to see you again. I have a suite for you at the Wellington Tower. It's a marvelous two bedroom suite with a lovely living room overlooking the city and central park." After he shows us to the suite, Sarah goes to her room to rest.

"Sue, I am glad you came," Jean-Louis says. "You will see so much that will change your life. I want you to have a private viewing of the gallery exhibit. Sarah agrees that you must view it alone. I will be nearby but not with you while you are viewing his works. It is to be a wonderful, private experience. When you arrive, I will spend a few minutes with you prior to your viewing of the exhibit." I am moved by his sensitivity toward my viewing the paintings alone. "Also, be aware that three major art critics have viewed the exhibit, which got outstanding reviews in the *New York Times*. Gary's work is intense, sensitive, and emotional. It showcases a man who could see beauty like no other painter. His unique style has been coined 'soft impact modern impressionism.' He never dominates anything in his painting, preferring to overwhelm the viewer with beautiful scenes of intense emotion. One critic wrote that his death now leaves us longing to treasure the gifts he left behind, which have now become invaluable to the art world."

Jean-Louis hands me a paper clipping. "Here, look at this. I found it in the *New York Fine Arts Review* while I was waiting for you at the airport."

Waltham's Works Undeniable Treasures

In 1969, Garrett D. Waltham painted Longing to Understand. *Waltham would undergo hours in the deep recesses of his memory to perfect his image before painting it. He was a painter who did not rely on elements and techniques of the greats. His paintings, solid in artistic quality, exemplify an effortless edification of beauty. His style was not wrapped in the exact representation of his vision but rather the intensity of a story he had to tell. Currently exhibited at the famed Jean-Louis Pacquet Gallery, his sequence of paintings gives way to understanding a painter who captured the immense beauty of life through his rich belief that what he had was "enough." Exhibit open to public the evening of July 23 and to remain open through November.*

I am stunned just seeing his name in print, evidence that he is someone of great importance to the world. I think of him as my quiet, sweet, humble, and very simple love. It's overwhelming to think he will be renowned for the art he has left behind. I start to feel detached, as if I am not a part of the Gary about whom I am learning. Where is the Gary I knew? As exciting as it is, there's sadness inside me. I came to New York to feel close to him, but style, technique, art critiques, and exhibits could never reveal the man I loved and now miss so much. It's as if I'm on a tour studying the life of a man in history. Although I find it interesting, it was not what I planned or sought.

Jean-Louis says a limo will pick me up tomorrow so that I may spend the morning alone at the exhibit. The opening reception would be that evening. He mentions the Benoit LeBranche exhibit in the West Hall of the gallery. I could tell he was filled with excitement about both exhibits.

Sarah and I have dinner, and I tell her about the following day's arrangements. She says she'll be resting at the suite and that after lunch we can talk about my experience with Gary's paintings. I show her the small newspaper article that Jean-Louis tore out of the *New York Fine Arts Review*.

"My dear Sue, you must not keep him to yourself. He lived a life away from you. Both of you grew in different directions. The Gary you loved was the boy from Beckenburg, Ohio. The man Jean-Louis and the critics write about is the passionate painter. You cannot see him merely as the man you know, for that will limit your ability to celebrate all that he was. It is time for you to get to know the other parts of him."

She is right. I wanted Gary to be what I needed, and I needed to keep him small. There was always the fear that I'd be overwhelmed with the person he became. I kept moving, looking for someone who offered me more, when in all truth he was so much more than I knew. Now I am being confronted with a different Gary than the one I knew.

Sarah goes to bed early, and I sit in the dark and look down upon the lighted city. It's an amazing view full of lights, motion, and activity. I think about Gary and how unattractive this view must have been to him—or at least to the Gary I knew. He would see it as chaos, distracting the world from its view of the heavens. I realize we were so different. I could be drawn into city life out of sheer curiosity. So far my visit to New York has been so unpredictable. I had imagined that coming to celebrate Gary would bring him back to me. Looking downward, I wonder if all this stimulation may take him away from me. Surely his paintings will be scenes of New York: places that Jean-Louis thought were picturesque and ought to be captured in painting. How can anyone remember where he came from when he is lost in the lights and motion of New York?

I arise early and have breakfast with Sarah. When the car arrives, I ride to the gallery.

"I am looking for Jean-Louis Pacquet. My name is Sue Martin."

"Oh yes, Ms. Martin. Jean-Louis is in his corporate office on the second floor. Please take the elevator. The corporate offices are to the left." Upstairs, a receptionist takes me to Jean-Louis' office. It is huge, elegant, and filled with beautiful paintings. He hugs me and we sit.

"Sue, today will be very special for you. Not only do you enter the world of paintings that Gary created; you will enter his heart, his passion, and his rich celebration of how he saw beauty." He opens a drawer in his credenza and takes out the leather-bound journal I'd given Gary years ago. "I know you are familiar with this journal. He treasured it, recording in it descriptive narratives about each of his paintings. As a valuable key to his art, it is now priceless. I ask that you not read the entries until you have viewed the paintings. You will find each painting's title on a plaque beside it. Look at the painting, experience it fully for yourself, and only then open the journal to read about the painting. I feel that this is the best way for you to experience his magnificent work. Before you go, I want to read the first page of the journal to you:

The Journal of Garrett D. Waltham (Gary)
(A journal from Sue as a Christmas gift.)

It is with a profound sense of gratitude that I record the following events in my life. Everything about me changed because of love. I dedicate this journal to Sue Martin. It is not a daily journal, but special recordings of moments that reshaped my life forever. I have been inspired to paint many of them…Sue made my world come alive and simply made everything I had enough…

    Background: I met her at the age of five at school. I never talked to her until we were in high school, when I became captured by her depth and intelligence. She made classroom discussions fascinating. She is a deep thinker like me…She speaks elegantly and is not intimidated by anyone. I, on the other hand, was shy. Both of us seemed much older than we were. Finally, at the age of sixteen, I found the courage to ask her to a school dance. That night was so comfortable and the beginning of many wonderful times. From then we grew in love and shared in life. Christmas of 1969 she gave me this journal. Although we have had many special times prior to today that are worthy to be written about, it is today that I begin with this journal.

    While she was around, I was consumed with seeing her and celebrating life with her. After she left for college, I became overwhelmed with all my memories of being with her…Soon I found myself overloaded with images and visions of the times we were together. Needing to express the rich visions illuminated within me, I passionately turned to painting, splashing all my intensity into works that I consider an homage to her.

I am stunned and moved by what Jean-Louis read. As I stand, he hugs me and walks me to the exhibit. Outside the gallery stands a huge picture of Gary captioned, "The Garrett D. Waltham Exhibit." Leaving me at the door, Jean-Louis says he will be in his office, should I need him. Now shaking, I walk into this beautifully lit gallery. My eyes are immediately drawn to an amazing painting of a pine tree; looking up through the branches, I see the uniquely shaped pinecone. It is so beautiful: the tree, the light filtering through the branches…The plaque beside it reads: *Illuminating Beauty.* I open the journal and turn to the page with the same title.

Illuminating Beauty
    This was her park. Everywhere I looked, I saw her in the beauty of it all. Way up high in an enormous pine tree, I saw one very distinctive pinecone. Its shape was unique; it stood out from the others. It reminds me of how I see her in the world. She would say that this pinecone is not normal, that it's deformed and it distracts…She is wrong—it is this pinecone that makes me want to look at its surroundings. It uniqueness gives it a special beauty that stands out from all the others…Like her, it is uniquely beautiful. I took her to the tree and showed her the pinecone without telling her my thoughts about it. From time to time, we would be walking through the park and I would check to see how it was growing. It continued to grow in a unique shape, and it was beautiful. One day when I was alone, I went to see it, but it lay on the ground, fallen and fully grown. I took it home—after all it was from "her" park—because it was unique and very beautiful, like her. I displayed it in our family cornucopia of

plenty on Thanksgiving…She saw it and knew that it was special to me. She never knew that I related it to her beauty, which was unique, which stood out among others, which also had grown in the beauty of the sun in that park. I will never forget the day I saw it growing in the tree. I had to paint that first vision of the sun streaming through the branches illuminating it.

My heart is pounding as I move to the next painting. It is of a beautiful moonlight night with the light filtering through snow flurries. I know exactly where and when it took place. There is the brook with the moving water, and the ground is starting to freeze with the snow upon it. It is a beautiful painting—so emotional and romantic. Opening the journal, I find the narrative:

Romance of Nature's Art
*   We went to the dance, but the gently falling snow outside was far more fascinating, so we left early to go sit in the park. The light flurries gently danced as they fell to earth, most of them melting as they touched the ground. The wet, shiny earth slowly started to freeze into its coat of white. The moving brook, indifferent to the cold, swiftly churned with moving water. While the moon cast its light, it illuminated the earth. The romance of nature's art enhanced the overwhelming feelings we had for each other that night. I had to capture it in a painting so I would never forget.*

Tears are blinding my eyes. I feel ashamed that I ever thought he forgot me. Although his paintings were outstanding in quality and composition, they still reflected the simplistic beauty of everything he was. I couldn't believe that I was such a part of him. Wiping my eyes, I get up and walk around the corner to the next painting.

Now in *total dismay*, I am shocked at what I see: a painting so sensitive and so emotionally stirring that I can hardly breathe. It is a vision of the wild roses behind the church—not just any vision, but how they look from the oak tree in front of the church. I am seeing the exact vision I had of them when I was a child watching my mother among the roses. I have hidden behind this tree so many times, watching her. How did he know? It is a beautiful painting, with wild rose petals glistening in the sunlight, their rich branches falling precisely as they do. How could he have known that I watched my mom from behind the tree? Shaking, I hurry and open the journal.

Longing to Understand
*   Walking down the sidewalk, I saw her in the distance. She was standing behind a large oak tree, looking toward a huge area of wild roses. Reverently*

standing among those wild roses was her mother. She longs to understand why her mother comes to this special place. I am inspired to paint the beauty of the wild roses that captured her mother's attention. They both left that day, each in her turn. I went to the tree where she had stood, looking at the roses as she must have seen them. Looking down, I saw her footprints in the dirt. Fixing myself in her position, I knew I had to paint this scene of morning sun radiating the silkiness of the petals, of vines cascading in an architectural delight. All of this beauty was highlighted by the importance the wild roses play in both of their lives.

I barely can handle the emotion sweeping through me. I sit on the floor, emotionally shaking. I thought as a child that I went unnoticed. How obvious it is that he knew me and cared about my every thought. How can I come to deal with a love like he had for me? Slowly I get a hold of myself. Walking up to the next painting, I see a wonderful, romantic memory of our trip. I remember how he had me stand by the fountain for such a long time. The beauty of the vines and flowers are so vivid in the painting. I love the fact that he never forgot that special day.

Beauty Surrounding Beauty
It was an amazing trip. We had such a wonderful time. The beautiful garden was breathtaking, and my head was swimming…I captured that moment of her by the fountain, which no words can describe. So vivid are the details in my memory, and I love painting that memory of her…a beautiful place, a beautiful woman. Beauty Surrounding Beauty…

This painting leaves me feeling beautiful. Tears streaming down my face, I move to the next painting. Ah yes, the cherry blossoms of Washington DC. Thinking back, I remember that scene. We were having lunch. I read from the journal:

Cherry Blossoms
It was a wonderful trip to Washington DC. Technically, it was our senior trip. But I don't remember being with anyone but her. Cherry blossoms surrounded us. Sitting on the grass having a picnic lunch, I loved the cherry trees behind her. I remember her saying, "These are good enough to line heaven with." As I pulled her to me, the smell of the blossoms and feel of her body was simply heaven.

I remember everything about that day. He held me for a long time. He said, "Don't forget the smell; it will always remind you of this moment." Looking at the painting, I can smell the blossoms. He detailed each of them so precisely it is like I am there again. Wiping my eyes, I move around the corner to the next painting. I am shocked to discover a huge portrait of me, draped and partially nude. It was such an intimate experience that I had offered him. I don't feel embarrassed as much as overwhelmed that he painted me looking so soft and special. I can hardly breathe. It is done in such a beautiful way, only offering mysticism and elegance. Shaking, I hurry and open the journal.

A Portrait of Her
   She wanted to give me something, but she couldn't figure out what to give. I had dreamed about seeing her ever so softly draped, letting the shape of her taunt my senses. She offered herself as an art form for me to delight in. I trembled as I softly draped her. The material was crafted by the essence of her beauty and shape. The complexity behind her gentle smile beckons to be sorted out…Her body elongated with grace evokes beauty, and I gasp trying to take it all in. Her shoulders are sensuously shaped, with the rich curve of her breastbone edging the roundness of her breasts. She looked beautiful, vulnerable, trusting, and poetic. The rich pink-tan of her flesh looks sensual and soft. In silence I became lost in her for quite a period of time. Eventually, the real moments ended, but the vision was captured forever.

Still shaking, I sit on the floor. The painting looks exactly as he had described it in his narrative. I never thought of myself as visually attractive…I love it. I love that he painted what he saw. He told me many times I was beautiful. Compliments were never something I ever really valued. I tossed his compliments aside so many times, but now I'm forced to see how he sees me. It's wonderful.

As I move to the next painting, I smile as I see painted so perfectly the park of snow angels that we had made. It looks like he has captured all of them. It's a wonderful painting, detailed, with the snow on the limbs of the trees, the sky cottoned with moving clouds. Suddenly, I notice he painted the snowman on the other side of the brook—the one that Eric had made for me. I feel my heart drop. My God, he saw that! I look up the narrative.

Field of Angels
   The park was blanketed with perfect, untouched snow. It was just a matter of time before footprints and activity would be imprinted in it. Quickly, we fell hundreds of times to the earth and artistically created snow angels. Afterwards, we went up the water tower to look down upon our work. It was amazing looking out at all the snow angels that we sprinkled in patterns all over the park.

However, looking across the brook, I saw a huge snowman. Even with hundreds of snow angels, she was drawn to look at that one curious snowman on the other side. I would never forget that vision of our art and the mystery of her longing for something more.

Gary didn't miss anything about me. I love the fact that every detail was important to him. Moving to the next painting, I feel the warmth of him surrounding me. Such a soft and tender painting, it portrays the place where we folded ourselves into each other and celebrated the sun going down. Opening the journal, I was desperate to read his reflection:

Hammock and the Garden
We no longer were able to see each other much, as we now live many miles from each other. On special occasions, however, we came home to be with our families. We always made special plans that included a night for us to curl up together in the hammock in the garden, where we were surrounded by daffodils, marigolds, tulips, lilies, and mums. The fresh flowers of spring permeated the air as we watched the sun crawl into the earth, putting nature to rest. Her intensity always beckoned me to comfort her here. This beautiful scene of the garden is a tribute to one of our favorite places. Painting it, I am flooded with all those special times we silently delighted in the fragrance and beauty of this remarkable place.

I close my eyes and imagine his long arms pulling me into him. I recall him softly whispering in my ear, "Hmmm, I love to pull you into me," with his sweet breath on my neck and the warmth of our closeness putting us to sleep. This painting conveys all of that and more. It's full of the emotion of what those times felt like. I imagine he was lost in them when he was painting it.

Next he painted the vision from my favorite spot in the park. Seeing it is like being there. He painted every tree on the other side of the brook, every wildflower on the water's edge, and even the slight decline of the lawn. The rocks cause the water to cascade and ripple. I feel as if I could walk into the painting and be there. It is magnificent. However, I don't understand the title: *Squatter's Rights*. I open the journal and read:

Squatter's Rights
If ever anyone owned a piece of land, it was the very ground I sat on to paint this painting. It was the place she grew up on. It held her tears and was the place where she celebrated life. Running my hand through the lush, green grass, I wonder when her tears last watered it. I wanted to paint the rich beauty of this scene with the wooded area across the brook. I wanted to capture its pull

on her. I had to get everything—the peace and calm of where she sat, the refreshing brook, and the beautiful woods on the other side that pull at her...The brook was like a barrier representing life's challenges. Nothing would ever stop her from experiencing every side of life. I love her philosophies and analogies of the power of this vision. Surely it stands as a testimony to how she moved out and into life.

His insight is so amazing. Again the emotion I feel inside is overwhelming. My vision is blurred from crying, and I am overwhelmed. I had never taken the time to really know where his favorite places were. We were not equal in giving, caring, and understanding. Laying my head on the floor, I cry. How could I go on? This is too much for me to take in. How could anyone have loved me so much and how could I not know it? Glancing at my watch, I see it is already noon. I still had not seen all of the paintings. I get up and struggle to move to the next one.

Never Unnoticed
   She doesn't know that my favorite place has always been in the woods across from the brook, where I could look at her. I remember when I was only seven and my parents took me through the woods. We entered a mile down, where the bridge crossed the brook. No one ever went to the other side except my parents and me. She was always on the park side. Sometimes she would be singing, and I could faintly hear her; other times she would be writing. She always looked beautiful. Once my mom took a picture of me in the woods at the water's edge, and when the picture was developed, there she was—across the water, sitting in her favorite spot. I never needed to look at the picture again. It was embedded in my thoughts forever. I had to paint the memory of that. She was only seven.

Smiling, I feel something powerful. As a child, I thought I went unnoticed. How sweet to think that I had an admirer at such a young age. This is such a sweet and beautiful painting, with the lush woods and sunlight coming through the trees.

The next painting portrays an older me sitting in my spot. The view is from the other side of the brook. The journal reads:

Hopefully Me
   I was sixteen and adored her from afar. For years, I hiked into the woods not only to enjoy the natural beauty of the trees and wildflowers, but also to see her beauty from across the brook. There she sat, reading a book. I sat quietly on a trunk of a large tree that had fallen to the earth from a recent lightning

storm. I knew every tree, every plant in that woods across the brook from her place. When she closed her book, she gazed directly ahead, I wondered if she saw me. So often, she sat looking across the brook. I loved thinking it was me at whom she was looking. I will never forget how I felt with her eyes gazing my way...the sunlight shining on her face, her hand now shading her eyes as she continues to gaze forward. Slowly pulling her hand down, she lifted her book and returned to reading. I remember walking away that day wondering what she had been looking at. I remember thinking, "Hopefully me." It was such a powerful and touching thought; I had to paint it.

Destiny is a strange thing. All of these paintings reveal that our relationship was not trite, or just a moment in our life. It was all-encompassing to Gary. How beautifully he painted the scene.

Moving to the next one, I find a wonderful romantic scene of the two of us. I wondered how he had envisioned a scene with him in it.

Romance in the Park
My parents loved the woods and daily went for hikes, always taking their camera to capture pictures of nature. One day, from the other side of the brook, they saw us having a picnic. Mom said it was such a lovely romantic scene that she had to take a picture of it. A few months later, I had to say good-bye to her when she left for college. Afterwards at home, mom could tell that I was already missing her. She gave me the picture. I was overcome with the sweet memories of that day. Even from a distance, it was easy to see how she had altered every-thing about me. The memory of that day screamed to be painted.

Feeling my body tremble, I move to the next painting. There it was: the night sky with our star centered under the Big Dipper. My emotions begin to choke me, for I haven't looked at the night sky since he died. What a beautiful painting, the rich, blue, dark heavens with the star-jeweled sky. It was a paint-ing like no other.

Our Star
We wanted something that would always connect us. Lying under the stars, we decided to make the brightest star centered under the Big Dipper "our star." No matter where we were, we could look at it at the same time. As Vincent van Gogh had his Starry Night, so did we. The night after she left, I took my pal-ette, laid in the park, and painted our star.

Collapsing to the floor, I cry. How beautiful this painting is. All of them are so beautiful and important to me, but none would match the impact of this one. Finally I make my way to the last painting—a self-portrait. It looks peaceful, soft and giving. I cry as I look at it. He has captured the softness that always existed in his face.

> *Waiting on the Other Side*
> *Growing up, she spent her life wondering what was on the other side of the brook. She never really allowed herself to resolve that question, as she liked to suffer from curiosity. Her limited vision pulled at her, causing her to crave the unknowns. With all her childhood ponderings, she never considered that there was someone who loved her and who was waiting on the other side. I had spent my entire childhood watching her from the other side of the brook. What she does not know is that I will always be waiting.*

"Oh Gary, I love you, I love you," I cry out, hitting the carpet. "I am so sorry I did not love you the way you deserved to be loved. Thank you for seeing beauty in me and for wanting me. I promise to step up in life with courage," I say out loud. I look up through my blurred vision at his self-portrait. Standing, I gently kiss it. I turn around to see Jean-Louis wiping his eyes.

"My dear Sue, these last few minutes I have been here with you in silence in case you needed me. I let you have your privacy, but I felt the need to be around. How are you?"

"Oh Jean-Louis, they are marvelous. Unbelievable. He loved me so...I can hardly deal with it," I say, almost choking on the words. Jean-Louis puts his arms around me as we walk to his office. Sitting beside me on the couch, he talks about Gary.

"You were all he could see. He had nothing to paint until he was so full of you. He said he saw beauty, but he never felt or breathed it in until you came into his life. Surely you must have known the paintings were going to be a reflection of everything about you. My dear Sue, anyone can look at a beautiful flower, but only a few will be moved enough to see the remarkable creation it is. Gary said he saw a lot of beauty in the world, but he wasn't able to take it in until he was full of the wonderful emotions you stirred inside of him. Today you have gone through an experience of viewing the paintings. They come to you with your own memories and emotions. The art world, however, looks at them through other criteria: composition, color, light, technical skill, and optical proficiency. Art critics find Gary's work mesmerizing and wonderful, even perhaps a new way of painting. These are masterpieces from a heart that could not stop feeling overwhelmed by everything you gave him. This, no doubt, is powerful to you..."

"Oh it is, it is…I am left spinning, thrilled, elevated beyond anything I have ever experienced." I try to catch my breath.

"Gary has a few more paintings. They are not considered major works but learning pieces. They are at his apartment, where you will see them. This exhibit is the legacy of his passion for painting, a romantic series overwhelming in its entirety."

Reeling, I know I need more time with the paintings. "Jean-Louis, will there be any more time for me to spend alone in the exhibit? I want to study every detail, every brush stroke. Today I am overwhelmed with their beauty and with my memories."

"Certainly. The gallery does not open tomorrow until noon, so you could have the morning. Also, we have planned for the attorney to meet with the Walthams, you, and me in the morning. When Gary joined me, I emphasized the importance of his signing a contract and planning for his life. Art can be a very lucrative form of business as well as a purely spiritual creation of visual treasures. Gary was reluctant to imagine his works as important to anyone but himself. Nevertheless, I required him to have an attorney to represent his interests. Mr. Bateman will be here at 9:00 AM. Then you can spend the rest of morning in the exhibit."

"Sure. I understand the importance of the meeting," I say.

"My dear Sue, I am touched by the love that Gary had for you. Gary was a student who quickly became a brother to me. He and I poured our secrets out to each other. Although you don't know me, I feel like I know you so well. He knew you were out exploring life. He wanted you to have everything you wanted. Nothing ever distracted him from his love for you. As a child, he watched you from afar. You were enough for him—even when you were only a mere vision across a brook. As a child he pondered what you were thinking, how you felt. He talked about times when he saw you across the brook crying and how he always stayed until you gained your composure. You were never alone; he was always there. As he got older, he found the courage to ask you out. He just believed that you were his gift from God. He never defined the gift, always making whatever you could give him be enough…"

I can hardly believe that I was such a vital part of his growing up. I had never understood why Gary always insisted that whatever he had was enough. I used to feel sad that he didn't crave more. It drove me crazy to think he was settling for whatever he had. I, on the other hand, am restless, searching, and impatient to know all the options life offers. Thinking about both of our lives, I realize that it was he who had the most valuable gifts life offers. His way of life gave him such a strong sense of gratitude and peace. Mine has been a world of high-risk potholes, damaging to both my character and self-esteem. He is the necessary contrast that I needed to reshape my way of thinking. I am stunned at the impact all of this has on me.

I return to the hotel and tell Sarah everything. With tears streaming I give her all the details. I show her the journal of his writings about his paintings and me.

That evening, Sarah and I go back to the gallery. Many people are waiting in line. A doorman lets us in the side door. Mrs. Waltham comes over immediately and welcomes me. "Sue, I have a surprise for you," she beams. Coming around the corner are my mother, father, and brothers. I am so shocked. I didn't think about the possibility that they might receive an invitation.

"Oh, Mom, it's all so wonderful, so very wonderful!" I say, hugging her so hard.

"Sis, we wouldn't miss this for anything," Mark says, kissing me on the cheek.

My family has just toured the exhibit. Mr. and Mrs. Waltham had seen all the paintings over the months that Gary painted them, and Gary had shared with them the stories behind each painting.

Jean-Louis looks in on us. "The doors are about to open. Sue, do you have any questions, or do you need anything?"

"No, no…please let the people in."

The doorman opens the door. Inside the lobby stand two huge picture easels. One displays Gary's picture and the words, "The Garrett D. Waltham Exhibit—East Hall." On the other easel is a picture of Benoit and the words "The Benoit LeBranche Exhibit—West Hall." Jean-Louis takes my hand. We walk into the east hall, where Jean-Louis hands me a program. Inside is a picture of each painting next to the narrative from the journal that describes its genesis.

"Sue, would you like to show me the exhibit?" asks Sarah.

I enjoy walking her through it, telling her stories and recalling the memories. People are listening to me. Some realize I am the fortunate woman Gary loved. My father whispers in my ear, "He really loved you. This is so unbelievable."

As we walk by the large portrait of me draped, my mother comments, "Sue, you are as beautiful as this painting. Don't forget it."

I listen as people talk quietly about the paintings. "He was as sensitive a painter as I have ever seen," says one. Another says, "Oh, how romantic and breathtaking this garden scene is; the woman he speaks of must really be something." Another says "How could any human love this much? These are marvelous."

After the exhibit closes, I return to the hotel, where I spend time alone with my mother. Mom is moved by the whole exhibit. But she is particularly stunned by the painting of the wild roses.

"Sue, I had no idea that as a child you watched me from that oak tree. I am so touched by that painting. Did you have any idea he knew you went there and watched me?"

"No, Mom, I didn't think anyone saw me watching you with the wild roses. I often felt ashamed that I was intruding by watching you. You seemed happiest in that garden. Oh Mom, I loved you so much as a child, but I was always confused because you pushed me away. I never understood why." Saying these words out loud, I begin crying.

"Sue, I am so sorry. Let me try to explain. Just as you were turning seven, I went into a deep depression. The doctor thought it was a latent response to the death of my parents. After they died, I had to take care of my sister and many other matters. I never grieved; I was too busy taking care of everything else. Then one day I woke up, and I had no patience for you. The boys didn't bother me because they were out doing things with others and your father. You seemed to demand attention, though. You had every right to, of course, but I couldn't cope with your needs. I could give to the community—that was a job to me. My sister always asked why you never helped around the house and kitchen. I did not want anyone to know about my depression, so I often led her to believe you were problematic. I am so sorry, Sue. I went to the rose garden to get away from everything and everyone. In many ways it was cathartic. It was so beautiful sitting among the wild roses. Day after day, I tried to cope with the dark thoughts running in my head. The roses were beautiful and inspirational. Their powerful imagery—beauty in the midst of thorns—gave life to my feelings. I have known for a long time that I would need to talk to you someday about how I treated you. Please forgive me. I had no idea that you watched me from afar. Gary's painting has given us so much: it has brought us to each other." Mom hugs me in a way she never has before.

"I am so sorry that you went through such a depression. I thought you were sad because I was born, or because I wasn't good enough, or smart enough, or pretty enough. When I saw you with others, you seemed okay and happy. But you always pushed me away. As a kid, I just didn't know how to deal with it. I loved watching you in the wild roses. You looked happy, peaceful. The roses gave you what I couldn't. Gary's painting is the key to understanding all this."

It is as if a world of hurt has been lifted off my shoulders. Everything is changed because of Gary's paintings. Now forced to revisit my childhood issues through a painting, I finally clear things up with Mom. We needed this moment. I needed the affirmation that I was loved and good enough, and she needed the forgiveness.

As I crawl into bed, I am dazed. Absolutely everything about my life has changed because of Gary's paintings. For the first time ever, I am at peace with my life. I know now that I have been loved beyond all reason. Gary has had such a profound purpose in my life. He is the lifeline that brought healing from my childhood. His boundless love, captured in every nuance, every brushstroke, is the strongest affirmation that I was...am...important. All of this is no small thing.

Gary is more than a man whom I loved. He has been the angel watching over me my whole life, pulling together all the painful pieces of my life. It still amazes me that he followed me to the oak tree where I watched Mom in the wild roses, longing to understand her. He painted many things, each of them bringing a point of healing into my life. But that painting, more than any other, restored a sense of peace and wholeness to the most deeply wounded part of my soul.

A New Day, New Feelings

Groggy and tired, I awaken from a restless night of being overwhelmed at everything Gary had painted and written. Sarah has breakfast waiting for me, and we go to the gallery. Jean-Louis has also allowed Sarah to spend time looking around the gallery before it opens so that she may see all of Jean-Louis' paintings and the Benoit LeBranche exhibit as well. She heads off to see them as the rest of us prepare to hear the reading of Gary's will.

Mr. Bateman asks us all to take a seat, and he begins. "As you are aware, Gary made out a last will and testament. When I first met Gary, he was very modest and felt that having a will wasn't necessary. He said his paintings were simply for enjoyment, and he couldn't imagine they had much value to others. He did not see his work as a way of making a living. It turns out he was wrong. The Jean-Louis Pacquet Gallery insures all its artwork, and therefore all paintings are appraised. The Garrett D. Waltham exhibit that is now showing has been appraised by two of the most reputable appraising firms. One has the exhibit appraised for $1.5 million, and the other has it appraised for $2 million. Each painting is valued individually between $50,000 and $180,000. These appraisals were done after the passing of Mr. Waltham. The value of the paintings is expected to increase substantially as the years go by. We have already received two lucrative offers to purchase the entire exhibit at 75 percent of the appraisal price, should the inheritor like to sell. We are aware of five other paintings Gary did that may have immense value, but none of those paintings are part of the estate, as Gary gave them as gifts to others. His parents hold what are considered his most valuable paintings, as his first and last significant works. The first painting is valued at $150,000 and the last at $190,000, with two others appraised at $68,000 and $83,000. Jean-Louis was given the painting *Believe*, which was appraised at $200,000. As you can see, Gary's simple belief that his painting would not be lucrative shows Gary's humility and lack of awareness of his work's value. Gary also has many paintings of less value in his studio, which I have excluded. Now to the reading of the will."

My jaw drops when I learn how much the paintings are worth. Surely they are wonderful. My insight into the value of art is limited. Attorney Bateman starts to read the will:

> *I, Garrett D. Waltham, do hereby make, publish, and declare this to be my last will and testament.*
>
> *First: I direct that all my just debts and funeral expenses be paid out of my estate as soon after my death as is practicable.*
> *Second: I give, devise, and bequeath all my paintings that are noted and narrated in my journal to Susan Elizabeth Martin. These paintings were inspired by my deepest love and celebration of her, and include the following:*
>
> Illuminating Beauty
> Romance of Nature's Art
> Longing to Understand
> Beauty Surrounding Beauty
> Cherry Blossoms
> A Portrait of Her
> Field of Angels
> Hammock and the Garden
> Squatter's Rights
> Never Unnoticed
> Hopefully Me
> Romance in the Park
> Our Star
> Waiting on the Other Side
>
> *Third: I give, devise, and bequeath all my estate, real, personal, and mixed, of whatever kind and wherever situated, to my parents, or should their death precede mine, then I leave them to Susan Elizabeth Martin.*
> *Fourth: I leave all my other paintings, and items in my studio to Jean-Louis Pacquet, who is truly like a brother to me.*
> *Fifth: I hereby appoint attorney Robert Bateman as executor of this, my last will and testament.*
>
> *Garrett D. Waltham*

I am shocked that he has left the entire exhibit to me. I am speechless. My hands are shaking, and my heart is beating out of my chest. My eyes flood with tears. I am so overwhelmed.

"As executor of the Garrett D. Waltham estate, I will facilitate the movement of the property as stated in his last will to the appropriate recipients." Mr. Bateman concludes by asking if we have any questions or comments.

"Yes," Mr. Waltham interjects. "I would like to make a comment. I am pleased Sue was named the recipient of The Garrett D. Waltham exhibit that is now being seen here. Gary was very outspoken about all those paintings being a gift to her." Mr. Waltham wipes his eyes.

Jean-Louis concurs. "Yes, Gary was always outspoken about the paintings being for Sue. I am honored to exhibit them here. Gary planned on the exhibit opening a few weeks before his untimely death, but he wanted to surprise Sue. The proceeds of the exhibit admissions will pay for the insurance for the paintings. Also, they will generate a steady income if you allow them to be seen by the world through a touring art exhibit."

I don't know what to say. "I am still quite stunned. I need time to think about everything, but I certainly want them to complete their original debut exhibit through November here at the gallery. Right now, this is all too personal for me. My heart is so overwhelmed that I am incapable of thinking."

Jean-Louis nods. "We have a financial officer who oversees the gallery. He will be happy to show you the funds that the exhibit has generated. He will take all directions from you, as you are the sole proprietor of the Garrett D. Waltham exhibit."

"I value all of you and welcome your thoughts. For now, I'd like to go to the gallery and enjoy them, if there isn't anything else. I think I will do that," I say, as I get up.

"Sue, please keep in touch," Mrs. Waltham says. "We want you to do whatever you want with the paintings. I know that Gary would not give you any directions."

I say my good-byes to the Walthams, who are returning to Ohio. They tell me they have left the keys to Gary's apartment with Jean-Louis. As I walk into the exhibit, all my feelings for Gary come rushing to the surface, and my eyes flood with tears.

I spend time with each painting, breathing it in and recalling the memories of what is captured. As I complete my time at the exhibit, I start back to the main rotunda of the gallery. While I am walking, I see Sarah sitting on a bench outside the Benoit LeBranche exhibit. She is wiping her eyes. She sees me and immediately stands.

"My dear, how are you doing?"

"Fine. It is all so amazing. I have much to tell you. Before I do, tell me why you look upset. Are you feeling okay, Sarah."

"Oh yes. I was just resting after having enjoyed all these marvelous paintings of Jean-Louis and…Benoit LeBranche. Should we go have lunch?"

That afternoon, Sarah returns to the hotel while I take a cab to Gary's apartment. It feels eerie walking into his place. As soon as I get the door open, though, I feel at home. It's a small, quaint apartment, with a little living room decorated in light colors. There is a picture of us on the bed stand. As I walk through the double doors off his bedroom, I enter a small painting studio. It is bright with many windows that overlook New York. I lie on his bed and look through the double doors, where I can see the stool on which he sat to paint. It is positioned in front of the canvas he was last working on. It's so overwhelming to imagining him sitting there painting.

I somehow fall asleep, and when I awaken it's dark outside. I call Sarah at the hotel and tell her I will spend the night at Gary's place. I go to the kitchen and open the freezer. Just as I expected, he has ice cream—butter pecan, our favorite kind. I sit at his desk and eat a scoop. On the top of his papers is an unfinished letter he was writing me…

∾

My dear Sue,

Gosh I miss you. I look down upon New York, and it has so much going on. Yet there is nothing that can stir me like my thoughts of you. How are you doing? What have you been up to? I do so want you to come to New York. I have a surprise for you and can't wait until you can visit. When do you think you will be able to come?

Have you seen our star lately? I went out for a walk last night. It is hard to get away from the city lights to see the sky. It's a good thing we picked the brightest star…there it was in the sky. I was hoping that somehow you were united with me in looking at it. Life is so fun for me. I get up in the morning and daylight accents the beauty of the world. Then, when nighttime comes, I close my eyes, and all the wonderful memories of you rush over me. Sue, you have been with me forever; I know I have not explained that, but hopefully I will in the near future. I love you dearly. Please try to come to New York as soon as you can.

It's so emotional…seeing his pen beside the letter…a stamp waiting to be licked. He is everywhere. I go to his closet and put on his big, warm, cream-colored sweater. I remember how he'd wrap his arms around me and pull me into the warmth of its wool. I can smell him. Lying down, I drift off to sleep.

I awaken to the sunlight coming through the studio window. As I think about the exhibit, I know it has to be shared with others.

I return to the hotel and have brunch with Sarah. We spend the afternoon together at the studio talking about each painting. Eventually, Sarah leaves to give me time to be alone. She spends more time with the Jean-Louis and Benoit LeBranche exhibits. As we leave, Jean-Louis gives me an album of photos of each painting. It's wonderful to have them and the journal.

Jean-Louis will meet with the booking curators and put together the exhibit tour. As soon as it is completed, he will come to see me to go over every detail for approval. When Sarah invites him to the farm, he says it will be a perfect place to go over everything. The next morning, Sarah and I return to Broctren Harbor.

Everything about my life has changed. I feel resolved and at peace. Gary has been an integral part in helping me sort out things. The painting *Longing to Understand* was a key in bringing my mother and me together. The portrait he painted means everything, knowing that it was how he viewed me. All of his paintings are overwhelming, and I realize how much he loved me. I now know I have never gone unnoticed in this world. All my self-loathing has been unwarranted, for I was really loved beyond all reason. As overwhelming as all of this is, now I am challenged to get outside myself.

The next few weeks go by fast. I am excited about Jean-Louis' visit to Broctren Harbor. Jessie picks me up and we head to the farm. Jean-Louis, who will be driving in from the airport, has confirmed his arrangements with Sarah. Putting my things away, I hear a car pull up and rush down the stairs to greet him.

"My dear Sue, it is so wonderful seeing you. Gosh, it's been a couple of months. How are you doing?"

"You told me before I came to New York that everything about my life would change. You were so right. I left New York so full of life. Gary knew everything that I was wrestling with, and his paintings resolved so much in my life. I am at peace and so changed because of them." I say, trying to share the significance of everything.

That evening after dinner we sit on the patio and relax. The clean, cool evening breeze feels good as the sun slowly inches its way into the earth.

"Sue, I have the itinerary for a six-month tour of the exhibit," Jean-Louis says. "It will stop in Chicago, St. Louis, Washington DC, and Los Angeles. The exhibit will receive 50 percent of all the ticket sales—funds that will go into a foundation that is being set up for you. The other 50 percent goes to the institutions showing the exhibit, shipping, insurance, and other ancillary fees."

Sarah turns in early, and Jean-Louis and I continue talking about our grief and shock from death. Jean-Louis shares his struggles with trying to come to terms with his loss of Benoit and then Gary. Both of them had different life stories, yet with uncanny similarities. He tells me the story of Benoit's life.

"As a child he grew up wanting to paint but did not have the internal intensity that he needed. Benoit said his paintings were representations without passion. When he was nineteen years old, Benoit met a young woman in Paris. He first saw her sitting at the edge of a fountain in a lovely garden in the Rive Gauche. She was running her hand through the water as if to feel it. She was lost to the moment and did not notice anyone watching her. Benoit sat at a distance, wondering why she was so lost in the experience. He described for me how she lifted her hand from the cool water and rubbed it on the side of her face. Her eyes were closed, and the slow way she moved her hand down the side of her face was quite erotic, Benoit said. He was stirred by her intensity." Jean-Louis takes a drink of lemonade and continues. "The air was filled with music coming from a large speaker: Giacomo Puccini's *La Bohème*. She had her eyes closed and was lost in the music. At that moment he came alive; he felt more life inside him than he had ever felt. He watched her for well over an hour. Then, she stood up and vanished. A couple of days later, he was walking by a cafe and saw her sipping tea. Again he observed her as she delighted in the steam of her tea and smell of her hot croissant. Later that week, walking in the square, he came upon her while she was buying a scarf. This time he approached her and commented on the design. The woman told him she had to buy it because the design screams 'be alive.' They walked down the sidewalk together, and he invited her to have a spot of tea with him. That afternoon they walked the streets of Paris and relaxed in the park. Benoit said he was lost to her. He described her as beautiful, intelligent, vibrant, and so full of passion for life. The next few months their love grew. Benoit said she loved teasing him about his seriousness. All of that gave way to a new kind of passion that Benoit used in his painting. His works became extraordinary. Sue, I hope I'm not boring you with my rambling…" Jean-Louis says, aware of the time.

"Oh no, please do not stop. Tell me what happens to them. You said there are similarities between them and Gary and me...please continue." I'm dying to know what happened.

"Well, they grew deeply in love. For the next eight months, they spent an enormous amount of time with each other. She refused to allow him to talk about their future, always saying that their relationship was in the here and now. She was from the United States, and he knew that she would return in time. At the end of the eight months, she became ill and saw a doctor. She told Benoit that she needed to return to the States to see a specialist. She said she would be fine and refused to let him go with her. She wanted him to stay and paint. He was now commissioned to do paintings of historical land sites. Only after her many refusals of his pleas to go along did he say good-bye. He told her that he would wait to hear from her and that he would come to the United States when she was ready. Desperate to know how she was, he attempted to write her. Then one day he received a telegram informing him of her death. Benoit was beyond himself. In time, the rich gift of her intensity, beauty, and poetic nature became his inspiration for painting. He said that he gave his favorite painting to her upon her departure. It was a painting of her in the park. He described that painting in detail in a handwritten narrative in his portfolio that I now have. I have sought to find it throughout the years. I have art investigators and researchers trying to find it. I just want to see it. We assume that it is probably here in the United States. Unfortunately, Benoit did not have any address other than one he sent his telegrams to years ago, and that address no longer exists. After her death, he continued to paint with a reflection of her in his works. Did you get a chance to go to Benoit's exhibit?" Jean-Louis concludes.

"Oh no, I am so sorry. I did not take in anything but Gary's exhibit. I do hope to come back sometime and view them—and your works as well," I explain.

"Sue, you are not going to believe his paintings. They are breathtaking: so full of her intensity and life. Anyway, now the man who taught me and a man whom I taught are both gone. Although they only briefly met, their lives have rich similarities. Both of them received their inspiration and passion as a result of a deep love they had for a woman," Jean-Louis says, taking a deep breath.

The next morning Jean-Louis is having breakfast and talking with Jessie.

"Well, you won't have any problems, because Sue has become quite familiar with the grounds. I have both of your horses ready."

I have coffee and we head out. I'm on Freckle, who has become my friend. It is a fun morning. We stop in some of the more scenic areas.

"Oh Sue, I wish I had my palette and canvas. This is quite exquisite," he comments. Everywhere we ride, he is lost in the breathtaking beauty of the lush natural grounds. Finally, it is time to head to the lake. Riding toward it, we see Jessie bringing Sarah in the jeep. Sarah quickly sets up the blanket while Jessie gets a huge basket from the back.

"My lord, woman! How much food did you have them pack?" Jessie says, as he bends down to relieve himself of its weight. "Well, I'll be back to check on all of you in few hours. Have fun."

Relaxing under the shade tree, Sarah starts serving cold beverages. "Tell me, how was the morning?"

Jean-Louis is so descriptive in telling her of the visions he captured. Eventually we start talking about paintings. Jean-Louis talks about a painting of Benoit's that he has.

"You both would love this painting. It is in my apartment. Benoit painted it as an opposite reflection of his first serious painting of the woman he loved. Anyway, that painting could be taken from this exact place. It portrays a lovely, rustic lake like this one, with ducks floating on it and with the woman's reflection in the lake as she sat beside it. Sue, remember I told you about the first painting he did of her? Well, mine is a similar painting with the reflection of her in the water. I hope to find the original someday. I am dying to see it. Anyway, this place is so lovely and reminds me of that painting," he says.

Sarah walks down the incline to the water's edge. She sits on a rock staring into the water, lost in her thoughts. Then, reaching down into the clear lake, she runs her hand through the water. With her eyes closed, she brings her hand up to the side of her face and rubs its dampness ever so gently on it. I see Jean-Louis staring—almost gasping—yet trying to remain quiet.

I think about what he said last night and feel a moment of déjà vu as I am reminded of what Benoit had written about the woman he loved. Sarah, unaware of his staring, slowly gets up and returns to the blanket. Jean-Louis respects her personal moment and does not comment. Sarah and Jean-Louis have a final glass of wine as Jessie pulls up. Sarah is tired, so Jessie takes her back to the house while Jean-Louis and I ride the horses back to the farm.

I work on a paper and study for a test. Jean-Louis sketches the landscape from the balcony off his room. Later that evening, we all meet outside for a barbeque where Jessie shows off his rancher's qualities as a cook. Slowly, the darkness moves in until only the bright reflection of the campfire lights the area. Clem plays his guitar, and all of us sing. Sarah shows off her talent for yodeling. Next, Jessie sings the playful song "Clementine" and all of us join in. The warmth of the company resonates with Jean-Louis, who is moved by all of it.

"Okay Sue," Jessie says. "Since Bertha refuses to dance, it's time we do some stompin'. Girl, get up here and let's try doin' a jig. Come on…"

Clem starts playing, and Jessie and I dance. After it's over, everyone applauds, and Jessie and I take a bow. Finally, Clem plays a slow country love song, and Jean-Louis asks Sarah to dance. It's obvious that both of them are experienced dancers. At the end, he graciously bows, kissing her hand and thanking her. Jean-Louis borrows Clem's guitar and plays a lovely love song, singing it partly in English and partly in French.

"Jean-Louis, who were you really singing to?" Sarah asks.

"Oh, always to a love that is rich inside me, waiting to get out…no one specifically. Certainly, it's for anyone who is moved by it," he says.

We walk Sarah inside, where Jean-Louis and I decide to have a glass of iced tea on the patio. "You have a marvelous voice and are quite good at playing the guitar," I say.

"Oh, thank you. I do love music a lot. I have a guitar and play often, always allowing my emotions to come out. I don't play for anyone other than myself, but I felt so connected that I wanted to play tonight. I do see how special this place and these people are. You are fortunate to have them as part of your family," he says.

"I know. I met Sarah at college. I don't know if you know this, but she is the dean of women. How I got to know her personally is a long story. Someday, I will have to share it with you. It really is an amazing story."

"I will count on that. She is an amazing woman and quite a good dancer as well," he says. We say goodnight and turn in.

The next morning everyone comments on how much they enjoyed the previous evening. I tease Jessie about having sore feet.

"Girl, if I remember right, you were stompin' on mine, but I must admit you do sashay well. Anyway, all of you rest up. Tonight we are going to have fun. At twilight, we are going on a hay ride under the stars. Clem has promised us guitar music, and maybe we can get Jean-Louis to sing to us under the stars again," Jessie exclaims.

"That's a marvelous idea," Sarah says. "Please share a talent or a special thought tonight. Betsy, please make a basket full of snacks and a thermos of hot chocolate. We can make a campfire at the lake."

I spend the rest of the day finishing my paper. Jean-Louis is lost to his sketch of the landscape. Sarah rests up for the evening. The day goes by fast. As I go down the hall, I see Jean-Louis coming toward me with a box.

"I brought you something. I want to give it to you before I forget. Gary's parents cleaned out his apartment, and Mr. Waltham told me to give this to you. He said Gary always wore it when you two were in the hammock. He thought maybe you would like to have it."

"Oh yes, thank you so much Jean-Louis! I wore it while I was in his apartment that day. I thought of asking the Walthams about it. Oh gosh, thanks. It means so much."

Soon evening is here. We get upon the wagon. Jessie has one of the farm help drive us. The night air is full of fragrance from the wildflowers as we pass through the meadows. "I want to share something special. Look at the Big Dipper. See it right there? That really bright star centered underneath it will always be Gary's and my star."

"Sue, my dear Sue, he painted it in the painting *Our Star*," Jean-Louis says. "He always said that as Vincent van Gogh had his *Starry Night,* so did he. He made it sound like everything in the sky was put there for the sole purpose of contrasting your one bright star. I will sing a song as a tribute to Gary. This was one of his favorite songs, Sue, I am sure you'll remember it."

I knew it was going to be Don McLean's "Starry, Starry, Night." As Jean-Louis finishes his song, a respectful silence occurs, as all of us are moved by it. He wipes his eyes.

"Oh Jean-Louis, that's lovely. Thank you for sharing it with us," Sarah says. For the next few minutes we ride in silence, staring into the sky. It is nice to finally be at a point in my life where I can talk about Gary and celebrate him.

As we arrive at the river, everyone becomes busy getting the fire going. Finally, when everyone is roasting marshmallows, Clem starts to play music. Betsy and I decide to dance for the gang, and Jessie gets up to stomp with us. Jean-Louis pulls out a harmonica, and everyone is clapping. Afterwards, Sarah takes out a journal and shares a poem she had written years ago, titled, "Life Should Never Be Dimmed." It is beautiful, inspiring, and uplifting. As she is reading it, the wind picks up; she pulls a scarf from her pocket to put on head. I see a look on Jean-Louis' face, it as if he is shocked about something. A few more songs and we are on our way back. Jean-Louis turns to Sarah. "I'm still taken by your poem. Did you write it because you have always valued every day in your life, or did you write it because something happened, and from that point you learned never to let your life dim?"

"I wrote it many years ago, after I turned away from something important in my life."

The wind picks up as the hay wagon pulls up to the house. As we go in, Sarah lays her scarf and gloves on the table. She says "goodnight" and excuses herself. I'm tired and decide to turn in, but first I go to the kitchen to thank Betsy for everything. As I come back by the parlor, I see Jean-Louis looking at Sarah's scarf. Quickly, I pause and tuck myself behind the arch. He turns it over and looks inside at the small designer tag. He must like it, given his response when she put it on. He looks up.

"I just love this pattern. It would make for a wonderful painting," he says, laying it down. "Have a nice night, Jean-Louis."

The next morning, I open the doors to the balcony off my room. I can see Jean-Louis on his balcony sketching. I sit and watch him from afar. I think about Gary and how I wish I had memories of him painting. Gazing downward, I see Sarah walking to her flower garden. It's a bright and sunny day. Betsy rushes out to bring her a parasol. I glance back at the balcony where Jean-Louis is sketching. All of a sudden, he jumps to his feet with a stunned look. I look down. Sarah is now walking under her parasol. What is there about Sarah that always seems to arouse something in Jean-Louis? I didn't understand his reactions when she was sitting at the water's edge feeling the water, nor how he reacted when she was reading her poem and put on her scarf. I wonder what is going on? I decide to walk to his room and attempt to talk with him about her. Maybe I can find out what's going on.

As I come out into the hall, the light casts a glow on a painting that I now remember seeing a long time go when I first visited Sarah. I had forgotten that it was a Benoit LeBranche painting. Now the sunlight is shining brightly upon it, and I see it in my peripheral vision. I turn to look directly at it. With shock, I realize that this is the very painting that Jean-Louis has been searching for. It is Benoit's first painting of the lady he loved as she sat by the water's edge. My heart is pounding as I rush down the corridor to Jean-Louis' room.

"Jean-Louis, hurry! I have something to show you. It's important," I say, now out of breath. I take his hand as I am unable to talk.

"Sue, are you okay? What's wrong?" he asks, as we hurry down the corridor.

"I found it, I found it!" I gasp.

When we arrive at the painting, I do not have to say anything more. He rushes up to it, tears rolling down his face.

"Oh my, oh my, it is it! It is the painting I have been trying to find. Oh, how lovely. Oh, how wonderful. I just can't believe I finally found it," he cries out.

"I am so sorry Jean-Louis. I do faintly remember seeing it a long time ago when I first came here. I have walked by it many times since but never really thought about it. I am so sad that I have never asked Sarah about it. Oh Jean-Louis, are you going to ask Sarah how she came to own it?"

Turning to me, he has an intense look—one that, in fact, is rather scary.

"No, Sue. I am not going to ask her that question. I know how she got it." He wipes his eyes and takes a deep breath. "Sue, look at this painting. Look closely. Now come with me."

He takes my hand and walks me back to his room and out onto the balcony.

"My dear, do you not see the truth? Remember when we were having the picnic with Sarah at the lake? Remember how she walked down to the water's edge? Did you see how she played with the water with her hand and then slowly got lost in the experience? She brought the dampness of her hand to the side of her face and with her eyes closed appeared to be somewhere else. Remember last night, how she took that scarf out of her pocket? The design is very unusual. Please look out there and see if anything reminds you of that painting you just showed me." Jean-Louis says, pointing out toward Sarah in the garden.

Shockingly, Sarah is under the parasol that's in the painting. It's a unique print.

"Jean-Louis, what are you saying? What does it mean?"

"Sue, I find myself disturbed, confused, and rather miffed that Sarah would have done such a thing to Benoit who loved her beyond all reason. Maybe there is some explanation. As excited as I am to finally find the painting, I find myself pained that Benoit was forced to believe she had died," Jean-Louis adds, choking on emotion and sitting bent over with his head in his hands.

"Oh Jean-Louis, I know there's an explanation. I even think I may know what it is. But it is not my story to tell. We must tell her what we know and—out of respect—allow her to share with us the truth. Oh, please—it could not be an act of cruelty. She is not capable of such a thing. Please. Turn from your pain and allow her to tell us her story," I plead.

"You are right, Sue. I have to give her a chance. Why didn't she mention this, though? She spent so much time at his exhibit. I just thought she was appreciating his art. I had no idea it was personal. Why has she never told us that she knew him? Why? What is her secret? Why did she betray him by telling him she was dead? Oh, Sue—so many questions, and I fear the answers. If you only you knew Benoit, you would know how hard it would be to leave such a sweet, gentle man. I am pained that anyone could deceive him like that." Jean-Louis spits out these last words with contempt.

"Jean-Louis, listen. As I was leaving Gary's exhibit, I saw her sitting at the door of Benoit's exhibit. She was wiping her eyes as if she had been crying. When I asked if she was feeling all right, she brushed it away. I thought she was just exhausted. Immediately she recommended we go to lunch, so I assumed she was just hungry. Now I believe she was overwhelmed by the exhibit and her memories. I know some things about Sarah, but as I have said her story is not mine to tell. I can't be sure of everything. I didn't know about her relationship with Benoit. Nevertheless, I'll stake everything on her and her decisions in life. I assure you that there is some reason for what she did. In fact, she probably did it for him rather than for herself. I won't allow your suspicions to override my sound knowledge of her. She is one of the most extraordinary women I have ever met. Now, let's go talk with her."

As we walk, I start thinking about Sarah. She wasn't trying to hide anything. She knew all along that painting was there. She wasn't trying to keep us away from the facts. I remember Sarah telling me that she doesn't share her life with others because she doesn't want them to have to deal with all she has been through. She also said that if ever I wanted to know anything I should ask and that she would be happy to share.

"Oh, I saw you both up on the balconies in the morning sun," Sarah says, as we approach her. "I do hope you had a wonderful night of sleep." I can see that Jean-Louis is still upset. He is unable to respond with his normal graciousness.

"Sarah, Jean-Louis and I found Benoit LeBranche's painting in the corridor. Actually, on my first visit I noticed it but have since forgotten about it and have walked by it many times without a thought. You must have bought it at an auction or something. The sunlight on it today drew me toward it, and when I realized it was the painting Jean-Louis was searching for…I went and showed it to him," I say.

"Oh, my. I heard you speak of one of Benoit's paintings that you were trying to find, but I had no idea that it was this one. Actually, no one has ever seen it but me, so I did not assume anyone really knew about it. By the look on your face, I can tell you are quite disturbed. Please, let's go into the house and have some tea. I will be happy to address any questions you may have about it," Sarah says.

"Thank you. I am quite perplexed and do so appreciate the opportunity to express my thoughts," Jean-Louis answers curtly.

We sit in the living room, and Sarah closes the doors for privacy. Jean-Louis begins to describe Benoit's portfolio of writings and the painting he left to him.

"Sarah, Benoit spent many hours, many days—a whole lifetime—talking about the woman who enriched him with the greatest kind of love that life offers. It changed him, and he painfully shared how she became ill and returned to the States and died. He spoke of every detail of every moment he was with her. Not only did he tell me, he went through the emotions of reliving his love for her over and over again before my eyes. I saw firsthand his pain at the loss of her. Although I did not know this woman, she played a role in my life through Benoit's encapsulation of her. She became my ideal woman, in fact—the kind of woman that I could love. Knowing Benoit's observations of her, I was stunned when I saw you at the picnic. You sat at the water's edge with your eyes closed and ran your hand gently through the water, playing with it and then sensually lifting it to dampen the side of your face. I saw how you were lost in the experience. It reminded me of the story he told of the first time he watched her sitting on the edge of a fountain. She too was lost to the moment. What he described was exactly like what I saw last night. Also, your poem appeared to be written as a learning experience from a time when you let your life dim. If that had not taken my breath away, then watching you pull that scarf from your pocket shocked me. It looked like the one Benoit wrote about, its every detail in the design a perfect match. He wrote how the fuchsia and pink unite with the rose-colored evening sun. I thought I must be delusional until we got back, and I examined the scarf you left on the table more closely. He had described it perfectly, saying she had to have it because it screamed out at her *"Be Alive!"* I went to bed last night thinking I was overreacting, and that all of this was purely coincidental. I concluded I was making it all up out of my desperation to find the painting he gave her." His hand shakes as he takes a drink of tea.

Taking a breath, he continues. "I have read his writings over and over, looking for any details that might help me find the painting. Then, this morning I saw you open the parasol in the garden—the exact parasol I knew was in that painting. I could hardly breathe until I was shaken by Sue's panicked knocking at my door. Quickly, I refocused as she took me down the hall to the painting. All at once, everything became clear. I believe that you are indeed the woman whom Benoit spent his whole lifetime loving. I must admit I am confused by learning that you are alive. I find myself struggling to cope with this knowledge. In fact, I feel painfully disturbed that you would have let him think you were dead. I don't believe you knew the Benoit I did. He loved you beyond all reason. You never died to him. Every painting, every writing, every detail of his life was full of you." Jean-Louis' voice breaks with emotion. "Why, Sarah? Why? Please help me with all of this—please…" Trembling, he wipes his eyes.

I am lost in Jean-Louis' intensity, emotions, and words. Turning to look at Sarah, I see the tears streaming down her face.

"Oh, Jean-Louis. Let me say I am sad to see you so upset. Yes, I am she. This is going to take a bit of time to explain, but I want you both to know everything. I was a very sick child. When I turned fifteen years old I was diagnosed with a rare form of leukemia. Even when I was in remission I was told that my respite from the disease would be short-lived. My life expectancy was often a month or two. It was awful living around people who were so frightened and sad for me. I could hardly forget my death sentence with everyone so pained. Still, I made it into remission, though the doctors said it would only be temporary. Eventually, I decided to get away and be with people who did not know about my condition. They wouldn't have on their faces that horrible sadness of knowing about my illness. I made a decision to spend what I thought were to be my last days in Paris, free from the reflection of my impending death. I wanted to pretend my life was normal. I had no desire to fall in love or grow close to anyone. As a matter of fact, that was the last thing I wanted. That would require me to be honest. Once again, I did not want to see my fragility darken the face of someone I love." Jean-Louis looks lost in what Sarah is saying.

"Paris was wonderful. I loved its rich beauty, the music in the streets, its art and museums. I got a small apartment that overlooked a beautiful part of the city. It was marvelous. Every morning I took a long walk, stopping at a cafe for morning tea and a hot croissant. Benoit introduced himself one day. I was unaware he had seen me at the fountain. He was persistent in getting to know me. I delighted in his pursuit but feared he would get too close. I refused to talk about my past or my future. I thought my closed nature and limited disclosure would push him away. I was totally definitive about only having the moment, so I pledged nothing beyond it. But love can't be contained, now can it? It slowly engulfed us until we were filled with the richest feelings either of us had ever experienced. I know I was wrong to delight in it and turn away from the inevitable. But my God, it was the first time I had felt anything so special. I felt so alive—not sick, not dying. I was caught off guard by how much I loved him. It is hard to explain how it gave me life and hope. Benoit took me away from my dismal reality, even if the escape was temporary. I know it was wrong, but it was so horrible knowing my life was going to vanish soon. Being with him removed me from my thinking about it. His love altered everything in my life. I found genuine laughter; he stirred every romantic cell inside me, making me feel like I was the most important person in the world. Most of all, when we made love, he elevated me beyond my painful reality." Sarah pauses, wiping her eyes.

"I know I rationalized all of this, believing him to be a gift from God who was sent to spare me from suffering day in and day out with my horrible reality. I let his love wash over me and breathe life into me. Never did I tell him the truth. I could not bear to see him suffer from it. I believe he lengthened my life because my health got better for a while. We were inseparable; the morning sun woke us and the moon lullabied us to sleep. He made everything so much better. I teased him that the food he fed me tasted better than food coming from my own hand. The way he pulled me into him and covered me tightly at night was warmer than all the blankets that I used to keep me from trembling. He would whisper poetry in my ear as I went to sleep and often woke me with verse. His soft, gentle touch sweeping over my body felt so healing. Oh, I loved him…he was everything to me…The day came when I was weakening. I knew what was going on. I could feel the sickness returning to my body. It all came rushing at me one night while he was sleeping. I snuck out of bed, went to the window, and sat looking into the darkness. There was nothing I wanted more than to tell him and have him to be there for me. I couldn't bear the thought of letting him go, but that would have been all about me and my needs. I felt I had been selfish in my indulgence of him already, especially knowing that I could not give back anything long-lasting. The truth would only offer him an opportunity to watch me die," Sarah says. She takes a sip of her tea before continuing.

"Benoit had just been commissioned by the government to paint five historical paintings. His work was so wanted by so many. He loved painting; it was his ultimate passion. I had watched him get lost in it so many times. Anyway, I felt to tell him the truth would take him from his painting. I knew how it was to watch people suffer by my bedside. It felt horrible that I could not save them from my illness. I needed to visualize him painting and going on with his life. I could not cope with the thought of him suffering with me," Sarah explains, now collapsed and trembling.

"With all that I have said, I had no idea that Benoit would never really move beyond me. That is a most troublesome thought to me now. I had thought in time he would accept my death and eventually be open to a life with someone else. I received all his telegrams. I so wanted to write him and beg that he come to the States. But I wouldn't do it. I loved him enough that I wanted what was best for him. I myself sent him the telegram announcing my death. It was the hardest thing I have ever done. After that, I promised God I would never put myself in a position where I would have to lie to protect someone from my illness. Even today, I watch every word I say to others to keep them at a distance so that no one must suffer with me. I have watched Jessie, Bertha, Betsy, Clara, and Clem's lives darken at any sign of physical weakness moving in me. They have all had to go through it with me. I believe it has taken some of their life away from them; that pains me. I would never wish that on anyone else. A few weeks after sending the telegram, I went into remission. Doctors warned me that I was weak and continued to insist my life was tenuous. My dear Jean-Louis, I have lived with the prediction of my death all my life. I have been in and out of remission four times. About three years after I sent the telegram, I decided that I no longer would be immobilized by the predictions of physicians. I had already lived much longer than anyone would have imagined. That death sentence had already taken more of my life than my illness. I continue to have bouts of illness, but today I feel better than I have in a long time. Trust me—had I ever considered that I would outlive Benoit, surely I would have never let him go." At this, Sarah breaks down at last, sobbing uncontrollably.

Jean-Louis moves over to her to hold her. "Oh Sarah, I am so sorry for misjudging you. You loved him as deeply as he loved you. Humans do not have the power to see into the future. Your act of love is as beautiful and rich as his was," Jean-Louis exclaims, as he takes his handkerchief and wipes her eyes. "It's wonderful that your life has not been taken from you, even though you continue to battle your condition. How fortunate for the college that you have been able to be there. Your life, your determination, and your wonderful way of living are a testimony to everything Benoit said about you. You were immortalized by him in his paintings. Did you not see that at the exhibit?"

"Oh, yes. I was stunned, honored, and pained. It was sad to think he spent his life in the shadows of our short period together. It was no more than eight months at the most. Like him, I treasured those months as the most powerful and the best time in my life as well. I often think that those memories are more healing than the medicine I take and the doctors I see. They've always sustained me at my most fragile times. It is nice to talk about all of this. This is the first time I have ever shared it with anyone. Jessie, who is like a brother, has no idea about my time in Paris. It was so special that I protected it, never wanting the judgment of others to dim it. It was not something I wanted anyone to interpret or frame. It was the most personal, wonderful experience of my life. When I was at the exhibit, I was totally overcome by the paintings. Benoit had painted another one like the one he gave me. The only difference was it was closer to the water and it contained my reflection rather than my presence. Same trees, same formation of ducks, same rocks with rippling water, same sun slicing through the tree branches and casting shadows. I also saw the large portrait of me. Of course, it looks nothing like the old lady I am now, but I think it looks exactly like I did in Paris years ago. The exhibit was so intimate and personal—as if he and I were alone again. I felt so much." Sarah falters, as tears continue to fall.

She gathers herself again. "Remember the night in New York when Sue stayed at Gary's apartment? I was so glad that I had the necessary time to think about all his paintings. I was so overwhelmed. I do not want either of you to be alarmed that I did not share this with you. It is not my nature to open up. Being with Benoit was the most treasured period in my life, and I held onto it tightly. One reason I did not tell Jessie back then is because he would have seen how much Benoit meant to me. He would have overridden my decision and brought him to me. I could not let anyone change or alter what I did. I really believed it was best for Benoit," Sarah explains.

Jean-Louis is clearly moved. "Oh, Sarah, you are an amazing woman. I can't imagine what it has been like to live with such a realization of your illness. Oh, I know that Benoit would have hoped that he had given you as much as you gave him. When he talked about you he was always lost for words to describe you. It was as if I wasn't there, as if you were something he had to describe for his own pleasure. He was always desperate to make his words bring you to life. Sarah, if you could have seen him talking about you, how his thoughts always brought him to his feet. His eyes closed as he visualized you. He would make you so tangible that even *I* felt like I could touch and see you right there before my eyes. Both of us gasped as we delighted in you. You were an illuminated vision from his thoughts. Never did I see him sad in his recollection of you. I longed to attain what he was feeling when he talked about you. He would go to his canvas and it was like you were his oxygen from which he would breathe life into his paintings. Then at nighttime, we would sit outside in the cool Paris evenings, both of us with a snifter of brandy and smoking cigars. Slowly, he would exhale the smoke with great intent, his hand ever so gently reaching out into the billowing smoke, crafting it as he described in detail how it felt to touch your face. His hand was cupped, and his fingers arched perfectly as they lightly drifted through the edges of the smoke. I could tell he was watching the art of his smoke as if it were you. It was as if he brought you back to him so he could caress your face. He was so lost in it. Often, I would say, 'Let's gets some brandy and a cigar, and you bring her back to us.' Every story was wrapped around you." Jean-Louis is lost in his memories too.

Silence falls upon the room. Sarah is so moved by what Jean-Louis says that she asks if it would be okay if she went to her room to rest for a bit. Jean-Louis takes her by the arm and walks her to the elevator. I see them embrace; he holds her for a few minutes. He comes back into the living room and pours himself some brandy.

"My dear Sue, Benoit was so right about Sarah. She is even more amazing than Benoit's words describe. How could anyone face what she has faced and still choose to do what is best for others first," Jean-Louis says, shaking his head in astonishment.

"Oh, Jean-Louis. You don't even know the half of what she has done at Broctren Harbor College. She has helped me through the worst times of my life. She is nonjudgmental, kind, gracious, and she knows how to love. All of the people who live here on the farm adore and love her so. I have changed a lot from just being around her. I feel so honored to be part of her life." Talking this way gives me such a strong sense of gratitude.

"Sue, I am so stirred right now. I know so much about her through Benoit's eyes. It is as if I know her personally and intimately. I do hope that I have not hurt her in any way by forcing her to open up and explain things. I don't know her, yet I know her more than I know anyone. It's all so unbelievable. I loved listening to Benoit. I always wondered if I would ever be able to feel the way he felt for her. I often thought of it in terms of being about him and his qualities. It was as if he possessed an extraordinary sensitivity that allowed him to feel so much. But now, I realize it is all about her. She brings out these wonderful feelings inside me. They flood me, and I feel so full of life…such benevolence…it all tugs at me. It arouses every positive emotion inside me. My God, such graciousness…compassion…gentleness…the altruistic actions pour from her heart. Everything Benoit said is true. I now understand how he was so taken by her. What is it that lets her transcend her painful reality? How truly extraordinary she is! Everything about her is simply exquisite. Oh, Sue. It's such a privilege to know the personal side of Sarah," Jean-Louis emotionally explains.

We continue to talk until its time for lunch. Sarah doesn't come down; Betsy says she is still resting. The rest of day I spend in my room trying to study, but my mind drifts back to the morning. How does one attain such depth and beauty as Sarah possesses? She knew how important and passionate Benoit was about painting. She has vivid memories from over thirty years ago of that eight-month period in her life. I had four and a half years with Gary that ended only months ago, and I don't have any memories of him painting.

Never did I take the time or care to understand his life. I loved him but only because he met my needs. I am glad that somehow through our time together he was able to be inspired to paint. It's true that God can use us even when we aren't aware of it.

I take a nap. When I awake, I sit on the balcony. Below, Jean-Louis is smelling the flowers and walking alone in Sarah's garden. I watch him, and he still seems so lost to his thoughts. Gary, Benoit, Jean-Louis, and Sarah have a sensitivity that makes their life so rich and full. How can some humans feel so much more than the rest of us feel? How can a sunset be so breathtaking to some and never be noticed by others? How can the smell of a hot croissant provide an experience for Sarah when I rarely smell any of the food I eat? How is it that all of this rich way of breathing in life is tangible to some while others walk despairingly along the same route and never see or feel any of it? My eyes flood with tears. I want to be stirred by a smile or the beauty of a flower. I want to be lost in the smell of hot croissant or captured by the look on the face of someone who exudes passion.

All at once, it becomes so apparent what it was all about. When we are self-absorbed, we are only as rich as our life is. Being self-absorbed limits us to a very small reality. That smallness will not get bigger; it can't. Unless we can get outside ourselves, we will die in a void, rotting away with the littleness of who we are. Any happiness or joy must surely be short-lived because individually we have fewer resources to sustain us. Only by opening ourselves up to the gift of others can we really expand who we are.

I see Jean-Louis reach inside his pocket for his handkerchief and wipe his eyes. Today has been overwhelming for him. Slowly, he turns to walk back to the house, but Sarah is coming toward him. He takes her arm, and they continue to walk to the gazebo and sit. Now they can talk privately. Although I have been instrumental in bringing them together, now they have a relationship that's filled with a richer reality than anyone could have imagined.

CHAPTER 30

At Peace

As my junior year comes to the end, it seems that everything has changed. My mother, now growing older, is becoming more frail all the time. Her headaches have changed how she lives her life. Unable to give to the community, she has the rich memories of endless hours of reaching out to others. She is at peace because she contributed so much while she could. She and I have grown very close.

Sarah is still working as the dean of women at Broctren Harbor College. She has found new energy in life and her health is holding steady. She has developed a wonderfully close relationship with Jean-Louis, who has given her much by sharing his many memories of Benoit. Sarah is a support to Jean-Louis, who is still trying to cope with the loss of both Benoit and Gary.

As always, Sarah continues to be a huge support and encouragement in my life. Although I don't get to spend as much time at the farm as I'd like, she rarely lets the week go by without calling me. Sarah will always have a special place in my life because she forced me to look at myself. Our lives have such a paralleling coincidence. Yet, we are very different in how we reacted. Sarah's nature and character put the needs of others first. I had become self-absorbed and unavailable to those around me. Now I have changed much. She has taught me everything about love by her example of how she lived. Forever I will be grateful for her presence in my life. In light of all she has been through, she never gave up. Her death sentence, predicted over and over in her lifetime, never destroyed her. She was relentless in her efforts to keep giving and living life. She is the greatest testimony to endurance, strength, and hope.

Still, out of all the people in my rich life, it is Gary whose unrelenting love is most overwhelming. How is it that a little boy would point out a little girl across the brook and determine that she would set the standard of beauty for him in his lifetime? He never surrendered his childhood dream of getting to know me. He never allowed his thoughts, beliefs, and dreams to be dimmed by anything. Eventually, he pursued me. How could he see so much in me when I felt anything but normal at that time?

I know the answer to the question. He consistently shared it over and over again. Gary learned early on that what he had in life was enough. Not having any siblings and being somewhat removed from others, Gary saw me always sitting in my favorite spot in the park. He celebrated my existence by believing that I was his gift and his friend. Even though I was on the other side of the brook and always in the distance, he internalized me, thus making me important. He was able to take the rich lessons of his parents and believe that what he had was all that he needed. Although he did not talk with me until my teenage years, he became emotionally involved with me though his observations, imagination, and hopes. He attentively watched how I moved and what I did. His emotions rode my smiles and tears from afar. I unknowingly expressed everything about myself through my actions in the park. That was my special place and it held all my childhood secrets. Also, in school he saw me defending my point of view.

It was not a mere coincidence that he one day asked me out on a date. Today, I understand why he always knew me better than I knew him. He grew up watching me from the other side of the brook, whereas I didn't get to know him until he was fifteen. I was a part of how he looked at the world and himself. Gary had written so much about all of this in his journal. He had grown to love me more than I thought was humanly possible.

With all the pieces of the puzzle in place, thanks to his paintings and journal, I feel honored that someone saw such value in me at a time when I thought I went unnoticed by everyone. Out of all the wonderful people whom God has seen fit to put in my life, Gary taught me the most. I never saw him down, feeling sorry for himself, or in real despair. He was full of everything that life had to offer. He enjoyed things that were different and had no desire to qualify beauty as others defined it to be. Never did he conform to or need to be part of the status quo. Yet he didn't judge it, either. He couldn't think in terms of comparing anything, for to do so would devalue one thing against the other. He saw beauty in everything, and somehow everything meant so much to him.

His life taught me that I was chasing an illusion. Life is not lived with something out there beyond who I am. It is not about the restless longings of something better than what God has already given me. Those were mere symptoms of my inability to be grateful for what I already had. He taught me that beauty surrounds all of us all the time. We simply have to be appreciative and sensitive enough to see it. The problem was my inability to see beauty until I finally realized it surrounded me in the gift of all that he was. My discontentment was not about what I was cheated out of, or what I did not receive from others. It is about my inability to appreciate what I already had.

Full of new insight, I feel I have grown so much. At no time can we afford to surrender to the thought that something more is out there. Sometimes we damn ourselves by being so ungrateful that it leads us searching for anything that will take us away from our reality. Painfully, I learned that running out into the unknown was the greatest act of self-indulgence. It bastardized everyone in my life, making all of them not enough for me. My lewd actions from my discontentment eroded my character. Gary showed me that living in the moment with gratitude will result in unbelievable peace. Had it not been for the unbelievable gift of his paintings and writings, I would not have been able to fully understand his life and lessons. He was the key to my understanding life.

I have often thought that we are put on this earth for some great purpose. It's a powerful thought that we could somehow have some significant role while we are here. Gary was a very shy, gentle man who really did not engage with others much. He was the type who would go unnoticed, for the most part. He would not be considered special and appeared rather insignificant compared with others. But Gary groomed himself for his purpose from a very young age. He honed in on me as a child and never lost sight of me. He watched me cry from afar and prayed for me. He watched me laugh, giggle, and play, and he delighted in me. Today I am filled with such a profound sense of gratitude. He had a purpose in my life. Because of his example, I've come to know that what I have in life is *always enough*.

About the Author

L. K. CRAFT's (Linda K. Craft-Hisayasu) career spans 27 years as a therapist, corporate management consultant, national lecturer and freelance writer. She received her Master's Degree in Communications from the University of Notre Dame. Her life experiences and creative thinking contributed to her rich desire to write fiction. In 2001, she stepped away from her long career to finally focus on her passion for writing.

L. K. Craft lives in Palm Springs, California with her husband. Now a full-time desert resident, she continues to provide some corporate consulting services, national lecturing, freelance writing and is working on a second literary fiction novel.

L. K. Craft-Hisayasu's Website: www.BrightReflection.com

978-0-595-39551-4
0-595-39551-1

Printed in the United States
52980LVS00003B/139-258